SHADES OF CIRCLE CITY

STEPHANIE A. CAIN

SHADES OF CIRCLE CITY
Circle City Magic: Book 1
Copyright 2016 Stephanie A. Cain

ISBN: 978-1-944774-00-4
First Print Edition, October 2016
Published by Cathartes Press

ALSO BY STEPHANIE A. CAIN

<u>Storms in Amethir</u>
The Midwinter Royal
Stormsinger
Stormshadow
Stormseer
The Weather War

<u>Faith and Fealty</u>
Sow the Wind

<u>Circle City Magic</u>
Shades of Circle City
Circle City Psychic (forthcoming)

<u>With Other Authors</u>
Equus (Rhonda Parrish's Magical Menageries #5)

For Lilliana

"One short sleep past, we wake eternally
And death shall be no more; Death, thou shalt die."

- John Donne

PROLOGUE

The problem wasn't, Victor thought, that Indianapolis was an unmagical city. The city was platted on a circle, that most magical of shapes, and was home to the second-largest cemetery in the United States. The White River provided its own magic, running through the city. No, there was plenty of magic in the Circle City. The problem was finding the right *sort* of magic. Or even deciding what *was* the right sort of magic. Was he looking for death magic? Or life magic? Was he looking for Faerie magic or demonic magic or divine magic or...

There was simply too much potential. Particularly for a man whose only previous brush with the supernatural had been agreeing to defend a woman after she summoned her husband's dead ghost to swear she hadn't poisoned him.

He didn't want riches or power; he had enough of those to suit him. He didn't want fame; he was well-known in the upper tiers of society as it was, and when he launched his Congressional campaign, he would have more of that by purely mortal means. He didn't want immortality or extraordinary beauty.

He wanted his little girl back.

He was a defense attorney. He had access to a small army of professional thieves, gangbangers, and heavies. Within that small army, he could certainly find a talent pool from which to draw support staff for this project.

He had begun acquiring occult texts the day after Alita's funeral two weeks ago—he had spent the time before the funeral drinking himself into a stupor—and he had been locked in his study with the texts since the funeral. But he had not gotten where he was in the world by believing a crash course would suffice for something so important. He had called his former client, who had been happy to give him guidance.

He wanted his little girl back, and he would move heaven and earth, and hell itself, if he had to, to accomplish that.

CHAPTER 1

Nothing worse than having your bra messed up under your Kevlar, Chloe Cole thought as she pounded along the sidewalk. Her Glock 19 was in her right hand while her left tried to dig under three layers of clothing and gear to fix the support garment. Her radio crackled and she gave the bra up as a lost cause.

"Cole—what's your twenty?" Jake's voice came in puffs. Her partner was a big bear of a man, and while he wasn't fat by any stretch, he could definitely stand to do a little endurance training.

Chloe keyed her mike. "Alley off Meridian. You feel like joining me any time soon, or are you just gonna hang around until the next robbery?"

"Shuddup."

Chloe had to bite back a grin, even though her heart was pounding in her chest. She was no rookie when it came to drawing her gun in the line of duty, but she'd never actually had to fire it.

The silent alarm at Rice and Cauldwell Jewelers had gone off six minutes earlier. Four minutes ago an eyewitness had called 911 and reported seeing a man with a ski mask and a pistol running out of the store and south along Meridian from Monument Circle. The suspect was wearing a blue shirt and jeans, which could describe any of a hundred Colts fans who were revving up for the weekend's game. Jake and Chloe had been grabbing coffee at City Market, east of the Circle, when the call came in. They'd left the confused barista holding their drinks and taken off on foot. Jake headed for the north end of the block, Chloe took off for the south end, and they headed west.

At two o'clock on a Friday afternoon, the streets weren't exactly crowded, but there were a few city employees and lawyers wearing pinstriped suits and walking shoes. The idea was to cut off the thief and trap him between them. It didn't quite work out that way.

As Chloe hugged the corner of a limestone building, she scanned the street for anyone who looked out of place or in a hurry. She saw two skateboarders and a stray dog, but no masked men.

A black guy with waist-long dreads shuffled along the gutter across the street, but he clearly wasn't her suspect. He was wearing stained clothes that were a decent fit, and he could have been anywhere from twenty to forty years old. A businesswoman in a skirt suit crossed the street to avoid him. He was muttering to himself, but he seemed entirely self-absorbed. Chloe turned to the right.

"Come on," she breathed, glancing up. A rusting fire escape, someone's years-old banner for the Colts at the Superbowl, a graceful winged shape against the sky that might have been one of Indy's resident peregrine falcons. There were fading paper signs fastened to the building with peeling masking tape. The traffic signal at the end of the block changed.

That was when the world exploded.

Chloe was a tall woman who lifted weights on a regular basis and could occasionally best Jake at arm-wrestling, but she was no match for the feeling of a giant fist coming out of nowhere and smashing into her chest. *That solves the bra problem,* she thought, already lifting her gun out of pure instinct as she staggered back and hit the wall.

Her vision went fuzzy black for a second as her brain bounced against the inside of her skull. When it grayed back in, she saw a guy twenty feet down the sidewalk. She registered a scraggly blond beard and bloodshot blue eyes and the .44 pointed at her.

She pulled the trigger until the gun clicked empty. Her lungs felt squished between the Kevlar and the limestone. She opened her mouth to scream or breathe, but another blast ripped through the air as something burned across the side of her neck.

He shot me. The bastard fucking shot me. She gasped out, "Drop your weapon," pretty sure she didn't sound as tough as she usually did. He laughed. He didn't drop the weapon. He pulled the trigger again. Luckily he was jerking it instead of squeezing, or his aim might have been better.

Chloe could hear Jake's voice. He was still far away, maybe at the end of the world, but he was screaming her name. The asshole with the gun was running. The limestone wall behind Chloe was snagging her hair out of its braid as she slid down. She ended up sitting on the sidewalk, one leg half folded under her, hair in her face.

I was wrong, she thought. *There are worse problems than stupid bras.*

* * *

"Hey, Wolfe, got a hot one for you." Shay Anderson handed Braxton her smartphone, which was opened to an alert about an IMPD officer who had been shot while intercepting a jewelry thief.

He frowned. "Chloe Cole...Rice and Cauldwell Jewelers." Braxton made a thoughtful noise. He'd been pursuing a suspect in what he was certain was a set of linked burglaries from various jewelers, pawn shops, and estate auctioneers. The first crimes had been less sophisticated, but the longer it went on, the more the thieves learned about their craft. There were never any fingerprints, but they had matching footprints outside a couple of the earliest locations. The Indiana State Police, namely Senior Trooper Braxton Wolfe, were officially stumped. And it was driving him crazy.

"She's listed as being in fair condition at Eskenazi," Shay said. "Maybe she got a look at your guy."

"If it *is* my guy. Worth a try, though."

Shay grinned at him. "And she's not bad to look at, either. Maybe she's single."

Braxton felt warmth spreading across his cheeks. He knew he couldn't possibly be the only single guy on the force, but some days his colleagues made him feel like it. "I'm feeling harassed," he complained, but Shay just laughed.

"It's not harassment, it's concern for a friend's happiness. Just like when you helped me get over my last girlfriend." She bumped his shoulder.

"That involved a lot more tequila, which helped," he said, grinning back at her finally. "All right, thanks for the tip. Maybe tomorrow I'll head down there and see if she'll talk to me."

"Not this afternoon?"

"Nah, I've got a thing. Took the afternoon off." He had to be home before two. Full moon was at 2:07 pm, and while most law enforcement paid attention to the moon phase because there were definite spikes in criminal activity and ER visits during the full moon, Braxton Wolfe had a much more personal reason to care.

"Oh, sorry," Shay said. Her tone went a little hushed the way it did whenever Braxton mentioned his dad. She must assume his 'thing' was something to do with settling the estate, and Braxton wasn't going to correct her.

He just shrugged. "Gotta do what you gotta do," he said, and gave her a faint smile. "Thanks, though. I probably won't make it in tomorrow until after I've headed downtown."

"See you then."

Braxton checked his watch and decided he had time to grab a meal on his way home. Full moons were always easier if he had red meat in his stomach beforehand. He sat down for the rarest steak he could order, skipped the fries, and went home.

The first thing he did when he got home was lock up the cat.

"C'mere, Fuzzy," he said, picking up the long-haired black and white cat. Fuzzy's official name was Obnoxious Fuzzy Creature of the Night, but he answered to anything that meant he got fed. Braxton settled all nineteen pounds of the cat in his arms, scratching behind his ears. Fuzzy jerked his head back and sniffed Braxton's fingers suspiciously for a long time. "I know. Full's close," he told the cat, and put him in the den with a can of food and plenty of water. "See you in the morning, bud."

Then it was time to hit the bathroom, strip down, and go to bed.

When the full occurred at night, Braxton and his pack ran at Eagle Creek Park on the northwest side of Indianapolis. When it occurred in broad daylight, like today, they rode it out indoors. The only wolves in the state of Indiana were captive, most of them up at Wolf Park about an hour north of Indianapolis. It would be far too dangerous to risk someone seeing a dozen wolves running wild, especially so close to the city. Not to mention werewolves were larger than their natural cousins; physics still applied, and the law of conservation of mass meant a 170-pound man wasn't going to turn into a ninety-pound wolf.

He checked his clock—fifteen minutes to go. His hands were shaking, his pulse racing. In a couple minutes he would break out into a sweat, and at 2:07

on the dot, the convulsions would start. By ten past two, he would be an actual wolf instead of a Wolfe in name only.

Hereditary werewolves had it easier than bitten wolves. Braxton had more control over the change, and it hurt less. He couldn't actually refuse to change during the full—there were stories of older werewolves who *had* been able to, but he'd never met one—but he could delay it if necessary. Not for very long, and it was harder the longer he delayed it, but it was a distinct advantage.

His stomach twisted and he checked the clock again. Five minutes to go. He wiped a hand across his face. The trick was to breathe through it.

Six changes, he thought, and a pang went through his chest. This was the sixth full moon since his father's death. His father, who had been the pack alpha. His father, whose death had made Braxton the alpha. Natural wolf packs were mostly an extended family group, but werewolf packs tended to pick up stragglers, since bitten wolves were generally unrelated.

Braxton sighed. "I miss you, Dad."

Then the first convulsion hit, and he curled into a ball in the middle of the bed. He kept his breathing as even as he could, letting himself experience the discomfort of muscle and bone reshaping itself without suffering through it.

The first thing he did as a wolf was hop down from the bed and trot through the house, sniffing everything to make sure all was well. Then he lapped water from the cat bowl in the kitchen—the change dehydrated him, and he wouldn't be replenishing it by hunting today. Finally, he curled up on the living room floor to wait it out.

* * *

Things were red for a long time. Chloe wasn't sure how long. Just that it was longer than she could keep breathing.

When she woke, she was colder than she could remember ever being in her life, and she was lying down. She couldn't remember the last time she'd woken up without her cat Whizz sprawling all sixteen pounds across her chest or stretched out against her side. She squinched her eyes closed more tightly and tried to will herself back to sleep. Maybe curling up would help her get warm. She started to roll onto her side and a breath-stealing pain shot through her. She made a noise that was supposed to be a scream, but came out more like a whimper.

Whizz got hungry and started eating my intestines, she thought. *It's the only explanation.*

Her answering machine was beeping, the only noise that broke through the haze in her head. On some level Chloe registered that if she could get to the answering machine to stop it beeping, maybe she could also call someone to make Whizz stop eating her guts. On an entirely more visceral level, she wondered if she could reach her Glock and finish the job Whizz had started.

That was about the time a voice said, "Chloe? You scared the shit out of me. Hold still, stupid."

Sweet little Martin. Her brother was always soft-spoken and considerate.

She stopped trying to move, more because her entire body was clenched than because he told her to hold still. After a dozen or so rapid heartbeats, the pain started receding. She still couldn't force her eyes open.

"Whizz," she mumbled. "Stop him." Talking made her neck hurt, so she stopped.

"Huh? Don't talk, Clo, you're high on morphine. I really don't want you to start spouting confessions. Just look at me. Come on, let me see those pretty baby browns."

As stupid as it was, those words were the ones that really made the fear kick in. As long as Chloe could remember, Martin had been telling her that her eyes were the color of shit. His saying something nice about her eyes without comparing them to excrement, made her realize things were more serious than Whizz eating her guts.

She peeled her eyes open and tried to find Martin in the sea of pukey green and white. It took a few blinks, but finally her eyes focused enough to see he was sitting in a vinyl-covered chair next to a silver pole. Crap, that was an IV pole. She heard the answering machine start beeping faster and that was when she put two and two together.

There was a nurse at the foot of the bed. She wasn't talking, but she was watching Chloe more like a mortician than a nurse. Chloe tried to ask her what had happened, but all that came out was "Wuh?" It started Chloe's neck throbbing again.

The nurse's dark brows pulled together. She said something, but the panic must have had Chloe's blood rushing too loud in her ears. Chloe didn't hear her. She sucked in a hard breath that seared her throat and lungs. She was so cold her body had started shivering without permission. She whimpered faintly.

"Hold still," Martin said. He pressed a hand against her forehead. "I'll get a nurse."

Chloe tried to tell him there was a nurse already, but when she looked again, the nurse was gone. Maybe she'd gone to get the doctor. Chloe didn't care too much at that point. Her muscles were seizing up, so she decided it was a good time to go away again.

The world went red for another long while.

The next time Chloe woke, her fingers lifted to touch the Saint Michael medallion at her throat...but it was gone. Her reaction was, unfortunately, not quite pious.

"The hell?" She fumbled heavily for the necklace and smacked herself in the face with something hard attached to her finger. Chloe tugged it off and stared fuzzily at it for a couple of moments and realized it was a pulse oximeter.

That was when she registered that her brother was laughing at her. It was a refreshing return to normal.

"You done flailing, or did that building give you brain damage when you hit it?" he asked.

"Shup," she ordered. That had been one of the first things she'd ever said to him when she started talking.

Marty had been her first word, even ahead of *Mama* or *Daddy*, but fourth or fifth came *shup*. Thirty-two years later they still used it. They took particular pleasure in resurrecting that in front of various boyfriends—hers *and* his.

Martin chuckled. Her brother had a rich voice that didn't quite match his tall, lean body. His laugh was a nice sound, the sort that filled all the corners of her heart that she didn't know were empty until just then. It made him great company, especially when she was sick or depressed.

"You got shot, you idiot," he said, his voice especially warm. "Ruiz's been pacing the floor all night. When are you going to get a hot partner, by the way? You know I like men in uniform."

"Close your mouth, Martin, it's gettin' hot in here." Jake's voice came from the opposite side of the hospital bed, and then one of his big hands took the pulse oximeter from Chloe's grasp and stuck it back on her index finger. He wrapped his hand around hers, pulse ox and all. Chloe was tall and muscular enough that she'd never felt like a delicate flower of a woman, but Jake was taller, and his hands were a little too big for him. It made a gun almost disappear when he was aiming at something, but it came in handy when they had to handcuff a combative suspect.

"The hell's my Saint Mike?" Chloe demanded, glaring at him. You could get half a dozen cops in the same room and you'd hear six different guns listed as the best, but at least three of them would agree a Saint Michael medallion was necessary equipment. He was

God's own cop, throwing the Devil out of Heaven and Adam and Eve out of the Garden. It stood to reason he'd take care of the boys and girls in blue.

Jake reached into his shirt pocket, which was when Chloe realized the shirt had spots of blood on it.

Oh Holy Mother, that's my blood. She took a deep breath, which was a bad idea. "Ouch," she gasped through the huge vise that was squeezing her lungs.

"Here, drink," Martin ordered, holding a straw to her lips. Chloe obeyed, keeping her eyes on Jake's face. Her best friend had circles under his eyes and a pretty good growth of stubble on his jaw. Jake was a suave-looking Mexican-American guy who had five o'clock shadow at nine in the morning, but this was the beginnings of a beard.

After a few sips of water the fire in her lungs eased and Chloe relaxed back against the bed. Jake pulled her Saint Michael medallion out of his shirt pocket. The chain hung from the medallion, broken ends trailing.

"San Miguel saved your life, partner," he said. "Kinda, anyway."

Chloe stared at the chain.

"Two bullets hit," Martin's voice said. It was uncommonly quiet. Chloe couldn't look at him for some reason. "One in the vest, didn't go through. That one bruised your lungs and broke a couple ribs. The other grazed your neck, nicked your carotid. If it hadn't been deflected by the medallion, it probably would have killed you."

Jake's hand tightened around Chloe's. She felt her stomach give a nasty lurch. Jake had kind eyes, but they were remarkably compassionate at the moment, even for him.

"What aren't you telling me, jerkface?" Chloe said, gaze still on Jake's.

"Nice." Martin's voice was appalled.

"Just tell me. If you keep dicking around, old age'll catch up with me and my pension will kick in." Chloe was in no mood for them to pussy-foot around. She hurt too much.

"You died," Jake blurted.

Chloe thought, *Well, okay, I wasn't expecting that.*

She hyperventilated for a while, which brought the nurses into the room and set off paroxysms of coughing and groaning. Eventually Chloe had more painkillers forced into her and was actually propped up a little in bed. Martin held up a mirror for her to examine the bruising on her face and the thick gauze taped to the side of her neck, while Jake explained what had happened.

Cutting through the medical jargon, Chloe learned she'd had no pulse or respiration for four minutes between when Jake started CPR and when the EMTs jump-started her again en route to Eskenazi. Jake had sent a friend over to get Martin at the garage he owned. They'd paced the ER waiting area for a couple hours while the doctors saved Chloe's life, then they'd traded time sitting next to her hospital bed all night.

When Jake got to that point in the retelling, he choked up, which was totally like him, but still got Chloe all teared up, too. Martin made a disgusted noise and stormed off to the bathroom. He'd always hated letting people see him get upset.

"I died," Chloe said. She was staring at the white drop-ceiling tiles. They were the sort that muffled sound, with the little, different-sized holes in them. It was easier looking at them than it was to look at Jake. "You tell Father Frank?"

She didn't pay attention to Martin's answer, though, because that was when the pale nurse from before showed up in the doorway. The woman just stood there, her thick brows drawn tightly together. Didn't she *ever* smile, Chloe wondered. She gave the nurse a wan smile, hoping she would return it, but if anything her scowl deepened. Her hair was a mess, tied back but falling out of the ponytail. Chloe wondered if it had been a bad day on the ward, or if that scowl was for Chloe in particular.

"—guess the morphine's kicking in," Jake rumbled. Chloe tried to look at him, but a yawn caught her. She blinked at the nurse.

"I already took my meds," Chloe said, and the nurse opened her mouth. It looked like she was saying something, but no sound came out. "It's okay," Chloe said. "You can come in. It's just my family."

Jake craned his neck to peer over his shoulder. "You hallucinating or something, C?" he asked.

"The nurse," Chloe told him, but got cut off by another yawn.

Martin chuckled. "Go to sleep, little sis," he said. Chloe felt his hand settle lightly on her shoulder and she closed her eyes. She *was* sleepy. It seemed like she'd spent a lot of time unconscious, though, so it didn't seem like she should need any more sleep.

The last thing Chloe thought as she slid under was that the nurse had disappeared again.

CHAPTER 2

Getting shot in the line of duty, Chloe decided, was not much fun.

She had emptied her magazine at the guy who shot her. She'd hit him twice, but hadn't killed him—a fact for which she was entirely grateful. No matter how justified the shooting would have been, it would still be her killing someone, and while she knew that was a risk in her line of work, it wasn't something she took lightly. The department had taken her gun for evidence and issued a replacement weapon, but Chloe felt weird knowing her Glock was in an evidence locker somewhere downtown.

Then again, she was also feeling weird about the knowledge that the ambulance crew had cut her shirt off in the process of saving her life. She was willing to bet she'd be hearing later from Crew Nineteen about her womanly endowments.

Lying around the hospital was boring. Her brother had had to go in to work that afternoon, and Jake had an approximate shit ton of paperwork to fill out about the shooting. They'd bought her a couple of steamy Harlequin romances from the hospital gift shop, which Jake had claimed embarrassed him to touch, but the morphine was making her vision swim a little, and even a mass market paperback felt too heavy for her to hold up for long. So she was watching *Scooby Doo* when an amazingly hot guy in a suit knocked on her door.

Okay, he was *short*, but still amazingly hot. He was leaning against the door, watching her. He had a trim, muscular build, and she could just tell he was short, maybe because he had a cocky air to him even as he gave her a friendly smile. Somehow that was more appealing than not. His hair was dark and just a little too long to be called a military cut. He was tanned, with little lines fanning out from the corners of his eyes. Chloe's hand flew up to pat at her hopelessly greasy and ratted hair, then she felt stupid. She hadn't thought about dating for a long time. She was happy with her job and her cat and her friends.

"Officer Cole?" he said, which gave him away immediately, of course.

Chloe groaned. "Let me guess. Internal Affairs. Or did the department already fix me up with a shrink?"

He laughed, earning him points in Chloe's book and showing off some even, white teeth. "Neither," he said. "I'm afraid it's worse than that."

"Oh, Mother of God, have mercy," she said.

He seemed to think that was an invitation to come in, instead of an appeal for holy intervention. He walked into the room and started to extend a hand, pulling out a badge to display for her.

"Braxton Wolfe. I'm with the State Police. I think you got shot by my bad guy." He said his name without a hint of self-consciousness. That alone was impressive. But his last words made Chloe scowl.

"Hey, I shot your bad guy back," she muttered.

"Yeah, thanks so much for not killing him," Braxton Wolfe said. He dragged an orange vinyl chair over so he could sit and look at her easily. "I think he and his partner have hit a couple of places in Avon and Plainfield. I've been chasing those two yahoos for a month now."

"Yahoos?" she said, staring at him. Who the hell said yahoos?

"Yahoos," he repeated firmly. "This was their first high-end job, and thank God they're not as smart as they thought they were. They've been hitting pawn shops and that sort of place up til now. Didn't know there'd be a silent alarm at Rice and Cauldwell."

Chloe's hair itched. She had a colleague of sorts sitting at her bedside, and with her itchy hair and gauze taped to her neck, she looked the complete opposite of professional. It made her feel twitchy.

"Well, it's just like you state guys," she said, trying to sound offhand. "I do all the hard shit and you just breeze right in and take the glory."

Dark eyebrows flew upward. "Maybe I wasn't clear enough," he said. His brown eyes were so light they almost looked amber. Chloe could definitely stand to keep looking at them. "I came to thank you. And to make sure you're okay." He shrugged, his gaze trailing down the length of the hospital bed. "If I'd caught the guys sooner, you wouldn't have gotten shot."

"Please tell me you didn't come down here to apologize because I'm a *girl*," Chloe blurted. It happened all the time, people thinking she wasn't as tough because she was female, or thinking the idea of her being injured was worse somehow than one of the guys getting hurt. It pissed her off.

His eyebrows went down again. "That hadn't occurred to me," he said.

Somehow, Chloe thought, those words weren't quite as comforting as he might have meant them to be. She glared at him.

"I mean, obviously you're a girl," he said. "Woman. You're female. But that's not *why* I felt bad."

The verbal fumbling somehow switched her mental assessment from 'gorgeous' to 'cute'. She raised both eyebrows in a skeptical expression.

"Honestly," he said, smoothing a hand back over his hair. "I would have apologized if it had been Ruiz who got shot instead."

"You know Jake?"

"Just his name and that you two work together a lot," he said. "And that he's a guy, which is the only reason I brought him up."

"Right, right, because you would have felt bad if he'd been shot," she said. She looked at the pitcher of water on the rolling bedside table, trying to decide if she wanted to attempt pouring a cup of water. The statie followed her glance.

"Let me," he said, and poured a cup.

"Thanks." Chloe took a couple of sips, glancing at the doorway. She hadn't seen the dark-haired, silent nurse for a while, but she was probably lurking around somewhere, and she had a couple of minions who prodded Chloe and checked vitals every once in a while. "So this is just a social call?"

"Er."

"Ha. I knew it wasn't," Chloe said. She took another sip of water.

"Well, I really did want to make sure you're okay," he said. He crossed one leg over the other, and Chloe noticed he was wearing cowboy boots. A suit and cowboy boots. It was so wrong that she found that adorable. She didn't even know this guy, for cripe's sake. He could be married with six kids and a drinking problem. Hell, most cops had drinking problems.

He wasn't wearing a ring though. She gave herself a mental shake. She wasn't in the market. She was just fine the way she was.

"But," she prompted.

He rubbed his hand over his hair again. "But... did you see what he did with the bag?"

Chloe blinked at him. That wasn't the question she'd been expecting, though she wasn't sure what she *had* expected. "What bag?" She thought back, trying to remember what she'd seen. The asshole had blue eyes and a scraggly blond beard. He had a black ski mask shoved up on his forehead like a stocking cap. And he'd had a huge-ass gun in his hands. The gun had made a pretty big impression on her.

"The bag with the jewelry. Well, pillowcase really. He used a pillowcase with Strawberry Shortcake characters on it. One of the witnesses mentioned it."

"Strawberry Shortcake characters. Someone's getting robbed at gunpoint and they remember what show the cartoon characters were from?" Chloe said.

The statie shot a pointed glance at the TV hanging in the upper corner of the room. It was still playing *Scooby Doo,* and a ghost was chasing Shaggy and Scooby around a castle. "You're telling me you wouldn't know the Mystery Machine if you saw it on a pillow case?"

Chloe sighed. It reminded her she had a broken rib as pain shot through her torso. "Point taken," she wheezed. It got her coughing and only the fire in her ribs kept her from jerking away as Wolfe leaned in, a hand brushing her shoulder.

"Should I call a nurse?" He sounded calm. Normally calm people sort of pissed her off, since she was so naturally expressive. But there was something reassuring about how he was unalarmed by the way she sounded like she was going to hack up a lung. *If the idea of getting spattered with lung gore doesn't flap a guy,* she thought, *what's going to?*

Chloe looked at him, and as her gaze passed the doorway, she saw that nurse again. Chloe had decided she must be in charge of the ward or something, because she always seemed to be around, but she never did anything. She looked in and her mouth moved, but Chloe couldn't hear her over the sound of her coughing.

"Ask... her..." Chloe managed, tilting her head in the woman's direction.

Wolfe turned and looked over his shoulder, then looked back at Chloe. "Who?"

She was standing right there in the door. Hadn't moved an inch.

"Her," Chloe repeated, gesturing. The nurse lifted a hand, mirroring Chloe's gesture. Chloe got the feeling she was making fun of her.

He looked over his shoulder again, then rested a palm on Chloe's shoulder. She could feel the warmth of his hand through the cloth of her thin hospital gown. "You should rest," he said. "I'll get someone to see if they can give you something for the pain."

Chloe hadn't actually mentioned pain, but it didn't take a perceptive person to tell she was pretty miserable at the moment. She nodded, not even caring why he was ignoring the head nurse. Except as she watched him walk out the door to the hallway, Chloe realized the nurse had gone away.

* * *

When they released Chloe from the hospital, she had enough stitches in her neck to make her feel like Frankenstein's monster. "Except I bet Frankenstein's monster didn't have a support problem due to not being allowed to wear a bra because of his broken ribs," she muttered. Then again, Frankenstein's monster had burned down a house and been chased by people by the end of his story, and Chloe was really hoping not to go that route herself.

Martin came to the hospital to drive her home. His car was an incredibly sweet Chevy Camaro that had been born before either of them. It was a hot and manly purple, with two white racing stripes that make it go perfectly with Martin's varsity jacket for cross country. He always swore that wasn't intentional, but Chloe liked to rib him about it even though he hadn't worn the jacket in at least a decade.

The passenger seat was cushioned with a puffy down blanket and a couple of pillows. He opened the car door for her and said, "Sit down. I'm not carrying your ass into your house." But there were pillows for her in his car. Chloe grinned at him and settled into the bucket seat, and pretty soon they were driving along 10th Street towards Lafayette Avenue, headed for Chloe's house on the northwest side of Indy.

The engine of a 1967 Camaro made a gorgeous sound. Martin had been tinkering with cars since they were teenagers, but the Camaro was his masterpiece, and the low grumble of that V-8 was one of Chloe's favorite sounds in the world. She was relaxing into the seat, head tipped back, eyes closed, listening to the reassuring growl of the engine as Martin turned onto High School Road. It was probably because she was listening so hard that she heard the sirens.

"Pull over," Chloe ordered Martin, reaching for the police scanner he never turned on unless she was in the car. An engine and a pumper truck roared past, lights blazing, followed by an ambulance. When the noise faded, Chloe could hear the scanner.

"All units in the area respond to Forty-Four-Eleven West Price," the dispatcher was saying. "Fire and rescue on scene. Ambulance and additional fire trucks requested."

My house. Chloe's eyes flew open and she jerked in her seat. "Martin—"

"Yeah," he said, and floored it. They swerved away from the curb with a move that threw Chloe against the door. She grunted and curved an arm across her ribs as pain shot through her, but she didn't complain. *Why did I have to think that about Frankenstein and fire?*

Martin Cole was a great mechanic. He was *not* a great driver. Chloe couldn't count the number of times he'd gotten away with speeding simply because he was her brother. She had tried to tell the other guys to slap him with a few tickets so he would learn his lesson, but either Chloe was just that popular or they were all secretly jealous of the Camaro. She had a feeling it was the latter.

All the same, Martin got them to Price Street in record time, but when they reached the end of Chloe's block, it was already closed. Two black and whites were parked across the travel lanes, an officer she didn't recognize holding up a hand to keep them from entering.

"Shit!" She threw open the door. She had forgotten to take her seatbelt off; it jerked her back so she had to struggle with it for a moment. The resulting blaze of pain through her neck had her gasping despite the painkillers. "Martin, I've got to get in there! They don't know about Whizz!"

"Chloe, Chloe," he was repeating. It didn't get her attention until she was unbuckled and half out of the car. "Chloe, *Whizz is at my place.*" His hand closed on her elbow. "I've had him since the day after you got shot."

Chloe slumped back into the seat. "Thank you, Saint Florian and Merciful Father," she mumbled, but in the next instant she tried to get up again. "But my things! My clothes and my books and—"

"Take a breath, Clo," Martin said, his hand sliding up to circle her bicep. She smacked at him until he let go. She heaved herself out of the car with a groan. After leaning on the car for a couple seconds she stumbled into motion.

Three pieces of fire apparatus were on the street in front of her house. It was almost entirely involved, flames shooting a good dozen feet up from the roof. Her house was a small two-bedroom on a postage stamp sized lot, but it was hers. There were flowers in the front yard that had been dead at least two months, and a mailbox that had been bashed by neighborhood kids last Halloween. But it was *home*.

"Ma'am, this street is closed," the uniformed officer told her firmly.

"That's my house!" Chloe shouted in his face. It occurred to her from a distance that she wasn't entirely calm.

The officer put his hands on her shoulder. "Ma'am, the firefighters are doing everything. You live at Forty-four-Eleven?"

"Didn't I just say that?" she snapped, and then regretted her attitude. She'd been in his shoes before, or at least similar ones in a smaller size. She took a deep breath and instantly regretted it, both because her ribs whined in protest and because it forced the smell of smoke into her nostrils. "Oh, shit," Chloe whimpered, and stopped struggling.

The Camaro's engine turned off. "Chloe!" Martin came around the car and touched the middle of her back. "Sorry, Officer... Hayden?" he said. Martin's arm slid around her as Officer Hayden let go of her shoulders and took a step back. "My sister's with IMPD," Martin continued. "She was shot last week, and I was just bringing her home."

"Wow, bad timing," Hayden said, then flushed. Chloe took a better look at him. He had buzz cut, strawberry blond hair and blue eyes and a muscled build. He looked to be about thirty or so. "Sorry, Officer Cole," he added.

"Oh, God," Chloe replied, and closed her eyes. "Whizz wasn't in there. That's all that matters, right?" She couldn't quite convince herself. "My scrapbooks. My clothes. Oh, my God, Mom's Bible." Her throat felt tight, but suddenly she was calm in the same way as when responding to a scene she knew would have injured children or victimized senior citizens. She could be angry or sad or sickened later, but right now she just had to keep it all inside and deal with what was at hand.

Martin's arm tightened around her. "Can we get a little closer?" he asked Officer Hayden.

Hayden studied Chloe's face for a moment, then turned a serious gaze on Martin. "*Don't* let her go in," he said. "Don't even let her on the driveway."

Martin led her closer. The garage door (at least forty years old, solid wood, and incredibly heavy) had fallen in. It was smoldering on the concrete driveway. Her mailbox, she noticed, had been smashed under a fire truck. Well, she'd been meaning to replace it for almost a year anyway.

"At least they're watering your flowers," Martin said. "It's more than you've managed this year."

Chloe's cell phone rang. She jumped at the vibration on her hip, then felt stupid. She answered without looking at the caller ID.

"Cole."

"Is this a bad time?" Chloe didn't recognize the voice. Masculine, the consonants crisp, but not familiar.

She uttered a disbelieving laugh. "Um, sorta. I'm watching my house burn down."

"I realize I might not have made the best impression the other day," the man said, and she realized it was the statie, Braxton Wolfe. He must not have taken her seriously about the house.

"I'm not kidding," she said. "Didn't you hear the call go out on the scanner? My house is literally in flames right in front of my eyes. This is so not a good time, Wolfe."

"You remembered me." His voice sounded pleased. Then he said, "Damn it. Your house is really on fire? I'm sorry, Cole. I'll call you back."

The line went dead. Chloe stared at her phone for a couple of seconds, then stuck it back in the holster.

"Sometimes," she told her brother, "real life is way weirder than I could ever make up."

It took almost an hour for the firefighters to extinguish the fire. By that time Chloe was hunched, shivering, on the hood of the Camaro, a blanket around her shoulders. Jake had arrived about twenty minutes after Chloe and Martin. He had brought coffee and burgers. Chloe's neck was throbbing, her ribs ached, and more than anything she wanted to cry.

"At least Whizz is safe," Jake said, for what had to be the fortieth time.

"And probably chewing my shoes right now," Martin muttered. He was working on his second burger and had a cup of coffee in his other hand.

"But my stuff," Chloe said, for what was probably the forty-first time. She hadn't been able to stomach even the smell of the burgers, but she was on her third cup of coffee.

"You ought to get some rest," Jake said. There were fire investigators on the scene, and Chloe could see Officer Hayden and someone else talking to them, standing at the end of the driveway. She knew she couldn't be any use there, but she couldn't make herself leave. The outside walls of the house were standing, but there were two gaping holes in the roof and the garage door was gone. Chloe kept imagining the local hoodlums picking through the charred ruins of her things.

Something occurred to her and she let out a little moan. "Oh shit. Every bra I own just burned to a crisp."

* * *

Braxton slid his car into a parallel parking spot in front of Barbecue and Bourbon, glancing at the dash clock. Two minutes past six, so he was early, but he liked being early. He'd taken over the leadership of the little group of werewolves by default, since his father had led them; that didn't exactly make him feel as though he deserved the role. He did his best to show his group that he respected them, and he hoped that meant they respected him in return.

"Been a few weeks since I've seen you all," said Suzanne as she dropped a stack of menus on the table at the back of the little restaurant. "How are you, hon?"

"Doing well, thanks," Braxton said, smiling at her. "How are the kids?"

"Little punks who won't do their homework, but otherwise delightful," she said. "Usual for you?"

"Thanks. I'm only expecting four others today."

Suzanne nodded and moved away, letting him flip open the menu in peace. Braxton stared at it, but his gaze was blank. He always got the breaded tenderloin.

Desperate to get away from Monteray's, where his father had always done full moon debriefs, Braxton had asked Elliott to find a place for them to start meeting. He should have known Ell would pick a place with the best bourbon, but he wouldn't complain. It was different from the greasy, all-night air of Monteray's, so mission accomplished. Plus, the tenderloins at Barbecue and Bourbon were the best in Indiana.

A svelte woman of nearly sixty slid into the seat across from him. She brushed a hand through her silver-black hair and sighed. "I'm getting too old for this, darling."

Braxton lowered his menu and studied her. There were deep shadows under Maura Schroeder's blue eyes, and uncharacteristic lines around her mouth. Braxton had been curious enough, once upon a time, to confirm that Maura's English accent was genuine, but he'd never had the guts to ask why Maura had settled in middle America. "Too old for what? The shifts, the dry summers, or the northside traffic?"

Maura gave him the glimmer of a smile, her gentle amusement deflecting the need to answer. A moment later, Elliott walked over from the bar, an old-fashioned already in hand.

"We don't need the big table?"

"Ximena and Estella had a family thing, and Theo's camping down in Brown County somewhere," Braxton said.

"Our little club keeps getting smaller," Maura observed, lifting a finger. As if by magic, Suzanne appeared and placed a manhattan at her elbow. "My thanks, love," she said, beaming up at her. Braxton bit back a grin and accepted his Coke and rye with his own murmured thanks. Suzanne was a good waitress, but he was certain Maura got the special treatment because of her accent.

Suzanne turned to check on another customer and almost bumped into Murphy O'Hare, who flinched and lifted his lip in what Braxton would have considered a sneer on anyone but a werewolf. Maybe it was just because he knew Murphy's temper, but on him, the expression looked like a snarl.

"Take it easy, Murph," said the tanned, busty redhead who was following him. She was in her early thirties, probably ten years older than Murphy, but they seemed to be a couple. At least, Tara was the only person who could always tame his ire, and she was good at making him laugh, too. The rest of them balanced somewhere on a scale of putting up with Murphy on one end and wanting to punch him on the other.

Murphy slouched into his chair, stark in the black leather jacket and black jeans he wore all year round. He wasn't what they would consider a pup, not anymore—he'd been a werewolf, a bitten wolf, for over a year now. But he was still unable to fully control his emotions, and he was still angry about the way he'd been turned. Braxton sand Elliott had done their best to mentor Murphy through all the changes in his life, but Braxton worried the most about Murphy, of all his little pack.

It was a serious offense to turn someone against their will, but once someone had been bitten, there was no reversing it. Braxton's father had dealt with the rogue werewolf who had turned Murphy, but dealing with the rogue had killed him, eventually. They'd never figured out what made his wounds go bad. As the pack doctor, Estella had been stymied and then horrified at his condition. Maura had since told Braxton she suspected his father had been cursed, but they'd never learned how Marcineau had managed that.

Braxton took a deep breath and leaned back a little in his chair, looking back at the menu and trying not to feel overwhelmed. What was he doing trying to guide this pack? His father had done it so effortlessly, but it seemed like people were drifting away under Braxton's watch. It was distracting him from his job, and his performance there was obviously suffering, since he hadn't managed to solve the series of burglaries. And when he was with the werewolves, he was distracted from the pack by worrying about the job.

"Why so morose, boss?" Tara said, flipping her hair back over her shoulder. She was pretty and she knew it, but she didn't take herself seriously, and she had a breezy sort of likability that let her get along with everyone. "You eat your Fuzzy Obnoxious Death Cat?"

Braxton frowned quellingly at her. "No."

"Get caught by a neighbor licking your butt?" she persisted.

Braxton rolled his eyes.

Elliott took a sip of his drink and thunked his glass down on the table. "Still pissed about your solve rate sucking?"

"Just shut up and decide what you're going to order," Braxton snapped, then instantly regretted it as Elliott gave him a thoughtful look. The others exchanged a glance that Braxton pretended not to see.

"But you didn't eat Fuzzy, right?" Maura said anxiously. "He's such a cute little thing."

Braxton's lips curled in a reluctant smile. "He's fine."

Suzanne came back to the table. "Had long enough?"

"Four meat platter," Maura said, nodding to Elliott to indicate they would share.

"Ribs. Full rack." Murphy's voice was terse. "And more shots."

Tara grinned broadly at Suzanne. "Oh, honey, you know I'm a Hot Mess every time." Suzanne laughed with her.

"The usual," Braxton said.

Suzanne headed off to turn in their order, and Braxton shook himself a little, sitting up straighter.

"So," he said. "How did it go? Any hitches?"

"There are never any hitches," Elliott said. "I had an attack of gastro at a convenient time."

Maura shrugged elegantly. "Dratted Jaguar. Always in the shop, you know. Had to leave early to pick it up."

"Punched a guy and got sent home," Murphy said. He tossed back a shot and shuddered.

"Pap smear," Tara said.

Braxton was sure the entire bar went just a little quiet as every man at their table turned to stare at her.

"What?" she said, shrugging. "No one asks you about those."

Braxton shook his head, trying to dismiss the discomfort. "Okay. Good. Another month in the clear." Another month without his dad. Another month when Braxton was responsible for more than just himself. He ought to be getting used to it by now.

Maura lifted her manhattan in a toast. "You worry too much, mate. We've all been at this for a while now. Well, except Murphy, but no one thinks twice about him acting odd."

Murphy raised one hand and stuck up two fingers, and Braxton felt the odd desire to laugh. Only Murphy would be crude enough to flip Maura off, but particular enough to do it in British fashion.

"You're a good leader of the pack," Elliott said, grinning, and Tara immediately chimed in, "VROOM VROOM."

Braxton laughed, shaking his head. "Cut it out, you two. You know I hate that."

"Well, we can't very well say you're the *alpha*," Maura pointed out, her thin lips stretching into genuine affection. "You aren't part of a breeding pair."

"Pedant," Braxton tossed at her. "I'm willing to trade a little inaccuracy to avoid maudlin Sixties song references."

Elliott snorted. "Just get a girlfriend. Then you can be accurate and modern."

Braxton glared at him, but his bad mood was failing in the face of their unflagging good cheer. They might bicker a lot, they might rub each other the wrong way. They might even come to blows from time to time. But they *were* a pack, and pack was family. In true wolf packs, out in the wild, the alpha male and female were simply the 'mom and dad' of the pack, which was made up, generally, of their offspring. Werewolf packs didn't work that way. For one thing, despite lycanthropy being genetically dominant, there *were* times when non-werewolf babies were born to two werewolf parents. Sometimes a werewolf fell in love with a regular human. Braxton found his mind wandering, thinking about how his mother had chosen to be bitten so her children would be more likely to be born wolves.

Murphy barked a sharp laugh at something Maura said, jerking Braxton's attention back to his pack. Werewolf packs were more like the human concept of family, with adoptions and blood-brothers and, occasionally, divorces and remarriages. But regardless, this pack was Braxton's family, and that had been true long before his father died.

By the time Suzanne came over with a tray loaded with their food—and more alcohol—he was laughing along with Tara at a story Elliott was relating. The rest of the meal was comfortable, and Braxton allowed his loneliness and self-doubt to be soothed away by their company.

As they broke up an hour and a half later, he said, "October fifteenth, 2325. I'll see you at the west end of the park."

CHAPTER 3

"This has gotten out of hand, Vic."

Victor Garza pushed back from his desk. "That doesn't sound like something Alfred would say to Bruce Wayne." His voice was sharp, which he instantly regretted. Fletcher was the only person he had left. Fletcher had proven more faithful than Victor's wife, and loyalty shouldn't be mistreated.

But Fletcher laughed. "You ain't read much Batman, have you?" He shook his head, grinning faintly at Victor. "I gotta get you some comic books."

Victor gave him a flat look, but Fletcher's personality was difficult to quell. A quiet, solid man, Carel Fletcher had been blessed with a lack of confusion about his place in the world. He liked helping people, and he didn't intimidate. He owned a car dealership that did well enough for him to make sizable donations to charity. Victor had always considered him a good partner, with his talent for scouting out volunteer opportunities and charity fundraisers that would benefit the most people locally. It didn't hurt that they were often high-profile events that made Victor look even more philanthropic than he was. Victor *did* make regular gifts to charity, but he had an image to maintain, after all.

Fletcher's talents didn't serve quite as well when he was trying to help Victor deal with his daughter's death.

Victor knew that was exactly how Fletcher viewed this. He thought Victor had gone off the deep end, so Fletcher was simply humoring him until he came to his senses. It was part of why Fletcher had been camped out in one of the guest bedrooms since Alita's death.

Victor scratched his jaw. He wasn't looking forward to this, but he valued Fletcher. He couldn't stand to alienate the one friend he had left. "All right, say what you have to say."

Fletcher folded his arms across his chest and leaned against the wall. "Stealing stuff, that's one thing. Not the Vic I grew up with, but it's not physically hurting anyone. But this time..." He shook his head. "A cop got shot, Vic. That is not good. They won't let this drop."

"No, they won't," Victor agreed. He had already decided what to do, but he would let Fletcher make his suggestions. He would listen and appear to consider them. It would make things easier. Fletcher was a simple man, though good-hearted; it occasionally made him too easy to manipulate. Victor guarded fiercely against anyone else who attempted to use Fletcher, but there were times he himself couldn't resist temptation.

"I think it's time to let this go." Fletcher rubbed a hand over his face, then pushed off the wall, wearing an earnest expression. "Vic, everyone goes through this at some point. You remember how I was when my dad died. It's easy to get caught up in the memories of how things were, to keep looking back and trying to make up for all the things you couldn't do when they were alive. But this kid you hired tried to *kill* someone. That's not right." He paused. "That's not *you*."

Victor stared at him. "You are telling me to give up on bringing Alita back."

"Man, I'm telling you that you *can't* bring Alita back. If they could bring people back from the dead, don't you think they'd have brought Alan Rickman and David Bowie back to life already? It ain't possible." Fletcher's tone made it clear that he shouldn't have to tell Victor this.

Victor stood slowly. "And I tell you that it is," he said quietly. "Are you calling me a liar?"

"You're not a liar. You're just...confused." Fletcher didn't look away, but his shoulders were slumped.

Victor didn't want to lose the trust of the only person he trusted completely. He pulled out his wallet and drew a card from it. It read, *Madame Yolanda, Oracle - Palm Readings, Tarot, Crystals.* He held it out to Fletcher.

"This is Yolanda Stevens. I defended her from a murder charge nine years ago."

Fletcher frowned down at the card. "You did?"

"It was shortly after leaving the public defender's office, but I was still taking on a pro bono case here and there. She begged me to believe that she hadn't killed her husband." Victor waited until Fletcher looked at him again. He wanted his friend to see his sincerity. "When I said I wanted to believe her, she proved it. She summoned her husband's spirit so he could vouch for her."

Fletcher's brow cleared. "Sure she did. She could say whatever—"

"I saw him," Victor interrupted, his voice calm. "Yolanda said it was because I had a touch of the sight that she had come to me, hoping I would believe her. Her husband swore that she hadn't poisoned him. He'd accidentally ingested it himself."

Fletcher was silent. He chewed his lower lip, frowning at the card again.

"I know how it sounds," Victor said. "But I witnessed it. I never forgot it. I knew better than to talk to anyone about it—even you—because I thought you would think I was insane. For a while, I thought I *was*. But sometimes, like on Day of the Dead, I can actually see spirits. So when Alita was killed, I knew what I had to do."

Fletcher shook his head. "Cody's still a problem," he said finally. "He can't exactly unshoot that cop, and if they start digging, he's not the kind of guy who'll take a fall for you."

Victor sighed. "I see that now. I thought, after all these years, that I was a good judge of the criminal character. I fear I failed."

"I could lean on him."

"No. I created this problem. I'll deal with it." Victor smiled at Fletcher. "You should go talk to Yolanda. Maybe she could call your father up for a conversation."

Fletcher's laugh was decidedly uneasy. "No, thanks. I prefer to keep thinkin' of him being happy in heaven."

Victor nodded. "As you wish." The doorbell rang, and he smoothed his jacket, then went back to sit in his desk chair. "That will be Cody. I asked him to meet me here. Would you show him in? Then it might be best if you made yourself scarce for a while. It would probably be easier for him if you weren't here to witness this."

Fletcher snorted. "A full-scale Garza Going-over, huh? No worries, Vic. I'll be back for supper."

* * *

Five minutes later, Victor tapped his fingers against his mahogany desktop, studying the scruffy-looking teenager standing in front of him. He had considered Cody an acceptable balance between being a fairly talented thief and being unlikely to challenge Victor's orders. He had *not* intended for Cody to be a self-starter, independently motivated, or any of half a dozen other qualities Victor looked for in his interns and paralegals. He certainly hadn't expected Cody to try knocking over a jewelry store.

"You shot a cop," Victor said, his voice deliberately cold. "You shot. A cop."

Cody's scraggly beard looked as if he'd been growing it out for weeks, but it was too sparse and blond to amount to much. He was nineteen, old enough to be tried as an adult, but Victor couldn't think of him as anything but a boy. Cody shifted his weight from one foot to the other, but he didn't say anything.

"Then, apparently deciding that wasn't *enough* trouble for you to be in," Victor continued, "you somehow settled on burning down her house as a good idea?" He made the last words crack out like a whip, and he was pleased when Cody flinched.

The boy cleared his throat. "Wanted to scare her," he mumbled.

Victor narrowed his eyes. "Excuse me?"

"I wanted to scare her," Cody repeated. "Make her leave it alone."

Victor let out a surprised laugh. It was one that had served him well in courtrooms, and it didn't fail him this time. Cody flinched again. "Make her 'leave it alone?'" Victor repeated in disbelief. "You just made her more determined, you little idiot."

Cody's unkempt eyebrows drew together. "She's just a girl."

"That makes her more dangerous, you fool! She'll work twice as hard to get the accolades her male counterparts take as their due."

Victor could see he wasn't getting through to Cody. Then again, he wasn't really interested in getting through to him. He was still fuming inwardly at the audacity of the punk to show up at Victor's home, demanding help extricating himself from the untenable situation he'd placed himself in. At this point, Victor was merely venting his rage before fixing the situation.

He pushed his desk chair back deliberately, giving Cody time to see that Victor was going to stand. To his pleasure, the boy took a couple of limping steps back, his eyes widening slightly. Victor took his time rising to his feet. He had practiced motions like this in the full-length mirror, learning to gauge the level of authority—or menace—in his movements. He was channeling more menace now than he used in the courtroom.

"I've looked into Chloe Cole," Victor said, making his voice conversational. He enjoyed speaking conversationally to someone he was about to crush. It gave him a satisfying little thrill to toy with his victims. "She's clever and tough. She has a very high success rate when it comes to her work. She's dependable and hard-working. And most importantly, she's *stubborn.* If she keeps investigating this, she'll get in my way. And when people get in my way..."

He turned his back on Cody to open the French doors that led out of his study into the backyard. Alita's play fortress was in easy view of the French doors; Victor had spent many happy hours watching his little girl play at being a pirate or a knight in shining armor in that fortress. The back yard had been designed specifically for Alita's safety and pleasure. It was surrounded by an eight-foot privacy fence, and inside the fence was a tall hedge of autumn olive bushes that kept prying eyes—or predators—from spying on the little girl's play. Victor gave the fortress only a passing glance now. Alita would learn to understand and appreciate everything he did for her.

Victor sighed and looked over his shoulder, catching Cody's gaze. He tilted his head in an invitation to walk outside with him. The young man followed him, his expression torn between fear and hope. "You screwed up, Cody," Victor said.

"No, I—" Cody began, but Victor didn't allow him to continue.

"You went outside my orders to you, then you shot a cop, and then you tried to intimidate her," he said, his voice cold. "You screwed up. I don't tolerate screwups."

Cody darted around to stand in front of Victor, his hands clutching each other in front of his stomach. "I'll fix it!" he began. "I can—"

"You can't fix this," Victor said derisively. "I didn't hire you to be smart. I hired you to do as you were told. You *didn't* do as you were told. Your job performance is unsatisfactory."

"Just give me another chance, Mister Garza! I can—"

"I don't do second chances, Cody."

Victor hadn't gotten where he was in life by being afraid to do the hard jobs. He believed completely in the power of delegation, but there were times when the old adage had it best. If you wanted something done right, you sometimes had to do it yourself. He reached inside his jacket and pulled out the silenced pistol. "I'm afraid, Cody, this is your termination notice," he said, and pulled the trigger.

Cody's bloodshot blue eyes widened, his mouth gaping open almost comically as he looked down at the crimson stain blossoming across his dirty Fallout Boy t-shirt. He swayed on his feet for a moment, began to lift his gaze back to Victor's face, then dropped to his knees. He toppled over, the body rolling onto its front.

Victor smoothed down the front of his shirt. "No severance package," he said, and slid the gun back into its holster. He drew his cell phone out of his pocket and thumbed open the contacts. First he speed-dialed Fletcher.

"Fletcher. New plan." He smiled at his friend's questioning noise. "I need to get something from the Mass Ave office. Let's meet for dinner in an hour." The Mass Ave office was actually an old building he had purchased years ago, intending to profit on the gentrification underway in the Mass Ave Historic District. It had proven too valuable, however, and Victor had never been able to part with it. The restaurant next door to the office was a favorite of Victor's.

After hanging up with Fletcher, he scrolled through his contacts and dialed another number. He had selected Cody's successor the moment Chloe Cole's house mysteriously caught fire. It was time for Deyonte Washington to earn that position.

"Deyonte," Victor said when the young man answered. "I have something for you to...remove. You know where I live? Good. I'll expect it taken care of before nightfall." He didn't bother listening to the eager assurances on the other end of the call. Deyonte would either work out or he wouldn't; Victor suspected Cody's demise would prove an excellent motivator. And if not...well, Fletcher would be watching him.

CHAPTER 4

"You're crazy. Eowyn is clearly the hottest hero in this movie." Celia tilted her head back and dropped a piece of popcorn in her mouth.

"She's not even *in* this movie," Lucia said. "Aragorn's the hottest." She was practically swooning as they watched said hero carve up a couple of orcs onscreen.

"Boromir," Chloe said, shifting gingerly in her seat. Celia and Lucia turned to stare at her. "What?"

"*Boromir?*" Celia shook her head. "Seriously?"

"He's proud and noble, and when he realizes he was wrong, he admits it and makes amends," Chloe said. She'd had a crush on Sean Bean since the Sharpe series, but she liked Boromir even when she read the books after seeing the movies.

"Um, and he's tempted by the ring and unavailable and loves his sword more than a woman," pointed out Celia, who Chloe had to admit was probably more qualified to say that since she'd read the books about a dozen times way before the movies came out.

"See? Sexy," Chloe said brightly, and turned her attention back to the screen.

She was feeling hazy from her pain pills and homesick for her house and her cat. Celia and Lucia were her best friends after their brother. The two sisters couldn't be less alike. Celia did some kind of computer work and played World of Warcraft obsessively; she had blue-streaked hair and Chloe considered her to be generally awesome. Lucia was a CPA and favored business suits for work and spent a lot of free time with a church group, and Chloe thought she was equally awesome in a completely different way.

"You know what you need?" Lucia said. "More popcorn and hot chocolate. With lots of butter and peppermint schnapps."

"Peppermint schnapps on popcorn?" Celia said, wrinkling her nose. Lucia threatened her with a pillow from the couch and went to the kitchen.

"You guys are talking through the saddest scene in the movie," Chloe complained. She still couldn't watch the end of the movie without sniffling, though, so she didn't mind the distraction. She had a feeling it would hurt a lot to cry, pain pills or no pain pills.

Celia looked at Chloe and leaned over to rummage in the bottom of the coffee table. Chloe was surprised when she pulled out a basket full of fingernail polish colors. "We need to cheer you up," she said. "It's been a pretty sucky week for you."

"No kidding," Chloe said, "but a manicure isn't really—"

"Manicure *and* pedicure," Celia interrupted, "and of course it'll help a little. Come on, Clo, you need a little bit of pampering." She fished through the colors, and Chloe's mind boggled at how many little bottles of polish Celia had. By the time she picked out a shade of blue—"since you bleed police blue," she teased—the credits were rolling on the movie and Chloe had given up arguing.

Lucia came back with three mugs balanced in her hands and a bowl of popcorn in the crook of one elbow. She stood over Celia and waited for her sister to take the popcorn and a mug, then carried the other mug over to Chloe.

"Not a good idea to let Celi get started on this," she warned, but she grinned in approval at the color choice.

An hour later Chloe had soaked and moisturized feet, deep blue fingernails and pink toenails, and was falling asleep in her recliner. She'd taken another painkiller with her peppermint hot chocolate, and— aided by the alcohol—it had kicked in big time. Lucia walked her back to the guest room they'd set up, thoughtfully making sure Chloe didn't fall over or walk into a wall.

"Get some rest," she said quietly. "Jacobo will catch whoever did this. And in the meantime we'll help out however we can."

"Thanks," Chloe mumbled, fumbling the covers down. "You guys are awesome."

Lucia gave her a smile that was more mischief than humility. "I know, but don't spread it around. Me and Celia already have too many fans."

Chloe laughed, then groaned. "Don' make me laugh. Hurts." She sat gingerly on the bed and started easing herself into a prone position.

"Sorry," Lucia said, her dark eyes sparkling. She patted Chloe's shoulder and helped pull up the covers so Chloe felt like she was being tucked into bed. *I ought to demand a bedtime story*, she thought hazily. *Maybe people in Mexico tell different bedtime stories. Goldilocks and the Three Coyotes maybe.*

"G'night, C." Lucia turned the lights out and pulled the door shut behind her as she left.

Despite the fact that Chloe had been practically comatose in the recliner, she had a hard time falling asleep. She had never slept well in strange beds. Listening to music might have helped, but her iPod was in her car, which was presumably parked downtown at the station.

She eased onto her back, staring up at the shadows and light dancing across the ceiling. There must have been a pretty good wind outside, because the tree branch shadows bounced more than they should. As silly as it was for a seasoned cop, Chloe creeped out easily in the dark. She'd never been fully convinced that there were no monsters under the bed or in the closet, and she couldn't sleep at all with the bedroom door open. Despite the fact that the human kind of monster wasn't generally deterred by locked doors.

After a while spent staring up at the ceiling, Chloe sighed and shifted over onto the side with the intact ribs. She ended up short of breath from the effort and the ache that started up. Her neck throbbed. Almost as soon as she succeeded in getting onto her side, she rolled back to her back.

She had so many things to do tomorrow that it made her mind spin. She had to talk to the insurance agent again. They'd only had a brief conversation about paperwork for the fire claim. She would also have to talk to the fire investigators again. And she should call and check on the status of her workman's comp claim.

Finally Chloe decided she might as well put this wakeful time to good use, so she decided to pray. "Maybe the Virgin Mother is as awake as I am," she mumbled.

About three minutes into it, she fell asleep.

She dreamed hard, about places and people she didn't recognize, except that—in the manner of dreams—she knew exactly who they were and why they were important. There were people who didn't quite look at her even though they talked to her. There was a guy with blond hair and blue eyes that Chloe knew was her best friend, right up until he shoved her into a wall and turned into a dog. There were girls with blue hair dancing the waltz with guys in hospital scrubs.

And there was *her*.

She had dark auburn hair and brown eyes and a mouth that was a little crooked. She had freckles kissing her cheeks like cinnamon sprinkles. She was wearing a white dress, her feet bare. She was perhaps fifteen years old, perhaps a little younger. And her expression was solemn; she looked directly at Chloe, unlike all the others.

Chloe wanted to ask who she was. She recognized the girl somehow. She felt a kicky little jump in her chest when she looked at the girl. But she had no idea who she was. She was just important somehow.

Chloe studied her, waiting for her to speak, but instead she just studied Chloe right back. Finally her blue violet-tinted lips parted. Her tongue flickered out to wet her lips. She said something, but Chloe couldn't hear. Chloe clutched at her ears. Was she deaf in her dreams? But she could hear a clock ticking behind her. After a while the girl took a few steps closer to Chloe. Chloe opened her mouth to ask who she was—

And then Chloe was awake, staring at the wall opposite her and clutching automatically at her ribs. She had sat up in her sleep and, awake, was paying the price. A glance at the clock told Chloe she had been in bed for less than an hour. It wasn't time to take the painkillers again.

How strange that someone she didn't even know would be the most striking image from her dream. She wanted to remember that sad light in the girl's eyes, the unusual color she wore on her lips. Chloe wanted her to exist in her memory, as if remembering her would mean she'd really existed somehow.

Chloe exhaled slowly, hoping it would hurt less that way. Maybe she should make a trip to the bathroom. Maybe she'd be able to get back to sleep more quickly. She eased her legs over the edge of the bed, then stared. The bedroom door was open just a little. Lucia had closed the door when she left. Chloe *knew* she had. She would have asked Lucia to close it if she hadn't.

After a moment, Chloe shook her head to clear it. Maybe not. The painkillers made her brain fuzzy. She pushed herself to her feet and shuffled to the door. It had been a long, crappy day, and she was probably just remembering things wrong.

All the same, when she got back from the bathroom, she made sure the door latched closed before she went back to bed.

* * *

The next day Celia fried up a ridiculously unhealthy breakfast and the best gourmet coffee Chloe had ever had in her life. Then again, anything would be a good change from the breakfasts they'd been feeding her at the hospital. Jake came in late, his hair still wet from the shower.

"What's on the agenda for today?" he asked, cutting his sausage without looking at any of the women. Jake had always been able to focus on food to the exclusion of anything else.

"Insurance paperwork, department paperwork, hospital paperwork," Chloe droned. Police work was actually a heck of a lot of paperwork, but that never made her enjoy it any better.

"Wow, sucks to be you," he said. "I'll be—oh, wait. Filling out paperwork."

Chloe snorted with laughter and then suppressed a groan. She had never realized how involved her ribs were in every movement she made. She turned her attention to eating, which at least didn't hurt.

"You want me to drop you off anywhere, Chloe?" Jake asked at the end of the meal.

"Would you mind taking me by Martin's?" she asked. "I want to see Whizz, and I think I might have some clothes over at Martin's."

Whizz came running to greet her as she was taking her key out of the lock at Martin's apartment. Whiz was a big cat, and he let out a loud, happy *mrow* as he ran towards her. His tail was straight up in the air. Chloe got creakily down to her knees and administered the full-body pets he loved, nose to tail.

"Hey, who's a good kitty?" Whizz was such a light yellow-orange that when she took him home, her brother said he was the color of pee, which was how her kitty got his name.

After a few minutes of him climbing into Chloe's lap and rubbing against her face, she set Whizz gently on the floor. "Okay." She wiped cat hair off her cheeks. "Time to dig up some clothes."

Her choices were the old, ratty clothes that she had worn a few weeks earlier when they painted Martin's kitchen, or a bag of clothes she hadn't worn in years that they had been preparing to donate to a local mission. Faced with the fact that she didn't *own* any other clothes any more, Chloe decided she could deal. She ended up in jeans that were a size too big, a tank top advertising a local winery, and her brother's socks. But finally—*finally*—she had a bra again.

She got her phone calls out of the way in the morning, despite a great deal of time spent on hold. She never would have expected, back in her oh-so-rebellious days of rolling her school uniform skirt up and sneaking lipstick in the girls' bathroom, to hear Aerosmith and Bon Jovi on the hold music of an insurance company. It was another reminder of the fact that thirty-five was fast approaching.

"Thirty-four and homeless," she told Whizz, who was twining himself around her feet. "And shot. This sucks."

Apparently he didn't agree, as long as his food dish stayed full. He let out a purry mrow and commenced his lunch.

"Fickle little shit," she sighed, and decided to see what Martin had in his pantry.

Chloe's cell phone rang while she was fishing Chex Mix off the top shelf.

"Cole? This is Braxton Wolfe. We spoke the other day..." He trailed off and Chloe smiled. It seemed bizarre that a man as handsome as he was should sound so unsure. *You mean hot guys are people too? Get outta here.*

"I remember. Did you get a lead on your robbery guys?" She pulled open the fridge and snagged a can of Coke. Caffeine would do in place of food while they talked. Having so many guy friends, she was used to men crunching things in her ear on the phone, but she'd never stopped thinking it was the height of rudeness.

"I wondered if we could get lunch or something and I could talk this over with you."

"I can't drive," she said. "Vicodin's my best friend right now."

"I could pick you up," he offered. "We could go somewhere close to where you are."

He didn't even know where she was. Or did he? Maybe he'd been keeping an eye on her. Or maybe he'd called the department first. He had to know she was on leave right now, though. "I'm at my brother's place," Chloe said. "In Broad Ripple. There's a great deli on Illinois Street."

"Sounds good," he said. "Give the address and I can be there in about twenty minutes."

She recited Martin's address for him and told him to take the walk along the side of the house, rather than the front door. "It's an apartment in an older house. The front door is someone else's place."

They hung up, and she rooted around in Martin's chest of drawers to find a shirt that didn't make her look silly. Martin favored jeans and button-up shirts when he wasn't at work, and he was taller than Chloe, but built about the same, so his shirts fit her pretty well. She found a blue and white striped shirt she had always liked and managed to get it on without too much pain.

Celia had put her hair in a French braid that morning, and it was still behaving, so Chloe didn't have to worry about that. Martin didn't exactly have much in the way of cosmetics, besides about half a dozen hair products, so she tried the old Victorian pinch your cheeks pink and bite your lips red thing, which—combined with the glassy thing the painkillers did to her eyes—had the end result of making her look a little feverish.

Braxton showed up promptly. When Chloe opened the door to say hello, Whizz barreled up and butted straight into his legs. Braxton's golden eyes widened a little as he looked down.

"Holy shit, you didn't tell me there was a tiger guarding the place," he blurted, and leaned down to pick Whizz up. He cradled Whizz in the crook of his arm, rubbing his ears with the other hand, and Chloe mentally awarded him major points for being a cat person.

"Whizz, this is Braxton. Don't bite him or he'll probably take you to the pound," she said.

Braxton laughed. "I wouldn't do that. If he was a dog, maybe. But I like cats." He gave Whizz one last scratch, then deposited him on the couch.

"Oh, man, Martin would kill you if he saw you do that," Chloe said, grinning. "He hates it when Whizz gets on the furniture. Quick, let's run away so if Whizz claws it, we won't be witnesses."

Braxton laughed again. He had a nice laugh, and the corners of his eyes crinkled pleasantly with it. He waited as Chloe locked the door, then escorted her out to a generic charcoal colored sedan that looked like a police pool vehicle. "Illinois Street?" he said, and she nodded.

"They have awesome chicken salad sandwiches, *and* you can get a beer there," she said. "Not that I'm going to be drinking Coors with the Vicodin, of course." *Way to sound like a lush there, Clo,* she thought. Ugh, it was like she had a brain-to-mouth disconnect switch that engaged every time she interacted with a good-looking guy.

It was a nice day for late September, so they decided to eat outside on the sidewalk. Once they were settled into their seats, she fixed an expectant look on Braxton's face. He'd been the one to call this meeting, so Chloe figured he could start the conversation.

Only he didn't. Instead he remarked on how nice it was, and how he hoped the weather held through Halloween for the trick-or-treaters. He mentioned a movie he'd seen recently and asked if Chloe had seen it. She found out he liked legal thrillers, and in return, she confessed she was hopelessly addicted to blazing hot bodice rippers. As she finished her croissant-wich, she realized this was feeling a lot like a social thing. That social thing where a guy and a girl eat a meal and talk. *Wait, what are those called again?* she thought.

Oh yeah. Dates.

"So about the jewelry bandits," she said, which was entirely graceless and lacking in subtlety—in other words, entirely fitting for Chloe when it came to social skills.

Braxton looked surprised, but he switched topics smoothly along with her. "We're still looking for the jerk who shot you, but I still don't understand *why* he shot you."

Chloe frowned and tapped her fork against the tabletop. "You think there's more to this than just a simple smash and grab thing."

"This *is* the first time they've had a weapon or hit while someone was in the store," he admitted. "In the past the burglaries have all occurred while the place was closed. The thieves force the back door and smash up the glass cases inside to get pieces."

"What kind of things are they taking?" she asked. It didn't make sense. Why would they go from simple B&Es to that kind of thing? The weapon alone automatically made it a felony, and then the genius had shot a cop on top of it.

Braxton shrugged. "Not necessarily things of any value, which is another weird thing. They take shiny stuff, old stuff, whatever tickles their fancy. They don't seem to have any concept of what's valuable."

"Or maybe they're just taking the stuff home for their moms to wear," she muttered. "Shit. Who does that? And why the switch in MO?"

"Something else I'm uncomfortable with," he said. He sipped his iced tea, then said, "Why did he shoot you? Even a small-time crook knows a cop-killer is going to be hunted down, no matter what resources it takes."

Chloe nodded absently. There were too many things that didn't make sense. She wondered if Jake had gotten a chance to talk to the asshole who shot her before he made bail. "I don't even know the guy's name."

"Wethering," Braxton said. "Cody Wethering. Scraped his way through high school but he had to finish via some kind of online program the school had for suspensions. You wouldn't call the guy smart, by any stretch of the imagination. Still, shooting a cop is just plain stupid."

She groaned, then pressed a palm to her ribs. "Crap, I keep forgetting about that."

"Hurts, doesn't it?" Braxton's tone was sympathetic. "I broke my collarbone playing football in college. Intramural, not even the big-time stuff. It's amazing how much you move parts of your body you don't normally pay attention to."

"No kidding. And the Vicodin's great, but not always great enough." She shook her head. "So did anyone find the Strawberry Shortcake pillow case?"

He looked grim. "Not yet. I retraced the route we think he took, but nothing. I retraced routes he *might* have taken. Nothing. Well, not nothing," he amended. "I did arrest a hooker and two drug dealers. But no jewelry and no pillow case."

"Cleaning up the city for us. Thanks," Chloe said, grinning faintly. "So where are we?"

Braxton shrugged. "I thought I'd see if you have any insights. And if I can do anything to help out with the fire investigation, I will." He gave her a diffident look.

Why? she wondered suddenly. This guy had shown up out of nowhere, except that he was looking for the same asshole who shot Chloe for what *seemed* like related crimes, but might not be. It was nice that he offered to help, but why? There was no guarantee she could help him with his case, not to mention he'd never seen her except when she was doped up on painkillers, when she definitely wasn't at her best. So why would he offer to help?

Chloe realized suddenly that she'd been silent for too long. His expression was starting to fade into something more reserved. She didn't want to hurt his feelings, but honestly, unlike Blanche DuBois, she'd never had much reason to trust in the kindness of strangers.

"It's nice of you to offer," she said finally, because it *was* nice. Just weird. "I don't know how much I can really help you though."

"I could use an extra pair of eyes when I go through the list of things they stole," he said. "You're not going to be up to anything but desk duty for a while anyway, right? Maybe you could take a look and see what you think."

"I think you're scraping the bottom of the barrel," Chloe said, but she couldn't help smiling. "All right, get me a copy of the list and I'll see if anything strikes me."

He nodded. He was way too agreeable. Chloe decided there had to be something wrong with him besides the fact that he was only about five foot nine. She just hadn't had a chance to see it yet.

* * *

Chloe and Braxton ended up back at Martin's apartment with a six-pack of Coke and the lists spread out on the coffee table. Two of them were inventory sheets printed off a computer, while the others were handwritten. Braxton passed the handwritten lists to Chloe and they settled down to analysis.

Chloe's frown deepened as she read. There were family heirlooms, lockets and pendants and pocket watches, cufflinks and crosses. Some of them must have been valuable, but there were no engagement rings or diamonds in the bunch. And there was just as much silver as there was gold; with the price of gold what it was recently, she would have expected more gold.

"Have you talked to Wethering's known associates?" Chloe asked, fingering the ragged edge of a paper that had been torn from a wire bound notebook. "Maybe one of them would have an idea what he's been up to."

Braxton nodded. "One of them said he thought Wethering had just gotten a regular job. Most said they hadn't seen him much lately. An ex-girlfriend said he'd asked her to get back together, and when they had dinner, he was flashing a lot of cash around."

"But it was more than he'd have made from fencing what he stole," Chloe guessed.

"Exactly."

"So what does all this add up to?" she asked in confusion. "Because I'm taking two and two and getting zilch."

Braxton grunted. Chloe never found out if he had more of an answer than that, because just then they heard a key in the lock and Martin let himself in. Her brother stopped in the entryway, surveying them, a smile spreading broadly across his face. He was wearing the blue jumpsuit of his garage and there was a smear of grease on his jaw. His hands were almost black at the fingertips. He lifted one in a wave.

"Hi there. I'm Martin. Chloe's brother. And you are...?" Chloe felt her stomach do a little jump at the smugness of Martin's expression. That couldn't bode well. If he flirted with Braxton, she might have to hurt him.

"Braxton Wolfe," he said, standing and holding out his hand to shake without any regard for the grease. "Chloe's helping me with a case that we think is related to the man who shot her."

"What's going on with that?" Martin asked, and Wolfe gave a quick run down of the situation. When Martin was up to speed, he shook his head. "Tell you what, I'm not a thinker, I'm a doer. So you two detect and I'm going to figure out something to eat."

"We just had lunch," Chloe protested.

"Three hours ago," Braxton said. She stared at him and he gave her a half smile "I guess you lost track of time."

"Great," she said, trying to stand up. Her body didn't want to straighten out after hunching over the coffee table for so long. "Time for more painkillers."

Braxton held out a hand to stop her. "Stay there and I'll get it. Where's the bottle?"

"Kitchen table." She watched him stand and go out to the kitchen. He moved smoothly, with an economy of motion that she had a feeling meant he could explode into action if it was called for. After a few moments she shook herself out of the little daze she'd fallen into and turned her attention back to the list.

You don't need to get distracted, she told herself. She had to concentrate on the task at hand.

Braxton returned a minute later with a mug of hot tea and her pill bottle. "Your brother says a splash of rum in your tea will actually make the Vicodin work better," he informed her. "And for what it's worth, he's absolutely right. It might be a good idea for a couple more days."

She sighed and took them. "Sure, as long as I don't turn into an addict while I'm at it." But he was right, and as long as he was suggesting it, he probably wouldn't judge her for it. She swallowed a pill and washed it down with a gulp of tea that was really too hot to drink.

"Ahhh," she managed, her eyes watering. "Shih— is hah." She fanned her mouth.

Braxton, to his credit, didn't laugh, but the corners of his mouth twitched. "I should probably let you get some rest," he said. "You haven't been out of the hospital very long."

"I have to go on record as saying that administrative leave is really boring," Chloe complained. She couldn't pretend she wasn't looking forward to just relaxing for a while after spending hours in the company of a guy who seemed too good to be true.

Braxton chuckled. "Why don't you keep the photocopies of what was stolen, and if you come up with anything, give me a call. And if I hear anything, I'll call you." He took his wallet out of his pocket and fished out a business card. Before handing it to her, he wrote another number on the back of it. "That's my home number, just in case you can't reach me otherwise."

Their fingers brushed when he handed it to her, and while normally she wouldn't go so far as to say there were instant sparks... It had actually been very dry lately, and they both saw the flash of light between their fingers. They both jumped, his amber eyes comically wide. Chloe's probably were too. That hurt, dammit! But it was funny too, and a moment later they were both laughing.

"I'll keep in touch," Chloe promised. She liked the way he smiled at that.

"Don't get up," he said. "I can find the door just fine. I hope you feel better soon, Chloe." And with that he scooped up his jacket and files and left.

Martin made her explain a little better what was going on, and he seized on the way Braxton had bought her lunch and given her his home phone number. Chloe had been looking forward to an evening chilling out in front of the TV, but instead Martin ordered a pizza and grilled her about Braxton Wolfe. In exasperation, she finally suggested she just do a background check to satisfy his curiosity. Martin tilted his head like he thought it was a good idea.

"No, absolutely not," she said. "First of all, I have no reason to do it, and second of all, it's just silly. The guy's a cop. A colleague, kind of. And that's it. There's no reason for you to get all fussed over this."

"Suuure," Martin said. A moment later he discovered she was still capable of throwing a pillow, even with her broken ribs. Unfortunately she was a lot slower than usual, so he had no trouble dodging.

As they were finishing up the pizza, Lucia arrived with bags of clothes hanging off her arms. Chloe had given her orders to not spend too much, but she had little confidence in that. Her taste was a little extravagant compared to Chloe's style, but Chloe had to ask her instead of Celia; if Chloe let Celia dress her, she'd end up looking like she was working Vice. Celia was a big believer in the if you've got it, flaunt it, philosophy.

Lucia spread everything on the couch for Chloe's approval. She'd ended up with three pairs of jeans, half a dozen tank tops and t-shirts, three button-down shirts, a pair of khakis, a pantsuit, and four bras.

"I'm rich," Chloe said, looking at the bras. "Thank God." That was when Chloe noticed Celia's sheepish expression. "What?"

"Well..." She drew the word out like a five-year-old about to be scolded. "It's just that I saw this when I was going through the dresses, and..."

"Lucia," Chloe said. "You did *not* buy me a dress."

Lucia gave her a sheepish look, then pulled it out. It was a deep emerald green, with a v-neck and a modest length flared skirt.

"What were you thinking?" Chloe demanded. "I don't wear those things!" Then again, she was lucky Lucia had bought so many jeans and only one pantsuit. *I suppose I ought to be grateful for small blessings.* "I don't even have any shoes to wear with that."

She coughed and drew out a pair of black pumps.

"Oh my God, you're trying to turn me into a *girl*," Chloe said in horror. Lucia and Martin both burst out laughing.

"She can probably find some reason to wear that," Martin said, his voice sly. "That state cop working her robbery case has a crush on her."

Chloe felt her cheeks get hot. "He does not. He just wanted my help."

"Help, right," Martin said. He described Braxton for Lucia, spending extra time on the gorgeous smile and very nice amber eyes.

"He's short," Chloe muttered.

Martin and Lucia just grinned.

CHAPTER 5

Braxton couldn't deny it was a relief to see the end of his shift arrive on Saturday. He was ready for a weekend away from the demands of his job and the prying eyes of his coworkers, who meant well but could never understand all the pressures he was under. Tonight he'd made the best plans of all—pizza, alcohol, and video games with Elliott and Murphy. Low-key and uncomplicated, it was just what he needed after a week of reeling emotionally.

He hadn't thought he had it all together, obviously. He was still coping with his dad's death and his new position with the pack. He was still trying to get back in the swing of things after taking weeks of accumulated vacation time following his dad's funeral. He certainly hadn't expected to meet a woman who was strong and smart and good-looking who knocked him entirely off-kilter. Thank God for the relatively easy relationships of packmates, people who were brothers through circumstance as much as choice, but had learned to lean on each other.

Even having Murphy in the mix wasn't bad. Elliott and Braxton had known each other since they were toddlers, their parents best friends, but their friendship had never been an exclusive one. It had been easy for them to expand or contract as their social circles—and pack circles—shifted. Murphy was an emotional thunderstorm, but Elliott helped him vent while Braxton grounded him, so it pretty much worked.

Still, Braxton should probably have known better than to expect *anything* to go smoothly this week.

The front door flung itself open hard enough to echo through the house, and footsteps stomped inside. The door slammed behind the precipitous entrance. As Braxton jogged up the steps from the basement, he heard the door open again, Elliott protesting loudly. The first person must have been Murphy, then. That didn't surprise him, exactly, but it didn't bode well, either.

"If you're breaking in, I'm armed," Braxton called. He rounded the corner to the first floor hallway and saw his guests.

Elliott was closing the front door. He met Braxton's gaze, his eyebrows raised, and gestured vaguely at Murphy.

Murphy's hands were shoved in his pockets, his shoulders tense. "Fucking Tara," he muttered.

Braxton held in a sigh. "Hello to you, too," he said. "Whiskey's downstairs."

"Good." Murphy stormed past him, just barely jerking away at the last minute to keep from bumping into Braxton.

Braxton turned slowly and watched him in bemusement. He wasn't the kind of so-called alpha male who bristled at any little challenge to his authority; he knew who he was and what he was capable of, and that was good enough for him. But Murphy had been just a little careful around him, ever since the pack had tacitly chosen Braxton to lead them. For a certain value of lead, anyway.

Braxton couldn't quite figure out what had changed between him and Murphy. He only wanted what was best for the younger man, but he would never try to force a path on Murphy. Surely Murphy knew that. Then again, Murphy hadn't been around as much lately.

"I didn't ask," Elliott said, coming up behind Braxton. He leaned gently against Braxton, a familiarity they only allowed themselves in private. Part of the upbringing of young werewolves involved teaching them what was acceptable in terms of public affection between platonic friends as well as romantic partners. Werewolves instinctively craved more contact than average humans, and were less body shy. More than once, Braxton and Elliott had been mistaken for a couple, before they learned the boundaries. It didn't bother Braxton, but Elliott had always been punctilious about it—maybe because he was flexible about the sex of his romantic partners and didn't want to make Braxton uncomfortable.

"You didn't ask what?" Braxton said.

"What set him off, specifically." Elliott followed Murphy down the hall, trailed by Braxton.

"Tara, presumably," Braxton said mildly.

"Sure, but they don't usually fight." Elliott shrugged.

"Not usually, but everyone has bad days." Braxton glanced back to make sure the front door was locked. "You planning to stay over?"

"I'm planning to drink my weight in whiskey, so yeah. I don't know about Murphy, but I would imagine so."

"Bad week?"

Elliott cast a sharp glance over his shoulder. "Just a colleague getting shot, almost fatally. No biggie."

Braxton jerked to attention. *Idiot*, he thought. Of *course* Elliott would be upset about Chloe Cole. They were both IMPD officers, even if they didn't work in the same department. Law enforcement officers tended to band together when they were under attack—maybe that was why werewolves did so well as cops—and Chloe's shooting would feel like an attack. "Sorry. I wasn't thinking."

Elliott grunted and went the rest of the way down the steps. Braxton followed him into the basement. The main room was set up as a rec room, complete with sixty-inch television, gaming system, dart board, pool table, and wet bar. The rest of the basement was a guest bedroom and bath, which might as well be labeled *Elliott's Crash Pad*.

Murphy was already slouched on the sofa in front of the television, bottle of Jim Beam in hand.

"So..." Braxton said. "Tara?"

"Fuck her," Murphy said automatically. "Wanting me to get a better job." He took a swig of whiskey. "I don't need another damn mother."

Braxton knew, theoretically, that Murphy had a mother somewhere. He'd never really thought in anything other than abstracts, though. He'd certainly never considered there might be someone worrying over his explosive temper and unexplainable mood swings.

He glanced at Elliott, who was looking back at him.

Elliott rolled his eyes. "Dude. At least get your GED. You don't want to be stuck slinging burgers all your life."

Murphy didn't look up from his whiskey. "Bite me."

Braxton frowned at Elliott.

"Everyone has to eat," Murphy continued. "As long as you can get the order right and fill in for the cook and waitstaff, you'll always have a job."

"You'll never be without debt collectors hounding you, either," Elliott said.

"Bite me," Murphy snapped again. "I might not drive a fancy car or own my own home, but I make my rent payments on time and have plenty left over for groceries and shit."

Braxton sighed. "Listen, I've already ordered the pizza. Let's not argue."

"Who's arguing?" Murphy said. He took another swig of whiskey and it occurred to Braxton that this really wasn't a terribly unfriendly exchange, in Murphy terms.

Elliott and Braxton glanced at each other again. Braxton wondered if it was just the age difference.

He'd been in college when he was Murphy's age, but he could remember thinking he owned the world and had all the answers. Murphy didn't usually give off that vibe, though. Murphy was a self-sufficient, keep-your-charity-to-yourself kind of guy. He wasn't stupid by any stretch, but he had no use for book learning or degrees.

"So..." Elliott said, drawing it out. "Met any nice girls since our last debrief, *Alpha*?"

Braxton started and glared at him. He could feel his face getting hot, and he cursed his inability to be as impassive in his personal life as he could be at work.

"Oh-ho-ho!" Elliott crowed. "I was joking, but..."

Murphy, picking up on it, turned to study Braxton, his thin lips curling in interest. "But you *have* met someone. Poor you."

"No." Braxton glared at both of them. "No. It isn't—"

"Sure it is," Elliott interrupted. "Who is it?"

"It isn't anything," Braxton insisted. "I'm in no place to figure out a relationship on top of the pack and the job and...and Dad."

Elliott's expression softened a little at the mention of Braxton's father, and Murphy slumped back against the couch. But Elliott didn't relent. "You wouldn't be talking like that if you didn't like her."

"Whoever she is," Murphy put in.

"Come on," Elliott ordered. "Spill. We can help."

Braxton laughed. "You think I want help from *you two*?"

"Thanks," Murphy muttered, though Braxton had the feeling he was amused more than hurt.

Elliott shrugged. "I'm hopeless for myself, but you have to admit, I'm good with advice." It was true, too. Elliott couldn't seem to help going for the bad girls—or bad boys, as it happened—but he was good at seeing people who complemented each other.

Braxton drew in a slow breath. "Yeah," he admitted. "But no. It isn't a thing."

Thank God, the doorbell rang at that moment. *Saved by the pizza,* he thought, checking his back pocket for his wallet.

"Mark my words, young Padawan," Elliott said to Murphy, "It's a thing."

Murphy snorted in agreement.

Braxton stalked off to get the pizza.

* * *

With a knock, Carel Fletcher stepped into Victor's study. "Vic." He didn't speak again until Victor looked up. Fletcher was one of the few people to whom Victor ever gave his full attention. Fletcher had never wasted Victor's time. Besides, they'd been friends since the eighth grade, when Victor made fun of his having a girl's first name—for which Fletcher's had promptly flattened him. Impressed at Fletcher's physical prowess, Victor had been very careful to keep Victor close since then.

"What is it, Fletcher?"

"Deyonte's here. Want me to keep him waiting? His appointment isn't for another ten minutes." Fletcher folded his arms across his chest, which emphasized his massive size.

Victor looked at the clock. "No, no, let him in. He did a good job with Wethering. We'll see how he does with this one."

Fletcher gave him an unhappy look, but he left the study. He had gone through the roof when he learned how Victor dealt with Wethering. He'd calmed down eventually, but he still wasn't happy about it.

A minute after Fletcher walked out of the study, a tall, lanky black man walked in.

"You're early, Mr. Washington. I'm impressed."

"Just because I'm an ex-con doesn't mean I've got no manners, Mr. Garza." Deyonte was in his mid-twenties. Victor had represented him after a fistfight went bad. He'd gotten Deyonte a plea deal for aggravated manslaughter and Deyonte had done his time. Prison had made him smarter, though, and Victor was certain Deyonte would know how to keep from getting caught again—and know that turning on Victor, in the event he *was* caught, would be a very bad idea. No plea deal would save Deyonte's life if he betrayed Victor.

"That's obvious," Victor said. "I'm also pleased that there has been no alarm raised regarding...the last job you did for me. You did well."

Deyonte smiled. "Do you have more work for me?"

Victor raised his eyebrow. "As a matter of fact, I do." Not only competent, but a willing worker, as well. Deyonte Washington gave Victor Garza a bit more confidence than Cody Wethering had. He was good at following orders, and he was smart enough to follow them capably but not creative enough to improvise.

He slid a paper across the desk to Deyonte. "This is the address of a pawn shop. I want you to go there after they close. I'm looking for a pendant made of silver."

"What's it look like?"

Victor slid a second piece of paper to him. "Here's a copy of a sketch that was made over one hundred years ago."

The pendant was almost three inches in diameter, in the shape of a poppy. Crossing the poppy in the shape of an X were a sword and an inverted torch—all symbols of Thanatos, the Greek god of death. Victor had been scouring the lineage of the pendant, and he had traced it to a Greek family living in Home Place. There had been a lot of Greek settlement in Home Place over the years.

Deyonte peered at the picture. "How old is this thing?"

"Very." Victor gave Deyonte a thin smile. "I will warn you that, while it is old, it has much more value to me than it would to anyone else."

Deyonte scowled at Victor. "I don't go behind people's backs, Mr. Garza. You hire me to do a job, I'm going to do it the way you want me to. You want the pendant, I'll get you the pendant."

Victor nodded. "You seem to be much smarter than your predecessor, Deyonte. I'm very glad to see that."

Deyonte gave him a tiny grin. "I don't want to end up like him, either."

It surprised a chuckle from Victor. He expected a certain amount of deference from his employees, but he was pleased to see a glimmer of humor in the other man. Victor might be driven and unyielding, but he wasn't a monster. He was just a man who wanted his little girl back.

"The pendant," Deyonte said. "Is it for sale at the pawn shop?"

"I'm not entirely certain. It seems that the family who owns the pawn shop has been in possession of it for many years, but it could be a display piece."

Deyonte's brows drew together as he studied the sketch again. "Any chance it could be at their house?"

Victor shrugged. "Anything is possible," he said. "If you don't find it at the pawn shop, call me before you do anything else. You still have the burner phone?"

"Yeah." Deyonte grinned at him. "Don't you worry, Mr. Garza. I won't let you down."

Victor watched the younger man leave the room. Fletcher would let the man out. Victor preferred to have his meetings in his study, where he was positioned to look powerful and wealthy. Being a successful courtroom lawyer was as much creating an image as it was knowledge of the law, and Victor was a very successful lawyer.

He slipped a hand into the pocket over his heart and drew out a delicate necklace on a slender gold chain. Holding it up in front of his face, he studied the tiny gold unicorn rearing up at the end of the chain. Its eyes were tiny chips of diamond. Alita had worn it every day for years. She was a rambunctious girl, athletic and energetic, but she had always taken good care of her possessions. Victor still had a complete set of her crayons—well-used, but none of them broken.

"Ah, Alita, I miss you, little girl." He sighed and rubbed a hand over his face. "I'll save you. I will. I swear."

Then he pulled out his cell phone and sent a text to Fletcher. *Keep an eye on him. Don't want another situation like W.*

CHAPTER 6

For the next few days, Chloe did nothing but lounge around catching up on the movies and books she had missed over the last year, in between phone calls to the insurance people and one trip to the mall to buy a few extra clothes. Martin spent two days combing through the wreckage of her house. Chloe tried to make him take her with him, but he said it would be dangerous for her to be in the house in her condition, and she couldn't really argue. Besides, she had the feeling if she saw their mother's Bible burned to a crisp, she would cry.

That was the first of the surprises from his clean up. The Bible didn't have so much as water damage, and there were three pictures of the family tucked inside the book of Daniel, even though she didn't remember putting them there.

Her CDs had survived, and there was a box of letters that the bed had sheltered from the spray of the hoses. Her gun safe turned out to be fireproof, even though all the ammunition, which she stored separately, had gone off in a series of mini-explosions during the fire. She was relieved her Smith and Wesson had made it.

Martin put all her things in boxes and brought them back to his place, where he started a stack in the spare room. Everything smelled smoky, and pretty soon his entire apartment was permeated with the odor. It didn't take long before Chloe had grown to hate that smell.

She didn't hear from Braxton Wolfe. Martin prodded at her to call him, but she had no reason, because she hadn't made any giant leaps of logic from the lists Braxton had left. She told herself she was much better off focusing on making an inventory of the things she'd lost in the fire. She had to turn that in before insurance would send a check, and though she was on paid leave and wouldn't get behind on bills, she didn't have the money to pay a restoration company to start work on the house.

For that matter, she hadn't even decided what to do. She was thinking about having them raze the house to the foundation and trying to sell the lot. She wasn't sure if she would ever feel secure living in a place that had burned down. On top of that, the fire investigator was taking his sweet time making any announcements regarding the cause.

They were never overly hasty when declaring arson.

Nine days after she got out of the hospital, she got the call. Thankfully, it was Jake who called instead of the fire inspector.

"Damn it!" Chloe shouted. She held the phone away from her mouth, but she could still picture him wincing at the volume. "Someone burned my house down."

"That's what the fire inspector says happened," Jake agreed.

"Some stupid asshole son of a bitch burned my house down."

"Clo—" Jake said.

"Dammit! Someone burned my fucking *house* down!" She could feel her face getting red. Some part of her knew it was ridiculous, considering she'd already been certain the fire was no accident. She didn't really need the fire investigator to tell her the point of origin had been in the living room, behind the TV, and that the flame had gone straight across the floor instead of rising the way fire, left to its own devices, always did. But hearing those words in her best friend's voice made her head feel like it was going to explode.

"Yeah, but they didn't get your cat, okay? And you weren't hurt. It sucks, and we'll catch the bastard and make him pay, but think how much worse it could have been." Jake sounded like he really wanted to believe that, but even he wasn't sure.

"Like it isn't enough that I got shot, but I have to be homeless too?" Chloe ranted. "Do you even *know* what it's like living with Martin? He's great, he really is, but he leaves his dirty socks in the middle of the living room! He doesn't put the toilet seat down! I'm about to go nuts!"

She had to stop shouting to catch her breath. Her side ached. Whizz had trotted in from the bathroom and was staring at her with his head cocked to one side like he was trying to decide if he should attack.

"Of course he does, Chloe, he's a man." Jake's voice was regaining its usual good humor. "Listen it sucks, and you know I won't say it doesn't. But you need to calm down. And by the way, you totally owe me Starbucks for not sending the fire investigator over to tell you this in person, or it would've gotten back to the Captain that you're totally unfit for duty."

"I am not, muffin brain," she snapped. "I'm just... perturbed."

"Perturbed," Jake repeated. His voice was suspiciously flat.

"Exactly," Chloe said. "Shut up. I got shot two weeks ago."

"Yeah, and you're clearly in the Bitch Phase of recovery," he muttered.

She growled. "Do you practice at being such a jerk, or does it come natural?"

"Born with it," he said, the tension leaching out of his voice. "Child prodigy."

"I can believe that." Chloe sighed and pushed her hair out of her face. "Jake, thank you for telling me yourself. Really." She had to grit her teeth in order to offer the semi-apology. She wasn't sorry for being pissed off. But logically she knew she shouldn't take it out on him.

"Just remember that, next time you try to wriggle out of something," he said, and hung up.

Whizz twined himself around her legs and she leaned down to scoop him up. She was still moving more slowly than usual, but considering it had only been two weeks since her ribs were broken, she figured that was doing pretty good. "We really are lucky," she whispered to the cat. "If I hadn't gotten shot first, you wouldn't have been living with Martin. And where would I be without you?"

Whizz didn't have an answer for that, but he purred and sprawled out on her lap, so she figured it was all good.

She was still on the couch two hours later when Martin got home. A purring cat cures a lot of ailments, including insomnia. Chloe yawned. "I swear there's some kind of soporific emitted when they purr. It spreads out over your lap and robs you of the ability to do, like, anything. It's part of their plan to take over the world."

Martin took one look at her and shooed the cat off her lap. "What's up, big sis?" he asked, sliding an arm around her shoulders. He was still treating her like she was made of china, but Chloe couldn't complain. She was still yelping in surprise occasionally when she moved wrong and her ribs twinged at her.

"Someone burned my house down," she said.

He took it stoically. "You already knew that, didn't you? I thought that sexy Master Trooper Wolfe was looking for the person who burned it down."

"Senior Trooper," She corrected. Then she rolled her eyes at herself. "Jake and Wolfe are both trying to figure it out, but Jake's the only one in the official investigation. Wolfe is just looking into it because he thinks—well, we both think—the fire is related to the guy who shot me."

"Whom the sexy Wolfe is looking for," Martin repeated.

"Shup," Chloe ordered, and used his boney knee to push herself to her feet. "I need a shower. When I'm clean and dressed, you'd better be ready to take me to dinner."

"Bossy, bossy," he said, but he was grinning as she headed down the hall.

An hour later, Chloe had just finished her second beer, which had made a larger than normal dent in her sobriety. When her cell phone vibrated at her hip, she checked the caller ID and grinned. It said, WOLFE, BRAX. Her grin widened as she took the call.

"Chloe, it's Braxton," he said. She had to strain to hear his voice over the noise of the crowded sports bar. His voice was low and tense.

"What's up?"

"There's been another robbery. Where are you?"

Another robbery. Martin was trying to get her attention. Chloe glanced at him, but when he made a 'come-here' gesture, she shook her head to dismiss it. She appreciated that he liked Wolfe and wanted him to join them, but he didn't know the whole story. "Martin and I are at dinner," she said, squeezing her eyes shut. *I need to get less tipsy, ASAP. Who's the patron saint of sobriety? Or beer? Hell, Saint Jude's the patron of lost causes. Might be the best choice at the moment.*

Wolfe sighed in her ear. "Look, it's complicated. Can I send someone to pick you up?"

He wanted her at a crime scene with alcohol in her system. She frowned. "I don't know if I'm allowed on crime scenes. Admin leave."

He grunted. "Hold on," he said, and she could hear him in the background issuing orders. He was telling someone not to move the shovel, and the medical examiner would be done in just a minute.

Chloe's stomach sank. The medical examiner meant someone was dead.

"Wolfe," she said. She had to raise her voice to get his attention. "*Wolfe!*" People at the tables nearby turned to stare at her. One of the women gave her an annoyed look and turned away. Chloe scooted her chair backwards and stood, turning towards the door. "I'm at Hannigan's in Broad Ripple. You know where it is?"

"Right on College, isn't it? I'm up in Home Place. I'll send someone. You don't have to step onto the crime scene, but I want your eyes."

"Why am I so important?" Chloe asked him. From the corner of her eye, she saw Martin slap a hand across his face in overly dramatic despair. She stuck her tongue out at him.

Wolfe paused for a long moment, then finally said, "Like I said, it's complicated. I'll have someone there in about fifteen minutes. Chloe, you have a personal sidearm, right?"

The question caught her off guard. She was wearing a tank top and jeans, her brother's leather jacket, and her new black Doc Martens. And she was wearing her pistol in a concealed carry holster at the small of her back.

"Yeah."

"On you?"

"Hell yeah." She didn't go anywhere without a weapon. She wasn't obligated to step into a dangerous situation if she was off-duty, but she didn't know any cops who would stand aside without acting while a crime was committed in their presence. Still, she didn't like his implication that somewhere between a sports bar in Broad Ripple and a crime scene in Home Place, she was going to need her gun.

"Good. See you in a while." He was about to hang up.

"Wolfe," she said hastily, "be careful."

There was a moment of silence, then he said, "Yeah." The phone call clicked off.

Chloe was beginning to realize that when Wolfe had something to say, he said it, and when he had nothing to say, he didn't pretend. He quit talking. It was actually a pretty admirable quality, but it did kind of leave a girl wondering where she stood with him.

Coffee ASAP, and my burger to go, she thought. She was hungry. Fifteen minutes wasn't a lot of time for the alcohol in her blood to wear off. She was glad she'd only had two beers. She turned back to the table and gestured at Martin.

He was scowling, but when he saw her face, he beckoned the waitress over. "Two coffees, black, please," Chloe said. "And the bill."

"What's going on?" Martin demanded as she walked away.

"Wolfe wants my eyes on a scene," she said. "He's sending a cruiser to pick me up."

"You sure going there tipsy is a good idea?" he asked.

"I'm not *that* tipsy," Chloe replied. "Anyway, I might not even get out of the car. He said it's complicated. I don't have any idea why he wants me there, but I trust him."

Martin's brows drew together, but he didn't say anything as the waitress brought the coffee over. She knew what he was thinking, and it was true. She didn't trust people easily. There were a lot of reasons, most of them dating back to college, and they were good ones. But she wasn't placing personal trust in Wolfe; she was trusting him professionally. There was a difference.

A guy could break your heart and still be the best cop in the world.

* * *

Chloe was sucking down her second cup of coffee when she saw the state trooper step into Hanigan's. He paused just inside the door, scanning the tall-ceilinged room. Chloe lifted a hand and caught his attention, then downed the rest of her coffee.

"Stick my burger in the fridge?" she asked Martin. He nodded and held his to-go coffee out for her to take. He knew what crazy hours she was used to working. Even working day shift, there were plenty of times she got called out in the middle of the night or had to leave during a social event.

Chloe bent, still a little stiffly, and dropped a kiss on his cheek. Then she went over to the trooper, who introduced himself as James Finney, holding his badge for her inspection. She followed Finney to his cruiser. They didn't make conversation, except for him to point out the heat if she needed it. She just tugged Martin's leather jacket closer around her.

She was pissed at herself for drinking beer at dinner. If she'd been totally sober, she would have less of an issue with the situation. She would still be reluctant to invade a crime scene, but after all, Wolfe wouldn't have invited her if it was someone else's crime scene, and he had the authority to consult with her if he wanted. But even though the alcohol would probably barely register, she was uncomfortable with the idea of doing anything that might make it more difficult to secure a conviction further along the road.

Chloe was very much a play-by-the-rules kind of girl. Maybe because any time she ever tried *not* playing by the rules, it caused a lot of heartache.

By the time they got to Jessup, a short street angling off College, she felt like she'd been lost in her thoughts for a long time, but it had been barely half an hour since Wolfe called her. She could see another state cruiser and two IMPD cars, along with the white coroner's van and an ambulance with its lights off. Crime scene tape cordoned off a building that had obviously seen better days. Then again, the building was better off than its neighbors; it still had an operational business in it.

A few years back, Carmel had tried to annex Home Place in a bid to increase the tax base to benefit some rich people who were too big for their britches. Home Place fought back, and it was kind of like the mouse that roared. Almost a hundred thousand dollars and years later, Carmel and Home Place had come to a temporary legal truce, but earlier this year a judge had ruled in favor of Carmel. Home Place had appealed, so for the moment this area of land, maybe two miles square, was proud of being an older, established neighborhood of brick ranches surrounded by six-bedroom Yuppiedom. All the same, to outsiders, Home Place didn't seem to have a lot going for it.

Chloe had always been fond of it, in an impersonal sort of way, mostly because the people of Home Place were a thumb up the nose at all the nearby rich bitches who lived in houses with white walls and hardly any furniture. Her former college roommate was one of those, and that friendship had ended badly.

Braxton Wolfe was standing in short, solid authority by the front door of a business that was clearly marked as Julian's Gold and Exchange. Chloe took a deep breath when she saw him. He was definitely the sort of guy who was in charge of every crime scene he ever walked onto. Probably even if it wasn't his crime scene.

He saw them pull up and raised a hand in acknowledgment. Chloe glanced at Finney, who put the cruiser in park and said nothing. She didn't get out of the car, though she did unfasten her seatbelt. Wolfe had said he wanted her eyes on the crime scene. He hadn't said why, but if he wanted her honest first impressions, he wouldn't. So she put her eyes on the scene.

The building had a stone front, the kind that was an obvious facade. Probably built in the late sixties or early seventies, though there was no telling if it had housed a pawn shop all that time. It had a flat roof and large windows without obvious bars. It was practically upscale for the kind of establishment it was. The sign was in good shape. The windows had signs in them announcing a sale on watches and the current exchange rate for gold. A sign in the door proclaimed that the safe was on a time lock after dark.

There was a white-haired man standing off to one side, his gaze on the huddle of cops, emergency medical personnel, and medical examiner. He was wringing his hands, so Chloe took him to be the owner or someone tied to the business somehow. His pants were too short by a good two inches, but he was tidy and stood up straight.

A group of onlookers had gathered at the other side of the property, a few feet outside the crime scene tape. Two or three teenagers, a couple of middle-aged women, a man in a white tee shirt and a beard that reached his chest. One of the uniformed officers was between them and the obvious focal point of the scene, which was a sheet-draped body.

She couldn't see the victim from where she sat, but blood was pooling out from under the sheet. The medical examiner obscured her view. Wolfe would have an approximate time of death soon, if he didn't already. To one side of the group, a crime scene tech was photographing a shovel that lay on the asphalt. Even from where Chloe sat, she could see blood glistening on the blade of the shovel.

Shit. Beaten to death with a shovel isn't a good way to go.

"Wolfe thinks this is related to our case?" she asked. Finney just grunted. She sighed and pushed the car door open, glad she didn't have a reason to get too close.

She made her way over to where Wolfe was watching her approach. He put his hands on his hips, drawing the bottom of his suit jacket out and displaying the Glock 40 on his hip.

Her Docs had an inch of heel, and she had about two inches over him anyway. So she decided he was looking at her chin when he said, "Nice outfit."

She immediately hunched into Martin's jacket and stuck her hands in the pockets to pull it tighter around her. "Sorry. I wasn't dressed for work."

Wolfe sighed. "I meant it, Cole," he said, but his gaze had already gone distant again. He glanced over his shoulder. "What do you think?"

She frowned. "You think this is our guy?"

"Uh-uh. What do *you* think?" he repeated, shaking his head.

"There's a body," she said. "None of the other robberies had fatalities."

Wolfe looked up at her again, his amber eyes flashing gold at her. She stared back at him for a couple of heartbeats, and then felt her face get hot. How could she have forgotten?

"You were almost a body, Chloe," he said.

She took a deep breath and cleared her throat. "Right." *Focus, Cole,* she told herself. She was too hung up on how good-looking he was; it was distracting her from the job. She took a couple of steps to the side, moving so he was out of her direct line of sight, and studied the scene.

"Right side of the door's broken," she said, thinking aloud. "So he went in after the place was closed. He wasn't expecting anyone to be inside, and there wasn't anyone. I'm guessing if I went inside, I'd see half a dozen or so smashed glass cases. Same sort of thing missing as there always has been." She listened. She didn't hear an alarm, but that might just mean it had already been silenced by the company. "With the place empty, maybe he hit the cash register before leaving. And that's when he ran into—" She frowned. "The owner? Or someone who just happened to be passing?"

Wolfe nodded. "Owner," he said. "It was bad luck, from what the wife told us. He'd forgotten his reading glasses and he was right in the middle of a Tom Clancy. She doesn't need readers, so after dinner he went back to get his."

"Damn," Chloe said, appalled. "Killed for a Tom Clancy novel. Poor guy."

Wolfe's lips tightened like he was trying not to be amused. It was instinct for both of them, she thought. Cops never got used to seeing death and violence. They just learned to deal with it as best they could. Sometimes a little morbid humor was the best way to distance themselves a little.

"Owner's name is Julian Nikolaou. He's got a computer system, so we should get a complete inventory to compare with what's missing. But you're reading this about the way I did."

She glanced over at the white-haired guy, who had taken a few steps closer to the body. He was still wringing his hands. "Who's the old guy?"

Wolfe turned to follow her gaze. "You've never seen Doc Solman?"

Chloe blinked at him, then looked from the old guy to the medical examiner and back. "Yeah, Doc Solman's the ME. I've met him," she said. "And he's not even sixty yet. I was talking about that guy." She nodded her head toward the old guy wringing his hands. She didn't want to point, because he might flee if he knew he'd drawn their attention.

Wolfe's expression was blank. "Chloe, Solman's the oldest guy over there."

She turned her head and stared at him. "Are you blind?" She turned back, ready to say the hell with it and point at the guy.

But he was gone.

* * *

The worst thing about it, Braxton thought, is that she's lying to me.

He'd sent Chloe to wait for him at his cruiser. He had a couple of things to wrap up with witness statements and sealing the crime scene, and she didn't need to know how angry he was.

She had definitely seen someone. She'd looked too surprised when he'd contradicted her. Braxton had heard her heart rate spike, had caught the piquant scent of confusion and fear.

But she'd just said she must have imagined it. She'd laughed it off.

It was disappointing. He couldn't deny he was attracted to her attitude as well as her looks. But he'd thought she shared his dedication to the job—to seeing justice done. Even if she was confused, she could have told him.

Instead she'd seen something that could be important to the case, and then she'd lied about it.

When he finally finished, he took a deep breath, quelling his anger. Everyone was gone. The bystanders had been shooed off to their houses. The medical examiner's van had driven away. The other cruisers were pulling away from the building. He strode back to the cruiser and jerked the driver's side door open. "You want to explain that?" he asked, sliding into his seat.

Chloe jerked upright and gasped. She'd obviously been asleep. Her hair was a little mussed, and Braxton felt his expression soften just a little. There were dark circles under her eyes.

She rubbed her hand over her face, then looked around. "What's going on?"

He started the car and reached past her to tug her seatbelt across her lap. "I asked first." He was proud at how level his voice was. She might not even register that he was angry.

"You asked what?"

"What's going on?" he repeated. "What old guy were you talking about? Why didn't you send someone to talk to him? If you saw someone who might have witnessed the crime—"

"I don't know, Wolfe," she interrupted. "I think it was just the lighting in the parking lot that made the guy look older than he was."

Braxton gave her a hard look, the one he normally reserved for recalcitrant witnesses. He saw her flinch a little and then she glanced away. The scent of fear hit his nose, surprising him.

He reached out and adjusted the temperature, then turned the radio down. "I'm sorry I interrupted your dinner for no good reason," he said after a moment. It was his nice-guy voice, the one meant to make witnesses feel like shit for lying to him. From the way she shrugged and turned her head to look out the window, it had worked.

"It's not a big deal," she said. "I'm used to crazy hours and interrupted dinners."

"But you're also on leave right now," he replied. "You shouldn't have to deal with interruptions while you're recovering from getting shot."

Chloe slanted a grin at him. "I'll live."

Braxton gave a reluctant laugh and shook his head. "You're pretty hard-headed, aren't you, Cole?" He checked for traffic and pulled out onto the street. He didn't know why she was lying to him, or even what she was lying about, but for some reason, it scared her. Braxton didn't think Chloe Cole was a woman who scared easily. He'd let it go for now. It would give him an excuse to call her tomorrow.

Not that I'm looking for an excuse to call her, he told himself. I just want to wrap this case.

He didn't need werewolf senses to detect *that* lie.

"Should I take you back to your brother's house?"

She chewed her lower lip for a second, thinking. "Maybe you could run me through a drive-through and drop me back at home? Er, my brother's house. He's probably headed down to Zonie's Closet by now."

Braxton felt his eyebrows go up. He hadn't seen *that* coming. "On a week night?"

"Zonie's has a drag show every Wednesday," she offered. "Lots of fun, actually, and Martin is friends with some of the kittens."

Braxton had been to more gay bars and drag shows than most straight guys he knew. But for some reason he hadn't picked up on Chloe's brother being gay.

"Huh. A gay mechanic."

"Did you think they were all hair stylists and fashion designers?"

"I can't say I've ever given it much thought one way or the other," he replied. "I just thought my gaydar was better tuned."

That made Chloe laugh. "You'd be surprised how many people say something like that when they find out."

Braxton snorted. "All right. Late-night drive-thru of choice?"

"White Castle, please," Chloe said. When they got there, she ordered chicken, onion petals, and a vanilla milkshake, which made Braxton like her even more, damn it. He shouldn't like her at all, since she was semi-involved in a case he was working. He'd hand-waved that since she was also a police officer, but now she was *lying* to him. He shouldn't let himself be attracted to a girl just because she mixed onion petals and vanilla milkshakes.

When he pulled up to the curb in front of her brother's house, he said, "Chloe, be careful. These guys are erratic, and that just makes them more dangerous. Don't go anywhere without your sidearm."

He heard her heartrate shift up again. "Don't worry." She looked at him for a moment, then said, "You be careful, too."

Braxton gave her a slow smile, touched at her concern, as he had been earlier on the phone. "Don't worry about me." He rested his hand on her arm. "I'll wait until you get in. Talk to you tomorrow."

Chloe's return smile was almost startled, and then she was out of the car and heading for the house.

CHAPTER 7

Thursday morning was rainy with a strong wind, so Chloe decided it was a good morning for strong coffee and cold pizza for breakfast. The *Indianapolis Star* was a rumpled heap on the kitchen table. She carried it out to the living room along with her breakfast, where she sat down and promptly got a face full of Whizz, who had grown up with the strong belief that he was people and should eat people food at every opportunity.

After Chloe satisfied him with enough pepperoni that he quit begging, she munched her denuded pizza and skimmed the headlines. The story just below the fold on the front page—or rather the picture accompanying the story—stopped her completely.

It was the old guy from the crime scene the night before. He had dark eyes and white hair and mustache, with deep lines beside his mouth. His cheekbones were prominent, his face just this side of gaunt, and there was absolutely no mistaking him. *So Wolfe found him,* Chloe thought, *and he's tied somehow to the pawnshop.* But when she read the caption under the picture, things got even more complicated.

He wasn't just some old guy who happened to be passing by the shop and witnessed the attack. *He was the owner.*

"Long-time Home Place businessman Julian Nikolaou, age 67, was found dead at his place of business at 7:14 pm. The alarm had sounded, prompting Nikolaou's security contractors to send emergency responders to the resale shop, located on Jessup Street. There police discovered Nikolaou's body and the apparent murder weapon, a long-handled shovel."

There was more to the story, but that was the part where Chloe started hyperventilating.

"Nikolaou's *body? Nikolaou's* body? What the *hell?*" She'd seen him standing there watching the scene, wringing his hands and...obviously very interested in what the medical examiner was doing.

"Oh God," Chloe whispered. "Holy Mother, Mary of God..." She was vaguely aware of Whizz dragging her pizza off the plate in her lap, but she couldn't make herself care. She just stared at that picture of Julian Nikolaou, who had been looking at his own body under a sheet.

No, it had to be something else. "A brother!" she exclaimed. Whizz jumped from her lap and she heard the plate hit the floor. She stood and started walking around the living room—her ribs were still too sore for actual pacing—thinking aloud.

"He has a brother, probably runs the store with him. The brother would have gotten a call from the security people when the alarm went off. Braxton's probably already talked to him. Maybe the wife forgot to mention him when she..." Chloe trailed off, staring blankly across the room. For some reason the girl with the sad smile came to mind. Why did Chloe keep thinking about her?

She pressed her hands against her eyes. "Not possible," she said. "Absolutely insane. Maybe I'm hallucinating because I almost died. Did die."

Whizz meowed at her. "You've had enough." She picked up the newspaper again and scanned the rest of the story, but it didn't tell her anything she didn't already know, except to say that Nikolaou was survived by a wife. *Shit*, she thought. It would have mentioned a brother, especially if said sibling helped run the shop.

"Do you know how stupid that sounds?" she asked Whizz. "So stupid I can't even say it out loud." She made two more circuits of the room, but when it came down to it, she *had* to say it out loud.

"I see dead people," Chloe whispered, and started laughing.

Okay, it was kind of a leap in logic. But the more she thought about it, the more true it felt. She flipped to the obituaries and scanned the faces of the recent dead, but she didn't recognize anyone else. The problem was, she couldn't really prove a negative. How could she go about testing the theory?

"Okay, I could hang out at a funeral home and see if the deceased show up for their own services. I could head over to the cemetery a few blocks from Martin's place. I could walk around examining the faces of strangers to see if I recognized anyone from the obituaries."

Funeral homes, cemeteries... or hospitals. As soon as she thought about going to the hospital to look for dead people, it hit her.

The head nurse on the ward had never spoken to her. She'd never actually interacted with Chloe at all outside of standing at the door to her hospital room and looking at her. What if she wasn't the head nurse at all? What if she'd been someone who died in that room and kept an eye on her old bed? Or maybe she *had* been a nurse, but years ago, and she still walked the ward to watch over the patients.

Chloe closed her eyes and stood still in the middle of the living room, trying to remember what she'd looked like. Thick, dark brows that seriously needed some grooming. Dark, wavy hair in a ponytail that was half falling down. And she always looked sad. Chloe hadn't scored a single smile off of her in the entire time she'd been at the hospital. Of course, if she was dead, Chloe could understand why.

Not much to smile about when you're dead.

Before she'd managed to get any further in thinking about dead people, her cell phone rang. She was really getting tired of the damn thing interrupting her paid administrative leave, but she checked the caller ID just in case. And of course—Braxton.

Damn it. Chloe hadn't forgotten that she had lied to him the night before. A cold thrill went through her stomach and she was grateful she'd had the instinct to lie. It wasn't like he was going to take her seriously if she tried to tell him she was seeing dead people. She looked down at her cat, who was gnawing on a pizza crust in the middle of Martin's beige carpeting. *Oops.* She took the call.

"Cole."

"Are you busy?"

"Never too busy for you," she said, and panic flashed through her. That sounded way too flirtatious.

"Um. Is this a bad time?"

"I'm not busy, and this isn't a bad time. What's up?"

"We have another dead guy. I've got a friend in Homicide with Metro, which is lucky, because he called me in. I want you down here." His words were clipped. Chloe wondered if he realized she'd lied to him or if he was just mad about the dead body.

"And you're calling me why? For that matter, why did your friend in homicide call you? Oh, and who's your friend in homicide?" Chloe was on her way down the hallway as she asked. She needed to wear something other than sweatpants and one of her brother's old shirts.

"Friend in homicide is Detective Blake. He called me because he thought I would be interested in the body. I'm calling you for the same reason. Can I pick you up?" He wasn't wasting words, and he definitely wasn't allaying any of Chloe's curiosity.

"Yeah, yeah, give me five minutes." She ended the call. He knew where to go and she needed both hands to scrape her hair into a ponytail.

She layered a tank top under a button-down shirt and wore her usual jeans and Docs, and she'd even managed some blush and lip gloss by the time Martin's doorbell rang. She checked her weapon and made sure she had her cell phone. On the way to the door she gave a goodbye pat to Whizz, who had proudly conquered the back of the couch.

"How'd you sleep?" Wolfe asked, which seemed like a weird question to open with.

Chloe blinked. "Hi to you too," she said. She locked the door behind her and followed him down to his car. "I had weird dreams. You?"

"Badly. I kept trying to think of what the connection might be between Nikolaou and the others. The shovel was just inside the front door, by the way. They'd been doing some landscaping around the front walk. So the killing was more a crime of opportunity, probably an effort to not get caught."

She pulled her lips tight. It wasn't exactly a smile but it wasn't quite a grimace either. "Doesn't make Mrs. Nikolaou any happier, I bet."

"Probably not." Wolfe glanced over at her, an odd light in his amber eyes. Every time Chloe thought she was done noticing how handsome he was, something else kicked her in the face all over again. This time it was the compassion in his gaze.

"I saw Nikolaou's picture in the paper this morning," she volunteered, biting back that she'd seen him last night as well.

"He'd never had any real trouble before," Wolfe said. "The occasional incident of vandalism, but never a robbery of any kind. From a quick look over the inventory list, he doesn't seem to have had anything more valuable than a few ounces of gold."

"Price of gold's been up lately, but I don't see that being the thief's goal," she agreed. "But he took a lot of things, right? Do you think the thieves are after some specific thing that's disappeared or something?"

She wasn't sure what made her say it, but the large number of pawn shops the thieves had hit made no sense when combined with upscale jewelry stores. Maybe they were easier for amateurs than a jewelry store would be, but then again, an amateur wouldn't have been willing to shoot a police officer.

Chloe looked around as Wolfe made a turn onto a much smaller street. They were heading for a park along the White River.

"Oh, shit, a floater?" she asked.

"Not exactly. That seems to have been the intent, but whoever disposed of the body can't be very good at it. You'll see."

She nodded and they fell silent. She couldn't help but dwell on the thought that she was keeping something from him. She had never been the lone wolf type of cop, going off on her own and breaking rules to solve a crime. Chloe preferred to have plenty of backup behind her, and someone to pawn the paperwork off on, whenever possible. Still, how did you explain ghosts without getting sent to the department shrink?

Orange and yellow leaves made a bright ceiling overhead, despite the rain, as they wound down a small paved lane towards the river. She laced her fingers together and told herself there had to be some other explanation besides ghosts.

When they rounded the last curve, there were two IMPD cruisers and a crime scene wagon parked at the edge of the river. Only then did Chloe realize she hadn't thought to grab Martin's raincoat. She hunched her shoulders and made herself climb out into the rain after Wolfe did.

The rain was cold; she hadn't even been out of the car for a full minute before she felt it dripping down the back of her collar. She squinted and held a hand up to keep water out of her eyes. Three crime scene techs were already collecting evidence and photographing the scene.

The medical examiner, Doctor Solman, was already straightening up over the body. "I won't know for certain until I get him on the table, but this guy's been dead a couple of days. Rigor has already come and gone, and lividity indicates he was facedown on a hard surface for quite some time." He paused. "He has a gunshot wound that appears to have partially healed. I would guess he was shot at least a week before his death."

Wolfe still hadn't told Chloe why they were interested in the dead guy. In Chloe's opinion, the homicide unit existed with its three shifts for a reason, and there were equally good reasons she never intended to work in homicide. Dead bodies were unavoidable in her profession, but generally speaking she avoided contact with them, and that suited her just fine.

"So who is this guy?" she said finally. She didn't step any closer. She could see him just fine from ten feet away, and she wasn't interested in getting mud jammed up in the tread of her boots.

"License says Cordel Wethering." Detective Elliott Blake glanced from Wolfe to Chloe. "Thought you might be interested in taking a good look at the guy who shot you, now that he's not moving too fast."

Chloe took a step backwards, caught her heel on her other foot, and sat down in the wet grass. *How embarrassing is that, tripping over my own feet.* Blake just watched her, a flicker of amusement on his face. It wasn't exactly a secret in Homicide that she was... well, squeamish was their word, not hers, but she couldn't deny it was close to accurate.

Wolfe had his hand around her upper arm before she even really hit the ground. He wasn't quite fast enough to keep her from falling, but he did keep her from landing too hard. A couple seconds later she felt wetness soaking into her underwear, but by then Wolfe was helping her up.

She got back to her feet and stood still, just breathing, for a couple of seconds. Her ribs hadn't liked the jarring they got, but the ache faded more quickly than it would have a week ago.

"Wethering," she said finally. "He's *dead*?"

"Looks like it," Blake said. He stood aside and Wolfe propelled Chloe forward to look down at the body.

It was definitely him. The blond hair was plastered to his forehead, the scraggly goatee streaked with mud, the bloodshot, red-rimmed eyes open and clouded over. There was no question about it being the guy who'd shot her.

"So much for interrogating him," she murmured.

Beside her, Wolfe sighed. "He was the best lead we had. What killed him?" The question was directed at Doc Solman, but it was Blake who answered.

"Single gunshot to the chest. It was definitely an execution." His expression didn't hold a shred of regret. "Teach him to gun down a cop."

It was an off-hand remark. Cop killers, even would-be cop killers, were not a beloved type of criminal. Part of a police officer's job was to protect and serve even the people who shoot at them, but that was a part of the job they did out of duty, not desire. Still, part of Chloe couldn't help being sad that someone was dead. Even if he was a small-time thief who'd been willing to kill her to get away, he'd been alive, and suddenly he wasn't.

If nothing else, he was someone's son, and out there in the city there might be a woman who would worry about him when he didn't come home tonight.

"Killed to keep him quiet," Wolfe murmured. "Or for something he had." It was quiet enough that Blake didn't seem to hear. Chloe just nodded.

It made sense. People like Wethering usually got killed for a reason. Maybe he'd pissed off a local boss or defaulted on a debt, but the chances were good that he'd been killed because of the jewelry store robbery. It reminded Chloe that they had never found the Strawberry Shortcake pillowcase.

"He couldn't have hit that pawn shop in Home Place," Chloe realized aloud. "He was already dead when Julian Nikolaou's alarm went off." When she had seen Julian Nikolaou standing over his own body, wringing his hands in upset over what had happened to him.

Oh God, maybe I'm going nuts.

Braxton was silent for a moment, then he swore explosively. It made Chloe aware that he hadn't let go of her arm. His hand was loose around her arm, but warm and steadying, until he exclaimed. Chloe looked over at him.

"This isn't a guy and his partner," he said. "This is bigger than that."

She frowned at him. "What do you mean?"

"Wethering's partner was never spotted," he said. "We only thought he had a partner because there was an unidentified set of prints on that shotgun he was carrying. There's always the chance that could have been the guy who sold it to him or something."

"Okay," she said again. "With you so far."

"If he just had a partner, though, why would the other guy shoot him? We have no way of knowing who the partner is. So why kill him?"

"Maybe Wethering had something the partner wanted, and wouldn't give it up," she suggested. Blake was watching them, his eyes bright with interest.

"We need to find the partner," Wolfe said. "The prints didn't get a hit in IAFIS though. Whoever the partner is, he doesn't have a record."

Chloe sniffed. The cold and rain had her nose running. She wanted to get away from Blake, who was a nice guy but always keen to rib her about her dislike of bodies. Her butt hurt and her underwear was working its way up the back. She was ready for a hot cup of coffee somewhere out of the rain.

That was when Cody Wethering showed up.

He didn't come walking up, he didn't even *appear*; he just wasn't there, then he was. His hair was dry, sticking up one one side of his head, and he was scowling. The rain didn't seem to touch him. He stared down at his body, then suddenly dropped to his knees. Chloe had had to deliver a few death notifications in her ten years as a patrol officer, but she'd never seen quite this reaction to death. Wethering dropped to his knees, rocked back on his heels, threw his head back, and howled.

It raised the hair on her arms and made the back of her neck prickle. Her stomach clenched up. She had the sudden urge to pee herself. But she couldn't hear him at all. The sight of that body-seizing, soul-wrenching sorrow made her want to puke.

"Chloe? Are you all right?" Wolfe's hand was tighter around her arm. She jerked her eyes away from Wethering's ghost and found herself staring into golden eyes that seemed to see into her.

"Sorry, I just—chill," she said. It was true, even if it avoided the reason for the chill. Let him think it was the rain. She wished it was the rain. She glanced back down at the body.

"She's scared of dead things," Blake informed Wolfe. For a minute Chloe considered shooting him, but with all the witnesses, she decided it wasn't worth it.

"I'm not *scared*," she said loudly. "I just think it's a waste."

It was a lie she'd been using for years, with varying levels of ineffectiveness.

"Let me know the autopsy results," Wolfe told Doc Solman.

"Come on. Let's get you warmed up. I wasn't thinking when I dragged you out into the rain." The pressure on her arm urged her back towards his car.

"I'm not fragile," she snapped, her voice a little sharper than she meant for it to be. She was still on the defensive from Blake's accusation. Blake, the jerk, let out a snort of laughter.

"You're not fragile, but you *are* still recovering from a gunshot wound, and all your rain gear is probably in your car downtown somewhere." He tugged on her arm again and this time she yielded.

"I want coffee before anything else," she told him. As they went back to his car, she extended a hand behind her and flipped Blake off behind her back. She heard him laughing.

Chloe sat on a plastic trash bag to keep her ass from soaking into the passenger seat of Wolfe's car. They got coffee at a drive-through. She cupped it between her hands, warming them up, while Wolfe drove. The rain was starting to come a little harder, and it felt cozy in the car.

They didn't talk. Chloe don't know why Braxton was so quiet, but her mind was still back with Cody Wethering, mourning over his own body. Every couple of minutes she shivered again, and the coffee couldn't drive the chill away.

When Wolfe pulled up in front of Martin's house, he put the car in park but left the engine running. He leaned an arm on the steering wheel and looked at Chloe, his golden eyes serious. "Go in and get warmed up," he said quietly. "And Chloe, make sure you keep the door locked. Whoever killed Wethering might have a reason to come looking for you."

She sniffled and held his gaze, feeling exposed. "I'll be fine, Wolfe. I'm not a rookie."

His brows squished together, then smoothed out again. "Why do you do that?" he asked, his voice softer.

"Do what?" Suddenly her heart was pounding in her chest, and she didn't have any idea why.

"You call me Wolfe," he said. "It's like you're deliberately keeping me at arm's length. Have I offended you somehow?"

Chloe swallowed. "No. Sorry. Braxton."

He was still frowning at her a little. "You're holding something back, though. I wish you could trust me."

She suddenly wanted to blurt out everything. His amber eyes looked golden in the watery afternoon light, and even though she felt stupidly anxious around him, she also felt oddly comfortable with him. She *did* trust him, more than she was used to trusting any man she found attractive. It was on the tip of her tongue, but then he touched her chin and she sucked in a breath. He was leaning closer, even though she hadn't noticed him moving.

"I need to go," Chloe blurted, and scrabbled behind her for the door handle. She all but tumbled out onto the strip of grass between road and sidewalk. "Let me know about the autopsy." And with that she'd swung the car door shut and was hurrying up the walk.

She paused and looked back when she got to the door. He was still sitting there, and through the rain dripping down the car windows, she thought his shoulders were slumped. Chloe bit her lower lip and waved, then let herself into the apartment.

* * *

"Fucking brilliant," Braxton muttered to himself. He drew in a sharp breath through his nose and huffed it out his mouth, trying to center himself. *Just because she's strong and attractive and mysterious is no reason to lose your objectivity, asshole,* he told himself. And touching her like that, thinking about *kissing* her like that... He shook his head and checked his mirrors before pulling away from the curb.

He pulled his phone out and dialed Elliott's number. He hadn't realized Chloe and Ell knew each other, but from the way she'd tensed up at seeing him, there was clearly some history there.

"Blake."

"It's me," Braxton said.

"Hey. Sorry about your dead suspect, man. That's a tough break."

Braxton grunted. "You know Chloe well?"

There was a moment of silence on the other end of the line, then Elliott began laughing. "You're kidding me."

"What?" Braxton said, and instantly knew he'd sounded too defensive.

"You and Cole. You like her."

"She's a tough cop who pulled through a bad situation. What's not to like?" Braxton said.

"Doth protest too much," Elliott said. "All right, I haven't had lunch yet. Meet me at Shalimar for the buffet and I'll fill you in."

"That's not what I—" Braxton began, but Elliott had hung up on him. Braxton swore and flicked on his turn signal to turn onto College.

When he got to Shalimar, Elliott was already at the buffet. Elliott saw Braxton and jerked his head in a come-here motion.

"Ordered you the buffet already," he said. "I've been craving Indian for a week." He grinned at Braxton.

Braxton sighed and grabbed a plate, loading it with various chicken and lamb dishes. "This is fine. I didn't really need to do lunch, though."

"Yes, you do," Elliott said. He led the way to a table where two glasses of tea were waiting for them. "You want the scoop on Cole, and I want the scoop on your case. Ergo, lunch."

"You're so annoying," Braxton said.

"It's a skill." Elliott took a bite of chicken tikka masala. "First of all, me and Cole, no. Never. She's a good cop, and she's got a good sense of humor, considering what a rough time we give her about being squeamish around bodies. She's clean, by the books. People like working with her." He shrugged. "But Sam was the first, last, and only time I date another cop. Too much rocky ground to navigate there. I want someone who works a normal nine-to-five where the biggest drama is who said what at the water cooler."

Braxton rolled his eyes, but he couldn't argue. Sam and Elliott had been bad for each other, no two ways about it. Elliott had a hard time resisting the broody, misunderstood type, and Sam had that shtick down pat. Sam had also ended up off the force for reasons unrelated to their relationship, but that didn't mean Elliott's reasoning was unsound. "So what do you want to know about the case?" he said.

Elliott snorted. "No skating the issue, Brax. You like her. I want to know more about you and Cole."

"There's nothing to know," Braxton lied. Elliott would see right through it. They'd gone on double dates together and played baseball together; Braxton had been the first person Elliott came out to. For that matter, Braxton wasn't even sure why he was trying to hide this from his best friend.

Oh, yeah. Maybe he wanted to hide it because Chloe had lied to him.

"Spill," Elliott ordered. "I saw that droop."

Braxton sighed and rubbed a hand over his face. "Fine. I like her. She's tough and funny and seems to be a good cop."

Elliott arched an eyebrow. "Seems to be."

Trust Elliott to cut right to the heart of it. "I had a call last night. B&E in Home Place."

"Right, the store owner was killed."

Braxton nodded. "I called Chloe to come consult. I don't know why, except that this case has me completely stymied and I figured another pair of eyes wouldn't hurt."

"Especially since they're pretty brown eyes," Elliott jabbed.

"Shut it," Braxton growled. "Anyway, I'm pretty sure she saw something or someone she thought was important, or else she...I dunno, hallucinated or something? She got kind of spooky. And then she lied to me."

Elliott was silent for a moment, then huffed and slumped back in his seat. "Huh."

Braxton tilted his head down, pretending he was having trouble scooping something on his naan. Not disclosing everything, he could understand. After all, he didn't go around handing out business cards that said BRAXTON WOLFE, WEREWOLF PACK LEADER AND DETECTIVE. But then again, no one had ever asked him outright if he was a werewolf. Lying point blank to someone's face, that was different than keeping information to yourself.

"So what did she see?" Elliott said after a while.

"Hell if I know. Someone I couldn't see or smell. She called him an old guy, but I didn't see anyone older than Doc Solman. What does it matter?"

Elliott shrugged. "Not sure it does. But I hear the gossip you might not. Scuttlebutt is that Cole actually died on the bus, and they had to resuscitate her. That's gotta fuck with a person's brain a little." He took a long sip of his tea. "Maybe just...give her a second chance."

Braxton glared at his plate. Second chances weren't his strong suit.

"I know," Elliott said, without Braxton having to say it. "But not everyone's going to abuse a second chance."

After several moments, Braxton sighed heavily. "The case is the same one I've been working," he said, and he could sense Elliott relaxing across the table from him. "It's the break-ins at pawn shops and antique dealers and all that."

"Wait, you think Cole's shooter was part of that? I thought he robbed an upscale place."

"He did. But I'm at the point I'll take any lead. I'm working a dozen other cases, and this is the oldest outstanding. Two months now, no break, and in the meantime they keep hitting. My ass is going to be in a fire pretty soon if I don't make some arrests."

They cleaned their plates in silence, and when they refilled at the buffet, Elliott made a remark about the Indy Eleven's fall season, which Braxton seized on as a welcome change of subject. By the time they left Shalimar, he was feeling more optimistic about things.

* * *

Victor Garza held the Thanatos pendant up to the light of the sunset, oddly disappointed by the dullness of the silver. Deyonte had brought it as ordered, though he'd had to kill the store owner to avoid discovery. Victor felt bad about that. Cody had been a criminal, but Julian Nikolaou had just been in the wrong place at the wrong time. Victor made a mental note to bring Nikolaou back, once he had harnessed the pendant's power.

If he could learn how.

He grinned fiercely at the pendant. He *would* learn how. He'd done the hard part—tracking the pendant down had involved a lot of mind-numbing research. And Deyonte had retrieved it without much trouble. Victor had added a bonus to his payment to thank him.

The chain clinked faintly as he lowered the pendant to his desktop. It looked shabby against the gleaming mahogany of the desk. But surely the shabbiness must be proof of the pendant's great age, and *that* must be proof of the pendant's power. He had traced it, and it looked exactly as described. The rest of his research must also be true.

"Please, let it be true," he whispered.

Victor took a deep breath and slipped the pendant inside the shallow middle desk drawer. He stood and crossed the room. After a moment, he poured himself two fingers of scotch, looked down at the amber liquid as it swirled in the glass, and downed it in two gulps. He exhaled heavily and poured himself another.

"Forty-seven days," he sighed. Forty-seven days without his little girl. Forty-seven days of searching —

No, that wasn't true. He'd wasted days too drunk to leave his chair. Forty-one days of searching for something, anything, to reverse the single worst thing that had ever happened to him. Forty-one days of trying to unlock death.

He lifted the glass to his nose, let the fumes waft against his skin, and lowered it again. Still carrying the bottle, he left his study and walked along the hall to the stairs. As he climbed, Alita aged in the pictures that decorated the wall to his left. Baby pictures, pre-school, kindergarten, first grade... He paused on the landing, resting his fingers against the last frame in the series. There would be no picture for this school year, the school year that had begun mere days after her death.

Swallowing a sob, he climbed the rest of the stairs and turned right along the upstairs hall. He paused outside Alita's room, decorated with a poster from the production of *Les Miserables* he'd taken her to for her birthday last October.

Oh, God, how would he get through her birthday? It was less than a month away.

"No," he breathed, clenching his free hand into a fist. The October full moon was an entire week before her birthday. The magic was strongest then, and he would have figured out the pendant by then. He would buy her something beautiful and frivolous for her birthday, something she would laugh at, and they would celebrate together.

He rested his forehead against the poster, remembering how many times over the years he had paused outside the door, listening to the sound of her voice, the bright ring of her laughter, just to reassure himself that it didn't matter if he lost cases or his wife took the Mercedes in the divorce. Victor had gotten custody of Alita, and that was the only triumph he needed. When she was little, the door had been wide open, and he would tap on it and she would giggle and invite him in for a tea party or to read her a story. Later he would step inside the cracked door to help her with her homework or let Alita read a story to him. It had only been in recent years that the door was closed to him, when he'd had to knock and knock and hope he was granted entrance.

He had stood outside the door, tapping gently, just two nights before she died.

He could hear her chattering away on the phone, her tone excited and resentful by turns. Everyone was going to the back-to-school party at Jacob Turner's house. Everyone who was anyone would be there. Her dad just didn't get that he was ruining her social life. Then she cheered up, presumably as one of her friends reassured her everyone would miss her. Victor hesitated, lifting his hand to knock again.

Maybe this was a mistake.

But she had been so heart-broken when he'd said no. She'd promised she would get home by midnight if he let her go, and she wouldn't even ask for new clothes for this school year. All her friends were going. Erica and Danyelle and Kiara would be there, and seriously, this was more important than homecoming, even, and wouldn't he please let her go?

Victor sighed and knocked harder on the door. There was a tiny pause in her conversation, then she started talking again. Victor knocked, pushing the door open.

"Dad!" she shrieked. "Knock!"

She was clutching her phone to her chest, glaring at him. She looked so young in the oversized t-shirt and shorts she wore to sleep in, her dark hair pulled up in a ponytail. But her dark eyes flashed fury that reminded him of her mother; Josephine had always looked at him like that, in the last months of their marriage.

"I did knock," Victor reminded his daughter. "You were ignoring me."

"For a reason! Get out!"

Victor drew himself up, frowning at her. "This is my house, little girl. And you are still my daughter. I will have some respect."

She muttered, "I've gotta go," into her phone and hung up, heaving a huge sigh. "What do you want?" she demanded.

Victor sighed, too, and walked into the room, settling gingerly on the white desk chair. He looked around the room, at the turquoise and green plaid curtains and the bulletin board with movie stubs and pictures pinned on it. His little girl was growing up.

"Daaaad."

Victor rubbed a hand across his face and looked back at his daughter. "I came to tell you I've decided to let you go to the party," he said. "As long as you promise there will be no drinking, and you will be home by midnight."

Alita stared at him for a moment, then shrieked and threw herself at him, hugging him. "Thank you! Thank you! Ohmigosh I have to call Kiara back! Thank you, Daddy!"

Victor felt the wetness trickle from his eyelids and wiped it away slowly. He had never made a worse mistake.

He pushed the door open and stood in the middle of the room, staring at the plaid curtains and the bed, carefully made with its matching plaid quilt.

Alita had been so promising, so pretty, so smart. So determined not to follow her old man into the law, but to do something that would make a difference in the world. Victor had liked to think he'd made a difference, but she always rolled her eyes at him and said no, she wasn't interested in getting criminals back on the street. Sometimes the words hurt him; other times they led to a spirited debate about due process and Constitutional rights and citizenship. Usually they just made him feel proud that his little girl was going to change the world.

Medicine, he'd asked her once, and she'd wrinkled her nose. Architecture, then? But no, she wasn't interested in architecture, or engineering, or the law, or even computer science.

"I want to help people," she had said, flipping her long, dark hair over one shoulder. "Join the Peace Corps, figure out how I can best make a difference.

Maybe work for an NGO for a while. Then maybe run for office. I want to change people's lives for the better."

They had ended up making a deal. Victor would pay for college. After she got her bachelor's degree, she could sign up for a two-year service with the Peace Corps.

But none of that had ended up happening. Instead, he'd let her go with her friends to that stupid party. He'd let her ride with Erica, even though he knew Erica was barely licensed. He'd waited by the front door until twelve-forty-five, when the uniformed officers had shown up at his door, a black cop named Jim Stone and his short, athletic partner Yasmina Hassan, to tell him his little girl was dead.

Victor drained the rest of his scotch and poured another. Then he sat on the bed, staring dully at the desk, where a stack of books and papers were just where she'd left them forty-seven days ago. As he stared, trying to get his breathing back under control, he realized he wasn't alone in the room.

Was the pendant already doing its work? He sucked in a breath and held it, unable to force himself to turn his head. The figure just visible at the corner of his vision seemed tall and a little wavery, but that might just be his tears obstructing his vision.

Would he turn his head and look on his daughter again? How would she be looking at him? With love? With sorrow? With blame?

Victor sucked in another breath and jerked his head to the right.

A lanky blond man, still in his late teens, stared back at him. His beard was so scraggly it barely deserved the name, and his Fallout Boy t-shirt was stained with blood. Cody Wethering's blue eyes were bloodshot and red-rimmed, and they pierced Victor.

"Get out!" Victor shouted.

Cody just stared back at him. His outline was faded, but he was definitely there. His gaze was accusing. His mouth was tight.

"Get out of my little girl's room!" Victor screamed. How *dare* this small-time thug defile his daughter's bedroom? How dare he stand before Victor after failing him?

"GET OUT!" Victor screamed, throwing the glass at Cody. Scotch spilled across the pale blue carpet. Cody disappeared.

Victor dropped to his knees and wailed in fury and heartbreak.

CHAPTER 8

After Braxton dropped Chloe off at her brother's place, she started going through the boxes of the stuff Martin had salvaged from the fire. She thought she could distract herself from thinking about how Wolfe—how *Braxton*—had touched her. Distraction didn't work, of course. She could still feel the warmth of his fingers on her chin, and the feeling he had woken in her chest had her cycling through excitement, fear, and regret.

It had been a long time since she'd dated anyone seriously, and no matter how many times she told herself she didn't need to punish herself for choices made when she was twenty-one and scared, and no matter how many times she told herself she was older and wiser now, she still struggled with trust and intimacy. With years of perspective, she could look back at her situation and know, intellectually, that she took the only option she thought she had. When a broke, nineteen-year-old, scholarship kid whose younger brother was still in high school, ended up pregnant...well, there didn't seem to be a lot of options. She was waiting other people's tables to keep food on her own and still trying to finish her own schooling and make sure Martin stayed in school himself.

She went by herself to the clinic, gritted her teeth and walked past the women handing out tracts, and cried despite—or maybe because of—the tremendous feeling of relief afterwards. And then she swore off romance and concentrated on school. She'd finished her criminology degree and started working for IMPD, and set her sights on being the best damn cop she could be. She took on extra shifts and worked as much overtime as she could get, especially after Martin graduated and immediately joined the Army. She told people she was too busy to date, and she said it to other people so many times that she almost believed it herself.

After meeting Jake and his sisters, she'd started going to church with them, and actually started forgiving herself for the mistakes she'd made. But forgiving herself was one thing; giving herself permission to fall for someone, to give part of herself to someone else...that was something else entirely. She'd screwed up massively the last time she'd tried to have a real relationship. Braxton Wolfe probably wouldn't be any different, no matter how handsome and kind he seemed to be.

When Martin got home from work, Chloe badgered him into driving her downtown to pick up her car from the parking garage. She was only taking the Vicodin at bedtime, so she wouldn't be driving impaired, and she desperately needed her independence back.

As soon as she was in the driver's seat, she headed out Interstate 70 to the 465 loop. Six lanes of freedom sounded like heaven. She spent some time driving fifteen miles over the speed limit along with most of the other drivers on the loop—she liked to joke that the *real* Indianapolis Motor Speedway was I-465. By the time she'd shaken off the worst of her melancholy, she was up by Eagle Creek Park. On impulse, she got off the interstate and headed for the park. Some time on the shooting range would do her even more good than driving, and even though the range had been closed to the public earlier in the year, it was still open to law enforcement.

When she got back to her car, she had a missed call from Jake. Lucia was making barbecue and wanted the Coles to come for supper. She texted Martin, *Dinner at Casa Ruiz*, and then called Jake to let him know they'd be there. She thought about swinging past the wreckage of her house on her way home, because it wasn't too far from Eagle Creek Park. But then she thought about Braxton's theory that whoever had killed Cody Wethering might be coming after her, and she decided to put it off until the next day. She could get Jake to come along as backup. Just in case.

She stopped at the grocery for a case of Coors Light and a bag of chips, and on impulse picked up a Jason Statham action flick she hadn't seen yet. If she wasn't in the mood for anything but crazy plots and long fight scenes, Jason Statham was always a good choice. Lucia and Celia loved his accent, Martin and Chloe loved his muscles, and Jake was blessedly uncomplicated in his enjoyment of the way Statham beat people up.

It was a good night. Regaining her car and independence had done a lot to restore her equilibrium. So she'd let Braxton shake her a little. Big deal. She just got shot two weeks ago, after all. It takes a while to recover from death. And so what if she was stuck living with her brother in a spare room that smelled like smoke? At least she had a brother who was willing to take her in. And she had good friends in the Ruiz family.

She did drag Jake into the kitchen with her partway through the movie, ostensibly to get another round of beers, but she really wanted to give him a rundown of what had been going on with the burglaries and Braxton Wolfe. She didn't tell him she was seeing spirits from beyond the veil, though. It was just too weird to try to explain that to anyone, even her best friend.

Jake filled her in on how the investigation was going back at the department. Wethering's death had thrown a wrench into the works. That was making everyone a little more meticulous in their work. Then he surprised her by saying he'd checked up on Wolfe. "Sounds like a stand up guy," he said, not looking at her as he opened a bottle for one of his sisters. "Solid detective, almost ten years on the force, good solve rate."

Chloe looked sideways at him and decided refilling the chips bowl was a better idea than replying.

"I hear he just lost his dad a while back. He was out on bereavement leave a few months ago. Other than that, he's single, seemingly well-adjusted, no wants or warrants..." Jake had kind eyes, but he also had a smirk that made Chloe want to smack him sometimes. He was using the smirk instead of the eyes at the moment. "And now he's asked you for help with his case instead of his own department."

Chloe shrugged. "I had an up close and personal encounter with his main suspect. He wanted to pick my brain. Nothing wrong with that."

"Yeah, except he's totally doing more than picking your brain, C. He's trying to pick you up." Jake gave her a big wink.

She tried to give a scornful, you-don't-know-what-you're-talking-about snort. It came out more like the sound Whizz made when he'd accidentally gotten water up his nose. *Chloe Cole: cool, confident, and oh-so-convincing*, she thought ruefully.

"You oughta know better than to doubt me on this," he said. "I'm a guy. I know these things."

"You're a dork," Chloe said. It was weak, as far as retorts go, but she started back out to the living room, where she could hear Lucia cooing over Statham's British accent.

"Hey, hang on." Jake's tone grew more serious. Warily, Chloe turned back. "How you doing? Really?" She felt her shoulders relax. It eased an ache in her ribs that she hadn't noticed until it went away.

"Um. Having some nightmares," she admitted. *About ghosts*, she didn't admit. "You know. I'm just trying to...let myself feel stuff, I guess."

Jake nodded. "Yeah. Good. That's good." He clenched his jaw briefly, then said, "Look, Chloe, you know if you want to talk about it. What happened, I mean." He rested a hand on her shoulder, then nodded. "Okay."

That was eloquent, Chloe thought. A few smartass words came to mind, maybe a remark about did he want to consider a career in speech writing after retirement. But as soon as she opened her mouth to say it, he glared at her.

She grinned at him and went back to the living room to admire the musclebound kickboxer in the movie.

* * *

The phone shrilled Braxton out of a sound sleep. He snapped awake and was reaching for it before he registered that it was still dark in his bedroom. He answered it automatically, heart pounding. "Wolfe." A moment later his eyes finally found the alarm clock, which told him it was just after four in the morning. Another jolt of adrenaline surged through him. Phone calls at this time were never good.

"Braxton. It's Murphy." The voice on the other end of the line sounded annoyed. "Sorry to wake you."

Braxton wiped a hand down his face. "It's fine. Are you in trouble?"

"Yeah, sorta." Murphy's voice took on a tinge of awkwardness.

Braxton threw back the covers and swung his legs over the edge of the bed. "What happened? Are you okay?"

"Oh. Um, non-life-threatening trouble," Murphy specified, and Braxton's steps slowed on his way to the dresser.

After a moment, the tension returned. Even non-life-threatening trouble that provoked Murphy to call Braxton at four in the morning had to be pretty bad. "Okay, what, then?"

There was silence as Braxton jerked open a drawer and started tugging on a pair of jeans. Then Murphy sighed explosively in his ear. "My damn car won't start."

"Are you still at work?" Braxton shifted the phone to the other ear so he could pull on a shirt.

He had time to open the top drawer and pull out a pair of socks before Murphy said, "Getting ready for work. I'm at home."

Braxton frowned. Murphy was skittish, all right, but he didn't usually hedge like this. Something was going on, but arguing about it on the phone wouldn't get Murphy to work. "All right. I'll be there in...say, half an hour?" Traffic would be light. It probably wouldn't take him quite that long to get to Murphy's, which was on the edge of the near north side of Indianapolis—one of the more dangerous neighborhoods in the city.

"Thanks. I've got coffee." Murphy hung up.

Braxton went to get his boots and almost tripped over Fuzzy, who was sprawled, as usual, in Braxton's direct path. Braxton swore, caught his balance, and grabbed the boots, then got his gun from the safe. On-duty or not, no police officer went anywhere unarmed, and there was no way in hell Braxton was going to the near north side without his sidearm.

Fortunately, the roads were clear. Indianapolis' morning rush hour didn't really get started until seven, and this early, there wasn't much traffic at all. Twenty-four minutes later, Braxton pulled up in a parking area behind Murphy's apartment building on North Meridian. To his surprise, Murphy was waiting for him outside the door, shoulders hunched against the morning chill. He got in the car and held out a cup of coffee.

"Thanks, man," he said, buckling his seatbelt. There were deep shadows under his eyes, and he looked a little rumpled, but wide awake—the latter being more than Braxton could say for himself.

"They switch shifts on you?" Braxton said, pulling out of the parking lot and automatically turning north to go to the Wendy's where Murphy worked.

"No, not Wendy's," Murphy said to the dashboard. He had his head ducked, shoulders still hunched. "Airport."

Braxton glanced at him in surprise, then flicked on his blinker and turned west on Thirty-Eighth Street so he could turn around. "Why are we going to the airport?"

Murphy huffed a sigh. "I got a second job, okay? I'm handling packages out there for FedEx. It's no big deal, except my car wouldn't start this morning, and I can't afford to be late. More late."

Braxton frowned, keeping his gaze on the road. Maybe Tara had had good reason to get on Murphy's case last week. Was Murphy having trouble making ends meet? And if so, why hadn't he just said something? Braxton wasn't rich, but the pack had resources. And most importantly, the pack took care of its own.

He turned south on MLK, Jr. and drove in silence, sipping his coffee, which was hot and black, the way he liked it. He could have jumped on the highway, but traffic on the surface streets was still light, so he took Washington west. It would make it easier to get to the freight areas of the airport. He decided to avoid conversation until they were on Morris Avenue and he could see the runway lights.

"If you needed money," he began, but Murphy didn't let him finish.

"I'm fine," he said, his voice flat.

"You're not fine if you're working two jobs," Braxton said. "The pack could float you for a month or two."

Murphy's fist lashed out and punched the dashboard. "I'm not a damn charity case." His voice was still flat, and he wasn't looking at Braxton. He was staring out the side window at the railroad lines north of the airport.

"No," Braxton said softly. "You're my pack."

"Fuck that, man!" Murphy snapped. "I'm just some stupid kid who was sneaking after hours into the park so I could get high. You don't know me from jack, so why should you give a shit about me?"

"The pack's code—" Braxton began.

"Shove your pack code! I was doing just fine until one of *your* Goddamn pack ruined my life!" Murphy sniffed hard and swiped a hand angrily at his face.

Braxton took a slow breath, telling himself to hold onto his temper. Murphy knew better, but he was too upset to watch what he said, and Braxton could understand. Braxton pulled the car into the Fedex parking lot and switched off the engine. "Not my pack," he said, his voice still calm, but a little cooler. "Not *this* pack."

In fact, it had been a bitter, power-hungry man who had been expelled from the pack a good eight years earlier. A man who had once been Braxton's father's best friend, before he began thinking himself above the law. Once Braxton's father drove him out, Claude Marcineau had disappeared for years. Braxton had since traced him to Quebec, and then to Sasketchewan, before he made his way back to Idaho and Montana, where there was enough wilderness that the werewolf packs didn't have to maintain quite the rigorous code that Indianapolis' pack had. Then Marcineau had come back to Indiana, where he'd tried to start his own pack by wilderness rules—that strength was all that mattered, and the weak were prey.

Braxton could feel Murphy tense next to him, but after a moment, Murphy muttered, "Fine, whatev, not *your* pack. It was still one of your kind. I don't want anything to do with it. I wouldn't even be in your damn pack if your father hadn't made it clear he'd have to kill me if I didn't get myself under control. So just take your pack code and your damn charity and shove it."

He got out of the car, not meeting Braxton's eyes. "Just leave me alone."

* * *

Chloe and Martin got home around ten and she pleaded exhaustion and retired to the guest room. She cracked the window to let out the smell of the smoky boxes before doing anything else. There was only one bathroom in the apartment, but the night stand had a mirror on it, so she used that to smear a thin layer of ointment over the stitches healing on her neck. She decided to go with Tylenol instead of Vicodin, since she'd had a couple of beers, and then she climbed in bed.

She left the window open even though it was getting down into the fifties at night. That gave her a good excuse to drag an extra blanket over her and snuggle in with Whizz, who had a habit of curling up against her butt when it was cold.

She did not have pleasant dreams.

Despite letting out the smell of the smoke, she dreamed she was trapped in her house as it burned. She could hear Whizz meowing from somewhere nearby, but the flames were too high. Then she was somewhere dark, clearing out a building, arms crossed at the wrist, Glock in her right hand, flashlight in the left. She heard a noise behind her and began to turn, but something hit her and she fell.

Then there was the girl. Her sad eyes were on Chloe, her mouth open as she spoke to Chloe, but Chloe couldn't hear her voice. She heard nothing but the wind as it whipped her hair into her eyes.

Chloe tried to ask who she was, her name, where Chloe knew her from. She reached out to touch the girl. She even shouted at the girl, demanding to know why she kept showing up.

The girl shook her head, watching Chloe, then sat down, cross-legged, and faded away.

Chloe woke up to the sun shining brightly in her eyes. The window was wide open, the curtains shoved back. Whizz was pawing at the bedroom door, obviously wanting his breakfast. She sat up, disoriented. It felt late. Why hadn't Martin woken her? He'd checked on her every morning so far.

She went out to the kitchen, Whizz trotting at her heels and between her feet, and put a can of cat food out for him. Her next priority was to check the coffee maker. Martin hadn't started any brewing before he left. Chloe remedied that, then checked the locks before stumbling into the shower.

Clean and caffeinated, she sat down at the kitchen table with a yellow tablet, a pencil, and the case files Braxton had given her. There was some connection, and she was damn well going to find it. She started making lists, grouping the stolen items by type or by material. Neither list told her much. It was a fairly even mix of each type.

There had to be a reason the thieves were choosing what they did, though. She made a list of all the stones that had been stolen, but there was nothing extraordinary about them. She pulled out a map of Marion County and marked the locations of all the robberies. Nothing special about that either.

After way too long, Chloe swore and tugged on her brother's leather jacket. She stuffed the case files into one of those reusable, ecologically sound shopping bags, since her brief bag had gone up in smoke. A bright green, hardware store bag wasn't exactly professional looking, but she would just leave it in the car and no one would know.

Braxton might have spoken with all the victims of the robberies, but Chloe hadn't. She hadn't even seen most of the places. She didn't have the authority to talk to the victims, as far as it was related to the investigation. If she did, it could hinder the DA's ability to get a conviction later on, if they thought Chloe was tampering with the investigation. But she could at least look.

She started with the first store that had been hit, out in Plainfield, and drove past each of the locations. She parked in front of every store, taking in the surroundings and any routes of egress. She checked out the back of the store to see what kind of security was in place. She reread the reports on each of them to see exactly what had happened.

Finally she made her way back to Meridian, where the robbery at Rice and Cauldwell had involved her in Braxton's case. She drove slowly around the traffic circle at the Soldiers and Sailors Monument. She witnessed three traffic violations that she had no current authority to address. She looked around for any of the peregrine falcons that lived on top of the Key Bank building.

Then she drove away from the circle without going past the jewelry store or the place she'd been shot.

* * *

The next day, annoyed with her cowardice, Chloe went back downtown and parked her car on the block where she'd been shot. She went and stood in the spot she'd been in when the first blast hit her vest. She looked up at the rusting fire escape and spotted the old Colts Super Bowl banner again. Everything looked the same as it had two weeks ago, except that no one was about to shoot her.

Her heart was pounding like she expected someone to, though. Having her handgun nestled in the small of her back didn't give her as much of a sense of security as she had expected. She took deep breaths, letting them out slowly, and sat down on the sidewalk, leaning against the brick building that had concussed her two weeks ago.

Chloe tented her legs and leaned her elbows against her knees, lowering her head. Her hair fell down over her face. After a moment she shoved her fingers through it, catching on a tangle and swearing under her breath.

When she looked up, Cody Wethering was standing over her.

She let out a little shriek. She couldn't help it. The guy shot her two weeks ago, ended up dead this week, and suddenly he was standing over her again. His eyes were as bloodshot as they had been, his beard scraggly. But he didn't look mean or desperate or strung out this time. He looked bewildered.

He was studying Chloe, his forehead wrinkled up. She wondered if he even recognized her. There was something about the set of his shoulders or how wide apart his feet were planted that suggested he was expecting trouble. Like he was in unfamiliar territory, or he'd been interrupted in the middle of something. It made Chloe wonder if she'd somehow drawn him there.

She glanced around. There was no one around, fortunately. If anyone had heard her yell like that, they probably would have thought she was nuts. But since no one seemed able to see the dead people but Chloe, she didn't want to be seen talking to thin air.

"What do you want?" she asked, looking back at Wethering. He recoiled, looking even more confused.

"Yeah, I can see you," she told him. "You're the scumbag who shot me. That was a dumbass thing to do, by the way. Probably why your partner decided you were a liability, since cop killers get hunted down relentlessly."

Wethering's expression was blank. She wondered suddenly if ghosts had thoughts and emotions, or if they were just memories of the person they'd been when they were alive. Or was there a more complicated explanation?

"Oh God, am I really thinking this?" she muttered. Wethering cocked his head to one side and looked at her. He opened his mouth and she could see words forming, but there was no sound to go along with it.

Great, so I can see dead people but I can't hear them. Figures. Being able to hold a conversation with someone who'd been murdered would have been too convenient. Oh, you've got a homicide? Sure, let me just dial up the dude's ghost and he can tell me who the killer was.

Not that the testimony of a dead guy would stand up in court as evidence, anyway.

Chloe sighed and rubbed her hands over her face. A sudden wind stirred her hair and sent shivers down her spine. It was only then that it occurred to her to wonder if dead people could hurt her somehow. She jerked her hands down. Wethering was gone.

"Shit," she muttered. She surveyed the entire block, but he was nowhere to be seen. Scowling, she shoved herself to her feet. Her ribs protested, but she took shallower breaths and headed in the direction of the jewelry store. There had to be some place the guys hadn't looked for the pillowcase.

Chloe spent the next two hours looking in gutter drains and behind Dumpsters and under steps. When she finally arrived in front of the Cauldwell and Rice jewelry store, she'd found a total of twenty-eight cents, dozens of cigarette butts, and a used condom, but nothing remotely resembling Strawberry Shortcake, Blueberry Muffin, or Huckleberry Pie.

She stopped outside the jewelry store and shoved her hands into the pockets of Martin's leather jacket. She stared at the signs for a while. "Established 1953" and "Purveyors of Fine Diamonds" and "Second Generation Family Business". What made them a target? Nothing with diamonds had been stolen from them, as far as she could remember. They were the sort of place socialites went to get their engagement rings custom designed, but they also did watch repair and heirloom and estate pieces. What might they have had—or more to the point, what did the thieves *think* they had—that made them the right people to steal from?

Chloe shook her head and walked away. Her ribs were aching and her nose was running from the chill in the air. The sun was out, though, and it felt good warming the shoulders of the black leather jacket. She crossed the traffic circle to the Soldiers and Sailors Monument and spent several minutes wandering around the base of the monument, studying the limestone carvings. She thought about going into the Civil War Museum in the bottom portion, because she'd always meant to go in there and had never gotten around to it. But in the end she just chose a different spoke of the streets radiating out from the monument, one a block over from the route she'd taken before, and walked back to her car.

Even though they were pretty sure Wethering had run along Meridian, she decided to do her sweep along Scioto Street as far as she could. It dead-ended a few blocks down, just north of the train tracks that ran to

Union Station. Still, it was basically an alley between parking lots, so maybe Wethering had taken that route instead, thinking there would be fewer witnesses if he dumped the pillowcase.

Of course, the problem with all this was that she was banking on the idea of Wethering and his partner not having had a chance to retrieve the bag. That was probably wishful thinking, when it came down to it. Wethering had had at least a week and a half to return and get the pillowcase back. Or maybe he and his partner had already arranged a pickup location, and the partner had the loot.

Either way, it was a long shot, and Chloe knew it. But a lot of police work was tedious and boring, and that tedious, boring work was what got the most results.

She ended up at the train tracks with nothing to show for all her searching, aside from a throbbing in her neck and an ache in her ribs. She went into the Claddagh Irish Pub and had some Guinness stew and a glass of Smithwicks. While she was waiting for the waitress to come back with her change, she dialed Braxton's number. She got his voice mail so she left a message about her new theories of the day.

Then, with nothing else to do, she headed to the library, picked out half a dozen steamy romance novels, and went home to take Vicodin and read until it knocked her out.

CHAPTER 9

Victor rubbed one reverent fingertip across the sword and inverted torch of the silver pendant. He kept taking deep breaths, attempting to calm his racing pulse, but he kept cycling between nervousness and excitement. Tonight, he would make the first attempt at using the Thanatos pendant. His research had been exhaustive—and exhausting, for that matter. He dared not outsource much of it, for fear someone would connect the dots and learn what he was up to.

He had been careful to obtain his translation of the inscription on the back of the pendant from one source—an online translation service that charged by the word—and the pronunciation of the incantation from other sources. It had taken some time to find enough Classics professors, from the departments at Indiana University and Purdue University, and when he'd finally obtained their translations of fragments he split between them, Victor had verified their work by consulting four separate Greek-speaking theology teachers at various religious colleges across the Bible Belt.

He studied the translation one more time. Merciful Thanatos, allow this humble petitioner to seek for lost love among the dead. Mighty Thanatos, grant this humble petitioner life anew for lost love.

It was simple enough. Almost too simple, to Victor's thinking, but the ancient text that had first mentioned this pendant had assured him it was among the most powerful of the death artifacts. One legend suggested it had belonged to Orpheus before he made his descent into Hades searching for Eurydice, and the possession of the pendant had been what inspired Hades to allow Eurydice to leave with her husband.

Victor's lips tightened. He did not intend for his story to have the same ending as Orpheus'. He would not look back. He would not lose his daughter again.

He checked the clock. Five minutes. Midnight was the in-between time, the witching hour. His research suggested this would be the most auspicious time for him to attempt this.

He took a deep breath. "I'm doing this for you, Alita," he murmured. "If I succeed, we'll never fight again." He knew that for a lie even as he spoke it; some part of him knew she would be angry about what he'd done to achieve his goal. But she would forgive him. She had to forgive him. He'd done all of this because he loved his daughter.

The grandfather clock in the downstairs hall chimed the Whittington pattern and then began striking the hour, its deep *bong* sounding throughout the house. Victor took another deep breath and looped the pendant around his neck.

He clutched the Thanatos pendant in his palm and took a deep breath to steady his voice. Then he began reciting the invocation and spoke Alita's name. Nothing happened with the first incantation, but he hadn't really expected it to. Three was the mystical number, after all. Peter had denied Christ three times. An oath made three times was binding with the Fae.

Heart pounding, Victor spoke the incantation again. His voice shook when he named Alita a second time. The pendant grew warm in his grasp. It was too warm for it to be just his body heat. The longer he held it, the hotter it felt, in fact. Victor winced and forced himself to tighten his fingers. He couldn't quite catch his breath.

That was when he noticed Cody Wethering lurking near the corner of the room. He looked like he was lounging against the bookshelves, his face twisted into a bored smirk. *This isn't for you*, Victor thought, but he didn't speak it aloud. He was afraid that saying anything in between recitations would break the spell. Instead he glared at Cody, wishing he could destroy the ratty little ghost forever.

Why aren't you here, Alita? he wondered. I do this for you. Can you not even come to lend your support? He felt a tear forming at the corner of one eye and blinked it away.

The third time he voiced the incantation, he was nearly shouting, partly out of his anguished need and partly because the pendant was searing his flesh, scorching his palm. He wanted nothing more than to drop it, but he refused to be bested—even by magic.

His stomach was churning, but he could almost feel her presence, almost smell the orange blossom shampoo she'd used. Alita was near, she was watching him. He could do this for her. Without opening his eyes, Victor screamed, "Alita Odilia Garza! My daughter! My little precious one!"

The power built, between his fingers and inside his chest. He arched his neck back, but he refused to open his eyes. He couldn't open his eyes unless he was sure he would see her. He wouldn't doubt Hades' word. He would trust that Alita was there. His pulse was racing, his breath coming fast. Inside his chest, his heart beat so fast it felt like it would explode. A cold sweat broke across Victor's face, and then his seared, cramping fingers opened of their own volition.

"*No!*" he screamed, his eyes jerking open. He grabbed after the pendant, and for just an instant, he thought he saw her dark hair and eyes. She looked sad, and his heart panged at the thought of his little angel suffering.

Then the room exploded with a darkness that was profoundly cold and searingly hot all at once. Victor felt his head explode, and then he lost himself entirely to the darkness.

"Vic. Hey, Vic." Something patted his cheek. "C'mon, Vic, wake up."

Victor's head was throbbing wildly and he felt like he might throw up. After several seconds, while he tried to mentally ascertain if he was still alive, his stomach gave a heaving jolt. Victor moaned and rolled over, vomiting on his Turkish rug.

He heard a noise of surprise and then nothing for several moments. When a cool, damp cloth wiped his face, Victor finally began coming back to himself.

Vic. No one called him Vic except Fletcher. He was in his own study, as evidenced by the carpet, and by the fact Fletcher had found him. He had attempted the incantation. It hadn't worked. Victor's throat seized up.

It hadn't worked—except he had, for that instant, seen Alita. He was sure of it.

"Almost," he choked out, and lifted a hand to cover his eyes. Fletcher had seen the depths of his grief, but Victor didn't want to weep in front of him. They were silent for a long time.

Eventually, Fletcher sighed. "You're bleeding," he said. "Or you were. How bad are you hurt? Can you sit up?"

Braced by one of Fletcher's meaty arms, Victor managed to sit, though his head spun like he'd drunk an entire bottle of whiskey. He touched his forehead gingerly, unsurprised by the bump there. Further exploration showed that his nose had bled copiously after the spell failed.

"It failed," Victor whispered.

Fletcher gave him a glass of water and rocked back on his heels once he was sure Victor could sit up on his own. He exclaimed over Victor's burned hand and went to get the first aid kit from the bathroom. It wasn't until Fletcher had finished wrapping gauze around his palm that Victor spoke.

"Why did it fail? I was so close." Victor met Fletcher's gaze. "I saw her, Fletch. I saw her face, her eyes."

Fletcher's face wasn't skeptical. It didn't show much expression at all, but what expression it did show was only concern for Victor. "Maybe you shouldn't of done it here," he said finally. "Maybe you should of done it in Alita's room. Or her fort. Or..." He trailed off, scratching his jaw. "Or her grave. I bet you should of done it at her grave."

Victor straightened, full of electrical resolve. "You're right. Of course you're right. Why didn't I think of that myself? Her grave, the resting place of her body, it would have to be there." He struggled to his feet and groaned.

"Maybe you'd better wait til tomorrow," Fletcher said, but froze when Victor cut a sharp glance at him.

"We'll go tonight."

"But it's not midnight anymore," Fletcher pointed out.

Victor shook his head, then regretted it as a wave of nausea threatened to swamp him. "Doesn't matter. It's the location, not the time. I'm sure of it."

He had Fletcher drive him to Crown Hill Cemetery, where Alita had been buried in the august company of James Whitcomb Riley, Benjamin Harrison, and Thomas R. Marshall. John Dillinger was buried there, as well, but Victor had kept Alita far from him.

Sneaking into the cemetery was easier than he had expected it to be, though he had a bad moment when his head started spinning and he thought he might pass out again. Fletcher steadied him and guided him to Alita's grave.

"Are you sure about this, Vic?" he asked softly. "We can wait until you're firmer on your feet. Do it tomorrow. It'll be just as easy—"

"No." Victor's voice was harsh. He wasn't usually harsh with Fletcher, but he was hurting and he was angry at himself for not realizing from the beginning that he couldn't perform this ritual just anywhere. "We'll do it now."

He knelt in front of Alita's grave, tracing the monument that he'd paid handsomely to have installed so quickly after Alita's death. The stone had been carved with the same symbols as the pendant. Thanatos would see how Victor honored him. It would work this time.

Victor drew in a deep breath and repeated the ritual, holding the pendant in both hands this time, because his burned right hand was too weak to hold it properly. He intoned each word carefully, speaking Alita's full name clearly at the end of each incantation. His breath was hissing through his teeth by the third repetition as he tried to keep from screaming or whimpering at the pain.

When Victor woke the second time, he was in the back seat of the car. Fletcher must have carried him. Victor tried to push himself up, but fell back, coughing. He wiped wet lips with his palm and it came away dark with blood.

"Did it work?" he rasped.

Fletcher didn't stop driving. "No. I'm sorry, Vic."

Victor subsided onto the back seat and let himself weep in the privacy of the darkness.

* * *

Chloe woke up Monday morning with Whizz sitting on her head. *Nothing says love like a cat butt in your face.*

After an extra long, extra hot shower, she had to go down to IMPD headquarters to fill out some paperwork. She was signing forms in her lieutenant's office when her cell phone rang. She ignored it, but within a few seconds it was ringing again. She glanced at the display, saw it was Braxton, and sent it to voice mail.

The third time the phone rang, Lieutenant Piper sighed and gestured at it. "Go ahead and answer it, Cole," she said. "I don't want to listen to it vibrate for the next twenty minutes."

Chloe made a face, which made Piper laugh. But Chloe answered it as directed.

"We've got another burglary," Braxton told her.

"This isn't really a good time."

"I've got permission to have you on scene," he said. "Cleared it with my supervisor."

"I'm in *my* supervisor's office right now." Chloe glanced at Lieutenant Piper, who looked unduly interested in the conversation. "Can I call you back when I'm done?"

"They'll get the crime scene processed without us if you wait." Braxton's words came quickly. "I thought you were on admin leave."

"I am. But there's paperwork." She could feel her fingers tightening on the phone and tried to relax.

"This is more important than paperwork."

Chloe closed her eyes and counted to three. "Braxton, if I don't finish my paperwork, I don't get paid. If I don't get paid, I'll have to eat what my brother picks out at the grocery store. His favorite aisles are the Chinese food and the produce section. I really want to be able to afford my freezer pizzas and cereal, okay?"

She got laughter in stereo as Braxton and Lieutenant Piper both reacted to what she'd said. Chloe glared at Piper, who was making no secret about the fact that she was eavesdropping. Piper just rolled her eyes, still grinning. She and Chloe both knew Chloe had been getting paid regularly over the past three weeks; the paperwork was just a formality.

"Okay, okay," Braxton said. "Listen, call me as soon as you get out of there, okay?"

"I promise," she said, rolling her eyes, and hung up.

"New boyfriend?" Piper asked. Chloe scowled at the automatic assumption and didn't answer, so Piper signed another paper and pushed it across the desk at her. "I won't keep you much longer," she promised.

"He's not my boyfriend," Chloe muttered, scribbling her initials next to a bunch of clauses and agreements. "I'm helping a statie with his investigation, since it ties into my getting shot, that's all."

Piper snorted. "That what Ruiz would tell me if I ask him?"

"Contrary to popular opinion, Jake doesn't know everything about me," Chloe said. It was a non-answer, and Piper totally caught that. But fortunately she shook her head and handed Chloe one last form.

"Take this down to payroll. Then I don't want to see you here for another two weeks. I've seen the doctor's report on your ribs."

"Whatever happened to HIPPA?" Chloe grumbled, but of course she'd signed off on letting the doctor share her medical records with her employer. She had to, since she wanted to get back her clearance to be in the field.

She tapped her fist gently against Jake's shoulder as she walked past his desk, then headed to payroll, where she arranged her paid administrative leave. She had her phone in her hand before she'd even cleared the building on her way out.

When he answered, he didn't bother with pleasantries. "Cole. I'm in Franklin. I got my boss to agree to calling you an outside consultant. There's an art gallery that was hit last night."

"An *art* gallery?" she asked, making her way to her car. "That's a little off the usual victimology. How'd you end up with it?"

"Their gift shop is full of handmade silver and pewter jewelry," he said. "Or, technically, *was*. Because almost all of it is gone."

"Okay, give me the address," she said, punching the button on her key fob. "I can be there in about half an hour."

With traffic it ended up being more like forty-five minutes. For the first time she was able to actually interview one of the victims herself, though she wasn't sure it would make any difference. The robbery had happened overnight. The alarm registered the break in, but for some reason it hadn't actually gone off. The gallery docent had come in at eleven that morning and discovered broken glass all over the back office.

"Most of the jewelry was done by one person," she explained, twisting her fingers together. "An artist named Rosemary Malher. She does a lot of mystic type stuff, trees of life and fairies and grim reapers and that sort of thing."

Chloe left the note-taking to Braxton and nodded encouragement. "What about other artists?"

"Well, there's someone who does masks. And then there's the miniature quilt squares made out of pewter."

"Huh." Seriously, miniature quilt squares made out of pewter? Chloe dismissed those being important right away, because she would remember if something that weird had been on the list of things that had been stolen at another shop. "Masks. Like theater masks, or what?"

"Well, some of them are Melpomene and Thalia, yes." The woman adjusted her glasses. "But most of them are green man masks, Mardi Gras masks, and beautiful masquerade ball pieces. Fancy, with feathers and sequins."

Chloe nodded slowly. She wasn't sure what the connection was, but somehow she was sure there *was* a connection. This was getting ridiculous, the way they'd stolen so much without Braxton and Chloe being any closer than they were two weeks ago. Braxton was probably feeling even more frustrated than she was.

She listened with half her attention as Braxton asked a few more questions, but she was already wandering around the shop, taking in the other items for sale and the general setup of the place. The gallery was two stories, with white walls and high ceilings. The shop had a lot of glass shelves that were a little too close together, like the shop was an afterthought and someone wanted to squeeze the most use out of the space possible. The shop was in the back part of the gallery, so anyone who just walked past on the street wouldn't know how many portable items were in the gallery. Okay, that meant their perp had some reason to have been in here before.

Or else maybe he was just looking so hard for whatever he wanted that he'd checked out all the galleries in Johnson County.

"They managed to get a couple of good fingerprints," Braxton told her, coming over to where she stood in front of a display of landscape watercolors.

"Any hits?"

"Not so far, but they've only run the local databases. We'll see if there's anything in IAFIS." The little lines around his eyes seemed deeper than usual, though, and she could tell he wasn't expecting any results. "Of course, it could be from one of the artists or a delivery driver or something."

IAFIS usually returned the results within ten or fifteen minutes. Chloe and Braxton spent that time prowling the gallery to see if anything there could give them clues about what the thieves were looking for. There was nothing in the gallery, and when they got the results from the fingerprints, they found out they were looking for an unidentified subject. They decided to eat lunch, and when Chloe suggested the Willard Pub, Braxton nodded.

They talked over the idea of the partner not wanting to have a potential cop-killer on his team. Braxton agreed it was a good theory, but his shoulders were slumped in discouragement.

"We're not getting anywhere," Chloe said, her voice tight. Two days ago she'd felt damn proud of herself for being all proactive and checking out all the locations. Yesterday she hadn't found anything, but at least she'd run into Cody Wethering, so she knew his spirit was sticking around.

"Usually when I got to this point in a case, I'd talk it over with my dad," Braxton said. He was turning his glass in slow circles. She hadn't noticed before how capable and strong his hands looked. "He retired from the Hendricks County sheriff's department about five years ago. Didn't quit until his arthritis got too bad for him to hold a gun." Golden eyes glanced up at her, a half-smile curling Braxton's mouth.

"Dedicated." She wasn't sure what she was supposed to say. Thanks to Jake, she knew Braxton's father was dead, but she couldn't let on without explaining that her partner had checked up on him. But she didn't want to be insensitive. "Why not call him this time?" she asked, feeling rotten about it.

"He died...almost six months ago. Cancer." Braxton was staring hard into his Coke. "As cliched as it sounds, I still sometimes have trouble remembering he's gone."

She shook her head. "No, I understand. Martin's and my folks died when he was still in high school. Drunk driver. You spend so much time thinking about things you wish you could tell them, or stuff you wish you hadn't said." She tapped a french fry against her plate. "I was in college, and I spent a lot of time wanting my mommy because she always made things hurt less...but she couldn't, because of course what hurt was that she was gone."

"Yeah." Braxton still wasn't looking at her. "Is it easier, being Catholic? I mean, believing they went to heaven?"

She chewed her lower lip. "In the grand scheme of things? Yeah. But it doesn't make you feel any better about wishing you could complain to your mom about the utterly horrible date you just went on, or ask your dad to help you study for a physics test. Or even just sit in the living room playing gin rummy and griping at your dad for calling you half pint."

Braxton nodded. "Dad grew up Baptist. I think the only Sundays he missed were the ones he had to work, and the one week every summer that he'd take me camping up in Minnesota. But he didn't make me go. Said he wanted me to think for myself and decide." He shrugged and ran a hand over his face. "God, sorry, I really don't know why I brought this up."

Before she'd even thought about it, she reached out and covered his free hand with hers. His skin was warm and sent a jolt of something all the way up her arm. She almost jerked back, but his lips had curved up, his other hand coming to rest on top of hers. She couldn't pull away after that. It would be more than rude. So they sat there for a minute or so, holding hands, with her heart feeling like it was going to jump out of her chest. It was beating so hard she could almost feel her ribs getting sore.

She was grateful when the waitress came over to make sure they didn't need anything else. Chloe extracted her hand gently from Braxton's and gave him a ten to pay for her lunch. Then she made a hasty retreat to the bathroom. When she came back out, he was waiting by the door.

They had one of those awkward moments on the sidewalk where neither person really wanted to leave, but they'd both run out of things to say. At least, that's how Chloe was feeling. She didn't know if he was feeling that way, too, but his lips were almost pursed like he was about to say something.

"Hey, I have tickets to the Indy Eleven match Saturday, and Elliott can't go. Do you like soccer?"

Chloe blinked at him. Was he asking her on a date? "Um," she said. "When is it?" Her heart started pounding harder.

"Kickoff at seven-thirty," he said. "They play downtown, at the IUPUI stadium."

"Okay, sure." As soon as the words were out of her mouth, Chloe wanted to recall them. Too late. She flashed him a smile that felt forced. "But I'll drive. I'm tired of having people schlep me around like a piece of luggage."

He grinned. "I get that." He shoved his hands in his pockets. "Good. I'll see you Saturday then."

* * *

"I can't believe my big sister has a date," Martin said. He walked into the bathroom, where Chloe was trying to remember how makeup worked, and started draping a red, white, and blue scarf around her neck.

"Hey, what—"

"You can't go to a football match without your team scarf," he said, grinning at her.

Chloe snorted. "I should have told Braxton to ask *you* out, if he wanted a real soccer fan," she teased.

"I don't think I'm his type, what with the penis and all," Martin said, and Chloe shook her head. She leaned in close to the mirror, brushing her mascara on gingerly. She didn't usually wear much makeup, just a little eyeshadow and lip gloss. She sighed and straightened, tucking her hair behind one ear.

"Okay. I can do this."

Martin draped an arm over her shoulders and kissed the side of her head. "You look gorgeous, big sis. Braxton won't know what hit him."

Chloe pursed her lips and made a face. "Well, I wasn't planning on punching him."

Martin snorted and let go. "Go. You're ready. Have fun. And remember, the team we like is the Indy Eleven."

Chloe rolled her eyes. "You act like I'm a complete moron."

"Not a *complete* moron, maybe," he teased, and left the bathroom as she threw her hairbrush at him. She checked her watch; it was almost 5:45, which meant it was probably time to leave for Braxton's. He'd given her an address in Avon, which would at least be an easy drive, but it was probably half an hour out and another half an hour back to the Indiana University-Purdue University-Indianapolis campus downtown. She wanted to make sure they had plenty of time to get inside the stadium and grab their food and drinks.

Braxton had asked if she wanted to get dinner before the game, but she'd declined. They had concessions at the game, and this season had added the Craft Brew Corner with Indiana craft beers on tap. As much as she teased Martin about his dedication to the team, which was in its third season, Chloe was a fan, too, and she enjoyed the complete gameday experience.

On the way out to Avon, she tried to psych herself up by listening to Janis Joplin at high volumes. At twenty past six, she pulled up in front of a nice split-level house. The yard was well-tended, with a profusion of day lilies in front, and a mailbox set into a solid-looking brick column. Braxton's car was parked in the driveway. A huge, long-haired, black and white cat was sitting in the front window. As Chloe walked up the drive, the cat jumped out of the window. A few moments later, Braxton opened the door. He was wearing an Indy Eleven t-shirt and jeans—still with his cowboy boots.

"Fuzzy told me you were here," he said, smiling at her, and Chloe couldn't ignore the little tug in her belly at that smile. Damn, he was handsome.

"Fuzzy?" she repeated, just for something to say. It was obvious the cat was Fuzzy.

To her surprise, Braxton colored a little. "His full name is Obnoxious Fuzzy Creature of the Night," he said. "But he answers to Fuzzy."

Chloe laughed. "He's huge," she said. "Bigger than Whizz, I'm pretty sure."

"Probably. The vet says he's a Maine Coon. They get pretty big." Braxton shrugged. "I found him as a kitten, at Eagle Creek. He was all by himself in the middle of nowhere, so I brought him home."

"Can't criticize a man who rescues stray kittens," Chloe said, smiling at him. She shoved her hands in her jean pockets. "You ready to go?"

"Yep." Braxton pulled the door shut behind him and locked the deadbolt. "Nice scarf."

Chloe grinned at him over her shoulder as she led the way back to her car. "Borrowed it from my brother. Martin's a *huge* soccer fan. We've gone to a few games together, but this year he's in the Brickyard Battalion, and they're too much for me."

Braxton chuckled. "I won't tell Elliott you said that."

They made small talk as she headed back along Rockville Road into the city. By the time they got to White River Parkway downtown, they were in game traffic, and Chloe just followed the car in front of her to a parking lot.

The Indy Eleven was a fairly new team, just in their third season; they didn't have a home stadium yet, so they were playing at the Michael A. Carroll Stadium, affectionately known as The Mike, on the IUPUI campus. Indy Eleven owner Ersal Ozdemir and his staff had tried hard to get a stadium approved, but even though Marion County had deemed an NFL stadium and NBA fieldhouse important enough to tax the citizens not only of Marion County but also the so-called doughnut counties surrounding Indianapolis, they hadn't thought an NASL stadium a good bet. Martin had been bitterly disappointed. He'd been on a one-man boycott of the Pacers and Colts since the decision earlier in the year.

Chloe was relating all this to Braxton as they made their way to the main gate and got through security. Braxton speculated that Martin and Elliott might have met through the Brickyard Battalion, the fan club that had existed even before Indianapolis got a pro soccer team. The Brickyard Battalion's grassroots efforts had been critical to the success of the Indy Eleven's launch as a new team.

"Martin can be downright obnoxious sometimes," Chloe confided to Braxton. "I'm a fan of the team and all, but please, don't ever get him started on the Lew Wallace connection and how all the BYB chants started. I think he has a freaking booth named after him at Chatham Tap." The bar on Massachusetts Avenue, colloquially called "Mass Ave," was an official affiliate of the Indy Eleven, as well as a good place to catch televised soccer matches.

Because Braxton had paid for their tickets, Chloe insisted on buying their supper of hot dogs, soft pretzels, and The Full 90 beers by Flat 12 Bierworks. She followed him to their seats, which were good ones—well out of Chloe's budget. Braxton explained that he and Elliott had one season ticket each, and she was using Elliott's, which made it a little better. Still, the Indy Eleven was a pro sports team that most average people actually *could* afford to watch live. Their cheapest seats were only ten dollars for a single game, which might be one of the reasons why they were consistently playing in front of large crowds.

They made small talk about the nice weather and good crowd as they got settled, and by the time they finished eating, Chloe was feeling a little more relaxed. Braxton was a nice guy, and she'd already spent plenty of time with him. This wasn't that much different from going to a game with Jake, really.

Okay, it was, but if she kept telling herself that, she might not freak out that she was on her first date in six years.

"So your brother's a soccer fan," Braxton said, and paused. "He seems nice. Where does he work?"

Chloe smiled. "He's a mechanic. Got his own shop. He went in with a friend a while back, but the friend decided he wanted to do something else, so Martin bought him out."

"That's pretty good for a guy who's—what, late twenties?"

"He just turned thirty a few days before I got shot, actually," Chloe said, "but thanks for thinking I'm younger than I am." When Braxton gave her an odd look, she said lightly, "Little brother, remember?"

Braxton's laugh was a little awkward, which made Chloe's stomach flip just a little. Were they flirting? It had been so long since she'd done it, she wasn't quite sure how flirting was different from being friendly.

"Anyway. Martin got his education courtesy of the United States Army, by way of Kandahar Province, so I think he earned a little good luck when it comes to the rest of his life." Chloe took a sip of her beer; she'd begged Martin not to enlist, but he'd been determined. He was tired of her worrying about him, so he'd decided to become self-sufficient—in the way best guaranteed to make Chloe worry about him for the next six years.

"I'd say so," Braxton said, his voice low. "That must have been rough."

Chloe shrugged, giving him a smile that felt too wide. "I guess he figured I was so focused on my career that it wouldn't matter." Her lips twisted. "It did matter, of course, but... Anyway, he made it home in one piece, which is more than I can say for a lot of his friends."

Braxton nodded. To Chloe's relief, she could see the honor guard carrying the flag out onto the field, and a moment later they were invited to stand for the National Anthem. Then it was time for kickoff, and she wouldn't be rude if she let the conversation drop.

The Eleven got off to a good start, and for a while she was able to lose herself in the game. She was aware of Braxton next to her, his thigh pressed lightly against hers as they cheered together, but he didn't try to keep an awkward conversation going. Late in the half, Braxton got up to get them each a second beer. When the halftime buzzer sounded, there was a commotion of people getting up to get refills or hit the restrooms, but Chloe and Braxton stayed in their seats.

"So..." Chloe said, searching for something to talk about. "You talked about your dad the other day, but I don't think you said anything about your mom. What's she like?"

A smile flitted across Braxton's face. "A force to be reckoned with," he said. He sighed and leaned back against the currently-empty row of bleachers behind them. "She's part White Earth Band Ojibwe, from western Minnesota. She met Dad while she was working at the casino on the reservation—he was traveling to Canada for a fishing trip and stopped in Minnesota." He chuckled. "You know, I don't think Dad ever made it back to Canada after that. Anyway, she left everything she'd ever known to move to

Indiana with him, and did it without a spark of fear, if you listened to Dad's stories."

Chloe couldn't help but smile at the look on his face. Clearly he loved and respected his mother. "Does she still live here in Indiana?"

Braxton shook his head. "She moved back to the rez to live with her sister, about two months after Dad died. Needed to get away for a while. I figure she'll stay up there for the winter, at least."

"Ugh. Why would anyone want *more* winter than we get here?" Chloe said, trying to keep her tone light. Braxton gave her an appreciative smile.

"Before you ask, I'm an only child," he said. "And you already know I was raised casual Baptist. Let's see, what else do you want to know?"

Chloe hooked one ankle around the other to keep from jiggling her legs. She wanted to bring the conversation around to the case, but she had the feeling that would hurt his feelings. This was a date, and you didn't talk shop on a date. That was one lesson she'd learned the hard way, after dating a couple of civilians who got bored with the minutiae of her work—or annoyed at how she could talk blood and gore over a steak. Maybe that was another reason she'd given up years ago on any thought of dating. It was just easier to focus on her career.

"Favorite color? Ooh, no, favorite band."

"Easy." He flashed his teeth in a grin. "U2. And yellow."

Chloe nodded slowly. "My favorite band is Led Zeppelin, and my favorite singer's a regional artist. Have you heard of Jennie DeVoe?"

Braxton nodded. "She's good. I'm more of a Why Store and Michael Kelsey guy, but I can see her appeal."

His hip pocket started ringing—"Werewolves of London" by Warren Zevon. "Damn," Braxton said, frowning, and pulled his phone out. "Sorry, I need to take this." Chloe waved in dismissal of his apology, and Braxton stood up, walking several feet away as he answered it.

He was too far away for her to hear what he was saying, especially given the half-time show, but she couldn't help being curious. He couldn't be on call or he wouldn't have drunk any beer. But this was clearly someone important. When he caught her watching him, he turned away. Chloe looked down, embarrassed at being caught. After a few moments, she glanced back. She could see his shoulders tense as he listened.

Ashamed of prying, Chloe looked back out at the field, carefully trying to pay attention to the half-time activities and not catch any snippet of what Braxton might say. A few minutes later, he sat down next to her. She looked over, but he stared out at the field for several moments. Finally he sighed.

"Sorry about that."

Chloe shook her head. "No problem. Anything I can help with?"

"No." His voice was clipped. He took a couple of deep breaths, then said, "Sorry. No, but thanks. It's just—there's a kid Elliott and I have been kind of mentoring, and it's...kind of rocky right now." He shook his head, obviously trying to dismiss it. "Never mind. I don't want it to ruin our date."

Chloe couldn't help smiling, even though the word 'date' sent a jolt of adrenaline or something through her. "It didn't. Don't worry." After a moment, she reached over and took his hand.

Braxton gave her a surprised look, and then he seemed to relax a lot more. He laced his fingers with hers, smiling. Without a word, they turned back to watch the second half of the game.

As the clock wound up closer to ninety minutes, Chloe felt herself tensing again. The Eleven were up one to nothing, and she really wanted a win. Not only would it feel like a good sign for their date, it would also ensure the Eleven stayed undefeated at home for one more week. They'd been Spring Champions, and she liked seeing them have a good season, even if she wasn't as dedicated a fan as her brother. They scored another goal in the last thirty seconds, and the crowd poured out of the Mike on a surge of victory-inspired goodwill.

Braxton was quiet on the way back to his house, but that was all right with Chloe. She could tell he was still preoccupied with his mentee, and she didn't want him to feel bad about it. She'd honestly had a good time, and there hadn't been the pressure or anxiety that she'd been expecting to go along with a date. They'd just had a nice, low-key, fun evening. When she pulled up in front of his driveway, she took the car out of gear, but didn't turn it off.

Braxton gave her a rueful smile. "I'd ask if you'd like to come in, but I probably should deal with that phone call from earlier," he said. His gaze flickered to the side a little as he spoke.

"It's all right. I'm a little tired. I don't have to get up early for work, so you'd think I could sleep in, but I still find myself waking up early." Chloe shrugged.

Braxton's gaze softened. "You're a kind person, Chloe. I enjoyed tonight."

She smiled crookedly at him. "I did, too. I'm glad Elliott couldn't make the game tonight."

He was leaning in, and she knew he was going to kiss her. She wanted him to kiss her. She was suddenly relieved that he hadn't asked her in. This situation felt a little more under her control in her car. Maybe that was why he'd done it.

"Relax," he whispered, touching her chin with two fingers. "I'm not going to bite."

She let out a giggle that only sounded a little nervous, and then his lips were on hers. They were warm and gentle, letting her decide how far to take the kiss. She parted her lips slightly against his, but made herself pull away before she really wanted to. His eyes flashed gold as he smiled at her, and Chloe felt herself grinning back at him.

"Good night, Chloe," he murmured.

"Good night, Braxton." She bit her lip to keep from inviting herself in as he climbed out of the car and headed up to the house.

She didn't put the car in first gear until he'd waved and closed the door.

CHAPTER 10

Chloe drove herself home feeling almost giddy, which wasn't a feeling she was used to. She kept turning over moments from the evening, lingering over the last few minutes. Martin would be insufferably smug about this, but Chloe couldn't even make herself care. She was attracted to Braxton, and more than that, she *liked* Braxton. She enjoyed spending time with him. In the face of that seeming miracle, Martin's teasing didn't really matter.

She let herself into the house, pleased to see Martin had fallen asleep in his recliner. Holding her breath, Chloe draped a blanket over him and tiptoed back to her room. She got ready for bed as silently as possible, hoping the post-date debrief could wait until tomorrow. She murmured a quick prayer and slid between cool sheets, shivering a little. She turned on her side and Whizz jumped up to the bed, walking delicately until he could settle into the curve of her hip.

"G'night, Whizz," she murmured, and closed her eyes. She wouldn't be able to sleep, the way her thoughts were going around in circles.

She fell asleep in minutes.

In her dream, Chloe was in a book store or library with the sad girl. The sad girl sat with one leg tucked under the other. She swung her foot, her attention on Chloe.

"Who are you?" Chloe asked, even though she knew by then she wouldn't get an answer.

The girl reached up and pushed her dark hair back from her face. Her lips were turned down, her eyes grave as she watched Chloe. Her eyes were brown, but not as dark as her hair. A necklace sparkled at the hollow of her throat. Or was it a saint's medal? Chloe squinted.

"Why do you look so familiar?" Chloe asked.

The girl looked down, then lifted her gaze to Chloe's again, and then the bookshop faded around them. Between one moment and the next, Chloe and the sad girl were in some sort of empty warehouse. In the middle of the concrete floor stood a steel table that made Chloe clench her fist. "No," she whispered, her stomach giving a leap like she'd reached the top of a roller coaster and gone sailing off the edge.

"No."

Was it possible?

I'm seeing dead people, Chloe thought. Cody Wethering has shown up twice. The woman at the hospital…I saw her at least half a dozen times. "Okay," she said. "You're dead. That makes sense. I mean, as much as anything makes sense anymore."

The girl was wearing jeans and an Earth Day t-shirt that looked very similar to one Chloe had owned back in high school. Was it possible for a memory to be passed down in the genes? Did ghosts age? Maybe ghosts got to choose what age they wanted to appear.

172

"You're my daughter," Chloe breathed.

The girl just kept looking at her, her gaze no less melancholy. She sat on the steel table and kicked one bare foot.

It was the kind of table the clinic had. Chloe squeezed her eyes shut for a moment, remembering how bone-chillingly cold she'd been that day. She'd hated herself, hated what she was doing, and hated Matt most of all, but she'd never hated her child. She'd imagined her baby as a girl from the moment the puking and missed period told her she was pregnant. Chloe had never had any real reason to think of the baby as a girl. She just had.

Chloe squeezed her eyes shut again, and when she opened them again, she was back in the guest room of her brother's apartment.

Whizz had wrapped himself around her neck, tucked under her chin. His tail was tickling her cheek, so she scooped up a handful of warm, limp kitty and deposited him next to her instead. As she did, the blanket slipped down to her waist, and she realized there was a cold breeze on her arms.

The window was wide open.

A visceral thrill shot through her. She hadn't opened that window. Suddenly she remembered waking up the other day with the window open wider than she'd left it.

"What the heck?" she whispered, watching the window to make sure it didn't open any further. She knew she should get up and close it, or at least check to make sure it hadn't been tampered with. But she couldn't seem to make herself move. What if someone had come in through the window and was hiding under her bed? What if Wethering's partner had found her? What if the ghosts—

Chloe cut herself off. "That's enough," she muttered. "Get up. You're lucky Whizz hasn't already jumped out the window."

She sat up, but it took her a couple of minutes to force herself to swing her legs over the edge. As her dream-clouded thoughts grew more alert, it occurred to her that with the dresser under the window, probably no one would be able to come in without her hearing them. She got up and closed the window, latching it properly and adjusting the curtains twice to make sure no one could see in.

Chloe went to the bathroom and got back in bed, trying to get back to sleep, but suddenly her brain wouldn't turn off. "I'm being haunted," she whispered. Her unborn daughter, whom Chloe had never known, was following her around, showing up in her dreams and at crime scenes. She was beautiful and sad, and even though Chloe could see her, they couldn't talk to each other.

Chloe tried to pray, but she felt too guilty and sad to pray, which was probably completely opposite how it ought to work. She finally got out of bed and went out to the kitchen to make herself a cup of tea. Tea had always been her mother's answer to a troubled spirit. It usually didn't work for Chloe, but at least it reminded her of her mother.

Martin had apparently woken at some point in the night, because he was no longer in the recliner as Chloe padded out to the kitchen. She didn't turn on the overhead light, just the dim light over the stove, as she turned on the kettle and waited for the water to boil. She rummaged through the pantry and found some bags of white Darjeeling. Martin *did* like tea, but his tastes were a little gourmet compared to Chloe's.

She poured the water into her cup, watched the tea brew for the one and a half minutes directed on the label, and then sat at the kitchen table, letting the steam wash over her face. Her shoulders and back muscles felt tight. The dream wouldn't let go of her.

Even though Chloe's parents had both been dead by the time Chloe got pregnant, Chloe had never doubted what her mother's reaction would be. Even at the time, Chloe had known what she would have told her to do. She'd have had Chloe quit school and have the baby, and her mom would have helped raise Chloe's child while Chloe tried to finish school and hold down a job and be a mother. Chloe would have failed miserably, probably at all three things. But her mother would have had her try, because it was the right thing to do.

Chloe sighed and pushed a hand through her hair. She still felt like that would have been the right thing to do. But it wouldn't have been the *best* thing to do. How would it have been better for her daughter to live a life of privation, her single mother never able to make ends meet, her clothes all hand-me-downs, and Chloe always gone because she had to work two or three jobs? That was no kind of life for a kid. Chloe didn't like abortion, and she didn't like that she'd had one, but she also hated that it felt like the only option for too many young women. Having a baby was expensive. Raising a child was even more expensive. And that was what she wanted to shout back at all those pro-lifers who picketed abortion clinics and then turned around and complained about welfare.

If you don't care about a child and its mother after the birth, then you're not really pro-life.

With a disgusted grunt, she got up to open the cabinet under the sink. Martin kept his alcohol under the sink, and even though Chloe knew it was a lousy idea, she didn't care. She added a healthy dose of whiskey to her tea, then swallowed another pain pill. If Vicodin and Maker's didn't help her sleep, nothing would.

She took Martin's place in the recliner, hoping the slight creak of the rocker wouldn't wake him. He'd always been able to sleep through thunderstorms as a kid, but after his years in Afghanistan, she didn't think he slept as well. She rocked and sipped her doctored tea and tried desperately not to think about a daughter who was suddenly part of her life even though she'd done her best to keep her out of it.

Had she been following Chloe around all this time? Did ghosts exist because they existed, or did they only become real because Chloe saw them? Did she haunt Chloe because of the abortion, or because Chloe was her mother?

Existential questions had never been her forte. She was a Catholic because she believed in God. She believed in God because that's how she was raised, and it felt right to her. Chloe knew plenty of people who believed God didn't exist, but Chloe couldn't argue with someone who said that, not with any rational argument. Trying to figure out the way her daughter's ghost had shown up in her life would drive her crazy.

If I'm not there already.

At some point, between the whiskey and the Vicodin, she fell asleep in the recliner. This time, she didn't dream.

* * *

Chloe woke up very late the next morning, still in the recliner. Whizz was tucked in between her thigh and the arm of the chair. To her astonishment, her brother had made coffee and left some for her. She raked her hair back into a sloppy pony tail and sat down at the kitchen table with her Bible and a huge mug of coffee.

She wasn't sure exactly what she was looking for, but she flipped through every scripture she could find on ghosts and spirits and death. Turned out, talking to ghosts was an abomination, and necromancy was forbidden. Mediums and spiritualists were evil too. Some lady called the Witch of Endor summoned up the prophet Samuel's ghost for King Saul, so the Bible was pretty clear that ghosts were *real*, but as far as being okay...not so much.

"So good news, bad news," Chloe told Whizz. "I'm not insane, but I'm apparently an abomination before the Lord."

Then again, a lot of Catholics believed her brother was an abomination before the Lord too, and Chloe definitely had a problem with that. She knew what the Bible supposedly said about homosexuals, but the Bible had been translated multiple times, and by humans—who might well have had an agenda as they translated. Chloe's position regarding her brother was simple: *I'm not God, so I don't get to judge, and in the meantime I love my brother and hope he finds a nice boyfriend who'll stick around.*

But saying she had no problem with her brother was completely different from feeling secure about the state of her own soul, particularly when she had dead people popping up all around her and the Bible said people like her were destined for the flames.

She did a little bit of praying over her coffee. After a while she remembered that Jesus had a parable about someone wanting a beggar to leave Paradise and carry messages to people on this side of the veil. Maybe it was thin evidence, but she decided that she might be okay as long as she was just seeing ghosts and not trying to summon them from the ether plane or Purgatory or wherever ghosts usually resided when they weren't plaguing poor, innocent Catholic girls.

Then again, it was entirely possible that being a police officer canceled out being a Catholic girl in

Chloe's case. Maybe her having shot a couple of people in the line of duty meant she deserved having dead people following her around. Though come to think of it, *she* hadn't *killed* Cody Wethering, and the man she *had* killed—five years ago in a shootout after a bank robbery and high speed chase—didn't seem to be angry that Chloe was still eating corn flakes and drinking coffee on a daily basis while he wasn't. At least, he hadn't showed up to tell her so.

It was right around her third cup of coffee that she remembered why she'd fallen asleep in the recliner during the wee small hours of the morning. The man she'd killed in the line of duty wasn't haunting her, but her daughter seemed to be.

I could be deceiving myself, she thought as she stirred creamer into her coffee. Usually she drank it black, but her stomach was more than a little unsettled, possibly some sort of painkiller-plus-alcohol hangover.

"So," she murmured, looking at the orange cover of her Bible. It was a hand-me-down from her father, who'd had it since his confirmation. She owned a couple of nicer-looking ones, including the white one with gold leaf that she'd been given at her own confirmation, but she could remember her father's hands picking idly at the corner of the onionskin pages while he read a passage. He'd never made a huge production of it, just like he'd only ever said grace over meals, but Chloe and Martin had grown up knowing their father believed what he read.

The orange, paperback Bible made her feel closer to her dad somehow. And that thought led her right around to Braxton Wolfe and how he'd said he missed talking cases over with his father.

Thinking of Braxton made Chloe smile involuntarily, even as her pulse jumped a little. Had she actually gone on a date with Braxton last night? It almost didn't seem possible, except she remembered the feel of his fingers laced with hers, and the warmth of his lips against her own. Still smiling, Chloe shivered happily and tried to drag her thoughts back to the scriptures, but thinking about the date got her thinking about the robberies and murders, and pretty soon she was thinking about all the things that had gone missing. Finally she shoved her chair back away from the table and went to shower and dress.

Her mind wouldn't stop circling around from the dead to the case to the dead to the case, though. She was sure that seeing dead people had something to do with dying herself. After all, she'd never been followed around by ghosts before that. The only thing that had changed was dying. *Maybe*, she thought as she toweled off, *maybe I'm not supposed to be alive. Maybe God meant for me to die, but modern medicine defied His plan.*

That didn't seem right to her, though. Chloe believed people could choose to do other than what God wanted; in the Catholic lexicon it was called sin. She didn't think someone else, even a doctor with power over life and death, could sin *for* her. So it must be God's will that she was alive.

But if God meant for her to survive being shot by Cody Wethering, why? Was it because there was still good she could do in the world? Was it because she would have insight into the robberies and could help Braxton? Was it because someone needed to see the dead people and do something about them? But if so, what? And how? Chloe couldn't even hear what they were trying to tell her. So if that was her new mission, God was going to have to give her a clearer message.

When it was all too tangled up in her head for her to think straight, Chloe decided the simplest explanation was probably the most likely—that there were still good things she could accomplish by not being dead. That didn't rule out her trying to do something about the robberies and the dead people both.

She combed her hair out and twisted it into two braids, opting for hippie casual. She didn't have any idea what to do next or where to look for answers, so she decided to do what she usually did in that situation. She pulled her phone out and called Jake.

They went to the range. Jake could usually outshoot Chloe, since he'd spent a couple of years with SWAT before deciding he wanted a slightly less stressful work day and opted to return to patrol. He was still among the top shooters in the state of Indiana, so Chloe felt good when she could manage to best him. It didn't happen all that often, but she'd been at the shooting range less than a week ago and it had been a little longer than that for Jake. She walked out of the gun range feeling good about that, at least.

"So let me get this straight," he said when they'd gone through all the ammunition they'd taken with them. "You think you're haunted because you didn't die?"

She shrugged gingerly. Her ribs had started out the day all right, but she was getting tired and she'd exerted herself a little more than she probably should have. They were starting to ache.

"Don't go all non-committal on me," he said, his hands moving like a dance over his weapon as he cleaned it. "Yes or no. You think you're haunted."

Chloe squished her mouth over to one side, looking at him like she'd smelled something bad. But finally she said, "Yeah."

At least he didn't laugh the way he had the first time she said it. He pursed his lips and nodded, his gaze on the gun instead of Chloe's face. "And yes or no, you think it's because you survived the shooting?"

She shrugged again. "Don't know," she admitted. "Seems like as decent a theory as any."

"Considering that the first part of the theory is that you're *haunted*, yeah, you're right," he said. His gaze flickered up to her face, then back down to his gun. She couldn't read his expression.

"I'm seeing people I can't explain, that apparently no one else sees. There has to be some kind of explanation for that, and considering how many times I've seen them, I don't think it's the painkillers. Besides, I'm taking the painkillers *less* often than directed, not more."

"So what do you expect me to do about it?" he said, pulling back the slide to make sure it was moving smoothly.

"I dunno, I thought maybe you'd help me do an exorcism, keep my head from spinning around while I spit pea soup." It was possible her tone was a wee bit sarcastic. Jake looked like he wanted to throw something at her. Or possibly send her down to the end of the shooting lane to use for target practice.

Finally he holstered his gun and turned his gaze on her. "Maybe you should just ask Father Frank what the hell's going on—pun totally intended—with the ghosts?"

"I'm not going to ask a priest about ghosts!" she hissed. The idea of Father Frank laughing at her was too much to bear. He could hang out with emo kids who wore their hair in mohawks without cracking a smile, but somehow she had a feeling that telling him, "I'm in contact with spirits from beyond the veil," would either have him crossing himself and her a few times, or else have him laughing so hard his collar fell off.

"Maybe they're hallucinations," Jake said. He was watching her clean her gun. She always took longer about cleaning her gun than he did—probably because he spent a lot more time tearing guns down and putting them back together when he was in SWAT, so he had muscle memory going for him.

She didn't dignify the hallucinations suggestion with a response. He was starting to annoy her, even though she'd called him. It wasn't really fair of her to get annoyed with him, because so far he hadn't outright called her crazy or suggested she needed a one-way trip to the funny farm. How many people would let you say you're seeing ghosts, but not tell you you're nuts? Since it wasn't really fair to snap at him, Chloe just kept cleaning her gun in silence.

Jake sighed. "Look, Clo, even if what you're seeing *are* ghosts, what exactly do you think we should do about it? You've already tried talking to them, and that hasn't worked, by your own admission. Do you want to try to get rid of them? Do some kind of seance or get a Ouija board or something? Buy ropes of garlic to string around your neck?"

"Garlic is for vampires, you doof, not ghosts." She scowled and shrugged. "I don't know. No seances or anything. That's not allowed."

"Not allowed by what?" he said, his eyes crinkling in amusement.

"By God." She pressed her lips together, tapping her fingers against her thigh. "Calling up the dead is forbidden. And I swear I didn't do anything to call them up. I didn't *ask* to start seeing ghosts. But I keep seeing these people, and it's like they want something from me, but they can't tell me and I can't ask, and I really, really don't want to go to Hell because I can see ghosts, Jake!" Her voice was rising throughout the entire speech, and as the last part burst out of her, she realized that was the real problem. She was scared of Hell.

She also realized, a couple beats later, that there were three fairly big guys with guns looking at her like maybe she needed to be subdued so they could call the men in white coats. She felt her face get hot. She must have been shouting pretty loudly if they heard her through their ear protection. She stomped out of the range area and didn't look to see if Jake was following her. He probably would be. If he wasn't, well, that was actually okay with her.

Chloe went over to Jake's truck and slumped on the tailgate, staring at the orange and yellow leaves on the maples surrounding the parking lot. She could hear some kind of bird chirping in the bushes. He sounded a lot happier than she was. She wished, miserably, that she could go back to the time when her biggest problem was coming home to find out Whizz had peed on the floor. No ghosts, no broken ribs, no really hot state troopers to complicate her life.

Jake came out and she heard the door locks click open. She got in the passenger side without speaking. As he pulled out headed for home, Chloe stared at the dusty red vinyl of the dashboard.

So she'd been lonely sometimes. Who wasn't? Loneliness was a part of life. Something you got used to because precious few people had ever been worthy of your trust, and none of them were people you wanted to go to bed with too. Despite the decision she made at nineteen not to become a mother, she wanted to keep her options open when it came to having a family. But finding someone to spend your life with was hard work, and it required too much going out on a limb and making yourself vulnerable. That wasn't something Chloe had ever liked doing—most people probably didn't. But it seemed so easy for some people. It had never been easy for Chloe, even when the drinking and the college parties made it seem that way.

One thing she'd always had to hold onto was her faith. When she was at college, she had questioned things, and even run away from the church after the abortion, sure that God hated her for what she'd done. Thanks to Father Frank, she'd learned to accept that God had forgiven her, and if she hadn't quite managed to forgive herself... well. She'd grown to feel secure in her beliefs, to feel close to Saint Michael, to live assured of her salvation.

Seeing ghosts... being exposed to something God had forbidden... having no apparent control over the ability to see them... it scared her. She didn't think anyone could retract her salvation but God... but what if He wanted to, because of the ghosts?

"I can hear you thinking all the way over here," Jake remarked. "Want to get something to eat?"

She shook her head. "I ought to buy cat food, but I just want to go home." *And hide under the covers,* she didn't add aloud.

"Your brain's gonna short out if you don't chill out." She could see Jake glancing between the road and her, but she didn't look up. Finally his hand closed on hers. "Come on, Clo, talk to me. You can't really think you're going to hell for... these visions or hallucinations or whatever."

"You don't believe me," she muttered. She didn't try to pull her hand away. He'd let go in a minute, but if she tried to pull away, he'd hold tighter.

"It's a little hard to wrap my brain around. That doesn't mean I don't believe you. It's obvious *you* believe you." That logic was so uniquely Jake that

Chloe couldn't quite suppress a tiny curving of her lips. He gave a crow of triumph. "Ah, I saw that! You were gonna smile. Careful, Chloe, if you smile it'll break your face. Don't smile! Don't do it! Oh nooo!"

She started laughing. She couldn't help it. There were a lot of reasons she spent so much time around Jake, and only one of those reasons was that he was a good cop. Another reason was his ability to keep her from taking herself too seriously. She could make fun of anything and everything except herself, most of the time, but only when she became friends with Jake did she learn that life was easier if you learned to laugh at yourself.

"God, you're such a jerk," she said, tugging her hand out of his.

"I know. It comes naturally."

"Doesn't hurt that you've had so much practice at it," she retorted.

Jake laughed. "Seriously, C, I really think you need to talk to Father Frank. I've never seen you scared or doubting yourself like this. It's okay to ask for reassurance sometimes."

"Maybe," she said. She still couldn't help thinking she might get excommunicated if she told Father Frank she saw dead people. Or at the very least committed.

He was silent for a few moments, then said, "So...I hear someone had a *date* last night. To be honest, I thought the shooting range was because of that." He was smirking out the windshield. "How did that go? You sure that's not really why you wanted to put some lead in bad guys today?"

Chloe felt her face heat. "Shut up," she said. "The Eleven won."

Jake's eyebrows shot up. "Oh, that is *so* not what I'm interested in hearing from you right now. Come on. We're going to go get some ice cream and you're going to tell me everything."

* * *

Braxton texted Chloe Sunday evening, just to say he'd had a nice time, and that he'd like to spend more time with her. Chloe had chewed one fingernail half off before she came up with the clever response of, *Me too. Without burglaries and homicides getting in the way. :)* Apparently it was an acceptable reply, because Braxton had sent her back a smiley-face emoji, and that was that.

Monday, Chloe didn't hear from Braxton. He did have a job, she reassured herself. And besides, going a day without hearing from him had never bothered her before. She forced herself to sit down at the kitchen table and make a list of all the things she needed to do. She was still waiting on insurance information regarding the house, but she would have to make a decision, at some point, whether she was going to rebuild or what. She also needed to start getting her sleeping pattern back under control, now that she was off the pain pills. And it wouldn't hurt her to start a light workout program to get back in shape for work.

And then there was the other requirement before she could go back to work. What with the dead people, robberies, and unexpected dates with a hot state trooper, there were some things Chloe had been putting off, and one of them was seeing the department shrink about her getting shot. Normally a visit to headshrinker would be the lowest thing on her list of "What I Want To Do Today," but if Chloe were honest with herself, it was all getting to be too much to think about, so she finally scheduled an appointment and went in.

Chloe spent a lot of time rehashing everything she'd already been angsting over in private, minus the part about spirits from beyond the veil. Dr. Jordan didn't seem to think Chloe was crazy. She assured Chloe that her ambivalence over Wethering's death was normal, and that the nightmares might continue for a while. Dr. Jordan's opinion was that the dreams were Chloe's subconscious' way of dealing with the trauma she'd been through. Chloe wondered if seeing dead people was another way of dealing with the trauma, but didn't ask.

Tuesday, Chloe got a text message mid-morning from Braxton. If you're free Friday, could we grab lunch? Assuming we don't get another call on the case.

Chloe was quick to text an acceptance, which got her another smiling emoji in return. *How do you feel about Jockamo's Pizza?* he asked, and Chloe grinned.

Read my mind, she replied. See you there at noon Friday.

Thus reassured that Braxton hadn't decided she was hopeless after their date, Chloe was able to turn her attention to other things. She mailed in a preliminary inventory of the things she'd lost in the fire. She went out for drinks with Celia and Lucia on Tuesday evening. They were appropriately excited about how things were developing with Braxton, and Lucia told them all about a mission trip she was organizing to the Gulf Coast of Louisiana, where flooding had created a lot of destruction.

Wednesday, Chloe was too antsy to stay inside, and it was a nice day, so she ambled around Broad Ripple for a couple of hours, window shopping in the little shops and enjoying the sunshine. She was starting to get worried about losing muscle tone, since she hadn't been able to do any lifting with her ribs broken. Maybe she wasn't quite ready to start that again, but she could at least start working to maintain her general fitness level. Wednesday and Thursday evenings, she and Martin went for long walks—one through Broad Ripple, and the other along the canal. At first they didn't do much more than amble, but the second evening, they were able to maintain a brisk walk the entire time. He waved off Chloe's gratitude, saying he could stand to lose the beer gut he'd been developing, and Chloe laughed. Her brother was skinnier than he'd been in his Army days, though he wasn't quite as toned. Still, she wasn't going to look a gift horse in the mouth.

On Friday, Chloe got up early and went to the grocery store, which was always an exercise in frustration and shopping cart aisle-rage. Once she was home and had the groceries put away, she sorted through the last of the boxes Martin had been able to salvage from her house—throwing away most of the stuff. By the time she finished that, it was time to shower and get ready to meet Braxton.

Jockamo's Upper Crust Pizza was in Irvington, one of the many small towns from a century ago that had been swallowed up by Indianapolis. Irvington still had the feel of a village, sort of the same way Broad Ripple did, which made Chloe like the neighborhood. She took 56th Street to Emerson Avenue, opting for surface streets instead of the 465 Loop. It took her a little longer to get there, but she was still there in half an hour.

Braxton was loitering outside the restaurant as she parallel parked in front of it. He gave her a smile that weakened her knees just a little. Damn, she had it bad, didn't she? Chloe shoved aside the thought and went to meet him.

"Hi," he said, reaching out to touch her arm. "You look nice."

Chloe glanced down at herself. She was wearing one of the nice shirts Lucia had bought her, but otherwise she'd stuck with her jeans and Doc Martens. "Thanks," she said, trying not to sound confused. "You too." That was the truth, at least. He pretty much always looked nice.

"So I've been worrying about how much we're going to fight about the pizza toppings," he said, holding the door for her. "I'm a fan of the Slaughterhouse Five, but I know it's not everyone's cup of tea." He paused and studied her. "You're probably...let's see...you're probably a Baja, aren't you?"

Chloe started laughing. "Right in one. How'd you know?" The Baja had chorizo, jalapeno, red onion, and homemade salsa on it, among other toppings, and it was Chloe's standard order.

Braxton grinned at her. "Seems like you'd want your pizza with as much bite as you have."

"Ouch," she said, pressing her hand against her chest in mock hurt, but she had to concede he had a good point. "Well, I have to say, I'm not really surprised you're a fan of the five-meat kind of pizza, but that's mostly just a feeling. No clues to go on."

He laughed. "Do we at least agree on the breadsticks and creamy Parmesan sauce?"

"No question." They settled at a table and gave their drink orders, then started catching up on the events of the week. Braxton talked about a couple of the other cases he was working, but true to their agreement, he didn't mention their case at all. Remembering the mysterious phone call he'd taken during the game, Chloe was curious about how his mentor situation was going, but he'd seemed a little touchy about it, so she didn't want to ask.

Braxton listened with interest as she told him all about the paperwork she was having to do regarding the fire and the insurance. When she remarked that she hadn't decided whether or not to rebuild, he shrugged.

"What else would you do?"

"Sell the empty lot? The foundation's still good, even if they couldn't save the structure itself. It's a nice neighborhood, safe and clean, even if the houses are older. Someone might be looking to build a new house in a place with mature trees and established grass." Chloe glanced at him through her eyelashes and stole the last breadstick. He grinned to let her know he'd seen it, but didn't remark otherwise.

"Then what would *you* do? Move in with your brother permanently?"

She laughed. "Lord, no. I don't think either one of us would like that, long-term. He's probably already hoping I'll get tired of him and get an apartment." She sipped her Coke. "I don't know, I'm just wondering if this is a sign that it's time I made a change. I know people say home equity's the way to go, but I was always having to replace an appliance or fix something that wasn't working. Why not rent and let my landlord deal with all that?"

Braxton was nodding thoughtfully. "My friend Shay's been renting for years for basically just those reasons. She seems happy enough with it."

Chloe swiped her breadstick in the Parmesan sauce and stuffed the last bite in her mouth. When she finished she said, "I'm still throwing around ideas right now. God knows I'm not really ready to make any decisions."

"Let me know if I can help with anything," he said, which gave her a ridiculous warm feeling in her chest.

"Thanks." Their pizzas arrived then, which silenced most of their conversation for several minutes. Looking at Braxton's Slaughterhouse Five—named after the novel by Indianapolis native Kurt Vonnegut—Chloe was tempted to try that next time.

The rest of their meal was spent in comfortable chatter, not talking about anything serious, just trading details about their lives, hobbies, reading preferences, and so on. She lost track of time as they talked. At some point, she noticed Braxton check his phone and realized it was the second time he'd done it. His jaw tightened a little as he read the screen, but he put it back on the table, where it had been lying face down until it had started vibrating.

"Crap, you're working today, aren't you?" she said. "I shouldn't keep you. Have you missed calls?"

Braxton grinned, but there were lines around his eyes that made it look strained. "If I had a trifle less honesty in me, I'd tell them I was having lunch with a consultant, but I can't bring myself to say it." He leaned in a little, lowering his voice. "Especially since I'd like to call this our second date, if that's all right with you."

"Definitely all right with me," Chloe said, her heart jumping a little. "I've had a good time."

"Me too." Braxton signaled their waiter to get the bill. "You interested in super-hero movies?"

Chloe was probably grinning a little too hard. "Got nothing against them," she said.

Braxton's teeth flashed, and she realized he was maybe grinning a little too hard, too. "Excellent. Want to catch a movie next weekend?"

"Sounds good to me," Chloe said. "Or Sunday. I know you have an Indy Eleven game tomorrow night."

"Oh, uh..." Braxton looked awkward, and then regretful, his brows drawing together. "I already have plans on Sunday. I'm sorry." He smoothed the bill against the table a couple of times, as if he didn't realize he was doing it, but he didn't look away from her gaze.

"No problem." Chloe felt her cheeks warming, but even though it had been a long time since she'd dated, she could tell Braxton wasn't just blowing her off. He wouldn't have asked her out for next weekend already if he wasn't enjoying her company. Still, his reaction seemed a little odd, even though she couldn't quite pinpoint why.

His expression cleared. "Good. In the meantime, you'll probably hear from me about the case. I closed a couple of cases this week, so I can focus on this one again." He touched her wrist lightly. "And then I *can* buy a cup of coffee for a consultant," he added.

Chloe grinned at him. "Sounds good to me."

CHAPTER 11

Braxton woke up snuggled against Elliott's back. He had one arm draped loosely over his best friend, who was snoring faintly. Braxton's mouth tasted like death, but he didn't want to move. Elliott was warm, and someone else—someone much curvier—was pressed against Braxton's back. Tara wasn't snoring, but she felt relaxed against him. Braxton closed his eyes again and smiled to himself. This was pack. It was the easy comfort they had in touching each other, the simple confidence that their packmates were with them.

A few moments later, the smile slipped off. This was his pack, yes, but it wasn't complete. Murphy hadn't run with them last night.

Murphy hadn't even answered his phone when Braxton tried calling. Braxton had paced the little clearing where they always began and ended their full moons, cell phone in one hand as he watched the time. At thirty minutes to full, he'd had Elliott call, but Murphy wasn't picking up for anyone. Tara had shrugged apologetically, but only said she hadn't heard from Murphy in a couple of days and she was sure he was on his way. There had been a sour note of doubt in her scent as she said it, though.

Then the shift had gotten too close. They'd stripped down and prepared, and the moon took them.

Braxton took a few delicate breaths, identifying by scent Ximena and Estella Bareira, Theo Smith, Maura Schroeder. With Tara and Elliott, that was the whole pack, except Murphy. He held in a sigh, but he must have tensed at least a little, because Elliott sighed for him.

"You can move," he mumbled. "M'awake."

Braxton grunted. "You're warm," he said, and yawned against Elliott's shoulder blade.

"Honey, the word you're looking for is hot," said Tara's sleepy but playful voice. One hand snaked across Braxton's side to pat Elliott's hip. Elliott just grunted his appreciation.

Braxton huffed a laugh, but it was melancholy. He couldn't stop thinking about Murphy. Had he just locked himself in his apartment for the night? It was possible to spend every full like that—werewolves, even the bitten ones, retained control of their senses throughout the change, once they learned how. That was what made it so much worse when Marcineau bit Murphy; Marcineau had *chosen* to turn someone, knowing it was against the rules. He'd deliberately ruined someone's life, or at least altered it forever. Braxton had never been of the opinion that lycanthropy was a curse, but he would never deny that it brought a lot of huge worldview shifts with it.

"Thinking 'bout Murphy," Elliott muttered. It wasn't a question. Elliott knew Braxton too well, and besides, Elliott must be worrying about Murphy, too.

"Yeah." Braxton squeezed his eyes shut. "I pissed him off a couple weeks ago. Offered him money." He wasn't sure that had been his real offense, but it had certainly triggered their argument.

Elliott hissed through his teeth.

"Yeah, I know. Should've known better."

Tara shifted behind Braxton, slipping her arms up between them to create a thin layer of modesty, even as she offered him comfort. He was grateful. Tara was beautiful, but Braxton had never had any feelings for her beyond pack and friendship, and Tara never pushed for anything else. Whether or not she wanted more, he'd honestly never been able to tell. "It's partly my fault, too," she said. "I've been on his case more. Sorry, B."

Braxton thought about Murphy's remarks about Tara last month. "He says he doesn't need mothering," he mused. "But...Do *you* know anything about his family? I don't."

"His folks split up years ago," Tara said. "They both love him, but loathe each other. Not exactly fun for him."

Elliott grunted. Good. At least he was still awake to hear this.

"Are they local?" Braxton asked.

"Dad's out west. His mom's here in Indy, though. I..." Tara hesitated, and Braxton could smell her sudden nervousness. "I'm friends with her, actually."

Braxton blinked, wondering why she was worried about admitting that. She didn't think Braxton would ask her to use that friendship, did she? He wouldn't refuse any insight Tara could give, but he also wasn't going to push into her private life, or the O'Hares' private lives. Then he registered what Tara had said. "Wait, does Murphy know that?"

Tara gave a low laugh. "I'm not sleeping with him, you know. That would be weird." Her tone, which began as amused, grew more pensive at the end.

Braxton wondered if Tara felt responsible for what happened to Murphy. Maybe she thought that somehow, by being a werewolf and friends with his family, she'd brought Marcineau's attention to Murphy. Braxton was pretty sure that wasn't the case, although he hadn't exactly pressed his dad for details while he was trying to save his father's life.

"Question now is, do we go to him, or wait for him to come back to us?" Elliott said, his voice rough. He was anything but a morning person. Braxton always brought an insulated canteen of black coffee just for Elliott after the full. He was still too comfortable to get up and find it, though.

"Hell if I know," Tara said. "He's been pricklier than usual since August. I have no idea what's going on with him, but I'm ready to smack him."

Braxton sighed. "Okay," he said at last. "I'll think about it some more."

They were silent for a while, except for the sound of breathing. Braxton could hear the other werewolves beginning to stir, but it was clear no one wanted to wake up yet. After several minutes, Tara let out a whimpery noise, then sat up. Braxton turned his head enough to see her give a long, languorous stretch and roll to her feet.

"Time to get moving, lads. Sun's almost up. There'll be people soon. You know those crazy joggers."

Braxton laughed and forced himself to sit up with a groan. "All right, you heard her, people! Up and at 'em."

There was a general shuffle as people began stirring, grumbling as they did so. Ximena was usually the first up, and her cousin Estella one of the last, depending on how quickly Elliott got his coffee. Braxton usually tried to be first up, to set a good example, but despite his anxiety over Murphy, he was too relaxed today. It wasn't long before everyone was dressed except Braxton and Elliott. The Barrera cousins were already making their silent way through the trees away from the camp, and Maura was draining her Thermos of tea.

Just before the shift, they always folded their clothes neatly and stored them in a metal footlocker Braxton's granddad had brought back from Vietnam. Also stored in the footlocker were provisions for breakfast—precooked bacon, sausage, hard-boiled eggs, and coffee and tea. Werewolves needed more calories than most humans, particularly around the full moon. Hunting while shifted helped, if you could bring yourself to do it. Not all werewolves could. Elliott had a hard time even killing a rabbit, and Maura was content to let the others bring something down and share it with her, if she ate at all. Tara and Braxton were both hunters, though, and Murphy, when he was with them.

Braxton felt another pang of anxiety about Murphy. Shoving it aside, he went to get clothes and coffee. He tossed Elliott's clothes at him before getting dressed himself. By the time he carried the coffee back over, Elliott was dressed and leaning against a tree. He wiped a hand over his face and stifled a yawn, and Braxton grinned. He knew he was biased, but he'd never understood why Elliott had such a hard time keeping relationships. He was smart, he had a good job and a great sense of humor, and he was, frankly, kind of adorable when he was sleepy.

"What?" Elliott asked, lowering his hand to take the coffee.

Braxton shook his head. "You about ready to head out? It'll be dawn soon."

Elliott shrugged. "You're driving, boss."

"Boss is a lot better than alpha," Braxton remarked. "Grab one end," he said, gesturing at the footlocker. Elliott snorted, but did as he asked. Braxton glanced around to make sure the others had all cleared out. Then they hiked the half-mile out to where he'd parked his truck.

"Speaking of alphas," Elliott said as they were shoving the footlocker into the back.

"Don't," Braxton said, though he didn't think it would stop him.

"What? I know you took Cole to the Eleven game last week. How was it?"

Braxton shrugged. "Good, except I got a pissed-off call from Theo at half-time. He said Murphy was giving him shit, and couldn't I do something about it."

Elliott snorted.

"Yeah, that was my reaction. I told Theo we'd talk about it at the full, but obviously Murphy wasn't here, so." They got in the car, and it took about five seconds for Elliott to start in again as Braxton pulled out onto Fifty-Sixth Street.

"So anyway. Date with Cole. You kiss her?"

Braxton felt his face get hot. "None of your business."

Elliott laughed. "Good. So you're going to see her again?"

"Already did."

"Yeah?"

Braxton wasn't sure if he should be pleased or annoyed at the surprise in Elliott's tone. "Yeah," he said, wishing he didn't sound so defensive. "We had lunch Friday."

"And..."

Braxton huffed out an exasperated sigh. "And we're going to see a movie next weekend."

"Why not this weekend?"

"Because I thought I was going to be dealing with Murphy and Theo today," Braxton snapped.

From the corner of his eye, he could see Elliott hold his hands up in surrender. "Sorry. Geez."

Braxton knew the reprieve he got from that wouldn't last long, but to his surprise, they were almost at the edge of Avon before Elliott spoke again.

He was fidgeting with his travel mug, turning it in his hands and tapping against the metal sides. Elliott drew in an audible breath and Braxton glanced over at him, but Elliott was looking out the side window as he said, "So. What about all this?"

"All this?" A jolt of outright terror went through him. Elliott didn't mean what Braxton thought he meant, did he? It was nowhere near that time yet.

Elliott made a gesture that encompassed both of them. "This. Us. Werewolves and shit."

Elliott *did* mean what Braxton thought he meant. Braxton knew Elliott would hear the way his heartrate jumped at the suggestion, but there was nothing he could do about it. "No way. She's not ready for 'werewolves and shit'."

As soon as he said it, Braxton realized he'd answered that wrong. Elliott knew him too well. If Braxton didn't like Chloe enough to tell her about werewolves, he would have said that outright. The way he phrased it, in terms of Chloe's being ready or not, told Elliott way more than Braxton had intended to give away, even to his best friend. It meant Braxton did like her, way more than he was letting on, and that he *did* see Chloe as a good candidate for a long-term relationship.

Elliott huffed. "It's a lot to take in, sure, but she's smart. She'd handle it." He still wasn't looking at Braxton.

"Way too early to make a decision like that," Braxton said. "Especially since I'd be outing you, too. Even if I didn't say anything, she'd figure it out."

He felt Elliott relax a little next to him. When he glanced over, Elliott was nodding slowly. "Yeah, she's smart," he repeated. He drew in another long breath. "I like her a lot, Brax. You know? I think she'll be good for you."

"Thanks for your approval," Braxton said. His tone was dry, but Elliott would know he really meant it. If your best friend didn't approve of the woman you were dating, it wasn't a good sign.

Elliott shrugged. "Will you just get us there already? I need breakfast."

* * *

One month and three days after getting shot, Chloe had a doctor's appointment. The x-rays cleared her to take her workout to the next level, though her doctor refused to clear her for work again. Chloe tried arguing for desk duty, but Dr. Surakanti said she had two more weeks of paid leave, and ordered her to use them. Chloe didn't keep arguing. At least she was allowed to hit the gym again.

She left the doctor's office and went straight to the gym, where she did some light cardio to warm up. She did low-weight reps on the leg weights, then headed for the free weights. Thankfully there were only two other people lifting, and they both seemed content to mind their own business. She wasn't in the mood to take shit from a couple of self-absorbed jocks about girls only being able to lift the bar. She was eager to get back into the swing of things, but she didn't want to re-injure her ribs, so she was going to start out slow.

By the time she left, her mood was spiraling downward. She knew she could come back from where she was, but it was discouraging to see how much muscle tone she'd lost in the past four weeks. She could usually free lift more than half the guys she worked with. She liked working out. She liked the way her arms looked in tank tops. But for the first time in a long time, she was glad tank top season was ending.

When she got out of the shower back at Martin's place, she saw she'd missed two calls from Braxton. He'd left a message, but she didn't bother listening to it. She just dialed his number.

"Chloe," he said in greeting. "Sorry if you're busy."

She found herself smiling at the sound of his voice. "Nope. What's up?"

"I left a message." She could hear the aggrieved tone in his voice, and she snorted.

"I don't listen to messages. If you don't get me when you call, text me."

He huffed. "I've heard of people like you, but I didn't believe they really existed."

"Sorry. I'm impatient." Chloe tucked the phone against her shoulder and brushed on some eyeshadow. She still didn't know why he was calling, but she hoped eyeshadow would be required. "So what's up?"

He made another noise, but finally answered her. "Another burglary. Fountain Square this time. You know the Black Cat Bookshop?"

Chloe frowned. She didn't spend much time in Fountain Square. "Doesn't ring a bell."

"Well, it's kind of eclectic. Used books, jewelry, hippie-looking clothes, incense, lots of loose teas, that kind of thing."

"Doesn't sound like your kind of place," she remarked, grinning.

"Not so much. But they got burglarized day before yesterday, and since they've got jewelry—"

"You wanted to check it out," she interrupted. "So what's the verdict?"

"Definitely connected. Can you meet me down here?"

"Sure." She glanced at the clock. It was getting close to eleven, but hopefully she'd be ahead of the lunch-time traffic. "See you in twenty-five minutes."

She threw on jeans, a black t-shirt, and her Docs, then grabbed a jacket. She knew they would have an Indian Summer—every year it happened just when she'd started thinking it was going to skip a year—but the days were a little cool, and the nights had been downright chilly for the past week. Better to have a jacket in the car than to miss it later. She grabbed a Dr. Pepper from the fridge on her way out the door, then headed down to Fountain Square.

The Black Cat Bookshop was exactly as Braxton had described. It was an eclectic mishmash of product, but aside from the patchouli-scented air, Chloe thought it had a welcoming feel to it. As soon as she walked in the door, a black cat—presumably the one the shop was named after—trotted up to sniff at her boots.

"Don't mind Merlin," called a voice. "He has to inspect everyone who comes in, but he's only thrown one customer out."

Chloe grinned at the green-haired woman who appeared a few moments later. "As long as he doesn't take an instant dislike based on my cat's scent on my shoes." She held out a hand to shake. "I'm Chloe Cole. Senior Trooper Wolfe called me in to consult."

"Oh, sure! Angela Hendry. Nice to meet you. Your partner's in the back office." Angela had a firm grip. She gave Chloe's hand a quick two-pump shake, then turned and led the way back to the office. Merlin trotted along at her heels, tail high. "We already had IMPD officers here. It's weird what they took. A few books, mostly from the psychology and sociology sections, which were sort of ransacked. Most of our new-age harp section of CDs—it wasn't very big to begin with, but still." Angela glanced over her shoulder to make sure Chloe was following.

"And Wolfe said there was jewelry?" Chloe said.

"Yeah, we have a lot of goth and emo customers," Angela said, "so we carry a lot of accessories and jewelry for them. Lots of black leather, black semi-precious stones, skulls, hearts, angel wings, ravens, that kind of thing."

"Sounds morbid," Chloe said.

"Oh, not really. I mean, they're mostly kids who've had it kind of tough growing up, but despite all the black lipstick and thick eyeliner, they're actually a lot of fun. Really smart, a lot of them, and nice. Not to mention, they pay my bills, so I'm not going to complain." Angela paused by a door and gave Chloe a smile. "Anyway, a lot of that stuff went missing. I honestly figured it was one of our regulars. We have a couple who don't really have much money, so I tend to let 'em sit and drink a cup of tea and read in the shop, but..." She shrugged.

"Doesn't that eat into your profits?" Chloe scanned some of the bookshelves. They were in the speculative fiction section, so the book covers had a lot of space ships, knights with big swords, and women in flowing dresses.

"Not as much as you'd think. The tea doesn't cost much, and they wouldn't buy the books anyway, so why not let them read?"

Chloe shrugged. "Sure." Merlin crouched, staring at something off to the right. It was a strange reaction, almost like the cat were assessing a threat. "Is Merlin your only cat?" Chloe asked, studying the sleek animal.

"Yeah." Angela laughed. "Otherwise it would be the Black *Cats* Bookshop." She leaned over to look where Chloe was looking. "He's probably just trying to freak us out. I swear they do that on purpose. You know, a lot of people think cats can see ghosts because of stuff like this." She went into the office.

Chloe gave one last glance to Merlin, then followed her.

Braxton was sitting in one of two chairs, poring over a piece of paper. "Hey," he said, giving Chloe a smile. "Thanks for coming."

"No problem." Chloe shoved her hands in her pockets, waiting to see what he wanted her to do. Before he could say anything, the bell on the door jangled.

Angela slipped past Chloe. "Excuse me. Let me know if you need anything." She disappeared to the front of the shop.

"So..." Chloe began. "This doesn't seem connected to the others, really. A bookstore?"

"It is," Braxton said. He flipped the paper over, frowning at the handwriting.

She raised her eyebrows, surprised by the confidence in that statement. With so little to go on, how could he be certain? Especially since a week ago, they'd both been frustrated. "Something new come up with the case?"

"Just this." He flipped the paper back over and wrote something.

"Oookay," she said, drawing it out. "I'll bite. How do you know?"

Braxton twitched and lowered the paper, then glanced up at her. "I just...I can just feel it."

That didn't seem like the kind of police work Braxton did, in Chloe's opinion. "Someone tip you off? What made you even notice this place?"

"I told you, someone stole jewelry. I have a flag on cases that involve jewelry, and today was a slow day, so I was scanning through some of the flagged cases. This one looked likely."

"Why, exactly?"

Braxton shrugged. "Our guys have been quiet for a while. Before this, they'd been hitting someplace new almost every week. It's been fifteen days since the Franklin burglary. But I haven't seen anything else between now and then."

"What if it's a coincidence?" Chloe said. "Maybe your guys are planning to hit a place tomorrow. Or tonight."

"Sure, maybe," he said, but she could tell he didn't mean it. He looked back at his list. "There has to be some kind of pattern I'm not seeing..."

She shook her head and glanced toward the door. "What convinced you..." she began, and then stopped as a cold thrill went through her. The ghost of her daughter was standing in the doorway of the office.

She looked unhappy, as usual, but she was fidgeting, her hands working at something Chloe couldn't see. What was she doing *here?* This place didn't have anything to do with her.

"You okay?" Braxton asked.

Chloe shook herself and turned to face him, putting her back partly to the door. It sent a crawling feeling up her spine, because her instinct was always to cover the exits, but she didn't want to look at the ghost. "Of course I'm okay. So what convinced you it's connected?"

Braxton studied her for a moment, and she noticed how bright his eyes were. Sometimes they looked more brown, but right now they were a warm golden-amber that seemed to see right through her. Chloe pushed at the guilt. Yes, she was lying to him. But how was she supposed to tell him she had just seen the ghost of her aborted daughter?

"What?" she snapped, and he shrugged.

"I want to get a complete list of missing items. Angela said it could take her a day or so, but she did give me a preliminary list, based on what she thought she had in inventory before." He broke off as his phone rang. "Excuse me," Braxton said. He glanced at the phone and his jaw tightened.

He didn't get up from his chair as he answered, so Chloe turned. Fortunately the doorway was empty of ghosts, so she stepped back out into the main room of the bookstore. The bookshelves were tall, almost taller than she could reach, and fairly narrow. She was pretty sure someone could get a wheelchair through the aisles, but there was no way someone shorter than her would be able to reach the top shelf.

She stood outside the office for a moment, curiosity eating at her. It had been the "Werewolves of London" ringtone again, and Chloe made a note to listen the next time Braxton got a call. She didn't think that was his standard ringtone, but she wasn't sure. But as much as she wanted to know what was going on, she didn't want to eavesdrop. She took several steps away from the door, ending up in the poetry section. She turned a corner and nearly tripped over Merlin.

The little cat was crouched, ears back, and staring at her daughter. Chloe scowled.

"What are you doing here?" she hissed. "This doesn't have anything to do with you." By now she didn't expect a response, but maybe she could make the ghost quit haunting her in public, at least.

The ghost stared at her, dark eyes solemn. She blinked slowly, and Chloe was flooded with grief. She pressed a hand to her breastbone and bowed her head, feeling the anguish physically as well as mentally. But it wasn't her own grief; even in the sudden onslaught of sorrow, she knew that. This was being pushed on her from someone—something—else. Chloe's heart started pounding, and she yawned like the air pressure had changed around her. The air seemed colder around her. She put out her free hand and fumbled for the bookshelf, trying to find a place to lean.

And then the sensation was gone.

The room grew brighter, and only then did Chloe realize her vision had darkened. She lifted her gaze to the ghost, suddenly panting for air. "Was that *you*?" she whispered.

The ghost gave a slow, grave nod. She was still fidgeting with something in her hands, but she looked a little more settled. Maybe it was something in the line of her shoulders, but if Chloe were talking about a living human, she would have said the girl had reached some resolution.

"So you can communicate a little," Chloe ventured, "even if you can't speak." The ghost shrugged one shoulder delicately. Chloe glanced around, hoping Angela and her customer were nowhere near the poetry section. "Why are you haunting me?"

This time, she braced for the onslaught of grief. Instead, she received a sensation that was almost...peaceful. Not quite. There was something too satisfied in it for peace, and there was a tinge of anger to it. Satisfaction? No—closure, maybe.

"So you want—"

"Talking to yourself?" Braxton interrupted, and Chloe jumped. She turned to look at him with a self-conscious laugh. "Oh. Just trying to work things out. What these guys are looking for, what they want out of whatever that is."

He gave her a little smirk. "And?"

She shook her head. "I still can't even imagine what it is they're after. Jewelry, but why? They can't be giving it to wives or girlfriends, because no woman needs this much. If they were pawning it, we would have seen it show up."

"At least some of the more distinctive pieces," Braxton agreed.

"If they were melting it down—"

"Not enough for it to be worthwhile," he said.

"Yeah. So what are they doing with it?" She shook her head. "It's crazy."

"Tell me about it." Braxton gave her a sardonic smile. "I've been on this case for weeks longer than you have, and I feel the same way."

Chloe shook her head again, at a loss for a response.

"Come on. Angela's going to do a full inventory and email the results, so the preliminary list is all we have to go on today. Let's go get some lunch."

As they headed for the front of the store, the shop cat dashed ahead of them, claws scrabbling on the hardwood floor. Chloe laughed, but the sound died when they reached the front. Her daughter's ghost was standing square in the door, and she wore a determined—almost stubborn—expression.

I can't give you closure here, Chloe wanted to say. She glared at the ghost. Of all the ghosts she could have gotten, why did it have to be the one who insisted on showing up in public?

Angela was ringing up a customer's sale at the register. "Thanks again," she called after them. "I'll get that info to you as soon as possible."

Braxton paused next to the register, so Chloe scrunched up her face and forced herself to walk right *through* her daughter's ghost. She got out to the sidewalk and shivered, clutching at her elbows.

Braxton came out of the store in time to see her shiver, apparently. He stepped closer and looked up at her oddly. "You okay?"

She scowled at him. "That's the second time you've asked me that today. I'm *fine.*"

"Okay, okay." He shrugged. "What do you want to do for lunch?"

"Have you ever been to B's Po Boy on Shelby? Martin and I love that place."

"Sounds good."

Chloe had been looking forward to spending more time with Braxton, but she felt twitchy and odd as they ate. She kept wondering what he would do if she told him she were seeing ghosts. Would he laugh at her and think she was joking, or would he take her seriously and decide she was insane? For his part, Braxton seemed preoccupied. That was partly a good thing, since it kept him from remarking on how she jumped every time someone walked past on the sidewalk, but it didn't leave much opportunity for dazzling conversation. Chloe was actually grateful when he glanced at his watch and said he had an appointment downtown in twenty minutes.

She drove home feeling guilty about the secret she was keeping from him...and wondering if he were keeping a secret of his own.

* * *

On Halloween, Martin dressed up as a vampire and Chloe put on an eyepatch and tied a scarf around her head to be a makeshift pirate. They watched horror flicks like *Ringu* and *Let the Right One In*, pausing to hand out candy to Red Riding Hoods and Avengers and X-Men and one exceptionally spotty cow. Some of Chloe's friends from the police department brought their kids around.

At one point they had two ninjas, a Jedi, and a cowboy play-brawling in the front yard. Later Peter Pan showed up and challenged Chloe to a sword fight, which he handily won, since her "sword" was an empty cardboard tube from the paper towel dispenser in the kitchen.

Around ten-thirty, when the doorbell was pretty much done ringing, aside from a few straggling teenagers, and they were trying to finish their movie, Chloe's cell phone rang.

"*Diadelosmuertos*!" Jake exclaimed when she answered the phone.

"Huh?" Chloe wasn't even sure if he was speaking Spanish or just gibberish.

"Dia de los Muertos," he repeated. "The holiday. I just realized it when we had a skeleton show up at the door for candy. You're seeing dead people, yeah? So Dia de los Muertos is when we hang out with our dead relatives."

Chloe glanced at Martin, who was totally engrossed in the movie, and went out to the kitchen. "Yeah, I know the holiday," she said. "With skulls and candles and picnics at the cemetery."

"Right, right," Jake said. "Well, Celia and me are going to our parents' graves in a couple days to leave the ofrendas and everything. I thought maybe you'd want to come partway with us and see if any of your dead people show up there. The veil between that world and this is thinnest at this time of year."

She blinked. "No offense, Jase, but do you believe that? About the veil and everything?"

"Eh. I don't know, Chloe. I've seen candles go out when there was no wind in the room, and I know my parents would have kicked my ass if I hadn't done the ofrendas for my grandparents. Whether or not I believe for sure... well, what does it hurt, huh? It's respect for the people who've come before you. And there's some good food."

She rubbed the bridge of her nose. It felt strange to be invited to something like that, something intimate and spiritual and ultimately about family. But maybe it would help. "So...what would it involve?" she asked finally.

"Well, I was thinking," he said. "The cemetery stuff is for family only, but you could come with us to Crown Hill. If ghosts exist, the place will be crawling with them. If you're really seeing ghosts, you'll see them, and I won't, and we'll be able to confirm it."

She frowned. He had a point. She'd considered hitting up the Irvington ghost tour, but who could guarantee there would be any ghosts?

"They're doing a Dia de los Muertos celebration at the Artspark there by your brother's place too," Jake added, when she didn't speak. "But that's tomorrow, I think. All Saints instead of All Souls. And who knows if any of the spirits would actually show up."

Chloe hummed. "I think I'd rather meet you at the cemetery. But don't tell Celia *why* I'm meeting you there. We can say it's case stuff."

"But you haven't gone back to work yet."

"She knows I'm consulting for Braxton. It'll be fine."

"Speaking of the statie...how's that going?" he said. She could hear the shit-eating grin in his voice. It kind of made her want to kick him. On the other hand, the thought of Braxton made her grin a little, so she couldn't really blame Jake.

"We're seeing a movie tomorrow."

"Dude. You really like him."

"Just because we're going on a second date?" she asked, feeling a little hurt. Just because she'd been too impatient to allow anyone to get close in a while...

"Third date," Jake corrected. "And yes, exactly because you're going on a third date. I can't remember the last time anyone got past a first date with you before you decided there was something wrong with him. Or that he wouldn't like your career choice. Or something."

Chloe snorted. "Fine, rub it in." She was still grinning as she hung up.

On Tuesday, Chloe met Jake and Celia on Boulevard Place, near the large stone gate that was the north entrance to Crown Hill Cemetery. Established in 1864, Crown Hill was the third largest cemetery in the United States, and Chloe had always thought it one of the most beautiful places in the city. Poet James Whitcomb Riley was buried on "The Crown," as the highest point in Marion County was called; his gravesite provided an outstanding view of the city. The cemetery was the final resting place of all kinds of famous people, including bank robber John Dillinger, Richard Gatling, President Benjamin Harrison, Colonel Eli Lilly, Mozel Sanders, Booth Tarkington, and plenty of Civil War generals, Indiana governors, and three United States Vice Presidents.

There was a trickle of people entering the gates, more than Chloe had really expected.

"Lucia's not coming?" Chloe asked, surprised.

"She doesn't like all this," Celia said. She had a picnic basket in her hands. "She thinks it's paganism.

But it was the Catholic priests who started Dia de los Muertos, so she can just get over herself."

"Hey, be nice," Jake said. He was wearing khakis and a sweater with a shirt collar peeking out from under it. Chloe was used to seeing him in suits for work, but he tended to be a sloppy dresser when he was at home, so it was kind of a jolt to see him dressed like that. A reminder that this was an important occasion for his family, not just a possible lead in her case. She glanced down at her jeans and Doc Martens and wished she'd dressed a little nicer, even though she wasn't planning on going inside the cemetery.

"You two discuss whatever it is you need to," Celia said. "I'm going to go on in. I want to get there before it's dark, so I don't have to walk out with just the candles." She looked at Chloe. "We don't stay all night like they do in Mexico. I mean, some people do. The older ones mostly. Some of them even spend all day and all night. But we'll just go and have our picnic at the grave and clean it up a little."

Chloe nodded. "I won't keep him too long," she promised.

Celia joined the trickle of people—which was becoming a small stream—entering the cemetery. Chloe watched her go for a few moments, then took a deep breath and scrubbed her hands down her jeans.

"Okay," she said, turning to face Jake. "So how will I know if I'm seeing a spirit?"

He tilted his head to one side. "Don't they look different from people?"

"Not enough. There was a nurse at the hospital that you guys never seemed to see, but I thought she was a real person." Chloe shrugged. "That was before I realized about the ghosts, but still. They look mostly like people, except if I look closely I can tell they're less substantial."

Jake hummed. "So let's follow Celia until she gets close to the gates. Maybe Mama and Papa will meet her there. You'd recognize them if you saw them, even if you wouldn't know Marc."

"Marc?"

"Oh." He shifted on his feet and shrugged. "Our little brother. There was something wrong with his lungs, so he'd always been sickly. He was older than the girls, but younger than me. He died when he was twelve. Anyway."

Chloe nodded. They were silent for a few moments, watching Celia as she got closer to the gate. Chloe cleared her throat. "So, if this isn't disrespectful, do you think it's just Latinx ghosts who show up tonight? I mean, I know it isn't just Mexico that celebrates Dia de los Muertos, but I know it isn't all Catholics, either. So what happens to the non-Latinx ghosts?"

Jake chuckled, his shoulders relaxing. "I have no idea. Maybe they just don't care about all you anglos like my ancestors do."

Chloe rolled her eyes at him, but she was glad she'd broken the odd tension that had materialized at the mention of Marc. She glanced around at the other people approaching the cemetery. It seemed the majority were over the age of fifty, but there were still quite a few people around her own age. They were in various styles of dress, and everyone carried something, whether it was a basket, a cooler, or a blanket.

With a start, she realized someone was staring at her. He was a tall man, about forty, with brown skin and black hair that already had a few threads of silver. He wore dress slacks and a polo shirt, and had an expensive-looking backpack slung over one shoulder. His eyes narrowed as she looked back at him. Next to her, Jake swore.

"That lowlife asshole," he growled.

Surprised, Chloe looked at him. "What?"

"You don't recognize him? That's Victor Garza. Asshole defense attorney."

Chloe swung around to look at the man again, but all she saw was his retreating back. He was walking next to a giant of a man, but Chloe couldn't tell if they were together on purpose, or just pressed together in the crush of people. "How do *you* know him?"

"He defended a guy a few years ago, someone I'd picked up after a bar fight. Deyonte something. A guy hit on Deyonte's girl, and Deyonte took exception. He called the guy a few impolite names, and the guy swung at him. It escalated from there, until the name-caller ended up dead. Bled out from the jugular after Deyonte put a broken beer bottle in it." Jake was scowling. "Garza tried to say I'd arrested the wrong guy, and I'd picked Deyonte just because he was black. I'm like, excuse me? Brown man making an arrest right here, don't try to pull the race card on me. I didn't arrest him because he was black, I arrested him because he was the asshole who did it."

Chloe grunted. She remembered the case, now that Jake filled in the details. "That's while I was on my National Park vacation, wasn't it?"

"Yeah." Jake hocked and spit on the sidewalk. "Garza's a lowlife."

"You said." Chloe looked back at the gate, but Garza was nowhere in sight. Celia was, though, and she'd nearly reached the gate. Chloe was grateful Garza hadn't made her miss seeing this.

"There, Celi's at the gate," Jake said, nudging her. "What do you see?"

Chloe squinted through the fading light. At first she just saw a jumble of people, both inside and outside the gates. But as Celia stepped under the arch, Chloe saw someone approach her from inside the cemetery. It was a boy who looked about twelve.

"I see...a boy," she whispered.

She stared until Celia had disappeared from view, her ancestral spirit following. Then she looked over at Jake.

He was staring after his sister, an expression of mixed jealousy and wistfulness on his face. Chloe felt a pang of guilt that she could see them and he couldn't.

"He looked so happy," she said. "And your brother, he was laughing. He's got a mohawk. He's wearing a Pokémon t-shirt?" Jake looked at her.

He quickly lowered his eyebrows and turned up the corners of his mouth, masking his expression.

Chloe stared at Jake, who stared back. Finally he gave a low whistle. "Okay, so. Wow. You're seeing real ghosts," he said. "There's your confirmation. Marc loved that game. It was something he could do even when he wasn't feeling good."

Chloe nodded, feeling as if she might lose her balance. Was the world suddenly spinning faster? She widened her stance. "Um. Thank you for letting me confirm it here," she said.

"No problem." Jake's tone was a little vague. He blinked and shook his head. "I'd better get in there, or Celia'll give me hell. I...This is a big deal for her, but I've always just kind of..." He trailed off and shook his head again. "I'll see you later, C."

* * *

Victor stared in shock at Chloe Cole. *Shit.* Had she connected him to the case? Was she following him? How had she come to be here at the exact same time as him, if she hadn't realized he was involved in her shooting? She was there with her partner, Ruiz. Victor remembered him; he was the cop who had arrested Deyonte. *Shit,* he thought again. He'd thought Deyonte had smartened up in the lockup. What if he'd been wrong? Had Deyonte ratted him out to Ruiz?

When Cole looked at her partner, Victor spun on his heel and strode to the gate as quickly as he could. Fletcher, who had paused when he paused, took a couple of moments to catch up to him.

"What's wrong?" he asked Victor.

Victor slipped a hand inside his coat, checking to be sure the Thanatos pendant was there. He didn't reply until they were inside and blocked from view. "Cole. The cop Wethering shot. She's out there."

"So? Maybe she's here for the same reason you are." Fletcher didn't sound as if he believed that.

"She's as white as you," Victor snapped.

"I'm still here, ain't I?" Fletcher reasoned. When Victor glared at him, he shrugged. "Okay, fine. She's not here to bring the offerings. So why *is* she here? She can't have connected her shooting to you. For one thing, you didn't tell Cody to shoot her. For another, you dealt with him."

Victor hissed at him, and Fletcher fell silent as a large family, talking softly and laughing, passed them. When they were gone, he filled Fletcher in on the connection with Ruiz. Fletcher mulled this over as they walked. When they were nearly to Alita's grave, he said, "I'll figure something out. You spend time with your little girl." He sat on a boulder and propped his chin on his fist.

Victor felt his stomach unclench just a little. Fletcher had way more street smarts than Victor. He would take care of this, like he took care of everything. *He's right*, he told himself. *Tonight is about Alita, letting her know I'm still here for her. Letting her know I'm going to bring her back. We'll worry about Cole tomorrow.*

He wished he'd thought to bring a camp stool. As he unfolded the little stadium blanket he'd brought, he felt foolish. He disliked sitting on the ground. With a sigh, he settled awkwardly on the blanket and pulled the other things he'd brought from his backpack.

He'd never done this before. His grandmother had observed Dia de los Muertos, but his mother had dismissed it as superstitious nonsense, and Victor had been happy to go along with her stance on it. Even after his mother's death, he'd avoided visiting the cemetery on All Souls' Day. He left her flowers on her birthday and at Christmas, and that was all. After losing Alita, though...

He sighed. He hadn't known what would be a good ofrenda, so he'd bought one of those pouty, sultry-looking dolls Alita had always liked. She was too old for them now, of course, but he'd made up for that by bringing a tube of lipstick from her bathroom.

"What's wrong with Barbie?" he'd asked once, faced with a wall of big-lipped, scantily-clad dolls at the store.

Alita tossed her hair. "Barbie's a ditz," she replied.

Privately, Victor had thought Alita's dolls looked like hussies, but he'd plunked down his money anyway, and she'd looked at him like he'd just slain a dragon for her, so he'd decided the doll was a good thing to bring her.

"I brought one of the books you like, too," he said to Alita's tombstone. He felt ridiculous talking to nothing, especially in this semi-public venue. It didn't matter that other people were doing the same; Victor was sitting by himself. At least the families looked like they were talking to living people.

He sighed and cracked open the book. It was one of those vampire novels all the girls had liked. Victor had taken Alita and her friends to see all four movies—or was it five? He wasn't sure anymore. He squeezed his eyes shut, fingering the pendant around his neck. How could his memories of her be slipping away like this?

"Shall I read to you?" he said, and began.

After a couple of chapters, he had to stop. His throat was dry, and it felt like he had a rock lodged in there, anyway. When was the last time he'd read aloud to his little girl? When she was tiny, she would creep into his study, holding a book and watching him silently until he noticed her there. It had become a game to see how long he could pretend to ignore her before she giggled and gave herself away. Then he'd drawn her into his lap. "Do you have time to read me a story?" she would ask, and Victor would reply, "I always have time to read you a story, baby."

As she got older, though, she'd been more interested in video games and riding her bike and playing with her friends. In sixth grade, she'd come down with strep throat, and Victor had offered to read to her. It was the last time he could remember her taking him up on the offer.

Victor wiped his eyes. When had he started crying? He blinked fiercely and looked around him—and swore.

Cody Wethering was sitting on his daughter's headstone.

"Fuck off," Victor snarled, glaring at him. "This is a family gathering."

Cody didn't speak, but Victor could feel himself being laughed at. Wethering was there just to provoke him. He knew how much Victor hated seeing him, and he appeared here anyway.

"As soon as I find a way to bring her back, I'm going to find a way to banish you," Victor said. He turned his back on the ghost, his stomach churning. He opened Alita's book again and read another chapter before his voice gave out.

As the night wore on, Victor could feel the dead growing closer. It came in a sense of gathering dread, the hair prickling along his arms, the urge to let his teeth chatter. There was nothing—no one—who felt like Alita. Just people like Cody. Dark people. Angry people. People who blamed and hated and haunted. Victor rubbed his hands over his arms, wishing he'd brought a jacket. Then he stood and wrapped his blanket around him. He didn't want to leave, not before midnight. He needed to see Alita. He *must* see her.

Midnight came, but nothing changed, except he felt sick to his stomach. He didn't see Alita. He didn't even see Cody any more. The feeling of dread, of wrongness, was so thick around him, Victor wasn't sure how he could see anything. He felt as though he were peering through a deep gloom or a thick fog. He left the book and the doll at the foot of Alita's headstone and went back to where he'd left Fletcher.

"Let's go," he said shortly. Fletcher didn't speak, just stood and fell in step beside him.

The cemetery wasn't nearly as crowded as it had been earlier. There were faint lights visible at scattered graves, but there didn't seem to be anyone nearby. Victor jumped when a woman stepped out from behind a tree directly into their path.

She was wearing jeans and a leather trench coat, her hair pulled back in a no-nonsense bun. She held a lantern in her hand that gave off a bluish light. She looked not at Victor, but at the air around him. She frowned as Victor and Fletcher halted to avoid walking into her.

"What the hell—" Fletcher began, but the woman cut him off.

"You don't know what you're doing," she told Victor.

Victor stared at her. "I beg your—"

"I can see the gloom around you. Whatever you're messing with, you're in over your head. You need to stop."

Victor scowled. "Mind your own business," he said, going to push past her.

She grabbed his elbow, her grip surprisingly tight. "You are dealing with powers beyond the mortal," she hissed. "Strong powers. *Amoral* powers. You know a lot about amorality, don't you, Victor Garza?" Her gaze was mocking.

Victor wrenched his arm from her grasp. "I said mind your own business, bitch!" He heard Fletcher stir behind him.

The woman peered up into Victor's face, tilting her head in a bird-like movement. "You are attracting malevolent beings to you. You're like a beacon to them. And they're hungry. They'll consume you."

Victor leaned in, narrowing his eyes. "Fuck. Off," he said, and pushed past her.

"Your funeral," she said, her voice sardonic. Then it grew sad. "I tried to warn you."

Against his will, Victor glanced over his shoulder at her. She was standing with her head bowed, but as he paused, she straightened, shrugged, and walked back the way Victor had come. Surprised that she'd given up so easily, Victor glanced up and to either side. What was it that she could see that he didn't? How did she know what he was doing? Was she, like Chloe Cole, a threat to his endeavor?

The woman had only taken half a dozen steps before she stopped. Victor heard her sigh. Then she turned and marched back to him. "Here," she said, holding something out. He took it reflexively. It was a piece of paper. "If you change your mind," she said, her gaze searching his. She turned again and left him.

Victor crumpled the paper in his fist without looking at it, but he didn't throw it on the grass. He was a lawyer. He knew the value of having an ace in the hole.

"Come on," he said. "Let's get out of here."

He would worry about this woman if she became a problem. In the meantime, he would have Fletcher deal with Chloe Cole. Obviously she was going to be a hindrance, and Fletcher was very good at removing hindrances.

He looked over his shoulder three times on his way back to the car.

CHAPTER 12

Wednesday afternoon, Chloe decided it was time to get serious about her living situation. She needed a place to live that she could call her own. She and Martin were starting to snap at each other, and he'd complained that morning about cat hair on his chair.

"It's time for us to venture forth," she told Whizz, and sat down at her brother's computer. After searching online for about an hour, she had found half a dozen places she wanted to check out. Apartment hunting wasn't much fun without someone else to go with her, though. After some thought, she texted Celia. *Want to help me find an apartment tomorrow? Short notice, sorry.*

The response came a few minutes later. *Sure! What time and where?*

They arranged for Chloe to pick Celi up at ten. Satisfied that she'd accomplished something, even if it was just in the planning stages, Chloe settled on the couch with Whizz and a book.

The next day was brisk, scattered clouds making the sun play peekaboo in the breeze. When Chloe picked Celi up, the younger woman was wearing a long, bulky cardigan with a silver-and-green striped scarf. She clutched a tall thermal coffee mug in her beringed fingers.

"Good morning," Chloe said, and Celi gave her a look from under lowered brows.

"It's morning," she replied, her tone flat.

Chloe grinned to herself and put the car in gear. "You can nap until we get downtown," she said. "I thought we'd start there and work our way out."

Celi just grunted and put her seat back a little.

By the time they reached downtown Indianapolis, Celi was actually speaking in complete sentences. She perked up even more when she realized Chloe was going to look at apartments on the canal.

The Central Canal had been built in the 1830s. It had been designed to connect the Wabash and Erie Canal to the Ohio River, but after a financial panic, it was abandoned with just eight miles completed. In the late 1980s and early 90s, the canal had been reclaimed. White River State Park had been established along some of the canal, and businesses and apartments had sprung up over the next fifteen years. Chloe had always liked the canal, with its gondolas and paddleboats and fountains. The idea of living along it was appealing.

There were several apartment complexes Chloe was interested in. She and Celi had fun touring the one-bedroom apartments available in each complex. She particularly liked one apartment with a balcony on the canal.

When they finished with the canal apartments, Chloe suggested they get lunch at the Rathskeller.

There were a couple of apartments she wanted to look at on Mass Ave. Housed in the 19th century Athenaeum Building, the Rathskeller was a live music hotspot and an Indianapolis landmark, but Chloe had never actually been there.

They split an appetizer plate, saving room for a Black Forest cake dessert. As they talked about Celi's job and Chloe's anxiousness to get back to work, Chloe found herself wondering why they had never really spent much time together one on one. Celi was younger than she was, but that didn't really matter. She was smart and fun, and they definitely shared a sense of humor.

"I'm starting to think about freelancing," Celi said, between bites of brats and hush puppies. "I think I could make way more money. I mean, not that I'm in bad shape as it is, but it would be awesome to be my own boss."

"What would you do?" Chloe asked.

Celi shrugged. "Troubleshooting. Build custom computers. Perform upgrades for people. Fix things. Basically what I do now, except with a little bit of fun added in."

"You'd have all the self-employment tax and health insurance expenses," Chloe said, thinking. "But you could operate out of the house, so you wouldn't need a building."

"I'd rather get a PO box and operate out of an apartment of my own," Celi replied. She tapped her copper fingernails against the table. "I'm sick of arguing about the temperature and sleeping in the same bedroom I grew up in."

"Yeah?" Chloe looked at her curiously. "I thought you were just coming along for moral support."

Celi grinned. "Oh, I was, basically, but I've been thinking about moving out for almost a year now, and seeing some of these apartments has kind of lit a fire under my ass." She shrugged. "I want to shape my own space, you know? Become the woman I know I am, but on my own. I love my sibs, but they can be a little... stifling."

"I get that," Chloe said, thinking she was probably making Martin feel the same way.

"I mean, I've always lived in that house, you know? Even when I got my computer programming degree, I was driving to Ivy Tech and living at home. My closet still has pink walls, for God's sake."

Chloe laughed. "We could paint."

"Oh, I could, but you know what I mean." Celi tossed her head to flip her hair out of her eyes. "Too much past there. I spent so much time trying to make myself like boys in that room. Worrying and crying and praying over why I wasn't normal. All that confusion and angst...it's weird, but even though I'm totally good with who I am now, it's like all that bad emotion is still in the walls of that room. Maybe painting and redecorating would help, but..."

Chloe looked down at her drink and traced a fingertip through the condensation on the glass. "You know, it *can* help to leave that behind physically, but...it doesn't erase that stuff." She glanced up to see

Celi watching her, forehead wrinkled in curiosity or concern. Chloe shrugged. "I've never felt unclear about my sexuality, but I made some...well, I made some choices in college. I can't even say they were bad choices, but they had consequences, you know?"

Celi leaned forward, gaze steady on Chloe's. "Go on."

Chloe took a deep breath. She'd never actually confessed this to anyone but Father Frank. But maybe it was time for her to open up with someone else. As much as she loved her friends, Chloe had always held herself a little bit apart. The more time she spent around Braxton, though, the more she realized she'd been holding *everyone* at arm's length, not just men.

"Well," she said, realizing Celi was still watching her. "I slept with a guy who wasn't much good. I mean, he wasn't too bad, either, but he wasn't a keep-forever kind of guy. Anyway, I got pregnant." She swallowed against a suddenly dry throat. "Martin was still in high school."

She got stuck there, not quite able to say the next words. She twitched when Celi's hand came into her field of vision and rested lightly on her wrist. It surprised her, but it gave Chloe the nerve to say, "I had an abortion. And it haunts me." She pressed her lips together for a moment, getting her emotions back under control. "Even though it felt like my only option."

She stopped talking and listened to the clatter of silverware against dishes, the low conversation of the other people in the restaurant. Then Celi blew out a short breath. "Wow. That sucks you had to go through that, C."

Chloe was startled into looking up at her. Celi gave her a crooked smile that was full of sympathy. "Hey, like I have the right to judge you. Like I'd *want* to judge you. I know you. I've known you for years now. I'm not going to stop loving you just because you have things you're ashamed of in your past. Don't we all?"

Chloe managed a shaky smile, but her eyes were stinging. She didn't want to get full-on emotional in public, so she patted Celi's hand and pulled back, shoving those feelings all back into the box she usually tried to keep them in. "Thanks," she croaked, and cleared her throat. "Anyway. You get what I mean about stuff staying with you."

"I do," Celi said mildly. "But I think in my case, moving out will help enough. I can reinvent myself in World of Warcraft no problem, but it's a lot harder to reinvent myself to my family."

"That makes sense. Family's used to seeing you the way you've always been. It's easier to make the transition stick if you're not living with them day in and day out. God knows, if you're apart long enough, you almost have to get to know each other again." Chloe stirred her drink idly with her straw. "At least, that's how it was when Martin came back from Afghanistan."

Celi nodded. "That could be a good thing, really. Anyway, it's awkward, trying to date anyone when I live with my sibs. It's not quite like living with my mom and dad, but in some ways it's almost weirder."

Chloe snorted. "I wouldn't know about that. I didn't even think about dating for ages after college, and by the time I did, Martin was overseas, so I didn't have that situation come up."

"Maybe I'll find a place I like today," Celi said. She gave Chloe an impish grin. "How would you feel about having me as a neighbor?"

Chloe laughed. "I'd love it! You could teach me how to actually cook."

"Ha. My idea of cooking is taking shit out of the freezer and putting it in the microwave. You want to know a secret? I eat frozen taquitos instead of making them myself, because it's easier. Plus, you can eat the frozen ones with one hand while you're running a raid."

They scoped out a couple more possibilities after lunch, but in the end, Celi's favorite was one of the apartment complexes along the Canal. She declared she was ready to move the next day, but Chloe had a feeling it would take a little longer than that for her to work up the courage to tell her brother and sister. Chloe liked the apartments Celi had chosen, but she wasn't quite ready to commit. She had the floorplans and paperwork, and she was going to take at least a day or two to mull it over.

On the way back to Jake's house, they discussed the best way for Celi to break the news to her sibs. That led to Celi asking how Chloe would tell Martin. Chloe smirked at the thought that Martin would somehow be bereft when she moved out.

"Oh, he'll probably be pushing me out the door as soon as I say the first word about it," Chloe said. "Remember, I only moved in with him because of the fire. He and I are both used to coming and going without telling anyone else what we're doing."

"I'm envious," Celi admitted.

Chloe made a noncommittal noise in acknowledgment and the conversation lapsed. Celi started humming along with the radio. Chloe found herself thinking about the case and how her daughter's ghost was following her around. At least she hadn't seen the ghost at all today. She'd half expected her to show up while telling the story to Celi. She huffed a sigh. What a mess. As if the case wouldn't be enough on its own, without the complication of ghosts.

"What's wrong?" Celi asked.

"Oh..." Chloe shook her head slightly. No way was she going to get into the ghost thing. She'd confessed enough for one day, thanks. "It's just...the case I'm working with Braxton," she said. "The shooting. The arson. There was another burglary back on the seventeenth, but there hasn't been anything since then, that we know of. I can't help wondering what's next."

"I don't know how you and Jake do this job. I mean, assholes are part of life, I know, but it seems like you guys have more contact than average citizens." Celi stretched. "I mean, if I get some Horde player griefing one of my low-level alts on WoW, I completely lose my shit. If it were about something that *really* mattered, something life and death..." She shook her head.

"Douchebags come with the territory," Chloe said philosophically. "It does help that we get to put a lot of them behind bars."

Celi snorted.

"Seriously, though, I know I'm making a difference," Chloe said. "Every domestic dispute I break up gives an abused woman a chance to change the direction of her life. Every drug dealer I get off the street makes that street safer for the school kids walking to school. It matters, knowing there are people I'm helping."

Celi was quiet for a moment. "When you put it that way, it's kind of awesome," she admitted. "You're awesome, Clo."

Chloe flashed her a grin. "I know, right?" she joked. They'd reached their exit. She flipped on her turn signal and switched lanes, easing off the gas. She hated this exit; it was a cloverleaf onto a busy four-lane street, and it seemed like there was always ridiculous traffic. She began to brake — or tried to.

Fuck, she thought as the brake pedal went all the way to the floor. The car wasn't decelerating, and the sharp curve was coming up way too fast. Chloe bit her lower lip hard. She couldn't freak out. She had to keep them from dying first.

"Uh, this is—" Celi began, and Chloe shushed her.

"Put down your window," she ordered, pumping the brake pedal several times. When she'd managed to build up a little pressure, she stomped the pedal to the floor. The car slowed, but not enough.

"What's—"

"Brakes are out," Chloe snapped. "Put down your window. Air resistance." She downshifted, wincing at the sudden screaming of the engine. The car slowed further, but she couldn't take that curve at fifty miles an hour. She'd roll the car.

Celi muttered a prayer under her breath as she put down her window, then reached back and hit the button to lower the back window, too. "What else?" she asked, her voice shaking.

"Hold on," Chloe ordered, hitting the button for the hazards. She tightened her grip on the steering wheel with her left hand and curled her right around the parking brake. "This isn't gonna be fun."

Holding in the release button, she eased up on the parking brake, trying to get it to engage gently. If she engaged it too fast, the tires could lock. On the other hand, she didn't have time for too much finesse. She steered into the curve as she began applying the parking brake with more pressure. The car responded, though the results weren't smooth.

"Oh, shit, Jesus save us," Celi muttered, clutching at the panic handle over the window.

"We're okay," Chloe said, steering the car tighter into the curve. Now that she wasn't going fast enough to kill them, she wanted the resistance of the grass in the median. Gritting her teeth, she coaxed the e-brake up one more click. Her arm muscles were killing her, but as it clicked into place, the car shuddered to a stop.

A car came down the ramp behind her, blaring its horn as he realized her rear end was still half in the lane.

Chloe's hands were shaking. She let out an explosive breath. "Thank you, Jesus and Saint Michael," she whispered. She looked over at Celi. "You okay?"

Celi's face was bloodless, her eyes wide as she stared at Chloe, but she nodded. "That...was..." She trailed off and shook her head.

Chloe hit the button to pop the trunk. Checking the mirror, she got out of the car and darted to the back, where her emergency kit was stowed. She set out a couple of flares, well back from the car to give approaching motorists plenty of warning. Then she pulled out her cell phone and dialed Braxton.

"We need to talk," she told him.

"Sure," he said, though he sounded a little nervous suddenly. "Where?"

"My brother's place, in an hour. I've got to arrange a ride home for Celi," she added. "My car's out of commission."

She heard him suck in a breath. "Are you okay?"

"I'm fine. Celi's fine. I'll fill you in when you get to my brother's place." Chloe squeezed her eyes shut and pinched the bridge of her nose. "Can you bring pizza and beer for three?"

"No problem. I'll see you there."

As she walked back towards the car, Chloe dialed her brother's favorite towing service and told them where they were. Rick promised he'd be there in twenty minutes. He even promised not to tell her brother until the next day. Chloe pocketed her phone and then grunted as Celi threw herself at Chloe.

"You are *seriously* awesome," Celi said, hugging her tightly. "Thank you for knowing how to do that." She pulled back, peering up at Chloe. "How *did* you know how to do that?"

Chloe shrugged, pleased. "They teach us that stuff. Special driving skills."

"It was awesome," Celi said. She turned and eyed the car. "Should we push it all the way to the shoulder?"

"Our ride's already on his way. He'll get this taken care of," Chloe said. "I need to make a few more calls. Can you grab all our stuff from the car?"

Celi nodded. Chloe was already sliding her thumb down her favorites list. Her next call was to Lieutenant Piper. She wanted her badge back.

If this guy thought he could get away with attempted murder, he had another think coming. His partner had killed her once. Chloe wasn't going to let it happen again.

* * *

Braxton ended the call from Chloe and frowned at his desk for a moment. "That was...weird," he remarked.

"What was?" Shay shoved away from her desk and swiveled her chair so she could look at him.

"Chloe. She just called and said we had to talk." He'd honestly expected this was going to be a 'let's just keep this professional' talk, but then she'd asked him to bring pizza...

"And?" Shay prompted.

"She asked me to bring pizza and beer for three people—me, her, and her brother."

"Rock on." Shay lifted a hand to offer a fist bump.

Braxton obliged absently. "Rock on what?"

"She's introducing you to her brother, dude! That's a good sign."

"I've already met her brother."

"Oh." Shay tilted her head back, studying the sound-absorbing drop-tile ceiling. "Huh. Okay, so maybe she...Nope, nevermind. I got nothing."

"You're helpful," Braxton muttered.

She grinned at him. "I know, right?"

He gave her a flat look. "That was my sarcastic voice."

He made arrangements for the pizza, then tried to focus on clearing up little five-minute tasks until it was time to leave. He picked up the pizza and beer on his way to Broad Ripple, only realizing after the fact that he'd forgotten to ask what Chloe and Martin liked. He gave a mental shrug. They'd have to put up with Sun King.

Traffic in Broad Ripple was bumper to bumper, as usual for the afternoon rush. Braxton kept checking the dash clock as he tapped his fingers against the steering wheel. He was going to be late.

That turned out not to matter. When he pulled up on the street in front of Martin Cole's place, he didn't see Chloe's car parked there, and he definitely didn't see the classic purple Camaro that Martin drove. Braxton switched off the ignition and settled in to wait. As he did, he scanned the area, looking for anyone who might be watching the apartment. No one looked out of place, though. There were a couple of pedestrians, but one was a jogger who was quickly out of sight, and the other was a harried-looking woman carrying two reusable grocery bags.

A black sedan pulled up a few minutes later and parked behind him. To his surprise, Chloe got out from behind the wheel. The passenger side opened to reveal a pretty Latina woman with blue-streaked hair. Braxton got out of his car, frowning for a moment before he remembered Chloe's remark that her car was out of commission.

"What happened to your car?" he asked.

"Broke down on US 31," Chloe said. "Come on, let's go inside. It's getting chilly out here. Oh. Celi, this is Braxton Wolfe. Braxton, Celia Ruiz—my partner Jake's sister."

They shook hands and then followed Chloe into the apartment. She scooped Whizz into her arms before he could trip Braxton, who put the pizza and beer on the table. "Shouldn't we have gotten enough pizza for your brother, too?" he asked.

"Oh, Celi's going home as soon as Jake gets here," Chloe said. She glanced from Celia to Braxton, her fingers twining around each other. "But we have time to tell you what happened."

Braxton listened in rising fury as Chloe told him about the brake failure, her police report style narrative punctuated by animated interruptions from Celia. Braxton got the distinct feeling that Celia hadn't thought about the wider context of Chloe's brake failure, so he bit back his temper. Maybe Chloe wasn't mentioning it to keep from scaring her. But when Chloe reached the end, she sat back in her chair and glanced at Celia, her brows drawing together.

"So here's the thing, Celi," she said. "I asked Rick to take a look while he was hooking the car up for the tow. He confirmed my suspicions." She licked her lips. "My brake lines were cut. Someone tried to kill me. Again."

The blood drained from Celia's face and she stared at Chloe. After a moment she looked at Braxton. He nodded slightly and she turned back to Chloe. "Because of the case?" she asked, twisting her fingers together. "Because of Braxton's case?"

"Yeah," he said. "I'm sorry." He looked over at Chloe. "I'm sorry for dragging you into this."

Her eyebrows went up. "You didn't drag me into anything," she said. "Cody Wethering shot me. I was already in it when you showed up at the hospital."

It was a good point, but it didn't make him feel any better. "But I kept you involved," he said. "I should have known better. You'd already been hurt enough. I shouldn't have kept you involved."

Chloe's brows snapped together. "Excuse me?" Her voice had an edge to it. "This is my job, Braxton, same as yours. I thought we'd already had this conversation. Would you apologize to Blake for involving *him* in one of your cases?"

Braxton tilted his head to one side. "I would, actually." He kept his voice mild. He wasn't angry at *her*, just at the situation, and he didn't want to pick a fight he didn't mean to. "And you can't really blame me for wanting to protect you. Even if I rationally know you're more than capable of protecting yourself, and I know that it's your job to get involved in situations like this, I'm not an entirely rational being." And he had to admit to himself, at least, that some of the wolfy instincts didn't help with that. Chloe was rapidly becoming someone he considered pack.

And that wasn't terrifying at all, he thought.

Chloe sighed, interrupting his thoughts. "I can't blame you, but I don't have to encourage it," she grumbled, and propped her elbow on the table. "So, okay. Our asshole hasn't given up on me, which means the only way to make him stop is to catch him."

Celia was shaking her head. "You guys are seriously not freaked out enough about this."

Braxton glanced at her. She was picking at her fingernail polish. He gave her what he hoped was a gentle smile. "It really is part of the job," he said. "It isn't that you ever really get used to it, but you learn how to cope with it. Granted, most of us aren't used to being targeted specifically, but we all know when we take on the badge that we're choosing to step into danger on a daily basis."

Celia sighed. "Well, you better hope Jake knows that, too, because he's going to be here any minute."

"Yeah, and we need to break this news to him and get you guys out the door—no offense—before my

246

brother gets home, or it'll get ugly," Chloe agreed. "He'll take it worse than Jake."

"Seriously," Celia said. She looked at Braxton. "Have you met Martin? He's awesome, but just a little uptight about some things."

Braxton nodded. "I've met him." He wondered if it was hypervigilance associated with PTSD. It wasn't really his business, but considering that Martin had spent three years in Kandahar Province, it was logical. *And if that's the case, it's also understandable,* he thought. *Not to mention Chloe being the only family he has left.*

"Want some pizza?" Chloe asked Celia, who shook her head. Braxton thought Chloe was trying to divert the conversation, so he asked Celia what she did for a living. That topic led into her hobbies, which kept them occupied until the doorbell rang. A moment later, Jake Ruiz entered the kitchen.

"So you want to tell me why I had to drive all the way up here to pick Celi up?" he asked Chloe. "And maybe where your car is parked?"

Chloe sighed and slid a can of beer in front of the empty chair at the table. "You're going to want to sit down while I explain this."

Jake took the news much worse than Braxton had expected. His face was red before Chloe even got to the point where her tow truck guy said the brake lines had been cut. By the time she finished the whole story, Jake was on his feet again and pacing the kitchen. When Chloe fell silent, he stood with his back to them for a moment, then let out a sharp breath. He spun around and glared at Chloe.

"Did you ever think, for one instant, that maybe you shouldn't be out gallivanting around in public with innocent people?"

Chloe arched an eyebrow at him. "Gallivanting? Really?"

"You think this is funny?" he snapped, and that made her scowl.

"No, actually, I don't think it's funny, Jake. I don't think any of this is funny, especially the part where I'm homeless and almost died! But I'm also not going to let this asshole ruin every aspect of my life. I have things I need to get on with—"

"And you don't have to drag my baby sister into it!" he broke in.

"Come on, Jacobo," Celia began, but he rounded on her. "You stay out of this," he snarled, and she was left blinking at him in silence.

"I haven't even been working the case for like two weeks," Chloe said. "How was I supposed to know he hadn't just given up or switched MOs or something? He could have thought I was—"

"No!" Jake shouted. "Just—no, Chloe." He wiped a hand down his face and took a deep breath. When he spoke again, he was calmer, but just barely. His voice was still hard. "Leave Celi out of it. Leave Lucia out of it. Until you deal with your ghosts and Wolfe gets his case closed, just leave my family out of this." He speared Celi with a look. "Come on, Celi." And he stormed out.

Celia had recovered from her shock and wore a look of disgusted disbelief. "Don't be an ass, Jacobo," she called after him, raising her voice. "You don't get to control my life!" She sighed and looked at Chloe. "I'm sorry, C. I'll get him out of here before your brother gets home. And no, I *don't* blame you. I'll text you later." She followed her brother out of the room, leaving Braxton and a shellshocked-looking Chloe.

Braxton gave her an awkward smile. "Your brother's going to be *worse?*"

Chloe gave a laugh that sounded shaky. "I'm glad I didn't offer him any pizza," she mumbled.

Braxton shifted his chair over so he could put an arm around her. "He wasn't fair. You didn't ask to be targeted. And he ought to know this is the job."

Chloe sniffled and leaned her head against his shoulder. "No, I should've guessed I'd be dangerous to the people around me."

Braxton sighed. He didn't know what to say that would make her feel better and not be empty comfort. Or worse, untrue. "I'm sorry, Chloe," he murmured.

She shook her head against his shoulder but didn't say anything. She stayed there, and Braxton drew some comfort from the fact that he must be making her feel a little better. He resolved to go over every aspect of the case again. They needed to solve this, and they needed to solve it now. He ought to call Elliott—Ell's homicide was tangled up in all this, after all, and another pair of eyes on the evidence couldn't hurt. But that could wait until Chloe didn't need him here.

* * *

Chloe let her eyes drift closed for a few minutes. Braxton's arm was warm around her, and she couldn't deny it felt good to have someone strong to lean on right now. She was exhausted. She'd done her best to hide it from Celi, because she didn't want to frighten Celi more than was necessary, but between the rush of adrenaline and the hassle of getting the car towed and getting a rental, she wanted to have a good stiff drink and curl up with her cat for the night.

"We have to have missed something," Chloe said. "I was telling Jake the truth—it's been so quiet since the Black Cat break-in that I haven't been poking around at all. I mean, I made a couple of phone calls, but that's it."

Braxton hummed thoughtfully, the sound a pleasant rumble in her ear. "Okay, so whoever this guy is, he's either following you, or he has an inside line on the investigation somehow."

"Oh, *hell*," she said, and straightened up. They stared at each other for a few heartbeats, but then Chloe said, "No. It can't be anyone inside. For one thing, I trust the guys I work with. For another, I've been on medical leave, so none of them know anything about this except Jake, and I trust him more than I do anyone but Martin."

The tightness around Braxton's eyes eased a little and he nodded. "Good," he said. "So whoever it is, if they know about the investigation, they know about it some other way."

"So following me," she said, and leaned on the table to prop her forehead in her hand. She hadn't seen anyone following her, but then, she hadn't been looking hard for that. Although Braxton had initially made her nervous when he'd made the remark about her having a firearm on her in Broad Ripple, and they had talked about Wethering's partner having an eye on her, she'd never seriously considered the idea of someone tailing her.

"I'll be more careful," she said. "I'll stay alert to anyone who might look suspicious."

"Maybe you *should* lay off for a while," Braxton mused. "You're still on leave, right? You could get out of town for a few days, relax on a beach somewhere. Take your brother with you."

"And that leaves no one watching your back," Chloe retorted. "Or Jake's. Or Martin's. Doesn't work for me. Anyway, I told you, I *have* been laying off for a while. So there was no reason for the guy to have contacted me." It was a simplification, but she couldn't imagine what Braxton would say if she tried to tell him about the ghosts.

"Maybe the guy doesn't like Catholics," Braxton said. That made Chloe grin involuntarily.

"Well, look," she said after a couple of minutes. "I'm not going to back off. I haven't been getting anywhere on it, but he must think I am. I'm not going to let him hurt people I care about just to save my own skin."

Braxton looked away, but she could see that he was smiling.

"What?" she demanded.

He shook his head. "Just glad to hear I'm someone you care about," he said, still not looking at her. The words made her catch her breath, but she couldn't deny it. Didn't even want to deny it. She *did* care.

When he turned back a moment later, his expression was serious. "But be careful, Chloe. Whoever the guy is, he's a puzzle. He's good at burglaries and bad at hiding bodies, but he—or his partner—managed to burn your house down just fine, not to mention cutting the brake line. And don't take any stupid risks."

She shook her head. "I promise. No stupid risks." She was tempted to make a smartass remark about whether or not there was any such thing as a smart risk, but she couldn't bring herself to do it. She couldn't look away from his eyes, and there was a softness around his lips that made her want to kiss him.

That was, of course, when Martin got home. Chloe straightened, and Braxton did too, which made Chloe wonder if his thoughts had been following the same line as hers. She cleared her throat and got up to get plates for the pizza.

"Let me handle him, okay? I'm not going to bring it up right away." She was relieved when Braxton nodded.

Martin came into the kitchen looking confused. "Clo? Who's here?"

"You remember Braxton," she said.

Martin nodded to Braxton, "Yeah. How's it going?"

While they exchanged pleasantries, Chloe took the opportunity to open a can of beer and set it at Martin's usual place. "Supper's courtesy of Braxton tonight," she said, giving Martin a smile. "Sit."

He looked distracted for a moment, then sat. Then there they were, the three of them sitting at the kitchen table, Chloe turning a beer can around and around in her hands while Braxton and her brother talked about the Indy Eleven. She'd suggested the pizza and beer mostly for Martin's benefit. She wasn't hungry, but she forced herself to eat two slices of pizza. Martin and Braxton finished off the rest of the pizza without any trouble. By the time the pizza was finished, they had trailed off into a silence that was a lot more comfortable than she'd been expecting. They sipped their drinks and gazed sort of vacantly at the table.

Finally Martin sighed and shoved his chair back enough to slouch down. "Okay, I'm not stupid. Either you two are announcing your elopement to Vegas, which knowing Chloe isn't very likely, or you've got some bad news you're just putting off telling me."

Chloe felt her face get hot, but she wasn't sure if it was for the eloping remark or the fact that he'd caught them out. She and Braxton looked at each other, then she sighed. "Okay," she said, and laid out the entire situation. Martin listened in silence until she was finished, then he got up and walked out of the kitchen.

Braxton stared after him, but Chloe shook her head. "He'll come back in a minute," she said. "He's just more pissed off than I expected." She paused, considering. "Or scared. But I'm betting on pissed off.

He's actually a lot better at controlling his temper than I am. He'll go be pissed for a minute, then get his temper under control so he can come back and discuss it rationally." She shrugged and finished her beer.

After a while Chloe got up and started the kettle. She didn't need more beer, but tea would be good. By the time the tea was brewing, Martin was back at the table, his expression hard.

"So what do we do?" he asked.

She gawped at him for a minute, then finally put the empty kettle down on the stove. "*We* do nothing," she said. "You're a mechanic. And I love you, but you are *not* getting involved in this. I ought to be sending you to Florida for a week."

"Maybe you ought to be serving and protecting, you slacker," he suggested, the faint traces of a smirk on his face.

Chloe mock-glared at him, though his teasing made her think things would be okay. "Maybe you ought to show some respect to the girl who almost died in the line of duty," she said. To her surprise, that wiped the smirk away.

"Who *did* die in the line of duty," Martin corrected, his voice low.

Oh yeah. It wasn't that she had forgotten that. She just didn't think of it that way, since she was still walking around and breathing. But Braxton hadn't known about that. He sucked in a sharp breath. She and Martin turned to look at him. Braxton was staring at them, his golden eyes narrowed. "What did you say?"

Chloe groaned and put a hand over her face.

It was Martin who answered. "After Cody Wethering shot Chloe, she died. Not permanently, obviously. They revived her in the ambulance before they even got to the hospital. But technically, she did die in the line of duty." He paused, and Chloe found herself afraid to look up. "She's been a little weird ever since, honestly."

Damn it. "Thanks a lot, you little shit," she muttered, and got up to pour them some tea.

"Weird how?" Braxton asked. She couldn't bring herself to look at him.

"Just weird. Jumpy. You know." Martin shrugged. "Hypervigilant."

Chloe carried a cup over to the table for Braxton and cuffed Martin on the back of the head as she passed, provoking a surprised yelp. When she returned to the table with her own cup, Martin was rubbing his head.

"I've never been shot, but I'd say that's probably normal," Braxton said. "After something like that, you're always expecting the worst out of situations. It just takes a little time to start feeling secure in life again."

He wasn't looking at Chloe as he said it, and she wondered if he'd realized that her brother had come back from Afghanistan with PTSD. Martin could joke all he wanted about her being weird since the shooting. She knew he understood, because she knew he was living it himself. Maybe Braxton got that, too.

Martin grunted and took the pizza box off the table.

Chloe cleared her throat. "So..." she said, running her finger back and forth along the edge of the table. The blue polish was mostly chipped off her nails. She licked her lips. Martin wasn't going to like what she had to say next. "You need to take a week off. You need to go get a hotel room somewhere that isn't here."

"And leave you here alone? Like hell," Martin growled. He folded his arms across his chest.

"Please," Chloe said, giving him a beseeching look. "I need you to be safe, Marty. Please."

He glowered at her. She knew she was playing dirty. He had stopped being a Marty when he was ten, and the only time he'd allowed it after that was just after their parents died. But she needed him safe. She'd play as dirty as it took to protect him.

"She shouldn't stay here either," Braxton put in. He looked at Chloe. "None of you should. I have a guest apartment in my basement. You and Whizz could come stay there until we get this bastard."

Some part of Chloe noted that their unknown subject had graduated from 'yahoo' to 'bastard' in Braxton's lexicon. That probably meant something. Then again, the fact that he was offering to let her stay at his place...that meant a heck of a lot more.

"I..." Chloe hesitated, looking back at him. She wanted to. She *really* wanted to. But that made her think maybe she shouldn't.

"If you don't go, I'm not going," Martin said, his voice flat. He leaned against the sink, and Chloe knew she could count on him to be every inch as stubborn as she was.

She sighed. "All right. Thank you, Braxton. I'll get some stuff together and come over tomorrow afternoon. I have my final checkup in the morning, and then I'm getting my badge back."

Braxton looked like he was poised to argue, but he slumped back in his chair and nodded. "Good. Okay."

Martin came over and pushed his chair in under the table. "If I'm going to go into hiding for a week, I have some calls to make. And stuff to pack." He glared at Braxton. "You'd better not let anything happen to my big sister. And you'd better solve this damn case *soon*." He walked out.

"Dumbass," she hurled after him, which wasn't the most eloquent of insults. "Can you believe he's my *younger* brother?" she muttered, glancing at Braxton as she tried to straighten her hair.

"Sure. Younger brothers are always a pain." His expression was deadpan, and she couldn't help laughing.

"How would you know? You don't have any."

He shook his head. "Elliott has two younger sisters, so I know how it goes. They were as good as siblings, really." She could hear the rasp of whiskers as he scratched his jaw. "Chloe, I know you said you haven't been working on the case, but you'll be really careful, right? I... I don't want to see you get hurt." He made a face. "Well, more than you already have."

"Don't worry," she said. "I don't really want to see me get hurt any more than I already am."

He nodded, his eyes crinkling at the corners. It was an expression she was starting to recognize on him. Not quite a smile, but just as good, because she could see the humor and warmth in the expression. Man, she really had it bad.

She managed to turn the conversation back to siblings, and more generally to family, which led into Braxton telling stories about his father, who had been a Civil War buff as well as an elder at his church. She didn't make the connection until he explained he'd been named after Braxton Bragg, who was apparently a Confederate General.

"Didn't do me any favors, though," Braxton said ruefully. "Not even with the history teachers, because Bragg wasn't all that popular a general. A lot of people actually blamed the guy for losing the war in the western theater. He technically won the battle of Perryville, but the Confederacy still had to withdraw. And with Indiana being a Union state and me being named after a Confederate..."

Chloe grinned. "You know, I can't say I'd ever heard of Braxton Bragg."

Braxton shrugged. "I don't suppose many people have. Ulysses Grant told a story about him that was sort of amusing, though. Apparently at some point Bragg was serving as quartermaster somewhere, and was also a unit commander. As unit commander, he wrote up papers requesting something or other in the way of supplies. Then when he was doing his quartermaster duties, he denied the request. So the next day he took the issue to his superior officer, who said something like, 'My God, General Bragg, you've quarreled with the entire army, and now you're quarreling with yourself!'"

He was grinning, his expression almost carefree. Chloe laughed as much because of his enjoyment of the story as because it was funny. "I've known guys who would be capable of that," she remarked.

"No kidding. I think there are some in my direct chain of command." He sipped his tea and shook his head.

They lapsed into silence. She listened to the sound of his breathing, which was slow and even. She wondered how it was even possible to feel so comfortable with someone and yet so unsettled by him at the same time. The kitchen was warmly lit by the lights over the sink and oven; having the overhead light off made it feel more intimate. Chloe felt her shoulders relaxing as they sat there, both of them looking at the table. Or at least, she thought he was looking at the table, until she lifted her eyes for a quick glance at Braxton.

He was looking back at her. Her stomach jolted and she gave him a quick smile that didn't feel right. There was too much affection in his gaze. Too much... familiarity. Like he knew her better than other people. Chloe swallowed and looked back down at her tea. It didn't feel safe. But she liked it.

Chloe forced her gaze back up to meet his. She hadn't had any problem leaning on him earlier. Why was it so hard to let her attraction to him show? Braxton's eyebrows and lips slanted up when she looked at him, and then he moved. His chair scraped loudly against the linoleum floor and she had just a moment to panic that Martin would hear it. Then Braxton's mouth was against hers.

She sucked in a breath through her nose and let her lips part against his. Heat raced through her from the top of her head to her feet. Braxton's lips were warm and slightly chapped. His whiskers scratched against her chin. She felt one of his hands in her hair, cradling the back of her head.

He didn't deepen the kiss. He pulled back just a fraction, just enough to breathe, then he kissed her again. Her heart felt like it was going to jump through her skin, and the new scar on her neck felt tight with the way her pulse raced. She wanted to put her arms around him and she wanted to push him away. Instead she curled her hand around the back of his arm and kissed him again.

In the back of the house, Martin's bathroom door shut loudly. It was enough to send her and Braxton both backwards away from each other. In the silence that followed, she could hear the tap turn on. After a couple of moments the water heater flared to wakefulness in the laundry room. Chloe couldn't stop looking at Braxton, whose golden eyes had lit with desire. She also couldn't catch her breath.

Braxton sighed and looked away. "I should go," he said. His voice was rough. Chloe didn't know if he expected her to protest, but she didn't. No way in hell was she going to make out with someone while her brother was home.

"Be careful," she said. Her voice didn't sound right. Too soft, too breathless. She pressed her lips together and looked at him until he looked back.

"You be careful," he replied. There was a frightening tenderness in his eyes as he lifted a hand and touched her cheek. Then he moved past her to the front door.

She got up and followed him. When they got to the door, neither of them seemed to want to say goodbye. Finally Chloe leaned down and brushed her lips against his. "I'll see you tomorrow."

After she closed the door behind him, Chloe leaned against the door until she heard Martin's shower turn off. She made herself finish cleaning the kitchen and go get ready for bed. Tomorrow could worry about itself.

* * *

Two days after his Day of the Dead failure, Victor Garza woke with a pounding headache, a dry mouth, and new resolve. He refused to give up on Alita. The amulet had failed him; very well, there were other avenues he could pursue. There would be no more drinking himself into a stupor over his failure.

He would go back to Fiefel and Landsberg. Fiefel's seminal work on thanatology, *The Meaning of Death*, had given Victor direction before. He had spent most of yesterday working his way through a large bottle of whiskey and rereading the poems of death and mourning he had collected over the past two months.

He'd had Deyonte bring several new books from the Black Cat Bookshop to add to the collection. Percy Bysshe Shelley, Gerard Manley Hopkins, John Donne, William Cullen Bryant...they had not comforted him, but they had sharpened his grief until he broke down. He had needed that catharsis in order to think clearly again.

But now it was time to regroup. He jerked the Thanatos amulet from around his neck and stared down at it. It was tempting to destroy it, since it had failed him. But he couldn't risk offending any of the powers, whether it had come to his aid or not. Besides, there was something about it...

When he looked up again, Cody Wethering was sitting on the corner of his desk, smirking at him. The ghost's bloodshot eyes bored into him. Victor clenched one fist, where it was hidden beneath the desk, and stood up. He wouldn't give Cody the satisfaction of railing against him. Especially not after last night.

Last night, deep in his cups, he had resorted to begging Cody to bring him news of his daughter, or, failing that, to carry a message to her that Victor would wake her soon. "I will unlock death," he had proclaimed, "if I have to go to hell itself to do it."

Wethering had laughed at him. Laughed.

Victor wanted him dead. Permanently dead, and banished or exorcised or whatever it was one did with annoying phantoms.

"You're not wanted," Victor told Cody now, his voice cold. Then he strode to the other side of the room and fished the crumpled paper from his jacket pocket.

That woman who had appeared in the cemetery while Victor and Fletcher were leaving had known far too much. Until Victor knew for sure what direction he was to travel next, he would investigate her.

The crumpled paper turned out to be a business card. THE MIND'S EYE OCCULT READINGS, it said, and listed an address in the historic Old Northside neighborhood of Indianapolis. How odd, he thought. For some reason, he wouldn't have expected it to be in that neighborhood, with its nineteenth century houses and prestigious history.

There was no phone number. Perhaps, he mused snidely, the woman believed she would anticipate visitors through her occult talent.

Victor showered and shaved before leaving the house. He had been careful not to let anyone see him fall apart, aside from Fletcher. He had already called his office and informed his secretary he wouldn't be in. He had no active cases, though he did have several awaiting trial; they could wait without him.

He arrived at The Mind's Eye shortly after four. The business was in a tall Victorian, painted purple with butter-yellow gingerbread trim and accents in green. It reminded Victor of a pansy or violet. He walked up the front steps to the wide front porch and hesitated.

Before he'd decided whether or not to go in, the door opened. Standing before him was the woman from the other night. She wore jeans and a black sweater. Her hair was pulled back again, and today he could see it was a light red-gold.

The woman smiled. "Mr. Garza. How lovely to see you again."

"How did you know what I was doing?" he blurted, and then felt his face get hot. He couldn't remember the last time he'd spoken without thinking like that.

She folded her arms across her chest. "Everyone who has any sensitivity at all knows what you're doing. You haven't exactly been subtle."

"I just want my daughter back," he protested.

"Oh, I know. How did the Thanatos pendant work for you? Congratulations on that, by the way, there are parties who have been looking for that for years. However did you learn it was hiding at the old Greek's pawn shop?"

"Research," Victor said, feeling a pang of pride, even though the pendant hadn't worked.

"If the most powerful magic-users in Indianapolis couldn't find it through their research, how did you manage it?" she scoffed.

"Through a different kind of research, I imagine," he said, straightening a little and letting a smirk creep into his voice. "I'm a lawyer. I searched wills and property records."

She lifted her head, a touch of respect coming into her eyes. Good. Victor wasn't used to being mocked. She tilted her head, studying him.

"You're being haunted by an angry young man," she said.

Cody flickered into visibility further down the porch. Had she made him show himself? Or had he just stopped hiding when he heard her mention him? Or perhaps he hadn't been there until then. Perhaps she had summoned him.

Victor gave a dismissive shrug. "I'll get rid of him eventually."

She seemed to listen for a moment, then said, "He accuses you of injustice. He calls others to bring misfortune on you."

Victor narrowed his eyes. "He was stupid as well as ungrateful."

"I could banish him for you."

"He's not worth the trouble," Victor said, and felt a stab of satisfaction as Cody went still at those words.

The woman shook her head, her lips curving in a reluctant smile. "You don't go out of your way to make friends, do you?"

Victor arched an eyebrow. "Why don't we take this discussion inside, Ms…"

"You may call me Teresia." She looked at him for a long moment, then tipped her head, indicating he should follow her.

"Would you like tea?" she asked as they made their way down the hall.

Victor wouldn't, but he thought he should attempt some manners after her observation of a moment ago. "Yes, thank you."

She led him to a kitchen with tall cabinets. A spaniel of some kind reclined on a rug in front of a fireplace. It thumped its tail when Teresia came in. She cupped her hand on the top of its head and crooned wordlessly to it.

"Since you know so much, why did the amulet fail?" Victor asked.

Teresia gave him an amused look as she walked to the stove. "You were too cheap, Mr. Garza."

He watched her in bewilderment as she poured two cups of tea. She sweetened her own and added a dash of milk. She dropped one sugar cube in his cup, and Victor thought about protesting that he didn't like things sweet. She gave him a knowing look. "You need sweetening up."

"Too cheap," he repeated, to get her back on track.

"Too cheap," she confirmed. She carried the tea back to the table and sat down, indicating he should sit across from her. "You can't simply ask and take from the god of the underworld, even if you have Thanatos on your side."

"Then what—" he began, but she cut him off.

"Sacrifice, Mr. Garza. Magic this powerful demands a very steep price. You must be willing to sacrifice deeply if you wish to bring someone back from the dead."

Victor leaned forward. "I will sacrifice *anything*."

"And if it isn't yours to give up?" she asked. She lifted her teacup and watched him over the brim.

"Immaterial," he dismissed.

She took a slow sip, still watching him. Her eyes were a strange purple-blue that mesmerized him. "And what if the price demanded of you…is your daughter's love?"

Victor stared at her, not understanding.

"Right now," Teresia said, "she is dead, but she died loving you. What you must do to get her back…most people would consider it evil."

Victor sat back slowly in his chair. "But you don't?"

She gave him a slow smile. "I am not most people."

He considered. It was true that he hadn't even blinked before killing Wethering. He had ordered Fletcher to take care of Chloe Cole without a further thought. He would do what he must, and he didn't think that made him a bad man—not when he did it all for his daughter. "How is killing Wethering to keep him from ruining my chances at bringing Alita back any different from killing someone to keep my daughter alive?" he said finally.

Teresia laughed. "How easily you rationalize!" she said, delighted. "But I'm afraid Alita may see it very differently."

Victor clenched his jaw. "I'll take that chance," he said. "If she comes back, I can deal with her being angry with me. Better angry and alive than dead and unable to feel anything."

Teresia arched an eyebrow. "How do you know what the dead feel or don't feel?"

He was tired of beating around the bush. "Just tell me what to do." He resisted the urge to pick up his teacup and fidget with it. What if she refused to help him? But why would she have offered the other night, if she wasn't willing to help?

Teresia sipped her tea and shrugged elegantly. "You must choose someone to offer as a substitute for Alita. Someone much like her. Someone loved by their parents. Someone talented and popular. It must not be an unequal trade."

Victor finally took a sip of his tea. It tasted like wet leaves. "And once I've picked?"

"You and I will go to Alita's grave. We will use the Thanatos amulet. We will replace Alita's risen body with that of your sacrifice."

"Good," Victor said. He drained his cup and stood. "Do you have a phone number?"

"Of course." Teresia produced another business card. This one had a phone number on it. She smiled at his look of annoyance. "I wanted to make you come to me," she said. "I had to know just how important this was to you."

Victor glowered at her. "I'll call you once I've selected my sacrifice."

Teresia smiled and stood. She walked him down the hall. Just before she closed the door behind him, she said, "Before the next full moon, Mr. Garza, or it will be too late."

CHAPTER 13

Braxton pulled into his neighborhood after work and was surprised to find Tara's Jeep parked in his driveway. He parked on the street and walked up to the house, where Tara and a very bloody Murphy were sitting on the front porch. Murphy sat hunched over, one arm curled around his stomach.

"What the hell happened to you?" Braxton blurted.

Murphy glared at him.

Tara answered for him. "Someone bigger and tougher."

"Shut up," Murphy muttered.

Braxton frowned, studying Murphy's injuries. He had a black eye, a puffy split lip, and lots of scrapes and bruises. When he lifted a hand to wipe his mouth, Braxton saw that his knuckles were bloodied. And from the way he was sitting, he probably had some bruised or cracked ribs.

Tara nudged Murphy. It didn't look hard, but it drew a grunt of pain. "Tell him," she ordered.

Murphy sighed, glowering at the sidewalk. "Marcineau wasn't working alone."

Braxton felt a chill run through him, followed by a flash of hot rage. "What?"

"Some necromancer or warlock or something was helping him," Murphy said with a shrug.

Braxton stared at him, his pulse jumping. Murphy glanced up through the fringe of his hair and twisted his lips unhappily.

"After the way things went with your dad, I knew it wasn't enough to stop Marcineau. I've been looking for the guy. I don't remember much from the night I was bit, but I know there was some kind of magic holding me. I couldn't move. I don't mean I was too scared to run. I couldn't even twitch a finger. And I've learned since then that wolves can't do that."

Braxton cleared his throat. "No, we can't." He felt like the earth was tilting. He'd thought the conflict with Marcineau had happened because the pack drove him out. What if Marcineau had other motives?

After a moment, Braxton shook himself and straightened. "We'd better get you cleaned up." He stepped past them and unlocked the front door. "Come on."

They followed him into the first floor bathroom, where he hauled out the first aid kit and went to work cleaning up Murphy's face.

"There's more," Tara said. Her voice was imperious. "Tell him all of it, Murph."

Murphy flinched as Braxton dabbed some wound wash against a raw cheekbone. "I was trying to find the magician. But she found me first."

"She?" Braxton tensed.

"I don't know her name, but I got a good look at her. I know her scent, and I know the feel of her magic. Bitch!" he spat.

"No, that's me," Tara said, a tinge of humor creeping into her voice.

Murphy gave a snort of reluctant laughter.

Braxton dabbed on some antibiotic ointment and moved on to the next wound. They were silent for a time as he worked on Murphy's knuckles. There was no bandaging most of the injuries, though there was a cut across Murphy's left eyebrow that he thought would probably need a butterfly bandage to keep from scarring.

As he worked, Braxton considered what should be done. There were plenty of magic-users in Indianapolis, and he didn't have a problem with most of them. The vast majority were benevolent types, or at the very least, petty in their selfish use of magic. People using their talent to make ends meet didn't bother him, as long as they weren't hurting anyone else. But now there was a magic-user who had hurt one of his pack. And not only that, but she had helped *turn* someone. It was inexcusable. Something would have to be done.

Finally he rocked back on his heels and rubbed a hand over his face. "Murphy," he said, trying to make his voice gentle but firm. "You aren't a lone wolf anymore. I appreciate what you were trying to do, but that isn't how we operate. We're creatures of the pack. We work better together."

Murphy met his gaze for half a second and then looked down. "I just...I owe you. I couldn't—"

"Yes," Braxton interrupted, "you could. We don't keep score. Not in this pack."

"Which is what I've been *trying* to tell you," Tara put in, her voice sardonic. Murphy's scowl deepened, but his shoulders relaxed.

"All right," Braxton said after a moment. "Tara, can you finish patching him up? We're pack, and this is pack business. The pack will deal with it together. I have to make a few calls."

Which was, of course, when Chloe arrived.

* * *

Chloe had just been finishing up at the police station when her cell phone rang. The caller ID read MASQUERADE LLC. Frowning, Chloe answered.

"Officer Cole? My name is Rosemary Malher. I'm one of the artists who exhibits at the gallery in Franklin. Trudy said you wanted people to call if we thought of anything."

Trudy, Chloe remembered, was the gallery owner. "Yes," she said. "Thank you for calling. I know this must have been very difficult for you."

"It has been, but at least I'm insured. Some of the other artists weren't."

"What is it that you thought of?" Chloe asked. She pulled out a pen and pocket notebook from her purse.

"Well, I have no idea if this is any help to you at all, but someone contacted me several weeks before the robbery. He wanted to commission something. I was fascinated by the project, but my sister has been ill and

I just couldn't commit to it at that time. He said he'd seen my art at the gallery, and he really liked a lot of the pieces, but none of them quite fit what he needed."

"Okay, and did he say what he needed?" Chloe wasn't sure how this was supposed to help the case, but she was willing to be open minded.

"That's the interesting part," Rosemary replied. "He wanted something that would symbolize the unlocking of death."

Chloe blinked. "The unlocking of death," she repeated. "I'm not even sure I know what that means."

"Well, a lot of the pieces I make are tied into the cycle of life. I started out with faeries and bats and witches, and they're still fun," Rosemary chuckled. "Honestly, they sell well, which is why I keep doing them. But as I've matured in my art, my main focus has been life, death, the unknown. Angels and Celtic trees of life and infinity symbols and grim reapers and skulls and Anubis and... The cycle of life." Rosemary's voice took on an air of mystery that made Chloe roll her eyes.

"Okay," Chloe prompted.

There was a pause. "Well, the man wanted something to unlock death. He was really specific. He wanted poppies and a sword and a torch... He even offered to give me a sketch. I was a little surprised by that, because if I were designing something to unlock death, I would probably have gone with things like crosses and skulls and maybe a lock and key. I would have asked for more details if I'd actually taken the commission."

Chloe started nodding thoughtfully as the woman described it. The more she talked, the more Chloe got an idea of what sort of things might symbolize this unlocking of death the guy wanted.

"This sounds really specific," Chloe remarked. "Do you get commissions like that often?"

Rosemary sighed. "To be honest, I don't get a lot of commissions, period. And I really could have used this one. But I had to go to Ohio. My sister's a single mom with two teenagers. I don't know how she does it. I'm child-free by choice, and I could barely keep up with them, but she'd been working full-time and driving them to after-school activities for three weeks before her pneumonia was diagnosed." She laughed. "I was relieved to get back to my two Dobermans. I'll never complain about how much work they are again."

Chloe couldn't help but laugh. "I hear you."

"Anyway," Rosemary continued, "Annette recovered and I came home, but he hasn't called me back."

"And you can't call him?" Chloe said.

"That's the thing, he didn't give me his name. He wouldn't give me his name. That's part of why it stuck in my mind. He contacted me by phone, didn't leave a callback number. I really wanted to take his name and phone number, but he said it was better if I didn't. He *said* it was a surprise for his wife and he didn't want her accidentally finding out. I thought it was more likely a gift for his mistress and he just didn't want his wife knowing he had one. But then after the robbery... well, I got to thinking, because out of all the artists, I was the one who lost the most. And my prices are frankly more reasonable than some of the other people who exhibit there. I mean, I know it isn't exactly easy to walk out with a pilfered oil painting, compared to my pieces, which are much smaller. But honestly, I don't think my pieces were stolen for the price tag. Most of my pieces on exhibit there had to do with death, because it was so close to Halloween."

"When he called, did he say how he got your phone number?" Chloe asked.

"Oh, that's not hard. They have a stack of my business cards at the gallery, and he could have found me on my website too."

"Okay. I don't suppose you have a phone number from caller ID or anything?" It was too much to hope, and Chloe knew it. She would try to run the phone records, but that required a subpoena, and Chloe wasn't sure she had enough to get that.

"I don't like caller ID," Rosemary said loftily. "It's just not for me. I don't have a cell phone or microwave or anything like that. The passage of time is part of the life cycle. I tend to avoid things that exist just to speed life up."

"Right. Thank you very much for this information, Ms. Malher. I'll need to discuss it with Detective Wolfe, but in the event we have more questions for you, is it all right to contact you again?"

"Oh, by all means," she said. "I'm glad to do anything I can to help the authorities. I do hope you can catch whoever's been doing this. My insurance company isn't very happy about the claim I filed with them. It would be great to recover some of those pieces."

Not to mention bringing someone to justice for two murders so far, Chloe thought, though she knew it wasn't fair. Rosemary didn't know about the murders. "Thank you again, Ms. Malher."

This had to be their guy. Chloe wasn't sure how the pieces all fit together, but clearly someone was looking for a piece of art that fit his exact requirements. It didn't sound like an art collector, though Chloe would check with an art dealer to be sure her instinct was correct. For one thing, art collectors tended to go for paintings by people who were already dead, didn't they?

She frowned and checked her watch. It was almost five. Braxton would probably be on his way home soon, if he wasn't already. She could swing by her brother's place and pick up Whizz, then drive down to Avon. She chewed her lower lip. She hoped this was the right call. She could have gone to the hotel with Martin, but Braxton had made the offer, and Chloe trusted him despite herself. The traffic would be bumper to bumper on Raceway Road, but that would give her time to think over this new development.

By the time Chloe got to Braxton's neighborhood, she'd put in a couple of calls to art dealers and confirmed her suspicions; no one would steal the small jewelry-type pieces of a relatively obscure artist. The man wanted something to represent unlocking death. Chloe still wasn't quite sure what that meant, but she was willing to live in uncertainty for now. She would sleep on it, and probably wake up with ideas in the morning; in the meantime, she'd tell Braxton about it and see what he thought.

There was a bright red Jeep parked in Braxton's driveway, and his truck was parked on the street. She pulled up behind his truck, wondering if he had company. He had never mentioned a roommate.

She left Whizz's carrier on the floor of the front seat for the moment and went up to ring the doorbell. Inside the house, she heard cat claws skitter across the hardwood floor of the entryway. She waited for what felt like a long time, then pressed the doorbell again.

After another minute, she heard footsteps approaching. Braxton opened the door. He looked a little flustered. His hair was messy, like he'd been running his hand through it.

"Chloe, hi." He smiled at her, but it seemed strained. Chloe wondered what had happened between last night and this afternoon that she didn't know about.

"Hi," she said, giving him a curious look. "Is everything okay?"

"Of course!" Braxton said. "What's up?"

Her stomach jumped a little. "Uh. You were expecting me, right?"

"Of course," he said again. "Sorry, I was just a little…preoccupied. Sorry."

Chloe shook her head, deliberately relaxing her shoulders. "No problem. Hey, I came over a little early because I got a really interesting phone call this afternoon. I'm pretty sure I've got some new clues."

"Really?" Braxton's eyes lit up. "That's great."

Before he could say anything else, a woman's voice called from further inside the house. "Braxton?" The voice was followed by a gorgeous redhead with curves in all the right places. As she approached, she said, "Is that Elliott already? I thought—Oh." She stopped speaking when she saw Chloe. She took a few more steps to stand right behind Braxton, her shoulder bumping his. "Hello."

Chloe stared at the woman, eyes wide. Was this the owner of the red Jeep? It would certainly fit her. She looked sporty and fun-loving and entirely too sexy for Chloe to be happy she was here. Suddenly Braxton's ruffled hair brought another, less pleasant possibility to mind.

"Um. Hi." She heard her voice go up in a question and wanted to kick herself. She didn't own Braxton. Just because they'd gone out a couple of times—

Braxton broke in hastily. "Chloe, this is Tara Storm. Tara, this is Chloe Cole." He gave Chloe an earnest smile. "Tara's an old friend. And I met Chloe through work," he added to Tara.

"Chloe Cole…Chloe… Why does that name sound familiar?" Tara said. Her lips formed a tiny, thoughtful pout, and then she snapped her fingers. "I remember! You're that cop. The one who got shot in a robbery last month. I remember Elliott was seriously upset about that."

Chloe coughed. "I had no idea he cared so much," she said dryly.

"He really is a good guy, Chloe," Braxton said. His voice was low, his expression hopeful. "He's my best friend."

Tara glanced from Chloe to Braxton and back. "Am I interrupting something?"

"Kind of," Chloe began, just as Braxton said, "Not at all." There was an awkward silence.

Tara gave Braxton a bewildered look, then smiled faintly at Chloe. "So…it's nice to meet you, Chloe." She turned to Braxton. "I'll just go check on Murphy." Murphy? Someone else was here, then. Chloe felt a flash of embarrassment that she'd been jealous about Tara.

She started back down the hall, but until then, none of them had noticed the tall, slender young man coming down the hallway. He saw Chloe and stopped short.

Chloe bit the inside of her cheek to keep from swearing. He had a black eye and several abrasions on his face, as well as a butterfly bandage over one eyebrow. And he wore a suspicious, almost hostile, expression.

"Who's she?" he demanded, narrowing his eyes. "New member?"

"Member of what?" Chloe said, but Tara talked over her.

"She's Braxton's girlfriend," Tara said brightly.

Chloe stared at Tara, shocked that she didn't seem jealous or possessive at all. What the hell was going on here? Who *were* these people?

Murphy barked a laugh. "Elliott was right. It *was* a thing." Then he grunted and put a hand to his side.

"Murphy?" Tara said.

Murphy responded by doubling over, letting out a hoarse groan that sounded like it was ripped from him. He was panting suddenly, and Chloe could see his muscles twitching.

"Shit," Braxton said. "Tara, get him—"

Tara was already lunging to grab Murphy, but he pulled away from her, snarling. Chloe gasped at the feral sound.

Braxton glanced back at her, white-faced. "Chloe, can you give us a minute?"

At that moment, Murphy dropped to his hands and knees and let out another groan. This one drew out until it sounded almost like a howl. He lifted his head and glared at Chloe with eyes that were a hot, bloodshot yellow. He opened his mouth, baring his teeth at her—teeth that were much sharper than any human's should be.

Chloe stared at him, her mouth dropping open. What the hell was going on?

Murphy snarled and lunged for her, but Tara stuck out a foot, catching his ankle so he fell. He hit the ground with a yelp, and then curled into a fetal position. Then he began convulsing.

Chloe couldn't tear her eyes away from him. "Do something!" she implored. "Help him!"

Tara sighed. "There's nothing we can do to help at this point," she said.

"If he's having a seizure, you need to keep him from choking on his tongue," Chloe said. She took a step forward. If they weren't going to help him, she would.

Braxton's hand closed around her elbow. "Don't." He sounded desperately unhappy. "It'll be over in a minute. He'll be fine."

Chloe swung around to stare at him in horror. "How can you say that?" she demanded.

Braxton was looking up at her, lines of tension around his mouth. "I've seen this before," he said.

Chloe realized the pained noises from Murphy had changed. They were more like whimpers now. She started to turn, and Braxton's grip on her elbow tightened slightly.

"Please don't," he said softly.

She shot him another disbelieving look and jerked out of his grip. She turned to see how Murphy was doing.

Except Murphy wasn't there. Instead, a scruffy, skinny dog crouched in the hall, its belly pressed against the floor. It looked terrified, and a bloody gash over one eye was oozing blood. Tara swore.

"What the fuck?" Chloe breathed.

"Tara, get Murphy out of here," Braxton ordered.

Tara nodded and coaxed the dog—no, not a dog. It looked like a coyote. Or— Chloe stepped hard on the thought that was trying to surface. She stared in silence as Tara coaxed the—Murphy—back down the hallway and out of sight.

"Uh…" said Chloe. She let it trail off, at a loss.

"I know how this must look," Braxton said lamely.

"Oh, you have no idea," Chloe said. Mostly because she had no idea, either.

"I can explain." Braxton ran his hand through his hair.

"I'd love to hear it," Chloe said. She actually felt like she might pass out. Or maybe throw up. Or possibly start shouting. She folded her arms across her chest to hide the way her hands were shaking.

"Okay," Braxton said. He straightened up, looking determined suddenly. "Uh. Well." He gave her a despairing look, then sighed. "I'm a werewolf. Murphy and Tara are part of my pack."

* * *

There was a shocked silence. Chloe was staring at him like he'd said he came from the moon and ate souls. Which, for all he knew, might be what she actually thought. His heart was pounding so hard he was afraid she'd be able to hear it, even without werewolf hearing. Damn it all, why couldn't this have waited until they'd solved the case? Once things were a little more settled, he could have done this properly. Though he wasn't sure how one actually told one's significant other that one turned into a huge, hairy beast every twenty-eight days or so. He'd given the matter some thought over the years, but he'd always thought it was likely he'd end up with another werewolf as his partner.

Chloe had gone very pale. He wondered if she was going to faint. She looked like she believed him, but she also looked like she didn't want to believe him.

"That's not funny," she said.

"It's not meant to be," Braxton said apologetically.

She stared at him, letting her gaze slide all the way down his body before coming back up to meet his eyes. Braxton wished he could read something sexy into that, but he knew she wasn't checking him out. She was assessing him, looking for signs.

She fixed on his eyes. Braxton knew they were probably a brighter gold than she'd ever seen them. The amount of adrenaline flowing through him had his entire body primed for fight-or-flight. He took a couple of deep breaths to try to calm himself.

"Murphy was turned against his will about a year ago," he said. "Not by us! We live by a code. That's very important to me. To us. All of us. But there was someone who hated our pack, and…anyway, he just ran into one of the people who did it. That's why he's so beat up."

He stopped babbling and watched her, shifting his feet. He felt like he was going to throw up.

"Oh my God," she said. "'Werewolves of London.'" She looked like she didn't know whether to laugh, cry, or shout.

"A lot of people like that song," he said defensively.

"It's a little obvious." She was obviously trying to joke, but her voice shook.

"You never suspected, did you?"

"Oh, God," she moaned suddenly, tilting her gaze up to the ceiling. "*Werewolves*. First ghosts and now werewolves. What next? Unicorns? Leprechauns?"

Ghosts? Braxton opened his mouth to ask, but she cut him off.

"You really believe that, don't you? That you turn into a wolf? Or do you just *act* like a wolf once a month?"

Braxton sighed. He really hadn't wanted to do this. "Tara," he called. There was no way Braxton was going to get naked in front of Chloe, not like this, and Murphy didn't have enough control.

Tara must have been eavesdropping. She padded back down the hallway already shifted into a gorgeous she-wolf. Her fur ranged from caramel and cream underneath to a deep russet along her back. She lifted her muzzle to scent the air and opened her mouth, flopping her tongue out. Then she bowed to Chloe. Braxton caught his breath. Chloe wouldn't know it, but Tara had just acknowledged Chloe's right to become alpha female. It wasn't really for Chloe, anyway; Tara had done it for Braxton.

He felt his face get hot. Were his feelings so transparent to everyone?

He lifted his gaze to Chloe's, and his embarrassment faded. She really looked like she was going to pass out now. She was staring at Tara, her mouth open. She must have felt Braxton watching her, because she met his gaze, her expression stricken. Then she jerked and looked past him down the hallway.

"Not you!" she exclaimed, and then she said. "This is too much. That's just the last fucking straw."

She spun on her heel and jerked the front door open. She was through it before Braxton could react. Tara barked at him and he darted after her.

"Chloe, wait!" he said, and she rounded on him.

"I didn't ask for *any* of this!" she said fiercely. "I don't want it! I had a nice life. I had my own house and a car that ran great and I loved my job. I hadn't died, I wasn't seeing things that aren't there, and I wasn't dating a fucking *werewolf!*"

"Let me explain," he said, but he could tell by her clenched fists and fighting stance that it was a lost cause.

"What is there to explain? You people *turn into wolves*." She hissed the last words, thankfully; he didn't want his neighbors overhearing this. "That is not okay. All of this is not okay. I am going home."

"Chloe—"

"Just leave me alone!" she shouted, and Braxton stopped following her. It hurt, and he knew some of his anger was because it hurt, but he wanted to punch something. He shoved his hands in his pockets.

"Fine," he muttered.

Her tires squealed as she pulled out.

He didn't know how long he'd been standing there, staring at the grass to keep from swearing or crying or something. He twitched when Murphy spoke behind him.

"Well. That was the most spectacular breakup I've ever witnessed," Murphy said. "You're out of whiskey."

CHAPTER 14

Chloe woke up the next morning cursing Braxton Wolfe and just about every man she'd ever known. She felt a little better after two cups of coffee, six strips of bacon, and four ibuprofen, but she still wasn't prepared to be charitable or even polite to Braxton.

She thought about collapsing into bed after she finished eating, but after brief consideration Chloe decided that one night of getting drunk and freaking out was all she was allowed. Besides, she really shouldn't be staying at Martin's place alone. He would flip out if he knew. Then again, she figured he'd flip out if he knew Braxton was a *werewolf*, so she thought that canceled out.

Still, she ought to be more careful. She got online and reserved a room at the same hotel her brother was staying in. Check-in time wasn't until four, so she had some time to kill.

Rosemary Malher's news about her potential commission and the bad guy wanting to unlock death gave Chloe a new angle from which to look at all the previous burglaries. In addition, she had to consider the possibility that, whatever he was looking for to unlock death, maybe he'd found it at the the Black Cat Bookshop, since he hadn't done anything for the past two weeks—except try to kill her. Well, not that they knew of, at least.

She started sorting through the lists of stolen items again, categorizing things with regards to whether they might be death-unlocking related or not. She wasn't really surprised to find that a large number of things had ties to religion or mysticism. Not all of them. Not even enough that Chloe felt stupid for missing that connection before, until she reached the books, which were all about death and dying and a discipline called thanatology, which was the study of death. It was a definite connection.

"Okay," she said aloud. She paced the living room while Whizz watched her from the back of the couch. "That pretty much seals the deal for me. The guy who wants to unlock death is the guy who has been breaking in all the jewelry stores and pawn shops around town. Oh shit."

She stopped pacing as another thought hit her. She *hadn't* been working the case over the weekend. She'd been pursuing the Sudden Occurrence of Ghosts side of her life. But their guy didn't know that. He thought she'd already made the connection and was a few steps ahead of where she actually was. He thought she was looking for him at places like the Dia de los Muertos celebration and cemeteries.

"So was he following me?" she asked Whizz. "Or did he see me at the cemetery? Maybe he was there trying to unlock death. That would have been the night to do it. Damn damn damn! Why didn't I realize this death connection sooner? What if he's not burglarizing people any more because he's done what he wanted to?"

She paused. "Shit. Did I actually say that? How the hell would you go about unlocking death, anyway? And what would happen if you did? Would I start seeing more ghosts? Would we have zombies shuffling around the Circle City trying to eat people's brains? Or would unlocking death actually give people true life back?" She could just imagine the problems that would arise from that. Forget wondering if you had a soul, you'd have to deal with the Social Security Administration and the IRS. That would be enough for the newly-reanimated to want to off themselves all over again.

She scraped her fingers through her hair. "So which is more likely? It seems too coincidental that I just happened to go to the same cemetery as our guy on Dia de los Muertos. Definitely more likely that he's following me. And the simplest explanation is usually the right one."

Whizz had curled into a ball, his chin up. He was clearly not interested in the fact that Chloe had had a major break in the case. She knew who would care, but there was no way she was going to call Braxton. She'd tried to tell him, and instead he'd dropped a supernatural bombshell on her.

She rubbed her face. How could she have let herself be taken in by a man yet again? She thought she'd developed better instincts since Matt. Not to mention she'd been just fine with being married to her job. She sighed.

"At least I won't have to explain the ghosts to him," she told Whizz. A little voice in the back of her head whispered that maybe a werewolf wouldn't mind that she saw ghosts, but she shoved it aside.

Forget Braxton. It was time to be proactive. Chloe shoved a protesting Whizz into his cat carrier—no way was she leaving him unguarded—and headed back downtown. She wanted to see if Cody Wethering's ghost would show up again at the site of her shooting. For that matter, it would be good to know if Wethering was still dead. After all, if his partner *had* succeeded in unlocking death—*and who am I to say it's impossible, since I'm seeing ghosts? Oh yeah, and fucking* werewolves *are real*—wouldn't he unlock Wethering? Or if he hadn't unlocked Wethering, that would either mean he'd been unsuccessful so far, or he and Wethering had been partners by convenience rather than closeness. Either would be good to know, though personally Chloe was hoping death's doors had stayed locked tight.

She sat around at the crime scene for about twenty minutes with no luck. *Doesn't necessarily mean anything,* she assured herself, and started doing another sweep of the area. She was pretty sure by now that she'd left no obvious stones unturned in her search for clues, but there was always the chance that she'd missed something before.

She turned up nothing, so her next step was to call a friend at the *Indianapolis Star* to check the obits and find out where Wethering had been interred. He gave Chloe the name of a Lutheran church on the near north side. He gave an address, too. One point in favor of making nice with the press.

As Chloe was driving, she kept an eye out for someone following her. She'd already determined that whoever might be watching her, they hadn't been following from Martin's place, but that was no reason to lower her alertness. Besides, as angry as she might be at Braxton *Werewolfe*, she *had* promised him she would be careful.

She found the church with no trouble and pulled into the parking lot. The church had been build out of limestone and looked like the sort of place she would expect to see in England, with crenelations at the top of the bell tower and large stained glass windows. The lich gate was located on the south side of the church. That was where Chloe headed.

Lich gates were built both as an entryway to cemeteries and as rain shelters for the pallbearers. Some of them could be pretty fancy. This one had a dead guy hanging out in it.

Chloe stopped walking when she was a few yards from the gate. She didn't know how she knew he was dead. There was no flickering or aura that made him look different from any other person she might encounter. Maybe it was the way the hair on her arms all stood up when she saw him. Whatever it was, she knew he was dead, and there was no way she was getting any closer to him. Someone was trying to unlock death. Hard to say how ghosts might react to living people if they'd been unlocked somehow.

The dead guy saw her about the same time she saw him. They looked at each other for a couple of heartbeats, and after a while it became obvious that he realized Chloe could see him. He recoiled, his expression almost frightened. Then he was gone.

Huh. That's a new one. A ghost is afraid of a person. Isn't it supposed to be the other way around?

She waited for a couple of minutes, but he didn't return, so she finally ventured through the lich gate and into the cemetery on the other side. It was a pretty cemetery, with lots of ornamental monuments and grave markers shaped like trees. There was a concrete bench at one point that had the name Elton St. Cloud and dates on it, and the inscription, "Set down, stranger, and pass a while." Out of a new respect for the dead, Chloe did as instructed and sat on the bench.

The weather was nothing remarkable, about fifty with some clouds in the sky. But as she sat there, Chloe felt like she could breathe a little easier. It was almost as if Elton St. Cloud was so pleased about having company that he was showing her some hospitality. She leaned her head back, looking up at the oak and chestnut trees that branched out over her.

She got another reward as she was sitting there with Elton St. Cloud. She'd been watching the wrought iron perimeter fence to make sure no one was staking out the cemetery. It really wouldn't be good to find herself in a cemetery if some guy who could raise or free the dead was here. As Chloe prepared to get up, she realized she was no longer alone.

Cody Wethering was sitting on the bench next to her.

"Holy Mother!" She jumped about a foot, making a complete ass of herself in front of the guy who'd tried to kill her. Well, his ghost, anyway.

He crossed his arms over his chest, and Chloe would swear she could see a faint smirk on his ghostly face. His hair was still sticking up on one side. She wondered if it had been that way when he died, and if he was stuck that way forever. Maybe it was just that whoever remembered him besides Chloe remembered him with his hair permanently sticking up. Maybe Chloe was the only one who remembered him. The thought made her unaccountably sad, despite what he'd done to her.

"I was looking for you, Cody. You mind if I call you Cody?" She made her tone as conversational as she could, considering that her heart was still going a mile a minute.

He just kept smirking at her, but Chloe took that as permission to continue, since he didn't go away.

"So I've figured some things out. One is that you had a partner in the burglaries you were committing. And he's kept going without you, while you ended up dead. So I'm guessing he killed you." Chloe leaned away from him just slightly, hoping it looked casual. She didn't know what ghosts might be able to do to people, but she wasn't really inclined to find out. It was entirely possible that she might just piss him off with her line of reasoning.

But he just cocked his head to one side and watched her.

"Okay...so I've been a little behind the times, but I finally realized what this guy is after. He's trying to bring back the dead, isn't he?"

This time Cody actually nodded. Then he caught himself and glared. Chloe shivered. Being the focus of undead ire left a prickly feeling along her spine, like someone had just dragged a safety pin up her back.

"I'm guessing you're a little pissed at the guy. I would be, at least. I mean, hell, you're dead and buried, and he hasn't done anything for you. For that matter, he's probably the one who killed you. And I'm guessing—just guessing—that you probably weren't worried about death, which is why you shot me instead of just surrendering." She was feeling her way through at this point. Cody didn't look too derisive, though—at least it didn't get any worse—so Chloe took that to be another confirmation.

"If you weren't worried about death," she continued, "that must mean that your partner was pretty sure he was on the right path. He probably promised you he'd take care of you if you got killed. So you could take risks you might not usually take. Like robbing a jewelry store in broad daylight in the middle of the city."

Cody shrugged. It was noncommittal, but she thought she was right.

"But here you are, still dead. If I were you, I'd want the guy to pay." And this was where Chloe was really taking a risk. If she pushed hard enough, he would jump one way or the other. There was a very good chance he would jump in the opposite direction and bet on his partner being successful and coming through for him. Chloe looked away from him, keeping him in her peripheral vision but taking a little of the pressure off.

"So here you are." She shrugged. "Here I am. I'm only not dead because Saint Michael was watching out for me." She pulled the repaired medallion from under her shirt and showed him. "You're only dead because your partner's an asshole." She looked over at him again. "I can't do anything about the dead part. I can see you, but I can't hear you and I can't bring you back. I'll be up front about that. But I can see that your partner pays for what he did to you."

And that was when Chloe's luck ran out. From behind her, she heard a voice. "Miss? Can I help you?" She jumped again and started to turn. Cody flickered out, goner than gone. Chloe plunged a hand inside her coat pocket and came up with her cell phone right before a white-haired man came around the tree she'd been sitting against.

Hoping against hope that he hadn't gotten a clear look at her before he spoke, she said, "Hang on," into the phone, then smiled at him. "Hi. My name's Chloe. I know this is weird, but I was just hanging out with Mr. St. Cloud."

To her surprise, the man's expression cleared and he smiled back at her. "It's a lovely bench, isn't it? When Elty said he wanted to do it, I thought he was crazy. But I think he gets a lot of visitors that way. It helps people remember him."

"You knew him?" She held up a finger and spoke into the phone again. "I'll call you later." She made a show of ending the call and sliding the phone back into her pocket. Hopefully she'd fooled him into thinking she was having a phone conversation instead of sitting there talking, apparently, to no one.

"He was a long-time parishioner. I'm the minister here." The man sat on the bench with her, though he maintained a comfortable distance.

"What was he like? A friendly guy?"

He laughed. "Oh, no. He was the curmudgeon's curmudgeon. I believe he spent more time telling teenagers to get off his lawn than he did sitting on the front porch passing the time of day. But he was lonely. He spent his last year in a nursing home, and I was his only visitor. I think it brought home to him how he'd pushed people away all his life." His expression sobered, but Chloe could tell there was genuine affection there for Elty the Curmudgeon.

Despite that, it left her a little chilled. In the past twenty-four hours she'd pissed off her best friend and walked away from the guy she thought she was falling for. Was she going to end up like Elty, trying to bribe people to spend time with her because she'd never been willing to let them get close? Maybe she really *would* die alone and be found half eaten by her cat. Maybe she should quit yelling at guys to get off her lawn and start sitting on the porch with them. Or with one guy, in particular.

Maybe she was taking the story a little too literally.

"Well, I'm glad people remember him now," she said honestly. "Thanks for telling me about him."

The minister nodded. "I need to lock the gates," he explained. "We don't like to leave them unlocked at night. Too much vandalism in the neighborhood, unfortunately. But you're welcome to come back another time."

"Oh." Chloe checked her watch. It was after five. She was probably lucky he hadn't locked her in. With Daylight Saving Time coming to an end, the sun was setting by six, and this guy probably wanted to go home. "Thank you," she said again.

He walked with her to the lich gate, where he stopped to lock the gates. Chloe had to fight a smirk at the idea of him locking death up. It would be nice if he could do that for her so she wouldn't have to worry about the dead walking around free. She wasn't exactly sure why that was *her* job, except that she seemed to be the only one, besides Cody Wethering's ghost and Rosemary Malher the death artist, who knew what was going on. Someone had to stop it, after all. And Chloe's job was to serve and protect.

She looked carefully both ways before she left the church. There didn't seem to be any cars following her, so she made her way to the hotel, swinging by a Pizza Hut on her way. She was hungry and tired, and her gambit with Cody Wethering's ghost seemed to have failed. Time for Plan B.

As soon as she thought of one.

* * *

"So what are we going to do about this?" Elliot said. He was leaning against the wall, his arms folded across his chest. "We can't let this jerk get away with beating Murphy up."

"Keep rubbing it in," Murphy groused.

Braxton didn't answer. He couldn't concentrate on the issue at hand, because he was still brooding over yesterday's argument with Chloe. He'd texted her once, asking if they could talk, but that didn't get a response, and he wasn't going to keep trying. She'd told him to leave her alone, after all. He didn't want to be the guy who acted like 'no' meant 'keep trying and I'll change my mind,' after all.

"I say we go back to the place Murphy ran into her this time," Tara said. "We could all get her scent. Maybe it's someone we've met before."

"I told you, I would have recognized her—"

"Yeah, if you'd met her," Tara said. "But, no offense, honey, we've been around a lot more magic-users in our time than you have."

Murphy gave a sullen shrug and lapsed into silence.

Braxton stirred, dragging his mind back to the conversation at hand. "It's not a bad idea. I wish we knew if the magic-user who hit Murphy was the only one involved. What if Marcineau recruited more than one person to his cause?"

"The Fort Harrison Pack swears they had nothing to do with him," Elliott said.

Braxton nodded. "I know, and I trust Peggy. But it wouldn't have to be werewolves. If he got a magic-user, he could have allied with all kinds of supernatural beings or talents."

"Except the Eagle Creek Pack has always respected the treaties and accords," Elliott pointed out. "I can't see any of the Others in town going back on that."

Tara cleared her throat. "I checked with a couple of sensitives I know, and nobody's said much of anything about Marcineau since your dad killed him. They're all talking about some idiot trying to raise the dead or enslave ghosts or something."

"Anyway," Murphy said, "it was just him and the magic-user the night I got bit."

"So we go back to Holliday Park," Elliott said, pushing away from the wall. "All of us. We should have Theo and Maura and the cousins meet us there."

Braxton nodded. He wasn't happy about everything they didn't know, but this was probably the best way to go about gathering more information. "Okay. Let's drive separately. We might find a trail that needs following."

"Yeah," Murphy said. "The trail of my blood that I left all over."

Elliott snorted. "I'll ride with Braxton. You two good?"

"We're good," Tara said.

To Braxton's surprise, Elliott seemed content to drive in silence for a while. His radio was tuned to Q95, the local classic rock station. Braxton closed his eyes and leaned his head back against the seat, humming along with "The Wall" by Pink Floyd. It wasn't until they were crossing Michigan Avenue that Elliot spoke.

"So she didn't take it well."

Braxton tensed but didn't say anything.

"I'm sure she just needs time to get used to it," Elliot said.

Braxton was startled into a bitter laugh. "Or she wants nothing to do with me."

"You're going to call her," Elliott said, in a tone of voice that made the *of course* at the end obvious.

"She said to leave her alone." The memory of the words still made Braxton's stomach churn.

Elliott was silent long enough to make Braxton curious. He opened his eyes and glanced over; his best friend was frowning. "Talk to her partner, then," he suggested finally.

"He's pissed at both of us after the brakes incident involving his sister."

"Understandable, I guess." Elliott sighed. "All right. I'll talk to her."

"You're not exactly her favorite person in the world, you know," Braxton pointed out.

"What? The dead body thing?" Elliott scoffed. "That's all in fun."

Braxton eyed him.

"Look, maybe this isn't about you," Elliott pointed out in a reasonable tone of voice. "She got shot in the line of duty. Almost died. That's a lot to deal with by itself. Then you throw in the house fire and sabotage and add werewolves on top of that, and she's holding up pretty well, I'd say."

Braxton frowned. Something was tickling at the edges of his memory. What was it? What… "And ghosts," he said.

Elliott swerved to avoid a pothole and then looked over at him. "Huh?"

"Ghosts," Braxton said. "I just remembered." He shook his head. "Ruiz said something the other day about ghosts, when he was shouting at Chloe. And then yesterday, Chloe said something, too."

"So there you go," Elliott said, looking smug. "There's something else going on. I'll talk to her. She'll come around."

Braxton rolled his eyes. "Leave her alone, Ell. You're not irresistible to *everyone*, you know."

"I know," Elliott sighed. "My life's quest is still unfulfilled."

CHAPTER 15

Pet-friendly hotels were not as pet-friendly as Chloe would like. Despite the fact that Whizz would be fine if she left him in his carrier unattended for an hour to go to dinner, the rules were clear: pets had to be supervised by their owners at all times. Chloe couldn't help but think snidely that those rules must make traveling as a werewolf difficult. Or maybe the human side would be considered to be supervising the wolf side.

Maybe you'd know if you'd stuck around to ask, whispered a little voice in the back of her mind, but she shoved it away. "C'mere, Whizz," she said, snapping her fingers to get his attention. She was sitting cross-legged on the king-sized bed, papers spread out in front of her. She'd been trying to work through the case again, giving a thorough look at everything that went missing and how it related to death—or the reversing of death.

"I'm surprised there aren't more crucifixes on this list," she told the cat, scratching behind his ears as he settled on her lap. Then again, she wasn't sure how many people actually believed in a literal resurrection of the body anymore. She'd even heard some of the people at church talking about Jesus' resurrection as something that had probably been faked by the disciples.

It might be old-fashioned, but Chloe *did* believe in a literal resurrection, both of Jesus back in the day and of Christians, at some unknown point after death. The mysticism and mythology appealed to her. *Then why do werewolves freak you out so much?* whispered a little voice in the back of her mind.

She shoved her musings aside. Their subject hadn't stolen many crucifixes at all, which presented Chloe with more questions instead of answers. Was he a Christian? Was he an atheist? Was he some other religion? If he was a Christian, why wouldn't he have chosen Jesus' resurrection as an event to model? Had he turned his back on God with whatever tragedy must have occurred? Was he *aware* that he was rebelling against God? Was he, on some level, ashamed of what he was doing?

Chloe sighed. "None of this is getting me anywhere," she said. She pulled out her phone and texted Martin, whose room was one floor up. *Get down here. Need someone to bounce ideas off of.*

A few minutes later, someone knocked at her door. Chloe carried Whizz over to check the peephole. Tucking the cat firmly under one arm so he couldn't get away, she let her brother in.

"You couldn't bother to put on shoes?" she asked, looking down.

"You couldn't bounce ideas off your partner instead of me?" he countered, shutting the door behind him.

Chloe snorted. "If you get some foot fungus from walking around a public hotel barefoot, don't come crying to me."

"Won't. I'll just piss on it."

"Ugh. So didn't need to know that." She put Whizz down on the bed and went to the mini-fridge, where she'd stored a six-pack of Coke. "Want a pop?"

"Yes. If you're going to bore me with police work, you might as well ply me with sugar to keep me awake." He took the bottle and dragged one of the room's chairs over so he could sit in the chair and prop his feet up on the edge of the bed. "All right, shoot."

Chloe sat down on the bed again, leaning against the headboard and stretching her legs out in front of her. Whizz climbed, purring, onto her knees, and she reflected that only a cat could make such a knobbly resting place seem so comfortable. She took a long sip of Coke and then ran through the basics of the case from her involvement forward. She reasoned that if something significant had happened before she was shot, the unknown subject would be targeting Braxton, not Chloe. That might be faulty logic, but she'd see what her brother thought about the theory.

"Hold on," Martin said, when she got to the part where she went back downtown and looked for the pillowcase. "What did you say was on that?"

"Strawberry Shortcake."

Martin rubbed his jaw. "That's fairly distinctive. Maybe it's just me, but if I were going to rob a jewelry store, I'd use a plain white pillowcase. Probably one stolen from a hotel, so it would have all kinds of DNA on it that didn't belong to me. Then if they arrested me based on DNA evidence, I could say I'd stayed at that hotel the night before."

Chloe stared at him, her eyebrows going up. "Okay, I hope you never decide to become a criminal," she remarked. "So the pillowcase was distinctive. Cody Wethering wasn't exactly a stellar criminal. No offense," she added, in case Cody was lingering around unseen.

Martin had started to take a sip of his drink, but at that last, he paused and lowered the bottle. "Why would that offend me? I never met the guy."

Oops. She'd said that out loud. "Uh. I meant, no offense that...I was arguing against your theory," she ventured, feeling her way through the excuse. Once it was out of her mouth, she wanted to smack herself in the forehead.

"Like you've ever apologized for that before," Martin said. He dropped his feet to the floor and leaned forward, peering at her. "Seriously, Clo, are you all right? I mean, I get that you and Braxton had an argument, but that'll blow over. It's good to get it out of the way this early, probably." He turned his head to look sideways at her. "You *did* go see the counselor after getting shot, right?"

"Yes, I went to see the counselor," Chloe huffed. "Geez."

Martin kept watching her. Chloe scowled at him. "What?"

"Something's going on that you're not telling me," he said. "And considering you told me about the brake lines being cut and your fight with Jake and your fight with Braxton, whatever you're not telling me has to be something really big."

Chloe's mouth went dry. Shit. She was used to protecting her little brother, but she wasn't good at actually lying to him. But if she told him about the ghosts, would he decide she was really insane and drag her back to the counselor? Or would he believe her? And did she want him to believe her? She'd told Jake, and that hadn't made him stick around. She could still feel the lash of his voice as he told her to stay away until she dealt with her ghosts.

"Uh-huh. Spill." Her silence had obviously been a tacit admission that Martin's surmise was correct.

Chloe sighed. "So...about how I died on the way to the hospital," she said. She licked her lips and gave him a nervous smile. "I think it did something to me."

Martin looked blankly at her for two seconds. "No shit. It killed you. Then it brought you back crazy."

"Thanks a lot," she said, glaring at him. "I was trying to be serious."

Martin cracked a smile. "Sorry. Go on." He patted her ankle.

She huffed. "It, uh." Crap. There was no way she could tell him this. But at this point, her partner wasn't talking to her, and neither was the guy she was dating. Who else *could* she tell? And she had to talk to someone about all this.

"Chloe." Martin's fingers curled around her ankle and squeezed gently. When she looked at him, he was watching her, his forehead creased with worry.

"Whatever you tell me, it can't be that bad. You're my sister. I love you."

Chloe licked her lips and sucked in a breath. *Okay,* she thought, and blurted it out. "After I died, I came back with the ability to see ghosts."

Then she held her breath. The heating unit turned off. In the sudden silence, she could hear a burst of laughter from the television in the room next door. Martin was staring at her, his mouth hanging open.

Chloe bit her lips together. *Say something,* she pleaded, watching his face for any change of expression.

Martin stared at her for several seconds, then closed his eyes. He gave his head a sharp shake and opened his eyes again. His gaze found hers and he finally said, "You see ghosts."

"I know it sounds crazy," Chloe said, but he lifted a hand.

"I didn't mean you really came back crazy," he said, holding her gaze.

"I...I know," she whispered. He never used the word crazy except in a joking sense; Chloe was sure it was because he felt his own sanity was hard-won. She had never taken him seriously when he called her crazy.

"So you talk to the dead. Like a medium or something?"

She shook her head. "I don't talk to them. Well, I talk to *them,* but they don't talk back. Not that I can hear, anyway."

"Huh." Martin sat back, rubbing his thumb against his lower lip. "Do you see any ghost you want?" He paused. "Have you seen Mom and Dad?"

"No." Chloe wasn't sure she wanted to see them. Ghost stories always made it sound like spirits had unfinished business. She didn't want to think that about their parents. "I saw Jake's, though. That's how I knew for sure."

"That would do it." Martin took a long drink of his pop and then snorted. "You gonna transfer to homicide? That should make it easier."

Chloe threw a pillow at him.

Martin caught it and shoved it behind his neck, leaning his head back to stare at the ceiling. "So Strawberry Shortcake pillowcase. No self-respecting guy would be using a Strawberry Shortcake pillowcase unless there was some reason for it."

"He stole it?" Chloe suggested.

"From who, his little sister? Anyway, regardless of how dumb this guy was, he'd have to know people would notice that."

"Maybe he was counting on the .44 to distract them."

Martin looked sideways at her and snorted. Chloe shrugged. They fell silent. Chloe studied her fingernails, picking at the chipped blue polish.

"Okay," Martin said after a while. "Here's what I've got. Your guy—the real guy, not the asshole who shot you—wants to unlock death. You die for a couple of minutes and come back seeing ghosts. What if he somehow unlocked your—your *deathsight* or whatever? He's trying to bring a ghost back to life, but what he ends up doing is letting you see ghosts when *you* come back to life."

Chloe stared at him. "Like...I *stole* from whoever he was trying to raise?"

Martin shrugged. "Not entirely clear on how this black magic thing works. But that seems reasonable."

"So it's *his* fault I'm seeing ghosts. Maybe if I solve the crime, it'll go away." Chloe sat up straighter.

Martin gave her a sympathetic look. "Maybe," he said, sounding dubious. "So the pillowcase. Not to be sexist, but it's fairly girly. Did the asshole who shot you have a sister or daughter?"

"His name is Cody," Chloe said. Maybe Cody was an asshole, but he was dead now. She thought that was more than enough punishment at this point. "And no, no siblings, no children. Just a divorced mother who's living in income-adjusted housing on the east side."

"So the girl the pillowcase belonged to, where'd she come from?" Martin scratched his chin. "And how old is she? What ages like Strawberry Shortcake?"

"That's hard to say." Chloe thought of the stuffed bear she'd slept with until she was in high school. She'd dragged that stuffed bear out of storage the night after the abortion. "Somewhere between five and fifteen. Old enough to like Strawberry Shortcake, but young enough that she still liked Strawberry Shortcake. That means probably not high school. Scratch that, probably not in junior high or older." She chewed her lower lip. "Fitting in's almost more important in junior high than it is in high school. In high school there's a certain cachet in being outside the crowd. In middle school, all you want is to have someone to sit with at the lunch table, and preferably not the fattest or weirdest or dumbest kid in school."

"An insensitive, but accurate, assessment," Martin commented.

"Then again," Chloe mused, "she could have kept the pillowcase hidden." She revised her age estimate again. "Yeah. Between five and fifteen. Oh, shit," she whispered as it hit her.

"What?" Martin sat up, watching her.

"Cody Wethering didn't have a child. But I bet the partner did. The partner had a daughter who liked Strawberry Shortcake." Chloe looked back at Martin, her eyes wide. "And whoever that little girl is, she's dead."

It made sense in the flash of intuition that only struck once in a decade or so. Plenty of police work was intuition and following her gut, but most of the time it was a slow, steady slog through witness statements and logistical reports and physical evidence. It was knocking on door after door, finding witnesses and corroborating statements, until she had a clear picture of what happened.

This time it was as if Chloe had had a camera out of focus and suddenly turned the ring around the lens that made everything clear. Someone was trying to unlock death to bring his child back to life.

"What?" Martin said when she repeated that aloud.

Chloe shook her head. "You might try to unlock death for a lover, sure, or to gain power. You might, maybe, do it for your parents or a sibling. But the one thing that throws your world topsy-turvy the fastest is losing a child." She should know. She'd lost one of her own, and by her own choice and actions. It made the entire world seem the wrong shade and every place you went feel too cold. It sent you into an emotional tailspin that warped every decision you made.

No parent should outlive her child.

Chloe was a fairly sane, fairly balanced individual—law abiding and adherent to a particular religious code—and she still would kill to protect her child, if she were in danger. If she thought she had a chance to bring her child back from the dead? To reverse the single worst decision of her entire thirty-four years of life?

She might do it. Fifteen years ago, she *would* have done it.

With the emotional and intellectual distance she'd gained in the intervening years, it was possible that, given the choice today, she would realize how insane that was. Becoming a mother at nineteen would have changed her life in ways so profound she had a feeling she wouldn't recognize herself now. She would have kept waiting tables until her feet were swollen and she was too big to walk. She'd have had to persuade Martin to room with her to make her money stretch further. She'd have dropped out of college. And since she didn't have benefits or paid time off as a waitress, she'd have gone back to work before she was ready.

She'd have gotten too little sleep for the next two years. She'd have been cranky and there would have eventually have been bitter custody battles with Matt, who at some point would have realized it looked bad for him to have a daughter that he wasn't in contact with.

Then again, she would have had a wonderful, amazing child to call her own. She might have just as difficult a time getting dates, but it would be because she spent Friday nights reading out loud and coloring and playing pretend. She would have traded the two or three major heartbreaks of her life for countless little ones over not being able to protect her child or give her the most fashionable clothes or pay for the sports she wanted to play. But she would be someone's mother.

Of course, she also probably wouldn't be a cop, and she wouldn't have met Braxton Wolfe. Which, she had to admit, were both pretty good things.

Life couldn't be lived in reverse. She'd learned to move on, and if she had regrets, she also had things that had brought her joy. But if, two months or two weeks or two minutes after the abortion, she'd been given a chance to go backwards and undo what she'd done?

In a heartbeat.

Chloe straightened. "Shit. The asshole's a parent."

Martin scowled. "Why does that that suddenly make him just a little bit less of an asshole?" he demanded.

"Because we can suddenly understand his motive. Or her motive," she added. Chloe suddenly felt just a tiny pang of sympathy for the parent, even if he—or she—had wiped out at least two people's lives in the course of the crime spree.

"Okay." She shook Whizz off her lap and folded her legs. "This guy didn't start looking for a way to reverse death ten or twenty years after his daughter died. He probably didn't even start it ten weeks after she died." She waved a hand. "As time passes, you learn to deal with what happened. We know that."

Martin nodded.

Even if it was your fault, Chloe thought, you went through the denial and bargaining and anger and all that, and started moving ahead with your life, because even if you wanted to die, every sane person knows you have to keep on living.

But the subject clearly *wasn't* sane. And he clearly hadn't grieved for his daughter, not properly. Not in a healthy way. Very soon after her death, maybe even before the funeral, he'd latched on to the idea of somehow reversing what had happened. Maybe her death was his fault and he couldn't deal with the grief. Maybe his wife was gone and he didn't have anyone but his daughter left to live for. Whatever the reason, he'd decided he could bring her back, and he'd never moved on emotionally from that moment.

"This gives us a starting point." Chloe tapped her fingers against her knee, then got up and started pacing. "The robberies would have started soon after he decided to bring her back."

"And it makes sense that he decided to bring her back very soon after her death," Martin agreed. He was bouncing one knee, looking almost as excited as she was.

"Logic dictates, then, that the robberies started shortly after the girl died," Chloe said.

Somehow the bereaved parent had hooked up with Cody Wethering. That probably meant the parent had a criminal history of some kind. She didn't have any idea why he'd decided he needed a partner in this venture. Maybe Cody had someone he wanted unlocked from death too. Maybe Cody just needed to pick up a few bucks and the bereaved parent needed a shooter. Either way, there was a reason, and she would need to figure that out too.

The robberies had started a few months ago. She would have to check the reports Braxton had given her, but she thought it was late August. She had a sudden shiver of doubt; what if there had been burglaries they didn't know about? It could screw up her pursuit of the theory she'd just developed. After a couple of seconds she shook it off. She couldn't think that way, or she wouldn't move forward at all. She had to go somewhere from here, and she might as well go in the direction she thought was right.

So it was time for some research skimming through the obituaries from the *Indianapolis Star*, looking for a girl roughly between the ages of six and sixteen, who had died in early to mid August. They were pretty big search parameters, but they were a heck of a lot smaller parameters than she'd been working with a few hours ago.

"Go get your laptop and order us a pizza," she said. "I have research to do."

* * *

Holliday Park was located on Spring Mill Road and stretched to the White River. It had pleasant walking trails in the wooded portions of the park, though the most famous feature of the park was The Ruins—three massive statues made of Indiana limestone that had originally graced the St. Paul building, the first skyscraper in New York City. The statues were called "The Races of Man" and represented the Asian, African-American, and Caucasian races working together.

Braxton had always felt disquieted by The Ruins, though he knew other people found them fascinating or even soothing. The Ruins had just been opened to the public as part of Holliday Park's centennial anniversary and the bicentennial of Indiana's statehood. Braxton had liked them better when they were behind the tall chain-link fence. He'd heard whispered legends about the statues coming to life due to some sort of curse. There were rumors something odd had happened during the restoration project, something about a woman whose ancestor had claimed the races weren't of *Man* but of some other creature.

"Will you stop twitching around?" Elliott muttered. "You're making the others nervous."

Braxton glanced sidelong at Theo and Estella, who were both watching him while trying not to look like they were watching him.

"Sorry," he said, and raised his voice. "Murphy! Where did you say she came after you? Down by the river?"

"Yeah." Murphy shoved his hands in his pockets and shuffled over. "I was running the trails, and she found me down under the 38th Street underpass."

Braxton nodded. That portion of the park was more remote. You could rarely visit The Ruins or the nature center without seeing a dozen or more people, even during the week, but the trails, especially trail eight, weren't as well-traveled.

"What was she doing under there?" Elliott said.

"Jeez, sorry I didn't stop to ask her," Murphy said. "As soon as she took a break from kicking my ass, I got the hell out of there."

"I don't blame you," Braxton said. "It's like I said, we're pack animals. We're meant to team up against threats. You did the right thing coming to me."

"I didn't," Murphy muttered.

Braxton ignored that. Murphy was still learning how to live with a pack, and even if he hadn't wanted to, he'd let Tara drag him to Braxton's house. "Lead us down there," he said. "Take the exact route you took. Hopefully we'll scent something."

Most of the trees had dropped their leaves, but the dry, brown oak leaves whispered against each other in the slight breeze as Murphy led the pack into the woods. Braxton didn't know this park well—his father had taken the west side as his territory, and Braxton had kept to it—but it obviously appealed to Murphy for some reason.

He couldn't imagine why. Murphy certainly wasn't affluent, and from the way he talked, his parents hadn't been either. The houses on Spring Mill were large and fancy—one of them even had a tower—and Braxton thought if he were poor, he would probably resent the people who clearly had more than he did.

He could hear nuthatches and woodpeckers in the trees, and leaves crunched underfoot. He thought that was Theo, and maybe Estella. The other members of the pack spent more time in the woods and were able to walk more quietly. Braxton couldn't even hear Murphy's footfalls, even though he was walking right behind Murphy.

Elliott stopped walking, grabbing Braxton's elbow. "Wait," he murmured. Braxton stopped and watched as Elliott lifted his head, nostrils flaring.

"What is it?" Braxton asked.

Elliott shook his head. "Can't you smell it?"

Braxton turned his nose to the sky, closing his eyes and breathing in. He *did* smell it now. There was something ancient and metallic to it. He shook himself, his skin crawling. It was familiar somehow, but he couldn't recall why.

"I'm going to shift," he said. There was no one human near enough to catch him at it. He stripped quickly. Elliott gathered the clothes as soon as Braxton discarded them, shoving them into a backpack.

Braxton took a deep breath, exhaled, and surrendered to the change.

The convulsions took him, and he breathed through it, feeling his fingernails lengthening and thickening. His muscles stretched and reshaped. Braxton grunted and let out an agonized groan. Then he dropped to his hands and knees, feeling his flesh prickle just before the fur sprouted. He squeezed his eyes shut, trying to breathe through it, but finally it was over.

He stood and shook himself, reveling in the clarity of his sharper senses. He could hear a squirrel scolding from half a mile away. He heard Murphy's rapid heartbeat, some part of the younger man still terrified of werewolves despite being one himself.

Then he took a deep breath and smelled the taint.

Braxton let out a whimper despite himself. There was a foulness to the scent here, something old, older than old, and malignant. What was it? And why did it tickle at the edges of his memory? And why couldn't he remember how he knew it?

"What is it, Brax?" Elliott's voice rumbled deeper to Braxton's lupine ears, and he smelled of piquant anxiety.

Braxton swung his head to look up at Elliott, then dropped his nose to the ground, picking up into a lope as he followed the scent.

"It wasn't that way," Murphy called after him, but Braxton ignored him.

He could hear Elliott's footfalls as his best friend ran to keep up with him. Braxton's human mind hoped he was doing something right, even as he surrendered to his lupine instincts. It was maybe the hardest part about being a werewolf, knowing that you were trying to give in to your instincts while your supposedly higher human intelligence tried to use logic to determine your actions. Braxton was grateful for the years he'd spent as a werewolf under his father's leadership, if only because his father had known when to obey the wolf's instincts and when to merely note them and make decisions based on human logic.

"Elliott," Murphy said, raising his voice, "I was on the other side of 38th Street when she found me."

"Fine," Braxton heard Elliott say, "but Braxton's picked up some scent. Maybe she was waiting here for you."

Murphy grumbled something that Braxton chose to ignore. There were human nuances to conversations that went right over the head of a shifted werewolf, but Braxton felt secure in the knowledge that Elliott was loyal to him and would tell Braxton whatever he needed to know.

Braxton shook himself and lowered his head to sniff at the narrow, weedy trail. The old, coppery scent demanded his attention, pulling him on like a magnet. He had no idea who this magic user was, but she was certainly strong, and the power she channeled was old and old. Werewolves had existed for centuries, but the blood magic scent Braxton followed was older still.

There were times that Braxton wished for some sort of telepathy or mental species communication, and today was one of those times. He trotted through weeds taller than his shoulders, hoping Elliott and Murphy would keep up with him. When he reached the banks of the White River, though, Braxton stopped walking and huffed in frustration.

The ancient, ravenous magic he scented had led him here, but it crossed the river in some fashion Braxton couldn't follow. He turned and looked unhappily at Elliott.

Elliott said, "Please don't jump into the river."

Braxton looked at him for several heartbeats, then turned his gaze on Murphy. Murphy looked unhappy, but he also looked frightened. Braxton wanted to ask him about it; since he obviously couldn't ask anything in his present state, Braxton whined an unhappy noise.

Murphy swallowed loud enough for Braxton to hear it. Then he stepped closer and rested a trembling hand on Braxton's shoulder. "Follow it the other way," he suggested.

Braxton wanted to get across the river to pick up the trail there, but something in him liked the tone of Murphy's voice. It was like he was offering something but also asking something. He chuffed once, leaning into Murphy's touch slightly, and took off back to where they had started.

As he trotted along the scent trail, he heard Murphy ask Elliott, "Will I ever have that much control?"

Braxton cocked an ear for Ell's answer, but between the noise of the pack and the rush of cars on the nearby 38th Street overpass, he didn't catch it.

Braxton loped along, nose stinging with the taint of that hungry magic. He was aware of weeds closing in around him, taller than him. This part of Holliday Park wasn't as frequented, and the trail showed it.

The ground underfoot turned to boardwalk; Braxton's nails scritched unpleasantly against the surface. He was aware of something blending into the tainted magic, but the taint was too overpowering to identify it. Then boardwalk turned into the cracking pavement of the handicap-accessible fishing pier. That was where Braxton stopped and sneezed. He suspected that was Murphy he smelled mingled with—or tangled around by—the taint.

He turned around and stuck his muzzle against Murphy's crotch, prompting an indignant, "Hey!" But it gave him Murphy's scent, and Braxton knew for sure that was Murphy he smelled in the magic.

He spun on his heels and took a deep scent. He lifted his upper lip in a silent snarl and dashed along the strengthening trail.

That taint had ambushed his packmate—had *hurt* his packmate. Braxton wanted to sink his teeth into that tainted magic user and shake her until her neck snapped. He stopped short at the spot where he knew Murphy's blood had been spilled. Forelegs locked, he bounced once and growled deep in his chest.

"Yeah." Murphy sounded out of breath and unnerved, but he had followed. Braxton was pleased and a little soothed by that. "This is where she jumped me."

Braxton shuddered and shook himself and gave in to the instinct to be human again. When he knelt breathless, muscles sore, but fully human, he lifted his head to look at Murphy.

"Yeah," Murphy said again. Elliott passed up the backpack and Murphy set it in front of Braxton.

"We'll take her down together," Braxton promised Murphy.

"You…why do you want to protect me?" Murphy whispered.

Braxton tugged on his boxers and t-shirt. He could hear footsteps approaching along the boardwalk and realized then that only Elliott and Murphy had followed him. Of course—Ell would have told the others to keep watch until he was human.

"Because you're my pack," he told Murphy. "And because we failed to protect you when it mattered. But mostly because I like you."

He held his breath after he said it. It could backfire, being that honest with Murphy. You could never quite predict how he would react to something. But to Braxton's surprise, Murphy's face flushed and he looked down.

"I don't know why I matter so much," Murphy muttered, but Braxton thought he sounded pleased.

Braxton finished dressing. "Whoever this woman is," he told Elliott—Murphy clearly already knew— "she's powerful, and she's old. Or else she's tapping into some power that's old. Older than us—than the magic that made us. And worse, it's hungrier than any magic I've ever met."

Elliott didn't flinch. "Then we hunt her together and we take her down," he said. He looked at Murphy.

Braxton felt a fierce grin stretching his lips and he looked at Murphy, narrowing his eyes.

"Together," Murphy said after a moment, "we'll take her down."

CHAPTER 16

It only took Chloe an hour and a half to find what she was looking for, which she thought was pretty amazing, considering she was reading the obituaries of the thirteenth-largest city in the United States plus outlying communities. There were a lot of obituaries that talked about the person's "courageous battle" with cancer, but she supposed whoever wrote the obituary wouldn't be likely to say the person had been a coward about it. There were obituaries that reminded her of news stories she'd seen, like the family killed by a drunk driver on the interstate, or the teenager who had just barely gotten his license and lost control on a rainy night. There were memorial contributions to Susan G. Komen and the Humane Society and mental health organizations and, in one rather interesting obituary, the National Rifle Association.

And then there was Alita.

Alita Lilliana Garza was fifteen years old and had died in a car accident along with two other teenagers. A fourth teen, who had been in the back seat with Alita, had survived with life-altering injuries. Alita's obituary was long and lovingly crafted, and mentioned her love of cats and reading and her intention to join the Peace Corps after college. Alita had been preceded in death by grandparents, and was survived by her mother Josephine Catrin, and her father, Victor Garza.

"Shit," Chloe whispered. Victor Garza was the high-powered lawyer she had seen at Crown Hill on Dia de los Muertos. Suddenly it all made sense.

Garza knew the legal system inside and out, and Wethering had a rap sheet full of small time burglaries and B&Es. Garza would have decided what he needed and gone hunting for someone who would have the know-how to accomplish it. He'd probably promised Wethering legal protection as well as being able to raise him from the dead if he were killed accomplishing the job. But he'd obviously decided Wethering was more of a liability than an asset—probably when Wethering burned down Chloe's house—so he'd put a bullet in him.

That was why her brake lines had been cut. Garza had seen her at the cemetery, and he'd thought she was working the case. He must have decided she was tailing him, or that she was surveilling the cemetery hoping her subject would show up. Either way, he'd decided Wethering was right, and she *was* a threat, and he'd decided to take care of her permanently.

"Bet he misses Cody now," she muttered, and sighed. "So what now?" She drummed fingers on the table. The obituary she'd found hadn't run with a picture, but there were bound to be photos somewhere. She started searching Alita's name, but she couldn't find anything. Plenty of pictures of Victor Garza, but even the stories about the car crash didn't have pictures of the teens involved.

Chloe rubbed her forehead and clicked one of the news stories about Victor Garza. There were a few articles related to his job, one talking about him appearing at a fundraiser for a prominent senatorial candidate, and one about his volunteer work at a soup kitchen downtown.

"What the hell?" Chloe muttered. How did someone who volunteered at a soup kitchen turn into the kind of guy who would kill other people in an insane attempt at bringing his daughter back from the dead? Grief could make you do crazy things, but could it alter your personality that much? Chloe sipped her Coke and pondered. Maybe he'd done the soup kitchen thing as a publicity thing. Maybe he'd really just gone off the deep end when Alita died.

A little voice in the back of Chloe's head whispered that she should call Braxton. She told that little voice to go screw itself, but it didn't really work. The voice was right. It was his case, and Chloe'd figured out who was behind the burglaries. There was no doubt in her mind that Garza had done it trying to bring Alita back from the dead. But she left her cell phone untouched. If she wanted Braxton to believe her that Garza was the guy, she would have to explain how she knew that. And that would take a hell of a lot more explaining than Chloe wanted to do.

"It's his case," she muttered, turning her Coke bottle in slow circles on the table. "He ought to be in on this."

Not to mention maybe she should take a leap of faith and trust him with her secret about dead people. He'd been honest with her, after all.

Yeah, about his being a damn werewolf. Chloe hadn't even tried to explain that one to Martin. It could wait until she figured out if things were going to work between her and Braxton.

If you're going to let him in, whispered that little voice. If you're going to take the time to ask what being a werewolf means, and if he's dangerous, and how exactly that explained that sexpot redhead and the scrawny, bloody guy being at his house.

Chloe sighed and glanced at her watch again. She wasn't going to call Braxton at nine o'clock in the evening. He was already pissed at her. She would call him tomorrow and see if he could have lunch. She could apologize then and tell him the entire thing.

On second thought, maybe she'd better make it drinks instead of lunch. She would probably need a drink to brace herself for telling him all that, and he would probably need a drink once she'd told him.

Chloe stood up and stretched. "I need to get out of here for a while," she told her brother, who was sprawled on the bed watching a documentary on television. "You'll stay with Whiz, won't you?"

Martin grunted. "Sure. Be careful. And bring back something chocolate with you, okay?"

"No problem." She pulled on a jacket and headed out to the hotel parking lot.

Alita Garza had been buried in Crown Hill Cemetery. The cemetery would be closed, of course, but Chloe was resourceful. She could spend the night staking out Alita's grave, just to see if anything was going on there. For that matter, it might be a good idea to make sure her grave hadn't been disturbed. She didn't know for sure whether or not Garza had succeeded in unlocking death. It would hardly be reported in the paper if he'd brought his daughter back to life.

She swung past a Starbucks for a couple of pastries and two large cups of coffee, which she dumped into a Thermos. Then she headed for the cemetery. She parked on Clarendon Road, well away from any entrances to the cemetery, and scaled the fence. It wasn't easy, but she managed it. Fortunately the wrought iron fence had gaps wide enough that she could reach through to pick up her backpack of provisions and the blanket she'd brought to sit on, so at least she didn't have to try carrying them over.

She had a flashlight, but she wouldn't use it except in an emergency. She let the dim glow of her cell phone display shine on the ground in front of her feet. She had a rough idea of where Alita's grave was, but it was a good half mile from where she'd entered the cemetery, and then there would be some searching to do before Chloe found the Garza Mausoleum.

While Chloe was athletic and getting back in shape, she wasn't particularly graceful. Especially not hiking through a cemetery in the middle of the night. By the time she got to the area where she knew the Garza Mausoleum to be, she'd tripped twice—once going all the way down to hands and knees—and bruised her hip against a headstone that had loomed closer than anticipated.

She'd also seen half a dozen ghosts. None of them seemed to have much interest in her. Two of them had noticed her, but the others had been oblivious to everything but what they were doing. One, for instance, had obviously been taking laundry off the line and folding it into a basket, even though Chloe could see nothing but his faintly luminescent outline. Another had been pacing in circles and had almost walked into her—or through her—but Chloe had swerved at the last minute. She might be getting used to this ghost thing (and how crazy was that, that she was *getting used* to seeing ghosts?) but she had her limits, and she didn't want to know what it would feel like to have a ghost walk through her.

But eventually she did find the Garza plot. There was a mausoleum and eight or ten graves surrounding it. A willow tree grew to the left of the mausoleum. Marigolds were planted carefully around several of the graves. A collection of Strawberry Shortcake dolls, Bratz dolls, and a few books were lined up on the stone knees of the building.

Chloe sighed.

Working as a cop, she saw death a lot. She had seen the full range of depravity that man was capable of inflicting on man. But she could never get used to dead children. If she ever got used to that, she would take her pension and find a job digging ditches or something. There was something about that rank and file of toys and books that made her heart twinge for

Victor Garza. Oh, he was a grade-A asshole, sure, but he was a grade-A asshole who loved his daughter.

Chloe knelt in front of the granite, pale amongst the shadows, and listened to the wind whisper willow leaves against the stone. If Garza had succeeded in bringing Alita back to life, her toys wouldn't still be sitting out here for anyone to see...sitting out here as if the angelita needed her companions to keep her company in the cold. Garza wouldn't have made an ofrenda if he'd unlocked death.

Or would he? Quiet doubt niggled in Chloe's mind. He was a smart man. Garza had handled the case of a millionaire who'd bilked people out of thousands of dollars, and everyone had been certain the millionaire would be found guilty. Through a series of technicalities and mishaps, Garza had managed to get the charges dismissed. So maybe he'd made the ofrenda in good faith, as a spiritual gesture of love for his child. Or maybe he'd done it as a neat bit of misdirection.

Who would come looking, though? No one suspected him of foul play. No one had made the connection but Chloe, and she still wasn't sure she would have made the connection, if it hadn't been for her ghosts. Then again, if it hadn't been for the mere *existence* of ghosts, maybe Garza wouldn't have gone off the deep end. How had he gotten the idea to unlock death in the first place? Most people didn't go around assuming there was a way to bring people back from the dead.

Thank God, she heard the footsteps approaching in time.

Chloe straightened, eyes widening, and locked her phone. Her gaze darted around, looking for a place to hide. A tiny glow drew her gaze to the willow tree, and there was her daughter. She looked anxiously at Chloe and beckoned for her to approach. Chloe glanced over her shoulder and dashed to the tree trunk. As she reached it, the girl drifted up, and Chloe realized she was supposed to climb the tree.

Crap. She hadn't climbed a tree in twenty years. The footsteps were getting louder, though, crunching through leaves. Chloe scrambled up the trunk to the first limb, then moved more slowly as she continued ascending. At least there were still leaves on the willow; they tended to hang on later than maples and hickories. Hopefully it would be enough to hide her in the darkness. She found a strong branch and sat on it, looping an arm around the trunk.

"Is this really necessary?" said a woman's voice.

A man's voice answered. "I just need to visit one more time. I've made my choice. I just need to explain it all to Alita before we go through with it."

Chloe drew in a slow breath as she realized Victor Garza was here. Chloe wasn't the only one watching Alita's grave, apparently.

"She still might not thank you," said the woman. Chloe wondered if it was Josephine Catrin, Alita's mother. The obituary had implied Alita's parents were estranged from one another, but stranger things had happened, Chloe thought.

"I don't question the things you're requiring," Garza snapped. "I'll thank you to not question what I need."

The woman gave a low laugh. "Very well."

Garza drew closer. He had a dim lantern in his hand, but his steps were sure. He was obviously very familiar with the way to Alita's grave.

"Wait—" hissed the woman. "There's someone here."

Chloe tensed, reaching to her hip, where her Glock nestled comfortingly.

"Who would be out here?" Garza scoffed.

"Be still and listen to me," the woman ordered. "You have been bashing about like a bull in a china shop, all unknowing of the consequences of your actions, and now I am attempting to create some order out of this chaos."

Garza folded his arms across his chest. "Fine. Who's out here?"

Chloe swallowed and held her breath. As she watched, Cody Wethering's ghost flicked into view, faintly luminescent, at the base of the willow. The woman let out a slow huff of breath.

"Just your pet haunt," she said. "You may never be quit of him."

Garza snorted. "He was nothing when he was alive. He's less than nothing now."

Chloe narrowed her eyes as she felt a surge of rage that certainly wasn't her own. What did she care what Garza thought of Cody Wethering? She eased out a quiet breath. She'd told her brother she couldn't communicate with them, but she wondered if that were true. Perhaps she just hadn't learned how yet.

She looked over at her daughter's ghost and smiled faintly at her. *Thank you,* she thought. The girl smiled back at her, face sad, and looked down at Cody. He glanced up, just for a moment, but Chloe felt a surge of something warm. It wasn't affection, nor gratitude exactly. Maybe regret and...apology? She realized suddenly that Cody had been protecting her by appearing at that moment.

Chloe aimed a wave of forgiveness at him. He'd shot her, but she still thought he'd gotten the worst of it. If her forgiveness could help him, she would give it.

Garza stood, and the movement made Chloe realize he'd been kneeling in front of Alita's grave. "I'll see you soon, Alita," he said. "We'll be together, and you'll be alive again."

He stared at the stone for a long moment, then turned and walked away. Chloe saw the woman go with him and gritted her teeth. She'd hoped for a good look at the woman's face so she could pass it along to a sketch artist.

A pang of grief struck her, so unexpected and palpable that she nearly fell off her tree branch. When she caught herself, she looked over at her daughter's ghost. The girl was watching Garza go, her face twisted in terrible sorrow.

"Oh, shit," Chloe whispered. "I got it all wrong. You're not *my* daughter. You're *his.*"

Alita turned and looked at her, the grief still strong on her face.

"Of course you are," Chloe said softly. "You're Alita Garza. You came to me because you knew I could help you, didn't you?" She wet her lips and shivered, suddenly aware of how cold it was. "Except it took me forever to figure it out, because I thought you were *my* ghost."

Alita watched her for several seconds before nodding slowly.

Chloe sighed. "This tree branch is killing my butt," she told Alita, and climbed down from the tree. When her feet touched the ground, Alita was there, standing next to Cody. They looked at each other, and Chloe would swear they were communicating with each other, but she couldn't hear or feel anything.

"Thank you for helping me, Cody," she said. "I'm not quite sure why you did, but I appreciate it."

He gave her a scornful look, lip curled, and she felt a sudden swell of appreciation.

Chloe laughed. "So I'm stupid for not understanding why you helped, but you appreciate me?" She said. He rolled his eyes. "Okay, um…you helped me because I appreciate *you?*"

That wiped the scorn from his face. He shoved his hands in his pockets—and it seemed weird, somehow, that ghosts could wear clothes and interact with their clothes just like a living person. Maybe that was just a mental projection, how Cody still thought of himself. But then why was he trapped with his hair sticking up on one side?

Chloe shook herself. "Okay. So I'm guessing, Alita, that you don't want to see your father succeed at bringing you back to life?"

Alita shook her head, projecting a sense of wrongness at Chloe.

"Yeah, I get it," Chloe said. "It's weird for me to see you guys. It must be even weirder for you all. Your father's fixation, is it keeping you from—you know, moving on? Being at peace?"

Alita shrugged and sent the feeling of wrongness again.

"Okay." Chloe fished the blanket out of her backpack and wrapped it around her. She hadn't anticipated how cold it got on a November night. This happened every winter; she forgot what cold weather was like until it was already on her. "Okay. I should probably get out of here. But this woman working with your dad—"

Alita and Cody both hit her with a blast of wrongness, of intensely perverse discord. Chloe doubled over, clutching at her chest and gasping for breath. "Okay, okay," she managed. "She's evil."

The feeling eased, though it didn't go away entirely. Chloe sucked in a few breaths and straightened slowly. Obviously the woman wasn't Alita's mother, or her feelings would be more ambiguous.

"So what now?" Chloe asked. She looked at Cody and Alita and they looked back at her. She scowled. "Okay, fine. I'll talk to Braxton. He'll know what to do."

A sudden thought hit her. "Alita, does this woman know you're hanging around?"

Alita shook her head, a wave of fear swamping Chloe.

"Good. If she did, I think you'd be in danger." Chloe shivered. "I think we all would."

* * *

Braxton's doorbell rang at ten pm.

Murphy and Elliott were both working their way steadily towards drunk. Braxton left them in the basement and went to open the door. He was surprised to see Chloe; if he'd been in her shoes, he would have run as far as possible after hearing the word 'werewolf.' But although Chloe met his gaze hesitantly, her twisted-together fingers and hunched shoulders suggested *she* was the one who felt guilty in some way. Braxton wasn't sure why, but he was glad enough to see her that he wouldn't question it.

"Chloe!" He smiled, hoping he didn't look too desperate.

"I hope I didn't wake you," she said. Her gaze was fixed on his face, her lower lip caught firmly between her teeth. She didn't make any move to step inside.

"No," Braxton said. "I have—well." He cleared his throat. "A couple of pack guys are here. Elliott and Murphy. But unless Elliott's passed out from too much bourbon, no one's asleep."

Chloe let out a startled laugh. "I'm not interrupting, am I?"

"Not at all." Braxton grinned. "Between you and me, I'm kind of hoping Elliott *has* passed out from too much bourbon."

She snorted. "If he has, you'll let me take blackmail pictures, right?"

They both laughed. "Come inside," Braxton said, shifting to make room. "It's chilly out there."

Chloe nodded and stepped inside, giving him a hesitant smile.

"Want something to drink? I have tea, or I can make a hot toddy." Braxton led the way to the kitchen as he spoke.

"Alcohol would be good," she said, sounding half joking and half nervous. She was silent as he switched on his electric kettle. Braxton focused on pulling a coffee cup and the nutmeg from the cabinets.

"Whiskey or rum?" he asked. "I have both, but the whiskey's downstairs, and Elliott would probably have questions."

"Rum is fine." Chloe sighed. "He'll have questions anyway."

"Doesn't mean I can't avoid them as long as possible," Braxton said, smiling as he got out the rum and eyeballed a couple of ounces. The kettle dinged and he dropped in a sugar cube, then added the water. As he sprinkled the nutmeg, he heard Chloe take a deep breath.

"Can we talk about something that isn't on the record? About Cody shooting me?"

"Of course," Braxton said without hesitation. Hopefully it would be something he could in good conscience keep secret. He finished mixing the toddy and turned, holding it out to her.

She took it, curling her fingers around the cup. There was a long silence between them then. Chloe looked everywhere but at Braxton. Braxton couldn't look anywhere but at Chloe's face. Something had prompted her to show up at ten at night, her nerves jangling and her eyes wider than they ought to be. She smelled of fear, anxiety, and determination, and Braxton could hear the rapid pounding of her heart. Whatever this was, it couldn't be good.

"What's going on?" Braxton finally asked.

Chloe huffed a sigh. "You know I coded in the ambulance on the way to the hospital, right?" When Braxton nodded, she did too. "So obviously they brought me back, but...I came back different."

Braxton heard her pulse spike, but he relaxed a little. Finally, she was going to tell him the truth she'd been keeping from him. He gave her an encouraging look.

"Ever since I woke up, I've been able to see things other people can't."

Braxton nodded. "I had a feeling it was something like that," he said. Maybe he could put her at ease. "Visions?"

She gave him a startled look. "Ghosts."

"Ah!" Braxton exclaimed as it clicked into place. "That explains it. You saw the pawn shop owner after he died, didn't you? I was furious that you'd lied to me, but when I thought it over, I decided you must have been afraid of something."

Chloe was staring at him, her mouth open. "'That *explains* it?'" she repeated. "That's it?"

Braxton arched an eyebrow. "Chloe, I'm a werewolf. Did you think I wouldn't believe you?" At her shamefaced grin, he laughed. "Anyway, I could tell you were hiding something. I figured—well, I hoped— you'd tell me when you were ready." He cocked his head, thinking. "So when you fell, that day Cody Wethering's body was found, was that him popping up and looking at himself?"

Chloe nodded. "And I..." She looked down at her mug and sipped. "I've had this girl following me around. I thought she was someone else, so it took me until tonight to figure out she's tied into the case."

Braxton leaned back against the counter. "So who is she?"

Chloe sipped her toddy again. "Her name's Alita Garza. She was killed about two months ago—"

"In a car crash," Braxton interrupted. "I remember. A high school party, and they were drinking. Three kids killed." He frowned. "Her dad's—"

"Victor Garza, high-powered defense attorney," Chloe said, nodding. "And, apparently, a dabbler in the dark arts."

"Huh?"

"Victor Garza's trying to bring his daughter back from the dead."

Braxton stared blankly at her. He definitely hadn't been expecting *that*. Bring his daughter back from the dead? Was it even possible? Braxton knew better than to automatically discount any supernatural phenomena, but aside from the stories in various mythologies, from Christian to Norse to Greek, he'd never heard of someone being raised from the dead.

Chloe giggled, surprising him. "What, you can be a werewolf and believe I see ghosts, but you can't believe in unlocking death?"

Braxton shook himself and grinned sheepishly at her. "I dunno, it just took me by surprise."

She grinned back at him for a few moments before her expression sobered. She took a sip of her toddy and said, "I can't prove it in a way a judge would accept, but I'd lay money Garza killed Cody himself. Cody's been haunting the guy, apparently. He saved my ass tonight, too—him and Alita."

Braxton held up a hand. "Do you mind telling Elliott all this? If he hasn't passed out?"

"Yeah, I expected to, since it affects his case," she said.

"All right, come on," he said, and led her downstairs.

To his relief, Elliott and Murphy were both still upright, sitting on one of the couches, and neither one seemed particularly drunk. He wouldn't give either of them a set of car keys, but their curiosity had obviously kept them from putting away any more shots.

"Chloe Cole," Elliott drawled, grinning lazily at her. "Good to see you."

She nodded at him, her expression cordial.

"Chloe, this is Murphy O'Hare. Murph, this is Chloe Cole."

Murphy looked her over, eyebrows raised, then said, "I'm glad you decided you didn't hate werewolves."

Braxton scowled at Murphy. When he glanced at Chloe, she was blushing.

"I know I didn't react well," she said. She took a seat on the empty couch. "And I'm sorry. I owe you all an apology, not just Braxton. All I can offer in my own defense is that I was dealing with some crazy stuff in my own life, and the news that werewolves are real kind of tipped me over the edge."

Murphy snorted. "No offense taken," he said. "Trust me, though, there are worse ways to find out werewolves are real."

Chloe still looked apologetic, but she nodded. "So the thing I was dealing with," she began, and launched into a more detailed story of her getting shot for Elliott and Murphy. She explained about the ghosts and shared her theory that Garza was not only responsible for the burglaries, but also Cody Wethering's death. When she finished speaking, Elliott leaned back against the sofa and whistled.

"So you're the ghost whisperer now," he said, his expression almost humorous. "Prettier than that chick who was in the show though." Chloe rolled her eyes at him and he laughed. "Yeah, don't worry, I already know you're immune to my charms, Cole."

"So you said Cody and Alita saved you tonight," Braxton remarked.

"She did?" Murphy said. He'd been following her story with a surprising amount of interest.

"Earlier," Braxton said.

Chloe nodded. "So...here's where I admit I did something kind of dumb," she said, and cleared her throat. "I went to Crown Hill to stake out Alita's mausoleum."

"In the dark?" Elliott said.

"By yourself?" Murphy said.

She shrugged. "I mean, now that I know ghosts and werewolves are real, maybe I should be afraid of zombies, too, but..."

They laughed.

"I really didn't expect anyone to be around," she went on. "But Garza came to visit his daughter, and he didn't come alone."

Murphy leaned forward as Chloe explained that a woman had accompanied Garza to the cemetery. Her ability to see ghosts—and the fact she'd somehow sensed that someone was there—alarmed Braxton.

"We should check it out," Murphy said. "If you got Garza's scent, you could check your other crime scenes, see if he was at those."

"Thanks, I hadn't thought of that," Braxton said, and Murphy snorted at his sarcastic tone.

"My problem is, I have no idea how to legally do anything with the information I have," Chloe said. She looked from Braxton to Elliott. "Checking for Garza's scent is great, but unless we find physical evidence..."

"Yeah." Braxton rubbed his hand through his hair. "We should start watching Garza. I'll put a couple of pack members on it. I have a couple who are small enough to pass for coyotes, if someone only gets a glimpse." He frowned at his watch. "In the meantime, Chloe, where are you staying?"

"I got a hotel room," she said. "I'm safe."

"And your brother?"

"Yep." She smiled at him.

Braxton nodded. "Okay. I think you said you're back on the job tomorrow?"

Chloe shrugged. "I've got my badge back, so I'm authorized to do what I have to. Lieutenant Piper said she didn't want me out on regular patrol until this case was closed. Why?"

"Can you be back here around ten tomorrow morning? I'm assuming you'll want to go to Crown Hill with us?"

"You assume correctly." She smiled and stood. "Walk me to the door?"

Elliott grinned, but fortunately, Chloe didn't see. Braxton followed Chloe upstairs, hoping this meant *everything* was back on, and not just their working the case together. Chloe didn't disappoint. When they reached the door, she leaned in to brush her lips against his.

"Thanks for understanding," she said.

"Thanks for telling me the truth," Braxton replied, slipping an arm around her waist. He pulled her closer for a longer kiss. "I'll see you tomorrow."

Chloe smiled. "Count on it."

CHAPTER 17

Their trip to Crown Hill the next day yielded more than Braxton had expected. Not only did they catch Garza's scent, but they also caught the foul, ancient scent of the woman who had attacked Murphy. Braxton felt a flash of fear at that, followed hard by anger. How dare this woman attack his pack? Braxton wanted to hunt this woman down and crush her throat between his teeth.

He shoved the feeling down. That was a last resort. Braxton, like his father before him, believed that peaceful solutions were best, despite the wolfish instinct to fight.

A hand rested on his shoulder and Braxton turned to force a smile for Chloe. She wore a heavy jacket and a stocking cap tugged low over her dark hair, and Braxton's smile became unforced in the wake of the happiness that hit him. She was adorable in the cap, but more than that, she was brave, and she somehow cared for him.

"What is it?" she asked, and Braxton shook himself.

"The woman who was with him," he said. "We've encountered her before. On Friday. She's the one who beat up Murphy."

Murphy made an unhappy noise, but didn't argue that she hadn't beaten him up.

Braxton shook his head. "I don't understand it. There's no reason for her to connect Murphy to the Garza situation. That leads me to believe her attack on Murphy wasn't connected to the case. But then why?"

Chloe shivered. "She scares me," she said unnecessarily. Braxton could smell her fear. He wrapped an arm around Chloe's waist.

"We'll figure it out," he promised. He scanned the area, taking in the willow tree that had provided Chloe cover, the Garza mausoleum near Alita's grave. "Let's get out of here. I want to do some digging, and we got what we came for."

When they got back to Braxton's house, they started digging back into Garza's public record, looking at the cases he'd argued, the charities he'd donated to, his clubs and church memberships—anything Braxton could think of that might pinpoint where Garza had first encountered the supernatural world. The man hadn't been born with his abilities, so there had to have been some introduction.

Late in the afternoon, Murphy showed up. "Trail from Holliday Park leads to a house near Lockerbie Square," he said. "The magic-user who attacked me is holed up in a house down there. Tall Victorian house painted purple, yellow, and green. Ugly as shit. Has a sign outside that says, The Mind's Eye."

Braxton scowled at him. "I thought I told you to go home and rest," he said.

"Yeah, and I decided not to do what you told me to," Murphy said. Despite that one eye was still swollen shut, he glared defensively at Braxton. It was hard not to admire such courage, even if Braxton thought Murphy needed to learn temperance. He sighed. "Fine. Rest now, okay?"

Murphy rolled his good eye and went off to the guest bedroom.

About twenty minutes later, Braxton hit gold. Chloe had gone back to the hotel to check on her brother and Whizz, so Elliott and Braxton were searching on their own.

"Hey," Braxton said. "Check it out. Yolanda Stevens."

Elliott looked up from his laptop screen. "She's the medium who was acquitted on her husband's death?"

Braxton nodded. "Acquaintance of mine, actually. If we'd pulled the case, I wouldn't have settled on her as the killer. She follows the Wiccan Rede."

"Doesn't mean she isn't capable of a crime of passion. Lots of people who otherwise wouldn't hurt someone have just snapped and killed a spouse or a parent."

Braxton waved a hand. "Beside the point. She was acquitted, thanks to the hard work of her lawyer—Victor Garza."

"Shit." Elliott straightened. "You think she's the one who told him about magic?"

"I think it's likely," Braxton said. "Worth giving her a call."

Elliott nodded. "While you do that, I'm going to go get us some supper." He stood, stretched, and left the house.

Braxton pulled out his phone and scrolled through his contacts until he found Yolanda.

It rang twice, and then Yolanda answered, a grin in her voice. "Why's the alpha of Eagle Creek Pack calling me?"

"I'm good, Yo, and how are you?" Braxton said.

She laughed. "I'm okay. And I was only really asking to be polite. You're calling me because of Victor Garza."

Braxton scowled. "If you know that, you could have called me first."

"I didn't know your pack was involved," Yolanda said. "Honestly. I've been aware of his actions for some time, but there was nothing to suggest pack involvement."

"We're involved," Braxton said grimly. "What can you tell me?"

Yolanda sighed. "He called me in August, just a couple of days after his daughter's death. You know what he's attempting?"

"Raising Alita from the dead."

"Right. I pointed him in a couple of different directions, gave him some leads to follow. What he's proposing isn't impossible, though I wouldn't advise it."

"Clearly, or you would've brought Chris back nine years ago," Braxton said.

There was regret in Yolanda's voice as she said, "Yes." She drew an audible breath, but said nothing else.

Braxton frowned. No need to ask Yolanda if she had been Garza's introduction to the supernatural. It seemed clear at this point that she was some sort of mentor to Garza. Still, she adhered to the Wiccan belief that, 'an it harm none, do as ye wilt.' She couldn't be condoning murder. It wasn't like her.

"So have you stayed involved?" he asked, knowing what she would say.

"No." She paused. "I gave him guidance, hoping to minimize the harm—to him and to others. But he hasn't called on me since he acquired the Thanatos pendant."

Braxton blinked. "Thanatos—"

"Pendant, yes. It gives him access to Thanatos, god of death. A lot of people have been trying for decades to get their hands on it, but it left Greece sometime around 1900, and no one had been able to track it. Everyone assumed it came to America, but no one knew for sure." She snorted. "Until a desperate lawyer decided he needed it."

"The pawn shop in Home Place," Braxton said, suddenly understanding. Julian Nikolaou had been the grandson of a Greek immigrant.

"Exactly," she said.

Braxton shook his head. "But Alita's still in her grave. We checked."

"For now," Yolanda agreed. "But he'll act soon. Before Monday."

Surprised, Braxton said, "The Full?"

"The third full moon since Alita's death. There is power in threes, you know. His window of opportunity is closing. If he doesn't raise her before Monday, he'll have to turn to much darker magic if he wants her back." She sniffed. "He was unhinged by her death, frankly, but he was basically a good man before that. Arrogant and manipulative, of course, as serves any lawyer well. But not evil. I hope that remains true."

"He's killed at least one person himself," Braxton said. "And he was responsible for Julian Nikolaou's death, even if he didn't wield the weapon that killed him. He's stolen thousands of dollars worth of jewelry before finding this pendant. I don't think he still counts as a good man, Yo."

Yolanda sighed. "It could be the influence of his new guide." She lowered her voice. "She frightens me. Frightens a lot of people. She came to town about eight months ago. She calls herself Teresia." She stopped talking.

Braxton scribbled the name on a piece of paper. "Teresia what?"

"I don't know. But she carries dark magic with her, Braxton. Old magic." Yolanda paused, and when she spoke again, her voice was a whisper. "Blood magic."

Braxton thought again of the scent there by the river that had so raised his hackles, and the coppery tinge of it in the cemetery this morning.

"I believe she will take him down a very dark path," Yolanda continued. "All magic comes with a price, and requires many sorts of sacrifice, but with her kind of magic—"

"Human sacrifice," Braxton said.

"Yes."

They were both silent a moment. Finally Braxton sucked in a breath. "Thanks for talking to me, Yolanda. We need to stop him."

"Good luck," she said quietly. "If she finds out what I told you—"

"She won't," Braxton promised. "Take care."

He ended the call and stared blankly at the tabletop. Garza on his own would have been difficult to take on. Garza with the help of a powerful dark magic user like Teresia... He rubbed his eyes and rested his face in his hand to think.

When Elliott returned, bringing sandwiches from a local deli, Braxton had formed a plan. Well, he admitted to himself, it wasn't a plan so much as he knew what the next step was, and he'd wing it from there.

"Let's go check out the place Murphy found," he said. "The Mind's Eye. We'll stake out Teresia's place and see what we can learn."

* * *

Friday afternoon, less than seventy-two hours before the full moon. Victor knew he was cutting it close, but he'd spent days researching what Teresia proposed. He'd found plenty of evidence to support the theory that a sacrifice was demanded. He'd found nothing that offered him an alternative. He had been wearing the Thanatos pendant around the clock since meeting with Teresia. The necromancer's words had made him wonder who else might be looking for the pendant. The safest place for it was around his neck, where he would know at once if someone were attempting to steal it.

He'd finally accepted that he would have to select someone to kill in Alita's place. Cody's death wouldn't do, because Cody wasn't worth as much as Alita. Besides, the killing had been deliberate, but unfocused, Teresia had said. Deyonte Washington wouldn't work, either, for similar reasons, so the young man had been given a handsome severance payout and told to forget he'd ever met Victor.

Briefly, Victor had toyed with the idea of snatching Chloe Cole for his sacrifice, but he had dismissed the notion almost at once. Although she'd done him the discourtesy to survive the brake sabotage that was supposed to kill her, she was apparently sensible enough to heed the warning it provided. She had gone into hiding, as had her brother. Victor had decided that as long as she obliged him in that way, he would ignore her.

That left one obvious choice for the sacrifice.

When Alita died, so had the boy who was driving and another girl. The fourth child in the car was a seventeen-year-old named Ken Wheeler. He had lost a leg in the accident, but he had survived. That was more than Alita got. It hadn't taken Victor long to decide Ken would be his daughter's sacrifice.

He left the house, locking the front door behind him. He was halfway to his Mercedes when he realized Fletcher was leaning against the driver's side door. Fletcher's arms were folded across his chest, and he was frowning at the driveway. Victor checked his steps, glancing around to see if any of his neighbors were out. His neighborhood was a friendly one; people walked their dogs and said hello to each other on the sidewalks. Fletcher didn't look as if he were anticipating a happy conversation, but Victor's neighbors would notice if he argued with someone in his driveway.

"We gotta talk," Fletcher said. His voice was pitched low, so Victor let his shoulders relax.

"I was on my way to meet Teresia," he said. "Ride along and we'll talk on the way."

Fletcher shook his head. "Can't do that. Let's go in the garage."

"You know I hate being late," Victor said, letting an edge creep into his voice.

"It'll be all right," Fletcher said. "She's definitely not gonna do it without you."

Victor sighed. "Very well, *Carel*. Lead on." The edge in his voice bit deeper, and he saw Fletcher's shoulders come up unhappily. The big man shook his head, but he led the way up to the garage, where he punched in the code to open the overhead door. Once they were both inside, Fletcher closed the door again.

Victor turned to face his best friend squarely. "What is this about?" he demanded.

"You know what it's about. This has gone far enough." Fletcher rubbed the back of his neck. "Too far, for that matter. Way too far." He shook his head. "This ain't you, Vic. How long I known you? And you been ambitious all that time, but you never been mean."

"Mean?" Victor repeated in disbelief. "You think I'm doing this out of meanness?"

What would he do if Fletcher tried to stop him? God, Victor wasn't sure if he could hurt his best friend, even for Alita's sake. Fletcher had been an uncle to her, had taught her how to fish and coached her through her basketball phase in sixth grade, since Victor had played baseball and knew next to nothing about basketball rules.

Searing rage flashed through him. How could Fletcher even *want* to stop him? Fletcher had helped raise Alita! What kind of loving uncle would refuse to help bring her back?

Victor stared at Fletcher, eyes narrowed. He wasn't sure what was on his face, but Fletcher actually flinched, just for a moment. Then he rubbed a hand over his head and sighed.

"I'm not going to turn you in, Vic," Fletcher said, his voice quiet. "I won't even try to stop you, because I can't bring myself to hurt you, and I don't want to force you to kill me. But I can't be part of it."

Victor lifted his head. "But I need your help."

"No." Fletcher shook his head. "You got Teresia now. That woman ain't right, Vic, and what you're doing with her ain't right. And as long as you got her, you can't have me. I want nothing to do with her."

"I'm only doing this to save Alita," Victor protested.

Fletcher shook his head slowly, watching him. "No," he said, his voice still soft, but sure. "No, you're doing it to save yourself. You think if you bring her back, you can live with yourself." He smiled sadly. "Fact is, Vic, you'll always blame yourself. That's just the truth. But I knew that little girl, and she had her own mind. Alita chose her path, Vic. You didn't." He met Victor's gaze. "It wasn't your fault."

"It wasn't Alita's fault!" Victor snapped. "Those boys must have put something in her drink or—or threatened her. She was an innocent victim!"

"Sometimes bad shit happens." Fletcher spoke calmly, but his shoulders hunched as if he knew he were treading thin ice. "It sucks, but it happens."

"How dare you blame her for this?" Victor demanded. His fingers were clenched around the Thanatos pendant. He didn't remember lifting his hand, but he was gripping the pendant so tightly the edges of the poppy were cutting into his flesh. He let it fall back against his chest, dropping his hand to his side. "It wasn't Alita's fault! I have to get her back!"

Fletcher shook his head. "I know you think this will help. But I promise you it won't." His lips drew down. "You've always trusted me before."

Victor wanted to howl. "You've always had my back before!"

"And I do now," Fletcher said. "Please. Trust me."

Victor clenched his fist, feeling his fingers stinging. He looked down at his hand, opening his palm to reveal the thin red lines of blood across his fingers. His stomach was roiling, and his head felt like it was caught in a vise. How could Fletcher be turning on him now? How could Fletcher just give up on Alita? His fingers hurt. He frowned at them. He was so tired. So tired. But Alita needed him...

He lifted his hand and darted a tongue out to soothe the sting of the cut. The taste of blood made his throat clench. He dropped his hand to the pendant again, and a wave of clarity washed over him.

"Damn you," he hissed. "You're just trying to keep me from succeeding. You'll perform the ritual when I'm not looking. I won't let you do it. If you try to stop me, I'll—"

Fletcher held up his hands, palms outward in surrender. "I won't," he said. He bowed his head. "I wish you well, Vic. Always will."

Victor stared at him for several seconds, breathing hard, and then stormed out of the garage. He was still fuming as he backed the Mercedes out of the driveway. After all the years they'd been friends, all the favors they'd done for each other, all the good times they'd shared, this was how Fletcher was going to end it? Victor wanted to punch him. He wanted to make Fletcher feel the pain of being stabbed in the back like Victor did.

But no, he told himself as he drove. He would have his revenge in a better way. He would bring Alita back, and then Fletcher would come crawling back to apologize. He would want to be by Victor's side then, but Victor would turn him away.

Yes, that would be much better. He stroked his fingertip against one smooth poppy petal. He would show everyone. Fletcher most of all.

CHAPTER 18

Braxton's phone shrilled with the emergency broadcast signal. He checked it and saw it was an Amber Alert for Ken Wheeler, seventeen. Frowning faintly, he dismissed the alert. It was sad, but he was off the clock, and he was frankly more worried about his own case. It sounded callous, but while he was always alert for situations that were off, he was going to focus on the one that affected him personally.

At least, that's what he was thinking until Chloe's footsteps pounded up the stairs from the basement.

"Ken Wheeler!" she shouted, and Braxton immediately began reassessing the situation. Obviously the name meant something to Chloe. If she said it was important, Braxton was prepared to act on it.

"Ken Wheeler what?"

"He was the only one who survived the wreck that killed Alita Garza," Chloe said. She was bouncing slightly on the balls of her feet as she watched him.

"You think he's the sacrifice," Braxton said, thinking back to the conversation he'd had several days earlier with Yolanda Stevens.

"He has to be," Chloe said. "It makes sense Garza would pick him to blame for the accident, since he's the only one who lived." She pursed her lips. "Lost a leg in the accident, and he's still recovering, poor kid. But I can see Garza blaming him. Like a projected version of survivor's guilt."

Braxton nodded slowly. "That makes sense."

"Right? So let's go!"

Braxton looked at her.

"We know where they'll be," Chloe said, her tone impatient. "We have to stop him."

Braxton caught and held her gaze. "We can't prove anything," he said. They were law enforcement officers. Their job was to catch the offender using the evidence they had so the prosecutor could mount a case against the offender.

"Who cares? We can stop him." Chloe scowled at him.

"And when we're asked why we were in Crown Hill to begin with?" Braxton asked, carefully keeping his tone mild. Chloe knew how this worked just as much as he did.

Chloe's face reddened, but she shook her head. "Date. We were going to picnic on the Crown."

Braxton raised his eyebrows, watching her. He couldn't help but be pleased she was willing to make their relationship so public. He couldn't deny, to himself at least, that he'd begun thinking long term when it came to his relationship with Chloe. But he'd been entirely unable to read her. She seemed so focused on her career that he hadn't been certain if she would let him in at all, let alone make things public.

"The alternative is letting him get away with it," Chloe said. Then she looked down. "Anyway, it's not like we're keeping this a secret, right?"

Braxton licked his lips and swallowed. "Fine. Let's go."

They grabbed Elliott from the upstairs guest bedroom, where he'd been sleeping since the weekend, and headed out.

There would be a lot of explaining to do, Braxton thought as he guided the truck along 38th Street. But Chloe was obviously so dedicated to bringing Garza to justice that she would out their relationship. Braxton couldn't be less willing. Especially since this was *his* case. Chloe didn't have any professional stake in resolving this. She just believed in the moral obligation to stop Garza. Braxton was the one who would profit by catching him. He'd like to think Chloe was doing this for him, but he knew better; she wanted to stop the bad guy. And when it came down to it, that was the best reason—the only reason—to do this.

He listened to Chloe's end of her phone conversation with Jake Ruiz. It sounded like she was explaining everything except werewolves to him, and Braxton admitted to himself that they would have to bring Jake into the secret if things were to continue between Braxton and Chloe. He caught her eye and tapped a finger against his chest to indicate she could tell Ruiz about him, but she shook her head. She said a couple more things to Jake, then ended the call.

"He'll meet us there," she said. "He can find out about werewolves later. I'm lucky he's talking to me at all right now."

Braxton snorted.

"Who's Elliott talking to?" Chloe asked, glancing over her shoulder to the back seat.

"Theo. He's going to call the rest of the pack and get them to meet us at the cemetery."

Chloe huffed. "So maybe Jake will learn about werewolves as soon as he gets there."

Braxton shrugged. What was important was catching Garza in the act. They'd get him on an insanity issue, and explanations could come afterward.

"So how do we do this?" Elliott said when he ended his call. "All of us converge on the grave and grab him, or what?"

"The mage will be there," Braxton said. "Maybe not openly. We need to hold at least a couple of people in reserve." He glanced at Chloe.

"Oh, no, don't you pull some kind of 'you're only human' crap on me," she said.

Braxton couldn't pretend he hadn't thought of that, but he shrugged. "I want to keep Murphy out of it, if possible. He's already been hurt enough."

"Good luck with that," Elliott said.

"I know," Braxton said. "We'll just...the main thing is that we stop Garza. I'd like to do it legally, but if we can't, we go with werewolf justice."

"Which means what?" Chloe asked.

Braxton glanced at Elliott, who said, "If the pack has a problem, the alpha deals with it. Usually by killing the problem."

Braxton saw Chloe twitch, and then she said, "And Braxton is your alpha."

"I am," Braxton said. "But I'd prefer to do this the human way."

He saw Chloe twist to trade a long look with Elliott. Then Chloe said, "Sure. A legal arrest would be ideal. But if we can't nail him on anything, you take him out, Alpha."

Braxton caught Elliott's fierce grin in the rearview mirror, but he just nodded.

The sun hadn't quite set when they arrived at Crown Hill. Elliott tossed Chloe up to catch the top of the fence and throw herself over, then Braxton. Braxton wanted to transform, but he would need to be there to make an arrest if they were able to take Garza legally. Chloe took off at a jog as soon as she was over, but Braxton waited until Elliott dropped down inside the fence.

"Whatever happens, protect Chloe," Braxton said. He held Elliott's gaze.

"You think she can't protect herself?" Elliott said, his chin lifted.

Braxton's lips quirked. When had Elliott become Chloe's defender? Braxton would have sworn that, at the beginning of this case, Chloe and Elliott weren't mutual fans. But he shook his head. "I know she can. But I know what a difference it can make to have someone watching your back. So I'm asking you to watch *her* back, Ell."

"And who's going to be watching yours?" Elliott demanded.

"Chloe," Braxton said, confident he was right.

Elliott met his gaze for several heartbeats, then nodded. "Make sure her partner doesn't shoot me when he shows up, yeah?" Then he dropped to hands and knees, tugging his sweatshirt over his head. Within a couple of minutes, he had transformed. Braxton scooped up Elliott's clothes and they both took off at a lope.

Chloe had a head start, but wolves ran faster than humans, so it wasn't long before Elliott caught up with her. Braxton would trust her to take care of herself, and he would trust Elliott to watch her back.

He wished he knew how many of the others had arrived. The pack was always better together. As he followed Chloe and Elliott, he scanned the cemetery through the fading light. They'd entered the cemetery far enough from Alita's grave that they wouldn't be seen.

Before he even got near the grave, he could feel the power emanating from the site. The hair prickled on the back of his neck and he drew his lips back from his teeth. That power was not right. Was it from the mage, or was it from that pendant Yolanda had mentioned? He saw Elliott, ahead of him, grab Chloe's wrist in his mouth. She drew up short and looked down at him. Everything in Elliott's stance, from his raised hackles to the silent snarl on his face, spoke of his unhappiness.

Braxton imagined it would be even worse to feel that as a wolf.

Braxton took several long steps and caught up with them.

"Do you feel that?" he asked Chloe, who shook her head. "Elliott was just warning you. Something truly awful is going down up there."

Chloe stared at him. "Do you suppose he's already killed Ken Wheeler?"

Braxton shrugged. "I just know someone's throwing around a lot of power at Alita's grave. Could be Garza's sacrifice, could be the mage, Teresia. For that matter, it could be that Thanatos pendant. I'm not a mage, I'm a magical being. I can feel it, but not use it or even understand what's happening."

Chloe gave a sharp nod. "We'll be careful," she said, "but we're here to stop him. We should interrupt before it gets worse, whatever he's doing."

Elliott let out an explosive huff of breath to get Braxton's attention. When Braxton looked down, Elliott had relaxed and was waving his tail. He must scent the others. Good. The more pack members who gathered, the stronger they would all be.

A moment later, a scruffy, skinny wolf trotted out of the shadows. He touched Elliott's nose, then stretched out her front legs and bowed to Braxton.

"Hi, Murphy," Chloe said. Braxton glanced at her in surprise, and she shrugged. "You don't forget the first werewolf you meet," she said, grinning faintly. Then her expression darkened. "Okay, let's go nail Garza."

Murphy looked over his shoulder. Braxton followed her gaze and saw the rest of the pack gathered under a statue of an angel. He counted them off aloud for Chloe. "Estella, almost white. Theo, the skinny one. Tara, you remember. Maura, almost all black. Ximena, the one hanging in the back."

"Hi," Chloe said to them. She was clearly impatient, but her scent didn't betray any hidden fear, or at least, not fear of the werewolves. She glanced over at Braxton. "How are we going to do this?"

He sighed. "We need to at least give him a chance to surrender. I'll confront him, give him the option of letting me arrest him peacefully."

Elliott's snort spoke his opinion of that likelihood.

"I know," Braxton said. "I don't expect him to go for it. But like I said, I'd rather resolve this peacefully."

"And when he refuses?" Chloe said.

"Tara comes in from behind him and takes him down." Braxton shot her a look. "Without killing him," he emphasized.

Tara nodded, an odd-looking gesture on a wolf.

"The rest of you," Braxton said, turning to look at them, "I want held in reserve. Murphy, you hang back, okay? Space yourselves out like in a hunt, surround him, and watch for the mage." He waited until he got a round of nods, then he headed towards Alita's grave.

* * *

Chloe's heart pounded as she followed Braxton through the cemetery. She didn't like the idea of his

364

putting himself in danger, but she couldn't think of a better plan. And he knew more about magic than she did, so he could probably protect himself better than she could. Still, she wasn't happy.

You're wandering around a cemetery trying to stop a kidnapper from performing human sacrifice to bring his daughter back from the dead, she thought. *What's there to be happy about?*

The scene was lit by garden torches that flickered and leapt in the light breeze. A fire burned in a cast-iron patio brazier. Chloe sucked in a silent breath.

The first thing she saw was that Ken Wheeler was sitting in his wheelchair, bound and gagged, but very much alive. His eyes were huge and he was trying to work a hand free, without success. The second thing she noticed was Garza kneeling on Alita's grave. He was mumbling, loud enough for her to hear but not understand his words. He clutched something to his chest in both hands.

Braxton strode into the light, self-assured and standing straight. "Victor Garza, you're under arrest. Please surrender peacefully." Chloe saw Ken straighten in his chair, face lighting up.

Garza laughed. "Under arrest? Oh, I think not."

Braxton shook his head. "I don't want to hurt you, Garza, but this stops now. By meddling with supernatural forces, you subject yourself to supernatural law. I would prefer to arrest you and handle this like humans, but if you won't surrender, you'll be taken forcibly."

Ken let out a muffled yell a second before sickly green light blazed out of the trees behind Garza. It hit Braxton, doubling him over. He bared his teeth, squeezing his eyes shut as his face twisted. Chloe had her gun in her hand, but she couldn't see anyone to target behind Garza. Besides, Tara was supposed to be circling behind him. Chloe didn't want to hit a friendly.

A low shape darted, snarling, into the torchlight. It was the black wolf, and it moved faster than Chloe would have expected. She snapped her teeth closed on Garza's wrist. He screamed, flailing at her, and the sickly green light snaked out to wrap around the black wolf as well.

The light broke off, releasing the black wolf and Braxton. He dropped to his knees, clutching his stomach and panting. A woman's voice swore, and then Chloe heard an awful yelp of pain. Tara must have attacked the mage, and now the mage had turned her attention on Tara.

Chloe thought anyone else in Garza's position would make a run for it. But he'd gone back to chanting. He drew a cruel-looking blade and climbed to his feet. Whatever he clutched in his left hand began glowing. Chloe squinted, trying to get a better look at it, but it seemed blurred by the glow.

Ken was twisting in his chair, watching Garza in horror. Cody materialized between Garza and Ken, both hands held up, palms outward, to tell Garza to stop. Chloe knew Garza would walk right through Cody, though. She took several steps to the right so she could get a clean shot at Garza without having anyone else in the line of fire. "Garza!" she shouted. "Drop it!"

To her surprise, he grinned at her. "Officer Cole, I'm not surprised to see you here. You don't scare easily, do you?"

"Not really," she said, though she could feel a cold sweat springing out, proving the lie. "I'm here to stop you. Like Braxton said, however necessary."

Green light flared in the trees behind Garza, and Chloe ducked automatically, but it wasn't aimed at her. Tara gave a high-pitched squeal. The scruffy, skinny wolf that Braxton had said was Murphy darted through the light, slashing his teeth at Garza on the way past. Garza tried to dodge and lost his balance, falling over.

Chloe swore. He'd fallen closer to Ken, spoiling her shot. She knew Murphy had just been trying to help, though. Snarls and growls erupted around the mage. Chloe relaxed a little; the wolves were taking care of the mage. She could handle Garza.

"Drop the knife," she ordered.

"Not going to happen," Garza said, struggling back to his feet. There was blood on his wrist and on his shirt. "You've figured it all out, haven't you, Cole? I want my little girl back."

"I understand," Chloe said. "But Alita doesn't want you to do this."

"She wouldn't want to be dead," Garza snarled. "She was going to change the world. I'm going to make sure she still can."

Red light blazed up behind him, making Chloe flinch. In that instant, Garza flung something at her. She ducked, half-turning so that it hit her shoulder. Tingles shot through her left arm. Had he thrown something magical, or just a rock? She turned back, glaring at him.

"What happened to you, Garza? You used to be the kind of guy who volunteered at soup kitchens and homeless shelters."

"What *happened* to me? My daughter died!" he shrieked.

Suddenly Chloe was enveloped by the green light. She gasped as her skin burned. It was like acid. Chloe dropped her gun and clawed at her face, trying to clear her eyes. The light died when a wolf snarled. She heard the thud of bodies colliding. Then she quit paying attention to the mage as Garza launched himself at her.

He wasn't a particularly tall man, but he was solid, and he was crazed. Chloe hit the ground with all his weight on her. Even though she couldn't catch her breath, she brought one leg up to knee him in the crotch. He let out a strangled cry and rolled away from her.

Chloe scrambled to her feet and scanned the area. Garza was clutching his groin, but he'd managed to get to his knees. He was glaring at Chloe, apparently unaware that Braxton was circling silently around behind him.

"Here's something you don't know, Garza," Chloe said loudly. "Ever since your boy Cody killed me, I've been able to see ghosts. I can see Cody. I know he's haunting you." She couldn't quite catch her breath; there was a hitch in her side, and she wondered if she'd recracked a rib. "I can see your daughter."

As if on cue, Alita flickered into view. Garza didn't react. He couldn't see her, Chloe realized. But he'd seen Cody easily enough. Was it because he'd killed Cody? Or was Alita hiding herself from him?

Braxton was almost in position. His gaze flickered to Chloe's and he nodded for her to go on.

"Alita hates what you're doing," Chloe said. "She doesn't want you to bring her back."

"You have no right—" Garza howled, and then Braxton's foot shot out, kicking the dagger out of Garza's hand. Garza started to turn, but Braxton got his left arm looped around Garza's neck. Chloe saw his muscles jump as he used his right hand to press Garza's head forward. His left arm applied pressure to the sides of Garza's neck. In just a few seconds, Garza sagged against Braxton.

"Cuff him," Braxton said, lowering Garza's body to the ground.

Chloe jumped forward, tugging her cuffs from her belt. "Nicely done," she said, and he gave her a brief smile.

"I need to help the others with the mage," he said. "Can you make sure Ken's okay?"

Chloe nodded. "Be careful."

* * *

Braxton's skin was still jumping from the green light the mage had hit him with, but his body was completely under his own control again. He'd felt the green light eating into him, twisting around his muscles, trying to force him to change. Thank God Tara had interrupted, or he would have lost control. But he'd heard the awful sounds of Tara's fight with the mage, and even with reinforcements, the wolves sounded like they were losing.

Chloe had been right to focus on Garza—he was the one trying to kill Ken Wheeler, after all—but clearly the mage was the bigger threat. Braxton sprinted through the trees towards the sounds of the struggle.

He found them just in time to see Estella fall, her pale fur pink with blood. "Estella!" he shouted, and launched himself at the mage.

It was stupid. He knew it, even as he leapt. But the instinct to protect his packmate was too strong. He managed to land a punch on the mage's shoulder, and then the green fire seized him. Braxton screamed, dropping to one knee, but he grabbed her hand, trying to push it away.

Blinded by tears of pain, he didn't see who jumped in to protect him, but suddenly the fire disappeared. Braxton panted for a couple of seconds, then forced himself to his feet. Tara was hanging by her teeth from the mage's shoulder. The mage, a woman with red-gold hair falling down from a tight bun, was blasting Tara with red energy that made the wolf whimper.

Tara didn't let go, though. She was too stubborn and too tough for that.

Braxton lunged, striking the woman in the lower back. "Leave my pack alone!" he snarled at her.

She let out a rippling, bell-like laugh. "Alpha Wolfe, I will make slaves of your pack." She sounded breathless but unafraid.

"We will die first," he replied, which provoked another laugh.

"Oh, I'm certain you'll try. But you must realize I can control death." She crooked her fingers and flames leapt up from Tara's muzzle. Tara yelped sharply and dropped to the ground, rolling and shaking her head.

"Bitch," Braxton growled, sweeping his leg at her ankles.

The mage side-stepped, still laughing. "Poor puppy. You're playing with fire." And abruptly Braxton *was* on fire as the mage thrust her hand against his chest. He screamed and lashed out blindly.

The fire cut off suddenly as the mage screamed. Braxton's spine crawled at the sound, and then he heard someone gagging. The mage's scream went on and on, finally subsiding into sobs. When Braxton looked over, he saw Murphy, back in human form, hunched over and throwing up. The mage had one hand clutched around her other wrist, which ended in a stump.

"Damn you!" she howled, glaring at Murphy. She swept the glare to include Braxton, who managed a very weak smirk at her.

She darted past him, too quickly for him to react. He turned, watching as she blasted Chloe with another shot of that green magic. Chloe yelped and threw herself sideways, avoiding most of the magic, but it left Garza unprotected. The mage swooped down on him, scrabbling with her free hand, and then dashed away. In moments, she had vanished.

Braxton slouched for a moment, trying to catch his breath. He ought to pursue the mage, but she was powerful, even injured. He would take the respite Murphy had given him. As Braxton turned to check on the younger man's condition, one of the wolves howled, raising the hair on the back of his neck. He spun to look and saw Ximena standing over Estella, her head lifted in mourning.

No, Braxton thought. He threw himself to his knees beside Estella, fingers searching through her blood-stained fur. There was no pulse, no breath of life. Braxton's throat seized up as tears stung his eyes. *No.*

One by one, the others joined in the lamentation. Braxton wanted to throw his own head back and howl. How could Estella be gone? Elliott limped over and leaned against Braxton's shoulder, muzzle pressed against his neck. Ximena nuzzled at her cousin's body, then howled again.

Braxton heard footsteps pounding towards them. "Oh, God," Chloe breathed, and knelt beside Braxton. She wrapped her arms around him and didn't speak.

He could hear sirens approaching. Probably Ruiz, coming to save the day, Braxton thought bitterly. His breath caught in his throat. Two sobs escaped before he got himself under control again. Too late. Help was too late.

* * *

Chloe stood awkwardly at the edge of the crowd, watching Braxton and Jake talk. She'd expected Estella to transform back into a human upon her death, but Tara, tears streaming down her cheek, had explained that your body retained whatever state you were in when you died. Chloe was almost ashamed of how much compassion Tara had spared for the ignorant human in their midst, despite her own obvious grief.

Elliott and Maura had both been badly injured in their fight with the mage. Transforming to their human forms was out of the question, Tara said; they would have to be transported to Braxton's house, where they could mend enough to eventually revert to human. Chloe didn't dare ask how the approaching full moon would affect their healing.

Murphy and Ximena had also returned to their human shapes. Murphy looked even more battered than before, but he seemed entirely pleased with himself despite that. He had, Tara said, bitten off the mage's hand while she was trying to kill Braxton. It had made him violently ill, but it had saved Braxton's life and sent the mage running.

"I just wish she hadn't gotten that Thanatos pendant," Chloe murmured to Tara.

The redhead shrugged. "She'll be back to cause more problems, I don't doubt that. But for now, we've beaten Garza, and we've got Teresia on the run. We'll be better prepared for her next time."

"I hope so," Chloe said. She had her doubts, but she kept them to herself.

Jake finished his conversation with Braxton and came over to Chloe. "Do you know how hard it's going to be to explain all this?" he demanded, a second before he enveloped her in a hug.

Chloe hugged him back. "I have an idea, yeah," she said. "But at least we got Garza."

Jake leaned back, studying her face, "Yeah, you got Garza. And started seeing ghosts and dating a werewolf. Your life is officially weird, Chloe Cole."

"It was already weird," Chloe said. "I think now it's finally starting to make sense."

He shook his head. "I'm sorry I was such a shit," he said.

Chloe punched him lightly on the arm. "Shut up."

He grinned at her, and she grinned back.

"Listen, do you think you can handle booking Garza for us?" she asked. "Braxton lost a packmate tonight. I don't want him to have to deal with red tape."

"And you want to be there for him," Jake said, nodding. "I'll take care of it."

"Thanks." Chloe smiled at him, then hugged him once more. "And thanks for coming."

Jake hugged her back. "Any time, partner."

CHAPTER 19

Barbecue and Bourbon didn't have a table large enough for the group that gathered there two days after the full moon. Chloe and Jake dragged two tables together as Martin found a parking spot. Braxton and Murphy arrived a few minutes later, followed shortly by Tara and Theo, who was supporting a limping Elliott.

"Ximena isn't coming," Braxton murmured as he slid into the chair next to Chloe's. "Estella's funeral is Thursday, and she's busy with arrangements."

Chloe curled her fingers around his, giving him a sympathetic smile. It must be hard to lose a packmate just a few months after his father's death. "Do you want me to come with you, or should I stay away?"

Braxton's eyes were a warm gold as he looked at her. "I think it would mean a lot to everyone if you came to the funeral," he said. "Thank you."

"You'll be the alpha female before you know it," Elliott remarked, then coughed as Tara poked him in the ribs. "Ouch. Hey, still healing."

"You're a brat," she remarked, and turned a warm smile on Chloe. "Seriously, welcome to the pack, Chloe."

Chloe wasn't sure why Murphy was snickering, or why Braxton was blushing, but she smiled back at Tara. "Um, thanks." *I think,* she added mentally.

"How did things play out with Garza?" Elliott asked quickly.

Chloe leveled a long look at him, but decided to let it go, whatever it was. "He gave the booking guys enough trouble that we're pretty sure he won't be getting bail. He says he's going to represent himself, which also looks pretty good for us. I don't know whether it was that pendant thing or his daughter's death or what, but something has clearly unhinged him."

"I wouldn't be surprised if we ended up with a not-guilty-by-reason-of-insanity plea in the end," Braxton added.

"Ken Wheeler's going to be a star witness," Chloe said. "Apparently Garza ranted all kinds of things at him about how Ken should be dead instead of Alita, and he was going to fix it, and Alita would have the life she'd been robbed of..."

"Thank God he wasn't hurt when Garza grabbed him," Jake said.

"I do wish you guys didn't have a vicious mage who wields blood magic running around with a grudge against you," Martin put in.

"So do I," Chloe said, frowning. She'd had Debby, their police artist, do a sketch of Teresia's face, but it hadn't turned up any matches so far. Chloe was definitely going to keep an eye out for the mage, as were Braxton and Elliott, but in the meantime, all they could do was watch and wait.

"On a happier note," Braxton said, squeezing Chloe's hand, "I'd like to officially invite you all to celebrate Thanksgiving at my place this year."

Jake snorted. "Only if I can invite my sisters and you promise not to make any werewolf jokes."

"I can safely promise that I won't make any werewolf jokes," Braxton said, and shot a look at Elliott, who blushed.

Chloe grinned. "They'd just think it was some weird inside joke," she said. "Anyway, Celi and Lucia are my closest friends. You'd be better off just telling them the truth, because to tell you the truth, I have a feeling you're all gonna be stuck with me for a long time."

Braxton's face lit up in a smile. "I think I can live with that."

Stay tuned for Circle City Psychic in 2017!

Author's Note

Thanks for reading my novel. If you enjoyed this, would you please take a moment to leave a review of my book at Amazon or Goodreads? Writing just two or three honest sentences is one of the best things you can do to support any author.

Thanks!

Stephanie

ACKNOWLEDGEMENTS

Shades of Circle City was written during NaNoWriMo 2010. Meg Burden, Larinzia Kimball, and Shelly Call provided feedback on the first draft. My fellow IndyScribes, who constantly challenge me to be a better writer, were directly responsible for the shaping of this novel. Peggy provided the werewolves and Marcia was kind enough to read the entire novel in just a few days to give her input.

A huge debt of gratitude is owed to Lilliana, who acted as sensitivity reader and critique partner.

My ever-supportive parents gave me a love of words and story-telling. My cats Eowyn, Strider, and Eustace Clarence Scrubb were always more than willing to chew up manuscript pages or sit on my keyboard.

And most of all, I am grateful for my readers. You enable me to keep telling stories that are close to my heart, and I would love to hear from you at stephanie@stephaniecainonline.com. You can also join my Circle City Magic advance release team by visiting http://bit.ly/SACfantasy.

About the Author

Stephanie A. Cain writes epic and urban fantasy. She lives in Indiana, where she works at a museum and is plotting the next book in the Storms in Amethir series and writing the next book in the Circle City Magic series. She enjoys hiking, reading, birdwatching, and general geekery. She has three cats, which she is well aware puts her firmly in crazy cat lady territory, and way more dice than she needs. She can be found online at www.stephaniecainonline.com, on Twitter @stephanie_cain, and on Facebook.

The Storms in Amethir series includes *The Midwinter Royal*, *Stormsinger*, *Stormshadow*, *Stormseer*, and *The Weather War*. Stephanie has also written an unrelated epic fantasy novella *Sow the Wind*.